KATRIN

# KNIVES, SEASONING, & A DASH OF Love

First published in the United States of America 2023 by Lake Country Press & Reviews.

Cataloging-in-Publication Data is on file with the Library of Congress.

ISBN 979-8-9877391-4-3 (paperback) 979-8-9877391-5-0 (e-book)

Publisher website: https://www.lakecountrypress.com

Editor: Borbala Branch

Cover Art: Vivsketchesss

Cover Design: Emily's World of Design

Internal Formatting: Dawn Lucous of Yours Truly Book Services

**Lake Country Press & Reviews**

*To 25-year-old me.*
*I'm glad you're still with us.*
*It really does get better.*

*For those who need it:*
*Dial 988 for the Suicide & Crisis Lifeline.*
*You're not alone.*

Dear reader, please be advised:

*Knives, Seasoning, and A Dash of Love* is an adult contemporary romance that deals with mature themes, explicit language, and explicit sexual content. Recommended for readers age 18+.

For a full list of content warnings (may contain spoilers), please visit:
www.lakecountrypress.com/bookcontentwarnings

# CHAPTER
## One

C ontrol. That's what he likes the most about running his own kitchen.

Everything has its place. Everyone has their roles to fulfill. Everything is measured and timed and seasoned.

Perfection.

He expects nothing less.

He likes his knives dangerously sharp—it's more dangerous to work with a dull blade—and he likes his waiters to pick up orders the second the plates hit the line. He's never bothered with a chef's hat because they're quite frankly pompous as fuck and it's hot enough in here as it is. He keeps his apron clean and the sleeves of his black chef jacket rolled up to just below his elbows.

Trained at the prestigious Gagnon-Allard School of Culinary Arts with three Michelin stars under his belt, he's the pristine image of the world-class chef everyone believes him to be. He's the great and mighty Head Chef of La Rouge, Alexander Chen.

But right now?

Right now, he's stressed as fuck, and *boy howdy* does his kitchen staff know it.

"What the hell is this?" he asks, voice booming over the roar of hood fans and sizzling skillets. While the noises of the kitchen don't stop, the talking does. None of the other chefs dare make a peep.

"A steak," Peter answers evenly, though the hard set of his jaw betrays his cool tone.

Alexander stiffens, staring down his nose at the rotisseur. He lowers his voice, quieter than before and somehow more frightening than when he was yelling. "I don't want to make a parody of myself, Drenton. But if this steak were any rarer, it'd still be alive on the damn pasture. The table wants it cooked well-done."

Peter looks like he wants to cry. Embarrassing for a man in his mid-thirties, but alas—Alexander has that effect on people.

"But these are prime triple A! Just look at the marbling! Cooking them well-done would be—"

"An absolute travesty and crime against God? I know. But it's what the customer wants. Do it again. I need another one on the fly."

Peter gestures to the stove beside him with a huff. "My station's swamped already. I've been trying to—"

"I don't need your excuses. I need a cook who can do their damn job."

Freddie, the pâtissier, hesitantly clears his throat. "Um, chef?"

Alexander turns in one swift motion, the movement both effortlessly aggressive and smooth. He's an owl making a pinpoint turn midair to lay its sights on new prey. Freddie is only a few inches shorter than Alexander, and just as broad. Nevertheless, he tries—and fails—to hide a grimace.

"The new hire is here. For the sous chef position."

Alexander's nostrils flare. "What sous chef?"

It's at this exact moment Alexander spots movement from out of his periphery. All he catches is a glimpse, but it's more than enough. A wisp of light brown hair. Tanned skin. The worn-down fabric of a white chef's coat that's seen better days.

Then he remembers. Alexander's last sous chef, Mitchell, left almost a week ago. He hadn't even bothered to tell Alexander that he quit in person. The sniveling weasel had stuffed his resignation letter into the pocket of one of Alexander's spare aprons, and that was that. Couldn't handle the demands of the job, apparently. Very few can.

Alexander can't say that it was a surprise. It was more of an inconvenience, if anything, trying to find a replacement. Despite his confidence as a chef, he knows handling an entire kitchen like this one without a second-in-command would be next to impossible. There are too many moving parts, too many chefs to keep in line. This kind of work requires a divide and conquer approach.

Hence the new, last-minute hire.

The new hire that's now staring up at him expectantly. There's something oddly familiar about her, but Alexander can't quite figure out why.

"You're not what I was expecting," Alexander states.

He half expects her to blanch or flush or quiver like a mouse beneath his intense scrutiny. Alexander's more than aware of the kind of effect he has on people. The kitchen is his kingdom, and as head chef, he's the rightful king.

He's intimidating. He's powerful. He's in his element.

The woman lifts her chin and holds his gaze instead, defiance in her eyes. "I get that a lot," she replies calmly, the lovely lilt of an accent gracing her words. It sounds southern, but it isn't distinct enough for Alexander to pinpoint.

She sticks her hand out and says, "I'm Eden. Eden Monroe. It's nice to meet you."

Alexander doesn't shake her hand. He glances at his watch instead. "You're late."

Eden frowns. "I'm on time for my scheduled shift. You said on the phone to be here at three."

He glares at the other kitchen staff. "What's rule one, people?" he prompts.

"Fifteen minutes early is on time, on time is late, and if you're late, don't show up at all," the chorus of chefs mumble in practiced unison. They sound like robots, his policy on tardiness so drilled into their brains that the response is automatic.

Again, Eden doesn't seem fazed. She takes it in stride, even going so far as to give Alexander a polite—albeit incredibly tight—smile. "Duly noted. Won't happen again, Chef."

*Chef.*

The way she says it makes his ears ring. It's gentle, but there's a hint of snark buried somewhere deep down.

He decides he doesn't like it.

Alexander gives her a disinterested once over. She's a scrawny little thing. Short, no more than five feet to his six. She's thin, too, any hint of her barely there curves hidden beneath her oversized chef's jacket. He notes the splash of faded freckles across the tops of her cheeks and bridge of her nose.

The more he stares, the more he thinks Eden doesn't look the part of a sous chef. If Alexander didn't know any better, he'd mistake her for the kitchen porter, or maybe even the dish-washer. She doesn't look like she belongs here.

It's not that he doesn't think women can cook. Far from it. Some of his greatest inspirations growing up were female chefs: Julia Child, Nigella Lawson, Christine Hà—his mother.

It's just that Eden's resumé boasted accolades and years of prior experience working in kitchens like this one. He has a hard time believing that the tiny woman standing before him is going to be his new sous. She's so small and quiet and—well—ordinary. Nothing about her screams haute cuisine.

Most sous chefs he's worked with have an air of authority

about them. It's not arrogance necessarily, though Alexander's no stranger to hotshot sous with egos too big for their aprons. They're the ones in charge of calling the shots when the head chef isn't there. They're the ones hungry and eager to move up the ladder, to learn all that they can and prove themselves in preparation for one day running kitchens of their own.

Eden is… *not* that.

But the night is young, and Eden hasn't even had the chance to prove she's not completely useless. If she is, Alexander will have her replaced. It's just that simple.

"Drenton," he snaps. "Give her a tour. Keep her at your station for tonight."

"And the steak?"

"I'll make the damn thing myself." Alexander turns to Eden, to the point and more than a little aware of all the chits printing out on the line. "Tomorrow, Monroe. Two hours early."

Her eyes widen ever so slightly. He finds satisfaction in finally eliciting a normal response. He's used to being on the receiving end of wide-eyed timidity.

"Two hours? I don't know if I can make it."

"Training starts bright and early. Unless you don't think you can handle it. If that's the case, you can just go. You'll only be in the way."

Eden licks her lips. His eyes accidentally flit down to follow the motion.

She crosses her arms. "Who says I can't handle it?"

Alexander doesn't bother responding. It's an abnormally busy day, and even though the restaurant has only been open for an hour, orders are piling up. There's still a million and one things to do, and answering rhetorical questions isn't on his list.

Tickets to call.

Dishes to verify and plate.

Steaks to not screw up.

Dinner rush hits them like a tidal wave, but Alexander's prepared. He always is. He's been doing this long enough to know how to keep things moving. Lack of momentum is the fastest way to ruin a night. Food stops going out, orders keep coming in, chefs become overwhelmed with ten different dishes they're trying to prepare at the exact same time. It's a nightmare.

So he keeps things moving, calling out times and demanding accountability, and more often than not yelling at his chefs to get their heads out of their asses and focus on the tables that have been waiting the longest. It's an extra headache not having a sous chef at the ready to help him with plating and putting out fires—one of them quite literal—but he manages somehow.

By the end of the night, his feet hurt. His arches ache and his back is sore from carrying his chefs through the worst of it. He doesn't even take his break because, for him, there's no such thing as sitting down on the job, not even for a breather.

He's tired and getting agitated, his fingers itching for a smoke. Even when there's a backup in the dish pit and one of the idiot waiters drops an entire tray of food out front, Alexander sucks it up, leans into the throbbing pain in his feet, and helps send out the last of the dessert that Freddie has diligently prepared. Alexander has to give credit where credit is due. Freddie's handmade éclairs are to die for. It's just a shame he takes forever to make them.

Alexander's about to ring the bell to call for a pick-up when something distracts him. A woman's laugh.

Eden's laugh.

It's light, and the sweetest sound he's ever heard.

He risks a glance over his shoulder as he stabs the last chit onto the check spindle. Eden and Peter are at the meat station, already cleaning up the area and preparing for closing. They speak in hushed tones, almost conspiratorial, looking at ease with one another. They look like this is perfectly natural, two old friends who've done this countless times before. It doesn't take long before Freddie wanders over and joins the conversation. Alexander briefly wonders what they're talking about. It's not like anyone willingly talks to him about non-work things.

Then he shakes his head. He doesn't care. He rings the bell and sends out the last order of the day.

Eden laughs again, bright and bubbly.

Alexander does his best to ignore her wide smile and concentrates on overseeing cleanup. He sincerely hopes she isn't this much of a chatterbox once she's fully trained. He doesn't like personal conversations during work hours. There's too much going on in a kitchen, lots of sharp objects and hot metal and scalding water. Unnecessary small talk will only get in his way of giving out clear, concise orders.

His dark brown eyes lock with her light hazel ones. Eden looks away quickly, and he suddenly realizes that he's been glaring this whole time. He turns to head toward the kitchen doors to check on the maître d'. The sooner the last customers eat, pay, and leave, the sooner they can all clock out and call it a night.

The sound of Eden's laugh echoes quietly in the back of his skull.

Somewhere deep down, Alexander knows that tomorrow's training will prove incredibly... *interesting*.

# CHAPTER
## Two

Eden has a confession to make. She may or may not have embellished a few things on her resumé to get this job.

Alright, fine. Who's she kidding?

She definitely embellished *a lot* of things on her resumé to get this job.

She really did attend the Gagnon-Allard School of Culinary Arts ten years ago. For all of two weeks. Had it not been for Parsons—the rat bastard—Eden would have been able to stay.

She should have known she could never be that lucky. She was admittedly worried when she got the call about the sous chef position, concerned that Shang would recognize her and realize how full of shit she was.

Except he didn't. There hadn't seemed to be an inkling of recognition in those cold, hard eyes.

He apparently goes by Alexander now, which she thinks is super weird, but Eden will always know him as Shang.

Shang, the mildly dorky, adorably sweet apprentice chef who shared a handful of classes with her—however brief her stint at Gagnon-Allard truly was. Even though Eden was forced to leave the school of her dreams, she'll always remember the way Shang helped point her in the right direction on her first day of class. Or the fact that he always seemed to smell like roasted hazelnuts and vanilla. Or the fact that his smile used to light up a room.

The contrast of who he was and who he is now is jarring.

A part of her wants to ask what the hell happened, but it will only expose her truth. Eden can already see how the conversation will pan out.

She'll ask why he turned into such a prick. He'll ask how they know each other. She'll say they met at school. And then he'll undoubtedly look into her credentials and realize exactly to what extent she's a fraud.

Half of her references are fake. She handed in a list of made-up names and dummy phone numbers that all linked back to her so she could pretend to be her own references. There are no shortage of websites online that generate fake, usable numbers and provide voice modifying programs. It's simply a matter of knowing where to look. It's probably illegal and definitely immoral, but...

But Eden needs this job.

So, as curious as she is, she keeps her mouth shut.

Getting to La Rouge two hours earlier than she'd planned is a giant pain in the ass. It's located in Seattle's downtown core, so she has to grab three different bus transfers followed by a quick sprint from the station to the restaurant's back doors to make it on time. The cold winter air burns her lungs and rips at her throat. By the time she arrives, Eden is out of breath and starting to sweat. Her hair—which she's thrown up into a bun to keep out of her eyes—is a windswept mess, flyaway strands everywhere.

She bursts through the doors to find Alexander leaning against the silver preparation table, looking at his watch while casually sipping a coffee in his other hand.

"You're a minute late, Monroe."

Eden isn't a violent person, but she really wants to kick him in the shin. She refrains because—yeah, no—kicking her new boss will probably be frowned upon.

*Probably.*

"It won't happen again," she says, but Alexander's already turning away.

"Drenton showed you where the walk-in fridge is, right?"

"Yes, he did."

Alexander nods once, not bothering to look directly at her. *Smug bastard.* "Good. Go make me something," he says.

Eden frowns. "What?"

"Consider it your interview."

"But you've already hired me."

"Talk is cheap. All I give a shit about is if you can cook."

Eden supposes that makes a lot of sense. She did think it was weird how quickly she landed the job. It was a brief phone call, a few simple questions about availability, and *bam!* Hired. It smells kind of desperate to be honest, but Eden isn't going to look a gift horse in the mouth.

If he wants her to whip up a meal for him to judge, fine. She's going to blow him away.

"Do you have a specific request?" she asks, shrugging off her winter coat to reveal a plain white tank top underneath. She wastes no time pulling her second-hand chef jacket out of her backpack and slipping it on.

His eyes shift from her collarbone to her exposed neck before looking away entirely. The glance makes her heart skip a beat. She tries not to think anything of it.

"Make whatever you want, just don't bore me. You have an hour."

"And I have free reign of ingredients?"

He glances at his watch again. "You have fifty-nine minutes," he corrects before taking another sip of his coffee.

Eden fights the urge to roll her eyes. Instead, she gets to work.

She's only mildly perturbed that Alexander remains where he is, watching her every move like a hawk. It's intense, his eyes. She can feel the heat of his stare on her skin, observing her. Is he waiting for her to make a mistake? Eden remembers how focused Shang used to be in class, but this is on a whole other level.

Her nerves—thankfully—don't win out.

Every measurement is precise. Every cut is clean. Every choice of herbs and spice is complimentary.

She tastes as she goes. Her palate is one of her greatest strengths. Eden knows exactly how much salt and pepper to add after half a bite. She knows how much chicken stock to add based off the texture on her tongue.

Alexander watches as she brings another spoon to her mouth. His gaze lingers on her lips. Eden, for a moment, fights the urge to squirm. Do the other chefs here not work the same way? It's imperative for a chef to taste their work. Sometimes that's the only way to know if a dish will turn out right. This is as much a science as it is an art-form, and minor verification tests along the way are perfectly acceptable.

*So why the hell is he staring at me like that?*

She wonders if she's made a mistake somewhere, if she's screwed up somehow and Alexander is the kind of asshole who won't point out the problem until *after* just so he can rub it in her face.

He definitely gives off that kind of vibe. This man is waiting for her to fail.

"What?" Eden asks, preparing to plate. She grabs a lovely ornate dish off the shelves below the cooking station, gilded filigree wrapping around the circumference.

"Licorice powder?" he replies flatly. "For a saffron risotto?"

"I was going to use white truffle shavings, but I know how expensive truffles are."

"Licorice powder," he says again, almost accusatory, in disbelief.

Eden hands him the plate and a clean spoon. "Don't knock it before you try it."

Alexander eyes the food. Eden knows she did everything right. This is exactly how her mother used to make it. At least, she thinks so. Her memories of her mother are fuzzy at best.

Chicken stock for saltiness. White wine for acidity. Butter for creaminess. Parmigiano-Reggiano for nuttiness. A pinch of saffron for earthiness and color. And the licorice powder? That's to add an unexpected hint of sweetness.

Perfectly balanced.

He takes a bite. She holds her breath.

His face is frigid and unreadable. Eden can't tell if he likes it or hates it. Somehow *not* knowing is the worst possible outcome. All she can do as he studies her dish is study him right back.

She remembers thinking that Shang was cute, but Alexander is *handsome*. If he smiled, she might even classify him as breathtaking—although she's pretty sure the effort of doing so might kill him.

His black hair is cropped short at the sides, but slightly longer up top, borderline militant in its neatness. He's got a strong jaw with trimmed stubble, also very neat and orderly. It's his eyes that makes Eden's stomach feel strange. They're not just dark and deep, but serious and cold.

As he takes another contemplative bite, there's a glint in his eyes. Whether it's a good or bad sign, she can't tell. She worries he sees right through her, knows her secret, remembers her from their time long since gone by.

She's about to ask for his opinion about the dish she's prepared when a group of chefs enter the restaurant through the back doors. She recognizes two of them, Freddie and Peter, having met them the day before. They're mid-conversation, sharing a hearty laugh. There's also a young Asian woman with cute, cropped bangs walking in front of them. Eden immediately smiles as they approach, even chancing a small wave.

Peter claps Eden on the shoulder and chuckles. "Looks like Hector owes me twenty bucks."

"Why?" she asks.

"We like to make bets on how long the newbies are going to last. Hector—that's the angry redhead over there—said you'd quit by morning."

The Asian woman grins. "I'm Rina, by the way, since dick-head over here hasn't bothered to introduce us. I'm one of the other pâtissiers. I had yesterday off, so it's nice to meet you."

"She works at my station," Freddie states proudly.

Rina scoffs. "You mean *my* station. I've been here longer."

"By, like, a day."

Eden laughs. "Oh, I think she's got you beat, then. Seniority is still seniority."

Rina smirks and nudges Eden in the arm with the tip of her elbow. "I knew I was going to like you."

"So," Peter says, "how did things go this morning? Did Chef give you the speech?"

Eden raises a brow, amused. "The speech?"

"You know. The *this-is-my-kitchen-so-you-need-to-follow-my-rules* speech."

"It's a right of passage," Rina adds.

"He likes to make you cry before you start here," Freddie notes. "To assert dominance."

"I nearly wet myself," Peter confesses, a hand over his heart. Eden can't tell if he's joking.

"That's terrible," she replies. "But, no. He didn't give me the speech. He just asked me to—"

Eden looks to where Alexander is standing. *Was* standing. He's disappeared without a trace, likely having slipped away while the others struck up conversation. Eden can see that the door to the kitchen office in the far corner has been shut and the lights are on, so she assumes that Alexander's retreated for the time being.

It looks like her role as sous chef is safe.

For now.

"Come on," Freddie says. "Everybody else should be arriving shortly. I'll introduce you."

Rina looks at Peter while gesturing at Freddie. "See? That's how *not* to be a dickhead."

"Yeah, yeah," Peter says dismissively.

Eden falls into the swing of things quickly. She's always had to be a fast learner. Necessity requires adaptation, after all. While the space is totally new to her, the functions of the equipment and the roles everyone plays is not. She can do this. She can be a second-in-command, even if she has to fake it until she makes it. The key is confidence. The second she wavers...

*I can't let that happen. I won't.*

So she watches and learns, rapidly acclimatizing to the way things work here.

Everyone's so efficient. It's a little frightening. People move fast and with purpose, preparing their mise-en-place for the night's service. She learns the names of all the chefs, the waitstaff, the dishwashers. She acquaints herself with the location of the produce in the walk-in fridge, as well as the dry goods in the storage room. She even gets her own locker in the staff room past the kitchen office.

Alexander is notably absent during prep.

"Who's the owner?" she asks Rina as she helps bring a huge bag of sugar over to the dessert station. "Or is this Alexander's restaurant?"

Rina visibly shivers. "No, he's not the owner. The real owner is..." She trails off. "Where did you work before this?" Rina asks instead, changing the topic completely.

"Oh, uh... Here and there."

"Did you specialize in a type of cuisine?"

"Not really. I dabbled in this and that. Italian, mostly. French. I worked at an Asian fusion restaurant for a few years, too."

It's all a lie, of course, but Eden doesn't want Rina to know that. If she keeps things general and non-specific, she figures she'll be able to fly under the radar for a while. Forever, if she's careful.

"Asian fusion," someone behind them scoffs.

Eden and Rina turn to find Alexander standing there, a gray plastic bin full of dirty prep dishes in his hands. He holds it out to Eden, and she has no choice but to take it. Not unless she wants dishes to come crashing down at her feet.

"Yes," she says, holding her head up high. *Confidence. The key is confidence.* "Do you have something against Asian fusion?" she asks lightly, putting on her best, most charming smile.

Alexander briefly swallows. "Take these to the dish pit," he tells her instead of answering. "When you're done, join me at the front of the line. We just heard from an unexpected party of fifty. They'll be coming in at the start of service."

Eden shifts. "Fifty? That's—"

Alexander frowns at her. "What? You're not nervous, are you?"

She *really* wants to kick him in the shin.

"No," she grumbles. "I just think it's inconsiderate to show up with a party like that unannounced."

He snorts. "You and me both. Up front. One minute. Let's see what you're made of, Monroe." He walks away without another word.

Eden takes the bin of dirty dishes to the pit as instructed, placing it down with a hard thump and rattle onto the metal counter. It's then that she notices the ornate plate she'd used before to serve Alexander the saffron risotto sitting atop the pile.

It's completely clean, every ounce of it savored.

Triumph rises in her chest. It feels like a win. Her head spins, high off the thrill.

*Maybe I can do this, after all.*

# CHAPTER
## Three

He loves his job.

He also really fucking hates it. Especially because of nights like this.

Eden wasn't wrong when she said an unexpected party of fifty—fucking *fifty*, what the fuck—was inconsiderate. It's probably the biggest asshole move in the history of asshole moves.

No reservation. Not even a courtesy call ahead of time. They apparently just showed up at the front door and gave the poor hostess, Kay, a seriously hard time when she said there might be a wait. Poor girl was half in tears by the time she managed to get a word out to inform him.

They're a bunch of hotshot investment bankers or something—Alexander doesn't give a shit how much cash they want to throw around—and they deliberately spread out across multiple tables, spanning different sections so the waitstaff has no idea who's responsible for whom.

He lets the maître d' handle the seating arrangements. It's in the kitchen that Alexander reigns supreme.

Unfortunately, it's a shitshow in here, too.

Fifty orders at once means there's no time to stagger. Food has to arrive at the same time—or just about—hot and ready for their patrons to eat. Alexander counts his lucky stars that the majority of the party's guests pick from the night's specials menu, ordering roughly twenty lobster tails that have been prepared earlier that day in anticipation of high seasonal demand. It's only a matter of time before they run out, however, and they still have an entire service to get through and other tables to worry about.

It's chaos in the making, and Alexander only has so much time.

"I want the orders for nine, eleven, and fifteen!" he shouts from the front of the kitchen. "Monroe, where's the escargot for table four?"

"Right here," Eden says, taking the plate from Laurie, the on-call boucher, so that the latter can get right back to making seven more orders.

He rings the bell for service. A waiter shows up out of nowhere, popping into existence to spirit the appetizer away.

Eden is everywhere and nowhere all at once, hopping from one station to another to ease the load wherever she can. She tries to be helpful, but more often than not only ends up getting in the way. It's clear that she doesn't know the kitchen well enough yet, struggling to find the exact ingredient she needs or sometimes failing to hear his ticket calls.

Eden's demonstration dish might have been the most delicious thing he's eaten in a very long time, but her disorganization is a huge detractor. The more he watches, the more annoyed he gets.

*I thought she was trained for this sort of thing.*

He pushes the thought away. That can't be right. It's probably just the unfortunate combination of stress due to her first day being on the kitchen floor and the asshole party of fifty out front. It's a terrible cocktail to be thrown into, but if there's one thing Alexander's always certain of, it's baptism by fire.

"Rina, where the hell is that crème brûlée?" he snaps. "Drenton, Jesus Christ, how is this steak undercooked again?"

Nobody responds, individual tunnel visions blocking him out. They're too focused on their tasks at hand to realize he's even speaking.

That just pisses him off more.

"What the fuck guys? I need you to pay attention!"

"They're doing their best," Eden says.

Her words take him by surprise.

"Their best clearly isn't good enough," he retorts. "This is unacceptable. If you guys don't get your shit together, you'll be working at McDonald's by the end of the week."

Eden huffs, exasperated. "Yelling at them isn't going to fix the problem, Chef."

For once in his life, Alexander doesn't have a response ready. His old sous chef never had the guts to talk back. It was always 'yes, chef' and of 'course, chef' and 'you're absolutely right, chef.'

Eden?

She's proving to have a backbone, and Alexander isn't sure how to deal with that.

He wants to yell at her, too, growing more and more frustrated with every passing second. But before he can even open his mouth, Eden expertly slips away to help the saucier like she knows he's about to throw a fit.

Service drags on for endless hours, never letting up to give them an opportunity to breathe. It's a marathon with no water available for its runners. It's just one problem after another, and—despite his years of experience—Alexander begins to feel uneasy.

Nothing's going right.

Peter nicks his finger with his knife and has to step away from his station to clean the wound and staunch the bleeding. Immediately after that, Rina and Freddie accidentally crash into each other, spilling massive amounts of whipped cream all over themselves and the floor. His chef de partie, Hector, slips in the mess, bringing a stack of plates tumbling down along with him. Shards of porcelain explode haphazardly across the tile floor.

"Stop! Everybody just fucking stop!"

His command slices through the kitchen. Nobody dares to move, not even to stir the pot that's very clearly about to boil over.

Just like his anger.

There's a throbbing pain behind his eyes, warning him of the skull-splitting headache awaiting him. He can feel his pulse in his *teeth*. His head is seconds away from imploding. His back hurts from having to carry this restaurant all by his damn self. Alexander wants to put his fist through a wall. He wants to sprint into the walk-in, lock the door behind him, and scream until his voice gives out.

The bitter fury almost gets the better of him. Just as he's about to open his mouth to scream a string of less-than-appropriate comments, his eyes lock with hers.

Eden observes him, big hazel eyes staring up and awaiting instruction. Her brows are pulled together in a question.

*What do you want us to do?*

He stares back.

*Fuck if I know.*

Alexander finally turns and leaves through the back doors of the kitchen, stepping out into the cold back alley. He needs a break, a breath of fresh air. He doesn't know what to do. Things have never fallen apart this badly before. He can already imagine the terrible reviews that are going to haunt La Rouge for years. People will no doubt complain about the slow service, receiving the wrong orders, or the god-awful wait times.

He doesn't end up putting his fist through a wall, mainly because his hands are too important to mess up. How can he hope to hold a knife or do anything else useful if he's accidentally broken a finger?

Outside, Alexander pulls out a small carton from the back pocket of his dark jeans and pulls out a cigarette. Leaning against the alleyway's brick wall, he lights it and takes a long, deep drag of smoke. He feels better, but just barely.

He just needs a second. He just needs a second to gather his thoughts, formulate a plan, and then he can get right back to—

"Alright, team. We've got this." Eden's voice is muffled and distant, but perfectly recognizable through the crack in the restaurant's back doors.

Curious, Alexander crushes his half-smoked cigarette beneath the heel of his shoe and goes back inside.

He's greeted by a cacophony of sound. Chefs hustle back and forth, moving with double the speed and triple the motivation. They communicate with one another, picking up the slack for each other so that nobody is left behind. The broken plates have been swept up and the spilled whipped cream has been mopped. There isn't a trace of a mess. Food is cooked, plates are arranged, orders are being sent out.

And above all the organized chaos, Eden's compliments are loud and clear.

"Good job on the dressing, Laurie. Be careful not to add too much lemon. Excellent work, Rina. I'm sure they'll love the tiramisu. That last dish was perfect, Peter. Try adding a bit more red wine to balance the flavor, though. That's fantastic, Freddie. Can you bring the extra macarons out from the fridge when you have a second? Oh, that's okay, Hector. Take five and put some ice on your wrist just in case."

She's at the front of the line, having assumed his position.

Alexander stands there, dumbfounded. He doesn't understand how she's doing his job so effortlessly. Things were a nightmare until a few minutes ago, so how the hell did she—

little, quiet, unassuming Eden—manage to turn it all around while he wasn't looking?

Eden waves Alexander over. He joins her at the front, silently nursing his neck from the whiplash.

"Kept your spot warm, Chef," she says, the faintest hint of a grin tugging at the corner of her lips. It's not arrogant, but it's certainly teasing.

"How did you do it?"

Eden pats him gently on the shoulder. It's a casual gesture, nothing to read into, and yet he suddenly feels hot under the collar.

"Come on," she says. "Just a few more chits and we'll be over the hill."

Alexander examines the printer sitting just beneath the line. She's right. The rate at which tickets are printing has slowed significantly. They're just about over the crest of this god-awful service.

"We can do this," she assures him. Soft, sweet.

He frowns, but nods once. How did Eden go from not knowing what she was doing to running the entire kitchen by herself? What had Alexander missed while out for a smoke?

And why is she still touching his shoulder? Were it anybody else, Alexander would have swatted her hand away by now like a gnat. He finds he can't bring himself to do it.

Maybe his brain's too fried to care anymore.

He clears his throat and takes a step away. The sudden lack of warmth from her fingers is noticeable, but he pretends not to care.

His new sous chef might be made of something special after all.

They get through it somehow. A miracle, all things considered. The party of asshat investment bankers at least had the decency to leave a generous tip atop their massive bill.

His staff is understandably exhausted, so they clean up for the night in silence. Everybody just wants to get out of here, so they close in record time. The majority of the chefs trickle out, hurriedly leaving to get to their cars. Alexander's waiting for the last couple of people to leave so he can turn off the lights and lock the door.

Peter, Freddie, and Rina are still gathering up their things. Eden's not five feet away.

"Shit," Peter sighs. "I need a drink. I need three drinks."

"I think O'Malley's might still be open," Rina notes.

"That sounds really tempting," Freddie adds, rubbing at the back of his neck. "Hey, Eden? Feel like grabbing a drink with us?"

Out of the corner of his eye, Alexander can see her smile politely. How she has the energy to be amicable is beyond him.

"Thanks for the offer, but I don't drink," she says. "And I have to be getting home, anyways."

Rina pumps her eyebrows. "Got a boyfriend at home waiting for you?"

Eden just laughs.

Alexander doesn't understand why the lack of an answer bothers him. He's probably just irritable because—yeah—fuck this night. His feet are killing him, his headache is in full force, and he just wants to—as Samuel L. Jackson famously once put it—go the fuck to sleep.

"Oh, well. Maybe next time, then." Freddie turns and grins at Hector. "Feel like tagging along?"

Hector slings the strap of his bag over his shoulder, grumbling a string of profanities under his breath that Alexander doesn't quite catch. He bumps into Eden on his way out, not bothering to apologize. When he passes Alexander by the door, Hector sneers, but doesn't look him in the eye.

"What's his problem?" Eden asks, slipping out of her chef jacket. It's covered in stains, and there are several loose threads at the seams.

Alexander notes that she doesn't seem to have a sweater or anything to put on, just her tank top and then her winter coat, which is in a similar state of disrepair like her work uniform. She really is just skin and bones. He briefly wonders if she managed to eat on her break. But the thought is immediately followed up with, *she's an adult, she can take care of herself.*

"Ignore him," Rina says to Eden. "Hector's just bitter that he didn't get his promotion to sous."

Eden blinks. "Oh."

Alexander sighs loudly. "Less talk. More walking."

He finally manages to usher everybody out the door. If he shuts it harder than necessary, nobody says anything. They exchange quick goodbyes and well wishes for good nights. Alexander doesn't stick around long enough to be extended an invitation for drinks, not that he expects to receive one. Not that he would care to join, either way. These are his employees. He's the boss.

They're not friends.

Freddie, Peter, and Rina depart in the opposite direction, throwing waves over their shoulders.

"I want you here two hours early tomorrow," he says to Eden before she can escape into the night.

"Again?"

"Got a problem with that?"

Eden chews on the inside of her cheek and glances down at her shoes. Her shoes are filthy and run-down. "No problem at all."

Alexander leaves it at that and heads to his car. His black Audi is parked in the same spot it always is: the back corner stall at the very back of the restaurant's parking lot. He lets out a long, deep breath the second he's in the driver's seat and the door's shut behind him. It feels good to sit down for the first time in hours.

"Christ," he grumbles to himself, closing his eyes.

He reviews the events of tonight's service like a play-by-play, determining where they went wrong and how he can fix things for tomorrow.

Drenton's still undercooking his plates. It's either borderline carelessness, or he's really losing his touch. Alexander's sure to have words with Drenton later. Rina and Freddie were behind for most of the night, and Alexander suspects it's because they're too damn chatty for their own good. He might have to put them in different sections if they keep distracting each other. Hector is a miserable little weasel, as per usual, but at least he knows he can handle the pressure.

Eden surprised him tonight.

Clumsy at times, a force to be reckoned with at others. She wasn't afraid to stand up to him, which was both inexplicably frustrating and refreshing at the same time. He wonders what surprises tomorrow will bring.

Alexander opens his eyes and prepares to twist the key in the ignition. He stops short when he spots Eden on the other side of the street, standing at the bus stop near the curb. The bus shows up not five seconds later—the last one of the night—opening its doors wide for her. The vehicle leaves and then she's gone.

As he starts the engine and pulls out of the lot, Alexander

thinks it's weird Eden can't afford her own transportation. She's apparently worked as a sous chef for several restaurants before, and her salary there alone would have been more than enough to afford her a cheap car. Or, at the very least, a chef jacket that doesn't look like it's about to fall apart.

Maybe she's bad with her money. Maybe she's just super frugal. Or maybe she's trying to reduce her carbon footprint by taking public transit. In the end, it's none of his business.

He lights a cigarette to make up for the one he didn't finish earlier. He lets the burn of smoke build in his lungs as the memory of Eden touching his arm flashes across his mind. His heart picks up speed, but he has no sweet clue why.

"Whatever," he mumbles to himself as he drives home.

# CHAPTER
## Four

The first thing Eden does when she gets back to the apartment is toe off her shoes, walk over to the back of the living room couch, and flop head-first over the back to bury her face in the cushions.

Every inch of her body is sore. Her hands are dry from constant washing, her hair is a knotted mess, and she still has the scent of murky dish water up her nose.

She contemplates falling asleep then and there, but not at the risk of waking up with a kink in her neck and a knot between her shoulders. Eden sits up, forces herself to stand, and slowly but surely drags her dead feet down the hall to the bedroom.

*Got a boyfriend at home waiting for you?*

Rina's question was perfectly innocent, but somewhere deep down, Eden could feel the sting in her chest. No, there was nobody at home waiting for her. Her cramped one-bedroom apartment can only boast one resident, and she isn't there half the time anyway thanks to work.

Fridge, empty.

Laundry, piling up.

Dust, everywhere.

Hotel, Trivago.

Eden has no time to clean. She has more important matters to take care of.

She heads over to her wardrobe—a white, four-drawer cabinet from Ikea she managed to score when one of her neighbors moved out— and pulls the top drawer open. Eden reaches to the back and fishes out the large coffee tin she's hidden there, popping the plastic lid off to peer at the contents inside.

Cash. Lots of it.

She adds what she earned from tonight's service—the kitchen gets 5% kickback of whatever the servers earn in tips—and closes the lid back up, replacing the coffee tin quickly.

"Only five thousand to go," she whispers to herself, half-reminder and half-assurance.

She forgoes taking a shower and decides to wash in the morning. Right now, her bed beckons.

He's there before she is, tall and alert and appearing well-rested. Eden doesn't understand how he looks so refreshed considering how late they worked last night. His dark black hair is washed and absurdly fluffy. His face is serene in the daylight. Practically sparkling.

Then there's her. She's more than aware that her hair is still wet from her shower, and her bangs are doing that weird cowlick thing she despises. There are dark circles beneath her eyes, her cheeks feel puffy, and she'd be willing to do just about anything to get one more hour of sleep.

*So unfair.*

Alexander sips at his coffee, observing the time on his watch. Eden's really starting to hate that damn thing.

"Congratulations," he says dryly. "You're only thirty seconds late."

"Traffic was awful," she replies, shrugging off her jacket to hang it up.

She's about to pull out her uniform jacket when Alexander shakes his head. "Stop."

"What?"

"You're not putting that thing on."

"Why not?"

"Because it's filthy."

"I washed it last night."

"Did you?"

"Yes..." she mumbles sheepishly.

"I expect my chefs to look the part. You look like you stepped off the line of a burger chain."

Eden glares at him. "So what?"

Alexander sets down his mug of coffee and tosses a plastic bag to her. Eden hadn't noticed the package sitting behind him because his wide shoulders and large chest obscured the view. Inside is a brand-new black chef jacket, much like his own.

It's the prettiest thing Eden's ever seen. La Rouge's logo is custom stitched beautifully into the front pen pocket in bright crimson thread. It has an asymmetrical collar with three-quarter length sleeves, made from a polyester and cotton blend. The fabric is soft beneath her fingers, and it smells like it was bought straight from the store. A bit like plastic, but miles better than her own questionable jacket.

"How much did this cost?" she asks, hoping that her voice comes out even.

"Don't worry about it," he says casually. "It'll come out of your first paycheck."

Eden swallows. She can't have that. She knows it's stupid to count her eggs before they've hatched, but as far as she's concerned, all of her paychecks are spoken for. She's calculated for every last penny.

Rent, utilities, bus and train fare, groceries.

The rest goes to her coffee tin. She should be able to save five thousand in a little over three months provided she doesn't have any unnecessary expenses crop up.

Like this new jacket, for instance. Even though it's lovely and she knows her old one is disgusting and ill-fitting and stained an unfortunate yellow in certain areas, she can't afford it. Custom, high-quality jackets like this one can be a couple hundred dollars. That's money she'd rather use elsewhere.

Eden has long since made peace with the fact that she quite literally can't have nice things.

She holds it back out to Alexander and glances at her shoes, which are also depressing to look at. "I can't accept this," she says. "My jacket's plenty fine."

When Alexander doesn't say anything, Eden glances up. She expects anger to be written all over his face. Instead, she finds bemused curiosity.

He takes it back with a shrug. "Fine. Let's get started, then."

Eden takes a deep breath, relieved to finally get to work. "Are you going to walk me through tonight's specials?"

Alexander shakes his head. "No. You're going to make me another dish."

"Did you like my risotto that much?"

"Don't get cocky, Monroe."

"You never told me what you thought about it."

"It was... satisfactory."

"You licked the plate clean," she counters with a smirk.

Alexander scoffs. "I did no such thing."

"Come on, admit it."

"Do you normally talk this much?"

Eden puts her hands on her hips, defiant. "Yes, because I'm

friendly. Do you know what that is? Or should I explain it to you?"

He holds her gaze for a few seconds, his hand dwarfing his coffee mug. "I gave you an instruction, chef. Don't make me tell you again."

With a resigned sigh, Eden asks, "Any requests?"

"Something that you enjoy."

Alexander takes a step back to lean against the prep counter as he sips at his coffee, observing in silence. Eden wastes no time and gets started, pulling out her leather knife roll from her backpack.

She has a preference for Japanese knives from Shun. They're lightweight and their slim pakkawood handles are comfortable to hold in her small hands. She's had these knives for a few years now, having found them for cheap at the local thrift store for nearly half of their actual value. Eden's grateful these knives found their way to her. They would have been wasted on anyone else.

She gathers the ingredients she needs from the walk-in and begins her prep, finely chopping stalks of green onion while she sautées minced chicken thighs in pad Thai sauce in a nonstick pan. Rich aromas fill the air, the hiss and sizzle of food over low heat music to hear ears.

Alexander grimaces. "You know this is a French cuisine restaurant, right?"

Eden grins, but keeps her eyes on the food in front of her. "I know. I just wanted to get back at you for scoffing at Asian fusion."

She thinks she hears him groan under his breath, "Ugh."

"What do you have against it? Oh, wait. Let me guess. You're a haute cuisine purist."

"Damn straight."

Alexander's phone dings a few times as she cooks, alerting

him of a new text message. After briefly glancing at the screen, he shoves the phone back into his pocket. All of the messages go ignored.

"Don't you need to get that?" she asks as she mixes in some freshly beaten eggs.

"Nope," he replies before downing the rest of his caffeine. "So, what happened last night?"

"What?"

"What did you do? To turn everything around."

Eden shrugs. "I told them to calm down. Said some encouraging things. People respond well to positive reinforcement, you know."

He visibly shifts his weight from foot to foot, but makes no comment. Eden chances a glance at him. He looks confused, like the concept of being nice to another living, breathing human being has never crossed his mind.

Eden plates everything up, bite-sized morsels perfect for sharing.

Alexander eyes the dish skeptically. "What the hell is it?"

"Pad Thai tacos," she says, beaming brightly.

He stares at her for a long while before sighing. "Christ."

"You said I could make something that I enjoy. I happen to enjoy these. You can't blame me if you're not going to be specific."

"Fair."

"Just try one. You'll like it, I promise."

Alexander takes a bite and chews. He says nothing, leaving Eden in anticipation.

"Well?" she prompts, hope rising in her chest. "Pretty good, right?"

"It's edible."

Eden deflates a little. That wasn't quite what she was expecting to hear. But then again, this isn't Shang she's talking to. Eden has to remind herself that the man standing before her, judging her food... They're two entirely different people.

Shang was encouraging, patient, and kind.

Alexander is—well—kind of a dick, to be honest.

Nevertheless, he ends up eating a quarter of the mini tacos before handing the plate back to her. Considering who she's dealing with, Eden takes it as a compliment that he didn't trash her efforts after the first bite.

"What do you want me to do with the rest?" she asks.

He wipes his large hands on the front of his apron. "Finish it off and then get started on prep. The others will be here in a few minutes."

"Finish it off? You mean I get to—"

Alexander's already gone, retreating into the shadows of the kitchen office.

Eden's mouth waters. She's been surviving on instant ramen and that cheap Indian restaurant around the corner from her apartment for months now. Even though she works in a five-star restaurant, Eden can't even begin to dream of affording something off of La Rouge's menu.

She takes Alexander up on the offer and eats up every last crumb, swallowing everything down in a hurry. Rich sauce coats her tongue, her grumbling belly thankful for the meal.

Today's shaping up to be a good day.

# CHAPTER
## Five

Today's most certainly *not* shaping up to be a good day.

Seeing the state of Eden's knives was physically painful for Alexander to stomach.

They were old as hell, sharpened within an inch of their life. Even the handles had been worn down from repeated use, dips in the wood where her fingers form a grip.

It's not uncommon for professional chefs to go through a new set once every three years or so. Alexander personally sharpens his work knives every day well before service starts. He prefers German knives to Japanese ones. They're heavy and thick, offering perfect balance in his large hands. A chef is only as good as his tools.

Which is exactly why Alexander has no idea how Eden's made it this far. She must be operating out of sheer stubbornness and talent alone. He recognizes that he's irritated, but not because of the damn toothpicks she calls knives.

He's irritated because there's clearly more going on than meets the eye. Eden obviously has the right not to open up about whatever's going on. It's her personal business, and Alexander has no right to pry. But this growing feeling of concern is beginning to eat at him. It sits in the pit of his stomach, quietly stewing.

Catching public transport. Sad uniform. Scarfing down food like she never gets to eat. Something isn't right.

Alexander may or may not have peeked out of the kitchen office to make sure Eden actually ate the rest of her Asian fusion abomination. Her *delicious* Asian fusion abomination.

As much as it bothers him to admit, Alexander has never tasted anything so amazing before. The sauce was tangy, notes of lime coming to the forefront without being overpowering.

The mini pita shells she'd used had been warmed on the skillet, offering a lovely crunchy texture to offset the softness of the Pad Thai. Alexander is pretty sure he would have finished the whole damn thing, but then he heard Eden's stomach grumble.

He couldn't quite understand the warmth that bloomed in his chest to see her so fully enjoying her meal. She looked so happy, so delighted. It made him feel... strange.

His phone dings again, and he knows he can't get away with hiding anymore. There are five new messages waiting for him, all from the same sender.

> Sebastian: How are things going with the new menu, my boy?

> Sebastian: I hope your new hire is helping to relieve some of your responsibilities.

> Sebastian: I expect great things. Winning another Michelin will be a feather in La Rouge's cap.

> Sebastian: Slow to respond today, eh? I hope you're managing.

> Sebastian: You're busy. I understand. Reply when you can.

Alexander drags a hand over his face.

*Fuck.*

He's been putting off coming up with a new menu for Sebastian for months now, and he doesn't know how much longer his excuses will hold up. At first, Alexander had argued that the lack of a sous chef placed too much work on his shoulders to fully concentrate on making new recipes. Now his excuse is that he's still busy training his sous, so he doesn't have time.

Allegedly.

He just doesn't want to admit that he's in a slump. He has been for a very long time, and he's just barely pulling things together to give the impression that nothing's wrong. Nobody knows that he's losing it, his passion for food. He just...

He simply doesn't care as much as he used to. All he cared about was earning his first Michelin. Now he has three. Earning another hardly carries the same motivation as it once did. If anything, Sebastian's more eager to win the damn thing because it means he can justify another menu price hike.

Sebastian owns La Rouge, just as much as he owns Alexander, and Sebastian takes every opportunity to remind him.

*I expect great things. I'm the one who saved you. You owe all of this—your career, your fame, your restaurant—to me.*

Alexander puts his phone away.

**D**inner service is busy, but it's not catastrophically unmanageable.

He holds back tonight, curious to see Eden in action. She's not as hesitant as the day before, and she already knows everybody by name. It's clear within thirty seconds of watching her that she's a people person. Always smiling, always complimenting, always supportive. When she turns to set the dishes for table ten on the line, Alexander suddenly remembers something.

A girl with brown hair. A sweet smile. The Gagnon-Allard school crest stitched onto the front pocket of her uniform. Brimming with life and possibility. He can't recall the finer details of her face, which he supposes makes sense. He graduated from Gagnon-Allard ten years ago. A lot has happened since then.

*Good job, Shang.*

It's a quick flash of a memory he isn't sure is real or if he made it up. He blinks and finds Eden peering up at him.

"What?" he asks.

"I said, can you please move over? I'm trying to get to the parsley."

"Oh."

Alexander moves to the side so that Eden can step forward and get to the garnish. It's a huge kitchen, but she stands not two inches away. She's close enough that he can admire her freckles. They're actually kind of cute.

*Wait, what?*

"Ah, shoot," Rina grumbles under her breath from her station. "Can somebody please grab the strawberry compôte from the fridge? I'm running low for the *flaugnarde aux fraises*, and my hands are kind of full right now."

Alexander almost scolds Rina for being so careless out of her pure habit, but before he can even open his mouth to get a word out, Eden raises her hand with a chipper smile.

"I'll get it for you," she offers, moving toward the walk-in with purpose.

He resumes work, calling out the next order that prints off the machine. They're working at a good pace, fast enough to keep things from piling up, but not so fast that his chefs will burn out before the rush is over. Alexander tries to concentrate on the final checks for table thirty-two, but his thoughts are hazy. It's just all so...

Repetitive.

Day in and day out. Opening the restaurant, closing the restaurant. The same food, the same people, the same routine.

It's no wonder he's in a slump. His mind is numb to the process. Running La Rouge isn't as thrilling of a challenge anymore, and Sebastian's demands for a new lineup only compounds his disinterest.

*Maybe I can try deconstructed recipes.*

*No, that's been done a thousand times before.*

He's pulled from his thoughts when he hears a woman yelp in surprise. The sound of something crashing loudly makes his heart spike.

Eden.

"Out of my way," he snaps, rushing toward the walk-in where the commotion originated. Alexander pulls open the door and freezes.

Eden's uniform is drenched, stained red from strawberry compôte. It drips and pools onto the tile floor, bits of sticky fruit scattered about. Hector is here, too, standing not three feet away while apologizing profusely.

"I'm so sorry," he repeats again and again. "I didn't mean—"

Alexander pushes Hector forcefully to the side, furious. "What's going on here?"

Eden shakes her head. "It was an accident," she says, voice quivering from the shock—and very likely from the chill. "I wasn't looking where I was going. I thought there'd be room."

"No, it was my fault," Hector mumbles quickly. "I should have just waited."

Alexander clenches his jaw when he sees Eden shiver. The fabric of her jacket is so thin, it's now see-through. He can make out the line of her bra strap, as well as the points of her breasts.

Eden crosses her arms over herself, her cheeks and the tips of her ears pink with embarrassment.

Alexander averts his eyes, ignoring the way his stomach flutters and his throat tightens. "Trisko, you stupid—"

"It's fine," Eden interrupts, placing a hand on his forearm. "Please, it's not a big deal."

"But you're—"

"Please." Eden swallows, casting her gaze to the floor.

Her discomfort is contagious. Alexander can feel the muscles in the back of his neck straining. He glares at his chef de partie. "Clean this up," he orders sharply.

Hector nods. "Right away, Chef. I'm so sorry, Eden."

Eden forces a smile, and Alexander has to fight against telling her not to do that. She isn't obligated to be polite in this situation. She should be angry. Lord knows Alexander would be if he were in her syrup-logged shoes.

"It's all right, Hector," she says softly. "Just be careful you don't slip in the mess."

"Sorry," Hector mutters one last time.

Except he doesn't *look* sorry.

"Come on," Alexander grumbles to her, guiding her out of the walk-in fridge.

He takes Eden around the perimeter of the busy kitchen—all of the other chefs are watching her with concern—and leads her to the staff room. There's a small men and women's bathroom just off to the side.

"Take your time cleaning up," he says. "There's no rush."

"We're in the middle of dinner service," she argues.

"I've got it covered."

"I'll just run this under the hand dryer. I'll be out in a few."

Alexander bites down on his tongue. He knows that isn't going to work, but says nothing. All he can do is watch as Eden hurriedly retreats into the women's bathroom and shuts the door behind her.

He goes back to the kitchen in a sour mood. The other chefs all stare at him, as if waiting for an explanation. He gives none. Instead, he shouts, "What the fuck are you all standing around for? Get back to work!"

People scurry back to their stations, but Alexander can't seem to shake the impossible knot in his guts.

"Man the line, Drenton," he snaps at Peter before rushing off to the kitchen office. He picks up the black chef jacket he tried to give to Eden earlier before slipping into the break area around back.

He knocks on the women's bathroom door. "Monroe?"

"Yeah?" Her voice comes as a muffle from the other side.

"I brought you something to—"

Eden opens the door quickly. She's stripped down to her sports bra, her jacket and undershirt wringed out and drying on the bathroom sink's edge. Alexander's eyes are immediately drawn to the graceful length of her neck, the delicate dip of her collar bone, and the peaks of her breasts.

She's so small, he'd have no problem picking her up if he wanted to. Alexander wonders what Eden's skin would feel like beneath his palms. He's suddenly curious to know if she's as soft as she looks, or what it would feel like to brush his fingers over the gentle curve of her breasts. Maybe he could venture down further, kiss marks against her belly, her inner thighs...

"Chef? You're staring."

Alexander rips his gaze away. Gulps. His whole face feels hot. "Take this," he grumbles, shoving the new jacket into her hands. "Cover up."

"But I—"

"Don't argue with me, Monroe. Just... put it on. Please."

Eden hesitates, her mouth opening only to snap shut again. She nods and accepts the gift.

Alexander leaves in a hurry, making a pit stop in the walk-in freezer so that he has a chance to calm down and ignore the growing stiffness in his pants. It takes him a minute—or five—before he manages to get everything under control and return to his spot at the head of the line.

Eden shows up a few minutes later, and she looks...

*Beautiful.*

It's a perfect fit and far more flattering than her previous jacket, which was clearly two sizes too large for her small frame. She looks elegant and professional, where before she looked inexperienced and barely keeping things together. Her hazel eyes look that much brighter in contrast—*dazzling*.

"It suits you," he says before he has the chance to think about it.

Eden laughs politely, her cheeks turning an even richer shade of pink. It's not a real laugh, he knows. Just one to ease her nervousness. "I don't know if that's true, but thanks. I promise to pay you back."

"Don't bother."

"I can't accept—"

"I'll write it off as a business expense."

"Chef—"

He turns to shout over his shoulder. "I need the appetizers for table four! Drenton, where's the filet mignon?"

"Twenty seconds out, Chef," Peter calls.

Eden hasn't moved an inch, prompting him to say, "Don't you have work to do?"

She nods, quietly getting back to it.

Alexander grins to himself when he catches Eden briefly admiring her blurry reflection against one of the large stainless-steel pots at the entremetier's station.

He's thankful when service is over. They had a good night. They all made plenty in tips, closing duties were taken care of quickly, and they were out and headed home in under twenty minutes.

Freddie, Peter, and Rina leave with Eden as one big group. Alexander is the last one out, locking the door behind him.

Rina slings an arm over Eden's shoulder. "Feel like joining us for drinks tonight?"

Peter smiles. "I scored some cheap beer. You a Jeopardy fan?"

"I am," Eden replies with a wry smile.

"Then you should join us at my place," Freddie says cheerfully. "Nothing beats a long day at work like getting buzzed and yelling at a TV screen."

"That sounds like fun, but I'm still all gross and sticky. I should probably shower and change."

"Then how about we go to your place?" Rina suggests. "Come on. We really want to hang with you."

"Yeah," Peter says with a nod. "You seem like a cool kid."

Eden laughs. "Do I?"

"Don't make him give you puppy eyes," Freddie warns. "You'll be a guaranteed goner."

"Fine," she relents. "I know I stink, but do you think you could give me a ride? I'll give you directions as we go."

Rina beams. "Oh, yay!"

Eden turns to Alexander, who's fishing for his car keys in his pockets. "Would you like to come?"

The invitation comes as a surprise to him. He never gets invited to these sorts of things. Alexander's sure he looks stupid, mouth hanging open slightly and caught off-guard.

His first instinct is to decline. He hates unnecessary social gatherings. They've all had a long day, and he just wants to go home.

But a smaller, quieter voice in the back of his head wants to say yes. It could turn out to be fun. Mildly amusing, at best.

Then he sees how uncomfortable Freddie, Peter, and Rina all are. They don't have to say anything, he just knows. It's in the way they stiffen, their eyes cast to the ground, to each other, to anywhere other than at him. Alexander's sure that hanging out with their boss after an eight-hour shift is the last thing they want.

Luckily, his phone dings again, giving him an out from responding right away. It's a text message. Much to his relief, not from Sebastian.

Bea: You up?

He texts a quick response and then shoves his phone back in his pocket. "Busy," he says before leaving for his car.

He pretends not to notice how relieved they appear. He also pretends not to notice how Eden is the only one who seems disappointed.

Alexander gets in his car and drives away, but doesn't head home.

He shows up at Bea's apartment not five blocks away. There's no passion in their kiss at the doorway when she lets him in. It's just how they say hello without having to worry about needless small talk. Bea is another head chef in town—working at some little place called The Lunchbox—so she's usually as tired as he is. It's perfunctory at this point, just the way they like it.

Their arrangement is simple.

She texts, he comes over, they fuck, they both get what they want, he leaves.

Rinse, recycle, repeat.

And it works for them. They're both too busy to date, but there's no denying that they still have physical needs. Alexander's never been keen on dating. Not when La Rouge takes up all his time and dedication. The restaurant is basically his wife—demanding and oftentimes unappreciative. Bea feels similarly.

There's also the fact that Alexander's familiar enough with Bea that he doesn't mind her touch. Not that she gets the chance to do it often. This isn't a touchy-feely sort of deal.

They're both undressed by the time they get to her bedroom. Alexander's so familiar with her apartment that he can navigate expertly in the dark. She has a nice place, but the bedroom is really the only area he's bothered getting to know.

Just like at work, everything has its place.

Condoms are in the left side drawer of the nightstand. Bathroom's across the hall. The apartment door is past the living room where it never seems to hit him on the way out.

Bea is a beautiful woman. Sharp cheekbones, pointed chin, strong brows. Physically speaking, she never fails to get his engine revving. It's just a shame that she's too damn loud for Alexander's liking.

He fucks her against the mattress, each thrust hard and practiced. He knows she likes it rough. She knows he prefers her on her hands and knees so he can pound her from behind. There are no surprises, as well as no need for exploration. Alexander can get her to come in under four minutes because that's just how routine this is.

"Oh, yes," she groans loudly, gripping at the sheets. "Yes! Right there! That's right, give me your fat cock."

God, he wishes she'd shut up.

Alexander grabs her by the waist and snaps his hips against her, chasing after more of that sweet friction. He can feel her pussy fluttering around his shaft, squeezing him tighter. She's close.

He isn't.

He's just not into it today. Much like everything else, this all feels so gray. Alexander closes his eyes and blocks out Bea's obnoxiously loud screams of pleasure—at least, he thinks it's pleasure... Sometimes he wonders if she's faking it. That, or she's dead set on pissing off the neighbors. He tries to concentrate, eagerly seeking release.

He imagines Bea's voice softer, sweeter. Maybe even with the hint of an accent. He pictures a woman, deconstructed. A wisp of light brown hair. Full lips. The scent of coffee and vanilla. Defiantly beautiful hazel eyes with a hint of freckles gracing her skin.

Alexander comes hard, a bright heat exploding from his core. His whole body shudders as ecstasy ripples through him, the tension in his muscles melting away in an instant. He remains there, his breathing labored. Alexander's not quite mortified, but he's certainly stunned.

*Where the hell did that come from?*

"Wow," Bea says with a content sigh. "What got you going there, tiger?"

Alexander doesn't answer. He gets dressed and dips down to kiss Bea on the cheek before he goes.

# CHAPTER
## Six

"Damn, girl. You live like this?"

Rina elbows Peter in the stomach. "Don't say that, you dick. You're so freaking rude."

He chuckles good-naturedly. "I was only joking. Trust me, my place is in rougher shape."

Eden smiles, though there's a tingle of bashful shame coloring her cheeks. She knows her apartment has seen better days. She counts her blessings that she did the dishes and took out the trash earlier that morning. It's not filthy, just a bit neglected. An abandoned home in the middle of nowhere.

"Don't worry," she says lightly. "I'll get him back for it later. Please make yourselves comfortable. I'll hop in the shower and be out in a second."

"I'll order Chinese," Freddie says. "Or should we just get KFC?"

"But I want nachos!" Rina protests.

"Get all three," Peter insists. "Beer and chicken wings are divine. And the more we order, the more we might actually get to eat before Rina breathes it all down."

Rina elbows Peter in the stomach again. "Shut up. I'm not that bad."

"Oh, please," Freddie says with a snort. "I've seen you down a whole-ass chicken all by yourself."

"I was *hungry*."

Eden holds back a laugh as she ventures down the hall, making a pitstop to her room. They're four highly trained chefs —well, maybe not her—arguing about what kind of fast-food they want to eat. She doesn't know why she feels like she's committing a cardinal sin, but screw it. A little chow mein, chicken wings, and fully loaded nachos to share doesn't sound half bad. Eden's in definite need of comfort food.

She deposits her tips for the night. Little by little, she's getting closer to her last five grand. It should feel like an achievement.

All she feels is tired.

She's so close she can taste it. She tells herself that she just has to put up with things for a little while longer. Once she has the funds...

*Then I can finally find them.*

Eden hides the coffee tin under a pile of old sweaters in the drawer before shutting it securely. She's sure that her new friends aren't going to snoop around and take what isn't theirs, but Eden's learned to be cautious. After the stunt Parsons pulled ten years ago, she can't even bring herself to trust the banks to keep an eye on her money. It's safer where she can see it, touch it, obsess over every penny.

She gets in the shower and lets the hot spray trickle over her, washing away the sticky strawberry mess she couldn't quite get rid of back at the restaurant. Eden shampoos her hair, massaging her scalp with the tips of her fingers.

She knows it wasn't an accident. Eden should have suspected right away that Hector was up to no good when he followed her into the walk-in, but she didn't know what to expect. Before she knew what was happening, she tripped over his extended foot, stumbled, and dropped the bin on herself. She didn't even remember screaming in shock, the sudden cold whiting her mind.

And then Alexander was there in the blink of an eye.

At first, Eden thought he was going to berate her for being careless. Instead, he put distance between her and Hector, standing in front of her like a shield. She couldn't remember the last time she'd felt more protected. She could sense the rage in his stance, in the way his fists were clenched, in the tightness of his jaw. He looked about ready to choke Hector to death.

Eden decides not to dwell on it. It's over now. If Hector tries something like that again, she'll deal with it appropriately. For now, all she can do is keep an eye out.

She gets out of the shower, dries off, and puts on a fresh set of sweatpants and her old Lady Gaga T-shirt she bought second hand at a thrift store. She used to dream about going to a big concert when she was a little girl, the idea of flashing lights and loud music and maybe even fireworks filling her with glee. It was a simpler time, back when she was still full of hope and had a bright future.

*Before my parents...*

"Eden!" Freddie shouts from the living room. "Show's starting!"

"Coming!" she calls back.

Rina scooches over on the couch to make room for her while Peter hands her a can of beer. Eden normally doesn't drink—mostly because she can't afford to—but she takes it and cracks it open. Freddie and Peter sit together on the floor in front of the coffee table, Peter's arm comfortably slung over Freddie's shoulder. Eden thinks they look cute together. The small TV—she got it for cheap at the local pawn shop—casts an array of light across their faces, the familiar blue of the Jeopardy title card filling the dimly lit living room. It's a late-night rerun, but she has zero complaints if it means getting the opportunity to hang out with her new friends.

Freddie laughs, pointing at the screen. "*Yo*. Doesn't that contestant look exactly like Patty?"

Peter squints. "The one on the end? Nah, I don't think so."

"Who's Patty?" Eden asks.

"She used to work with us," Rina explains. "She was our old sous chef. Total badass. The one before Mitchell."

"Mitchell?"

"He's the one you replaced."

"Oh. What happened to her?"

"She quit," says Freddie, leaning back to rest against Rina's knees.

"In the most spectacular fashion, too," Peter adds with a grin. "You should have seen it, Eden. It was like something out of a movie. A glorious trash fire I couldn't look away from. Damn near burned my retinas."

"What happened?" she asks.

"Alexander's what happened. Patty was probably one of the only people not afraid to challenge him. I think they got into an argument about the French onion soup—"

"It was the quiche, Lorraine," Freddie corrects. He looks off into the distance, clearly haunted. "I'll never forget."

"Sure. The quiche. Anyways, they had a huge fight right in front of all of us."

"Should have grabbed some popcorn," Rina says with a chuckle. "It was amazing."

"They really got into it," continues Peter. "They were so loud, some of the patrons out front actually called the cops."

Eden swallows. "Gosh, that's awful."

"No, it was spectacular," Peter says, dramatically waving his hands in the air. "Patty gave him a piece of her mind. Called him a prick to his face. '*An unfeeling, pretentious asshole whose food is unoriginal and overpriced.'* I couldn't have said it better myself."

Eden grimaces. "That seems... harsh."

Freddie shakes his head. "You're sweet, Eden, but you don't need to defend the second coming of the devil."

Peter and Rina laugh, like it's an inside joke. Eden doesn't think it's particularly funny, but only because she knows.

*He wasn't always like this.*

They don't dwell on the subject for much longer once the game show starts. Freddie, Peter, and Rina waste no time yelling answers at the screen. Eden joins them, chiming in only when she knows she has the right answer. Freddie makes wild guesses and gets lucky half the time. Peter answers every single time, but he's rarely right. Rina thinks aloud before answering, or outright admits that she doesn't know.

It's actually a lot of fun. Eden can't remember the last time she hung out for the sake of hanging out. It's surprisingly easy to be around them.

The first commercial break rolls around just in time for the food to arrive. Peter is the one who answers the door, and he eventually returns with three separate bags crammed full of greasy fast food.

Eden is ravenous.

They talk while they eat, occasionally making fun of the over-the-top gum commercial that plays twice in a row. Why does an ad for chewing gum need to be so damn cinematic?

"So," Rina says, practically slurping the meat clean off her hot wing. "Where did you go to culinary school, Eden?"

"Gagnon-Allard," Eden answers stiffly, deliberately stuffing her mouth full of chow mein so that she doesn't have to elaborate.

"Just like His Majesty, huh?" Peter chimes. "Glad you didn't come out of there like a tyrant, too."

"What about you guys?" Eden asks, hoping to take the spotlight off of her.

"Freddie and I studied at the NYC Institute," Peter says. "We were in the same class. Wound up landing our jobs at La Rouge at the exact same time."

"And you?" Eden asks, looking at Rina.

"I studied at Hayson Polytechnic with my sister, Penny. She used to work at La Rouge, too."

"Where's she at now?"

Rina beams. "In Paris. She's opening up her own restaurant come springtime."

Eden's eyes widen. "That's amazing!"

"Working at La Rouge does that for you," Freddie mentions, finishing off his first can of beer. "Like it or not, having La Rouge on your resumé can open a lot of doors."

"It's the only reason I'm still here," Peter admits, scoffing. "Just have to put up with Alexander's shit for a few years and then I'm packing up and working with someone who actually appreciates me."

"Don't forget to take me with you," Freddie reminds.

Peter kisses his cheek. "Don't worry. I wouldn't leave you behind to rot there."

"What about you?" Rina asks Eden. "Want to open your own place one day? I can't imagine you want to be a sous chef forever. Not for him, at least."

Eden shrugs. "I don't know. I haven't really thought about it much."

It's the truth. Right now, she only has a singular priority, one that involves an intense amount of savings before she can take the next step. Working at La Rouge is only a means to an end. She can't see that far into the future, so Eden doesn't bother thinking about it.

The game show comes back on to the screen. The host

speaks clearly, reading off of his prompt card. "This private investigator saw the safe return of actor Michael Blaine in 2019."

Before the contestants even get the chance to press their buzzers, Eden whispers, "Maxine Kendo."

"Who is Maxine Kendo?" the Patty lookalike asks.

"That's correct."

Freddie whistles. "Wow. How'd you know that?"

"I don't even know who that is," Peter admits.

"That's because you're dumb," Rina teases.

Eden shrugs her shoulders, sinking into the cushions behind her. "I'm just good at trivia," she lies.

"If that's the case, you should join us for trivia night at the pub next weekend," Freddie says. "You could help us break our losing streak."

Eden smiles. "Sure. Why not?"

They return to their food, eating and chatting and yelling at one of the contestants when they get an obvious answer wrong. For a moment, Eden forgets about everything else. Tonight, she allows herself to forget all about the private investigator's fees she's slowly been collecting.

E den's flustered.

She's at work, frantically searching through her assigned locker in the staff room. She's taken everything out and put everything back in twice, but she can't find her knife roll anywhere. This isn't an ideal start to her day. Eden won't be able to rest until she finds them.

"Fucking goddamn," she grumbles under her breath. "Shit! Asshat! Son of a bitch! I know it's in here somewhere. Sweet baby Jesus, why are you doing this to me?"

"Maybe you were an ax murderer in a previous life."

Eden whips around and finds Alexander leaning against the doorway, arms crossed over his chest. He once again looks stupidly well-rested. Eden doesn't understand how it's possible. After her friends left last night, she got a solid eight hours, and she still needs at least two more naps at some point to feel even remotely okay.

Alexander looks as severe as he always does, dressed in all black. It makes him look strong. Regal. Commanding.

Sexy, even.

She swallows.

*Stop it, Eden. One crisis at a time.*

Alexander also kind of looks pissed. Or, at the very least, perturbed at the sight of her. She wonders if she's done something wrong. She literally just walked in. What the hell's his problem? Then again, this is Alexander. She's pretty sure the frown he wears is permanent.

It's a lot for her to process. She sucks in a sharp breath when she realizes she's been staring for a little too long. "Huh? Oh, sorry you had to hear that."

"My poor virgin ears."

Eden snorts. "Like you're such an angel."

"Never claimed to be." Alexander's eyes drag over her before moving to her locker. "What are you doing?"

"I can't find my knife roll. I remember putting them here overnight. Maybe I brought them home with me?" She chews on the inside of her cheek, spiraling. "But then I would have... I'm losing my mind, sorry. I'll put this all away and be right there. I'm sure I'll figure it out."

He's as still as a statue, and she isn't sure why. His presence is hard to ignore. Just like how it's hard to ignore how heavy his gaze is upon her. There's something there, just past the dark of his eyes, but it's fleeting. Eden can't identify it in time. It makes her skin unbearably hot and her rabbit heart race.

"Grab your jacket," he finally says, voice firm, but soft. Softer than she's ever heard him speak.

A shiver slithers its way down her spine. She wants to hear him say it again. "Grab my jacket? Why?"

"Just do it. Don't keep me waiting."

She isn't sure why listening to his voice makes her face so warm. She doesn't like being ordered around by anybody, and yet... Eden does as she's asked, grabbing her jacket and putting it on before following him. She notes the width of his back. For a second, she wants to reach out, fingers curious to know what he feels like.

Eden thinks against it, instead bringing her cold palm to her cheek in an effort to cool down.

# CHAPTER
## Seven

It bothers Alexander just how much she looks like a child in a candy shop. Except she's not a child and there's no candy in sight. The awestruck joy on her face is no lie, though. Her smile makes his chest tight.

He can't say that he minds.

"Are you sure?" she asks for the umpteenth time.

"I'm sure."

"Because if this is some sort of practical joke..."

"Do I *look* like the kind of guy who jokes?"

"I don't know. Maybe?"

"No, Monroe. I'm not joking."

"But they're so much."

"I told you. Business expense."

"Alexander—"

"You're no good to me if you can't do your job properly," he says, sounding as indifferent as he can. "So pick something already. Service starts in half an hour."

Eden grins. She walks up to one of the many glass display cabinets, keeping her hands in her pockets like she's afraid she'll leave smudges. Alexander finds it adorable, not that he'd ever admit that aloud.

Sharp End is one of the fancier specialty shops in the city, carrying a wide range of brands to suit all sorts of chefs and their handling styles. Famous chefs from around the world have, at some point, graced the same tile floors. Only the finest can be found here, and Alexander fully intends to make sure Eden selects something complimentary to her talent.

Jacob Rochester, the owner of Sharp End, reminds Alexander of a crypt keeper. Hollow cheeks. Pale white skin. Sunken eyes and a scowl that scares him a little, and it takes a lot to scare a man like Alexander Chen, but Rochester *just might* make the cut.

Rochester smiles, but his impatience is made obvious in the strain of his voice. "See anything you like, dear?"

"Show her the Miyabi collection," Alexander says.

Eden gawks at the knives Rochester dutifully sets out for her. There's one of everything. A chef's knife, a prep, a utility, a nakiri, a santoku, one for paring, one for boning, and one for bread. There's also a sharpening steel to round it all off. They're all very beautiful, made with a flowering Damascus finish and gorgeous black ash wood handles. Alexander has half a mind to buy a set for himself. The only reason he doesn't is because his collection at home is massive enough as it is. If his knife collection grows any bigger, people might think he's a serial killer.

He watches as her fingers curl around the handle of the chef's knife. He's mesmerized by the smile that stretches across her lips. The blade is sleek, perfect in her expert hold.

A flash of something old passes through his mind. Alexander can picture someone before him. A young woman in a Gagnon-Allard uniform, diligently practicing her cuts at a workstation.

*What do you think of this, Shang?*

Maybe it's a memory, but it feels like a dream. Either way, the details are missing. The woman's words linger, but not the sound of her voice or the details of her face.

He snaps back to reality and regards Eden slowly. "Do you like it?"

"It's beautiful," she whispers. Her excitement is electric, practically crackling against his own skin.

It's all he needs to hear.

Alexander turns to Rochester and nods. "Pack it up."

"Which one, sir?"

"All of it."

Eden's eyes widen in horror. "No."

"This isn't up for debate."

"Alexander, this one alone is three hundred dollars."

"I'm well aware of tha—"

He stops short when he notices her eyes glossing over, red at the edges from the threat of tears. His heart sinks.

*What the fuck did I do?*

"What's wrong?" he asks, stepping forward. "Eden?"

Eden shakes her head. "Sorry. I'll pay you back."

"I already said you don't—"

"This is just overwhelming, okay? I'm not used to—" Eden presses her lips into a thin line, swallowing hard. She wipes at her eyes, refusing to let any traitorous tears fall.

"What?" Alexander presses.

"People don't do stuff like this for me. Ever. So, it's... It's just a lot."

Something akin to anger stirs in the pit of his stomach. "Ever? What, have your parents never given you a gift before?"

Eden pales, and he knows immediately that he's messed up.

*Touchy subject. Got it.*

He scratches at the back of his neck, straining to find the right thing to say. He's never been good with words, least of all comforting ones. "Look, you need these."

"I know, I just... I feel guilty."

"There isn't any need to be."

"That doesn't change the fact that I do."

Alexander sighs. It wasn't his intention to upset her. "What can I do to make this easier on you?"

"Let me pay you back."

He shakes his head. "Absolutely not."

"I can work for it."

"Last I checked, you're already one of my employees."

Alexander's phone buzzes in his pocket. He takes a quick glance and sees that it's Sebastian.

*Ugh, this guy again.*

> Sebastian: Any updates, my boy? I hope you're not working too hard.

He can already feel a tension headache coming on. Can he not go one day without Sebastian checking in on him? That's something he's never appreciated about restaurant owners who aren't chefs themselves. They treat it like a business. But cooking takes time and planning, trial and error. If Alexander could snap his fingers and have an entirely new menu in an instant, he would.

It's just that he's lacking inspiration. His senses have been dulled to the point where new ideas don't come to him as easily anymore, if at all. What he truly needs is a fresh perspective on things to get him started.

An idea suddenly pops into Alexander's head.

"Maybe there is something," he mumbles.

"What is it?"

"I have a project. I'm trying to come up with a new menu and I'm... stuck. So, let's make a deal. If you help me—"

"Yes," she answers immediately. "Absolutely, yes. It's the least I can do."

Alexander nods. "Excellent. We'll start tomorrow. Come in early like you usually do."

"Sure."

His eyes fall to her lips, and he swears it's an accident. Or perhaps not. She's only a foot away. All he'd have to do is dip down to kiss her, but he resists the urge.

*No. Not a good idea.*

"Thank you," she says, earnest and sweet. "Seriously. Thank you, Alexander."

He doesn't know what to say. He likes the way she's looking up at him, tilting her chin up so they have direct eye contact. Alexander takes a moment to admire her face, quietly noting how much he likes the lengthy curl of her lashes and the slope of her cute button nose.

"Don't mention it," he murmurs, so quiet that he barely hears himself.

"Woah," Rina gasps. "These are beautiful, Eden."

"Where'd you get them?" Freddie asks, gathering in close.

"Oh, um... They were a gift," Eden says.

"Damn," Peter says. "Whoever gave them to you has great taste."

There's a bit of a crowd around her. The other chefs are all amazed at Eden's new tools. Alexander didn't expect it to be such a massive distraction. It makes sense, though. They're a work of art in her hands. She was already able to create delicious meals with her old blades holding her back. Now there's nothing in her way to stop her from truly creating.

Alexander spots Hector lurking in his periphery. He seems to be the only one disinterested. In fact, he seems peeved for some reason.

Alexander clears his throat. "This isn't a museum," he snaps, though there's half the usual heat in his words. "Hang out on your own time. I don't pay you all to stand around."

"Yes, Chef," comes the chorus.

People scurry away to their stations just as the first chit of the night prints. It's a small order. Alexander calls for two medium-rare steaks with a side of potatoes au gratin, one escargot appetizer, one bowl of French onion soup, and a side Caesar salad with no bacon or croutons. It's a nice, simple start to the night.

In the meantime, he gets to work, occasionally distracted at the thought of how nice Eden looks working alongside him at the front of the line. She smells really nice. He really likes the way she pulls her hair up into a bun, exposing the nape of her neck. He mentally scolds himself when he thinks about giving her skin a good lick.

Service wraps up smoothly that day, and they're all out the door fifteen minutes after close. It's a new record. Save for the one asshole who returned their dish only after they'd eaten half —Alexander almost went out front to yell at the sorry bastard— tonight was mostly uneventful.

Freddie, Peter, and Rina leave with Eden ahead of him as always. Alexander locks the door behind him, fully prepared to head straight for his car. For the first time in forever, he's actually starting to think up possible recipes to try. He's sure his sudden burst of motivation has something to do with the fact that he'll now have Eden to hold him accountable. He's a little... excited. Eager to try.

He can't very well have nothing prepared for her tomorrow, now can he?

"Hey there, tiger."

Alexander hates being caught off-guard like this. He spins around, confused as fuck.

"Bea?"

The woman saunters over, the sharp click of her stiletto heels echoing against the cement. She's dressed up for the evening, hair pulled back into a sleek, high ponytail. She boasts a full face of makeup, complete with smoky eyes and dark black lipstick. Bea clearly wasn't at work today, nor does she look like she's on her way back home. She moves in like she wants a kiss, but Alexander takes a huge step out of the way.

Public displays of affection? No.

In front of his employees? Hell no.

In front of Eden?

*Absolutely not.*

"What are you doing here?" he asks curtly, more than aware of everybody's eyes on him and—to them—this mystery woman. Alexander's made a point of never even mentioning his private life. It's just his luck that his private life would show up at his front door.

Bea, unfazed, simply shrugs. "Me and a few of my girlfriends want to check out the new club that opened downtown. I was in the area and thought I'd stop by to invite you."

"Not interested. Goodnight."

She puts a hand on his shoulder, getting much too familiar for his liking. This wasn't a part of their arrangement. No dates. No hanging out as friends. This was supposed to be a no-strings-attached situation.

"Um, hi?"

Alexander sees Eden take a step forward, smiling sweetly. Somewhere deep down, there's a part of him that kind of wants to shrivel up into an angry little sesame seed ball.

Bea, cool and collected, grins. "Hello. Who might you be? Alexander never talks about his colleagues."

"Employees," he corrects coldly.

"I'm Eden. It's nice to meet you."

"I'm Bea," she says with a wink. "Lovely to meet you."

"What's this about a new club?" Peter chimes in.

Scratch that. Alexander just wants to shrivel up and plain old *die*. The last thing he wants is for his personal life to clash with his work life. "Nothing," he snaps. "She was just leaving."

Bea clicks her tongue. "Someone's cranky. If you want to be a party pooper, fine. I'll text you later, okay?"

Just as abruptly as she came, Bea walks away with a level of pep in her step that pisses Alexander off to no end. He's lost count of how many lines she just trampled over.

Totally unacceptable.

Eden stares at him. "Goodnight," she says softly. "I'll see you tomorrow."

"Right. Until then." Alexander doesn't understand why he's so unnerved.

"Who was the babe?" Rina asks in a hushed tone as the group walks away.

Alexander doesn't stick around. He's already formulating a strongly worded text to Bea never to do that again, all the while trying to decipher Eden's look of disappointment as she walks away.

# CHAPTER
## Eight

"Your girlfriend seems nice."

Eden mentally kicks herself. She's not sure what else to say.

She thought about Bea all night—as weird as that sounds—in awe of the easy confidence the latter radiated. Eden thought the woman had walked straight off the runway or off the cover of a fashion magazine. There was a graceful poise to the way she walked, a hypnotic sway to her hips and a worldly sophistication in the way she spoke. It makes sense that a man like Alexander would have a woman like that on his arm.

"She's not my girlfriend."

Eden perks up. "Oh? A friend, then?"

Alexander looks up from his work. There are several ingredients laid out in front of him on the prep table. He's pulled up a stool to sit. Like this, they come up to the same height. Eden's amazed to finally see him at eye-level. Being able to see the top of his head shouldn't be as amusing an experience as it is.

Eden really likes his hair. Always has. She has to stop herself from reaching out, combing her fingers through it. She imagines it must be incredibly soft.

Instead of answering, he says, "Try this." He quickly brings a spoonful of something up to her lips.

Eden opens her mouth instinctively, only realizing afterwards how odd it is to have the great Chef Alexander Chen feeding her so nonchalantly. Quite literally by his hand, too.

Alexander's eyes lock with hers, patiently awaiting a verdict. The intensity of his gaze makes her heart skip a beat. There's a certain nervousness in it. Maybe a dash of wanting to please?

Flavors wash over her tongue. She closes her eyes and concentrates. It's a creamy lobster mashed potato, but it's so much more than that. She can taste the sweet meat of the shellfish, the salinity of the butter, the earthiness of finely chopped chives. The potatoes are soft, lighter than air, almost like they've been whipped for hours. Eden determines that he's used brie instead of cheddar, giving the whole thing a much milder taste.

"What do you think?" he asks. He's quite literally on the edge of his seat.

Eden thinks he looks younger like this, boyish in his curiosity. She feels bad because he's so clearly looking for an honest response, but her opinion isn't exactly flattering.

The food is... underwhelming. She was expecting fireworks, but only got a few sparks. It's not terrible. It's quite nice, but hardly deserving of a place on La Rouge's menu.

"It's, um... It's good."

He arches a brow at her.

"It would be better with Roquefort," she continues.

Alexander frowns, nose crinkling slightly in contempt. "That'd be too overpowering."

She puts a hand on her hip. "I thought you said you wanted my help."

"I do."

"Then I think you should try a variation with Roquefort. Not a lot. Just to give it a nice tang."

Eden half expects him to ignore her. Much to her surprise, he pulls a pen from the front pocket of his chef jacket and starts writing notes down on a piece of paper next to him. Eden tries not to stare at the sheer size of his hands. Long fingers, thick knuckles, hard palms. His penmanship is gorgeous, she notices. Cursive letters gliding effortlessly into one another, looping and flowing like a dance. He presses the tip of the pen down hard, though, writing as aggressively as he speaks.

*Yeah, that checks out.*

He sets the pen down and hands her the spoon. He points to the next dish over. "Okay. Try that one next."

She does so, taking a sample. This time, it's some kind of dessert. Eden's always had a sweet tooth, and it shows. She moans, willingly drowning in the rich cocoa powder, icing sugar, and savoring the sourness of the raspberries baked in.

"Wow, that's good," she mumbles. She helps herself to a larger spoonful and sighs. "*Mm*, fuck me. More of where that came from, please."

She swears she sees the tips of his ears turn red. He shifts in his seat. Her breath hitches when her eyes flit down towards the growing tent in his pants.

*Oh?*

"How would—" His voice cracks. He clears his throat and tries again. "How would you improve it?"

"Me?" she asks, her face flooding with heat. Her heart's beating so hard and loud that she can't think straight.

"Yes. You."

Eden licks her lips. His eyes follow the motion. Her throat's uncomfortably dry all of a sudden. "I think it's kind of perfect, to be honest," she manages to answer. "I'd serve it with a side of vanilla bean ice cream, but that doesn't exactly scream fancy, does it?"

Alexander jots something else down. Eden really likes how his fingers look wrapped around his pen. The more she stares, the more she can imagine said fingers grazing against her cheek, dragging down waist, sliding down her legs to push her knees apart.

*Good Lord, it's hot in here.*

"Are you going after a specific theme?" she asks, licking her spoon clean.

Alexander is most definitely staring. His nostrils flare as he glares at the utensil.

*Is he... jealous of a spoon?*

"No, not yet," he answers finally, voice strained. "I'm just trying to determine my flavor palate first. I'm hoping the theme comes to me soon, though."

"Is this a total overhaul of the set menu we have now?"

"Yes. Everything from hors d'œuvres to specialty cocktails to desserts. They just need to be new."

"Ah, plenty of room to play, then."

Alexander looks up at her, slightly wide-eyed. "Room to play?"

Eden shifts her weight from foot to foot. "You sound confused. Should I say it again slowly?"

He smirks. It's such a rare sight that Eden's heart almost bursts.

"I've never thought about it that way before, is all."

She shrugs. "I mean, yeah. Coming up with new recipes is always fun, isn't it?"

"Fun?"

"Mm-hmm. Ever heard of it?"

Eden says this like a joke, but Alexander doesn't react in the slightest. In fact, he looks deep in thought. Maybe even troubled. Before she can ask what's bothering him, Alexander stands.

"What did you eat for breakfast this morning?" he asks.

"Nothing."

"Nothing?"

"I usually sleep in and miss breakfast entirely, so yeah. It's not a big deal, though."

"Then what did you have for lunch before you got here?"

Eden doesn't know why she feels so exposed. "Nothing. I had to hurry and catch the bus to get here early, so I didn't—"

Alexander walks away before she's finished speaking. At first, Eden's miffed. Didn't his parents ever teach him it's rude to leave in the middle of a conversation? But then Alexander returns not one minute later from the walk-in fridge with a few ingredients. He sets everything down and gets to work, first by placing a non-stick skillet on the stove to heat.

"What are you doing?" Eden asks.

"You a pasta fan?"

"Who's *not* a pasta fan?"

"Hm. Good. Sit here and wait."

Eden doesn't argue. She's curious to see him at work. She's admittedly been so busy learning the ropes as his sous chef that she's never taken the opportunity to see him in action. Alexander's always at the front of the line, delegating and organizing. She sits on the stool he once occupied, hands on her lap as she watches him move expertly about the space.

He boils a pot of salted water and cooks fresh spaghetti under a rolling boil. He slices garlic cloves into precise, paper-thin pieces. Next is a generous glug of olive oil, coating the bottom of the skillet until it starts to pop and hiss. In goes the garlic to fry, turning a beautiful golden brown as the air fills with its aromatic scent. Alexander tosses a pinch of red pepper in as well, the sizzling sound filling Eden's ears.

Once the sauce is done, he turns off the heat, drains the cooked pasta—al dente—and adds the spaghetti to the skillet. He tosses it all around with a pair of tongs, making sure to coat every noodle with the light sauce. He plates without too much showmanship—Eden isn't exactly a customer—but Alexander takes great care in drizzling freshly squeezed lemon juice over it all, as well as garnishing with finely chopped parsley.

Eden is completely still, in awe. His timing is perfect. It has to be, in order to juggle twenty different steps at once. Practiced and calculated and totally in control. Alexander could cook in his sleep if he wanted to, and the meal would still come out as amazing as ever.

She wants to watch him all day.

He sets the meal down in front of Eden and hands her a clean fork from a nearby utensil bin. It's precision on a plate.

"Eat," he says.

"Aren't you going to have some?"

"I'm not the one who didn't have lunch."

"Th-thank you."

"Make sure to eat before you come into work next time," he says sternly. "I don't need you passing out on me."

Eden smiles, more than a little aware of the warm giddiness bubbling in her chest. She can't remember the last time someone cooked her a meal, and completely from scratch, no less.

"Thank you," she says again, softer.

"When you're done, start prep for the filet mignon special tonight."

"Yes, chef."

She watches as Alexander leaves, disappearing to the kitchen office. She can't stop smiling. Eden takes one bite and is lost to her senses.

This is the most delicious thing she's ever eaten in her entire life.

# CHAPTER
## Nine

E den arrives the next day to some sort of commotion.

"Did you really think that was going to fly?" Hector says with a snarl. He's yelling at a young woman, probably no older than twenty, who's doing her best to hide her tears behind her hands. Eden recognizes her as the part-time boulangier, Amanda.

"Please, Hector," she whimpers. "All I'm asking for is a chance. Can't I talk to the head chef?"

"You'd only be wasting his time." Hector waves a sheet paper around in one hand, pinched between his thumb and forefinger like it's a piece of trash. "Did you seriously think we wouldn't check your references?"

There's a sticky lump lodged in the back of Eden's throat. She swallows, but it won't go away. She steps into the kitchen, doing her best to hide how shaky she feels.

"What's going on?" she demands.

Hector glares at her and snorts. "We brought her on almost a month ago to prepare our bread in-house. Turns out, she's been faking her references and lied about where she went to culinary school."

Panic rises in Eden's chest, her heart pounding in her ear.

"Please, Eden," Amanda rasps, grasping her hands. "I just really wanted this job. I didn't think it would matter!"

"You're fired, Amanda," Hector snaps. "Get the hell out of here."

"That's not your decision to make," Eden snaps.

He glares at her. "Fine. *You* fire her."

She blanches. Fire her? Why would she do such a thing? As far as Eden can tell, Amanda's perfectly adequate at her job. So what if there was a little white lie on her resumé? Eden pities the poor girl. They're kindred spirits, after all. The thought of firing someone for things she's done herself doesn't sit right with her.

*I'd be a hypocrite.*

Eden snatches the resumé out of Hector's hands. Just because he's been here longer doesn't mean he has authority over her. *She* was chosen to be Alexander's sous chef, not him. There's a chain of command here. She better start acting like it.

"I'll deal with the matter," she says firmly, not once lowering her gaze.

"There's nothing *to* deal with. She lied to get the job. She needs to be terminated."

"Is your home life okay?"

"What?"

"Your home life. Are you doing okay, man? Because if the only way to make yourself feel better is to yell at women and get high off the power-trip, might I suggest therapy?"

Hector grinds his teeth. The vein at his temple looks like it's two seconds away from bursting. "Bitch," he hisses as he stalks off, bumping Eden's shoulder harshly.

She can't say she's a big fan of his, either. "Dick," she grumbles as he trudges off.

Amanda sniffles beside her. "Thank you, Eden."

"You keep this between you and me, alright? As far as I'm concerned, I didn't see anyth—"

"Didn't see what?"

Eden nearly jumps out of her skin at the sound of Alexander's voice. One would think that a man of his size would make some noise when he walks.

"Nothing!" she says all too quickly.

Alexander squints his eyes at her, his jaw a hard line. "Monroe, with me."

Eden's stomach flips. She decides not to argue.

"W-what about me, Chef?" Amanda asks.

"Get to work. We'll talk later."

"Yes, Chef."

The corner kitchen office is cramped, just barely big enough to fit the two of them. The desk is built into the wall, covered from corner to corner in all sorts of documents—order forms, handwritten book out requests from the staff, a couple of one-star reviews printed off of Yelp to be addressed at a later time. There's a metal filing cabinet next to the door, several shelves just above Eden's head containing thick navy blue binders full of things like first aid instructions, OSHA regulations, and various other food safety manuals.

Alexander closes the door. It occurs to her just how close he is.

*Really* close.

"What happened?" he asks. "And don't you dare try to tell me it was nothing."

Eden chews on her bottom lip. She doesn't miss the way his eyes flit down to follow the movement. She takes a slow, deep breath. "Hector thinks that Amanda lied about her references and training when she got hired. He tried to fire her."

Alexander's jaw tenses. "That's not his call to make."

"That's what I said."

"So, did you?"

"What?"

71

"Fire her."

Eden shivers, her whole body suddenly turning cold. "No."

He doesn't say anything. Not right away. Instead, he stares at her, his brows knit together into a steep and severe frown. Alexander crosses his arms over his chest, his thoughts a mystery to her.

Eden's eyes wander over the expanse of his broad chest, his strong shoulders. His arms are massive, the curve of muscles obvious beneath the black material of his chef jacket.

She takes a step forward, determined and unperturbed. "You said all that matters is if someone can cook!"

"Yes, but that doesn't include lying on one's job application. It's a violation of our code of conduct. She has to go, Monroe. No exceptions."

Her head swims. The sudden queasiness in her stomach leaves her winded. What will happen to her if she's found out just like Amanda? Will she lose her job, too?

"There has to be something we can do for her," she insists. "She just wants to work. Is it really such a big deal?"

"This is La Rouge."

"You say that like it means something."

Alexander's eye twitches. He straightens his back, stands at full height. There's barely two inches between the two of them. Eden swallows. Her throat's awfully dry all of a sudden.

"La Rouge is a fine dining establishment," he says, an edge to his tone. "Our patrons come here expecting the best of the best. An *experience*. One that they're willing to shell out top dollar for. They come with the expectation that they're being served by some of the most talented chefs in the world, not someone who weaseled their way into our kitchen by luck."

Eden furrows her brows. Doesn't he know that talent and pedigree aren't the same thing?

"Kind of pompous, isn't it?" she asks tersely.

"Welcome to the world of haute cuisine, sweetheart."

Her breath catches in her throat.

*Sweetheart.*

She knows he's being sarcastic, but the word echoes around inside her skull and makes her feel so terribly strange. Tingly. Oddly *warm*. Her heart picks up in pace and her skin burns like soft fire. A tiny voice in the back of her head craves to hear him say it again.

Alexander leans forward, officially leaving no space between them. They're so close that all it would take is for Eden to tilt her chin up just so for their lips to touch.

"Here's what's going to happen," he says, tone low and smooth. He smells like peppermint toothpaste and clean laundry, hints of hazelnuts and vanilla lingering just beneath the surface.

"Chef?" she mumbles, mesmerized by the warmth radiating off of his body.

"You're going to go out there and you're going to fire Amanda."

"But—"

"But what, Monroe?"

"I don't *want* to."

His hands graze her hips on either side, his dark eyes glued to her lips. "You know what your problem is?"

Eden's knees tremble as a wet heat pools between her legs. *God*, what is even happening right now? "What?" she rasps.

"You're too soft."

"What's wrong with being soft?"

Alexander's lips whisper across hers. It's not quite a kiss, but it's pretty damn close. She can feel his breath against her cheeks as he speaks, the tips of their noses bumping lightly against each other.

"You're my sous chef," he grumbles, almost like it's a reminder to himself. "Start acting like one."

He pulls away.

Disappointment floods her veins, a cold chill racing straight through her body.

*Oh, shit.*

"Tell Amanda she can work her shift, but after that, we're letting her go." Alexander's voice is tight and thin. "The best I can do for her is write up a letter of recommendation, but she can't stay here."

Eden nods stiffly, her fists clenched up tight. She turns and leaves, thanking her gelatinous legs for not giving out then and there. There's no time to decompress, to truly reflect on what just happened. Maybe she's overthinking things? It's a small office space, after all, and Alexander's a big man. It wasn't like he was *actually* kissing her. They were simply having a serious, face-to-face conversation.

*Literally.*

She pushes the whole thing to the back of her mind. She'll deal with it later—or maybe not at all. Right now, she has to find Amanda. She can't allow herself to think about the throbbing between her legs and the thunderous roar of blood rushing past her ears.

Eden hates being the bearer of bad news.

She finds the boulangier outside, seated on an overturned milk crate with her head in her hands. Eden doesn't even get a word out before she asks, "I'm fired, aren't I?"

"I'm sorry. I really did try to fight for you."

"I believe you." Amanda offers a sad smile.

"Sha—I mean, Alexander said you can work your shift, but then after that..."

She nods solemnly. "I understand. Thank you for sticking up for me."

The queasiness in the pit of Eden's stomach still hasn't gone away.

Hector.

Alexander.

The lies that got her here to La Rouge.

Eden decides she's going to have to be a hell of a lot more careful, otherwise she can kiss her job—and the money she's so desperately trying to save—goodbye.

# CHAPTER
## Ten

The kitchen is slammed. One of the hood fans isn't working, it's torturously hot, dirty dishes are piling up in the pit and not getting washed right away, which means his staff don't have new, clean plates to use for their own prep or plating. The restaurant itself isn't even that busy. They have no waitlist, nor any huge reservations taking up their time. In Alexander's experience, this can only mean one thing.

Someone isn't pulling their weight.

His kitchen is a well-oiled machine. All of his staff may be in charge of their own stations, but they have to move as one. If appetizers aren't sent out fast enough, that means entrées are held back, which means dessert production is paused even longer. It's like a traffic jam. If some asshole decides to slam on the brakes, everyone behind them has to slam on the brakes as well. As head chef, he's the traffic controller and police officer all in one.

It doesn't take him very long to figure out who the hell is dropping the ball.

"Hector!" he seethes. "Where are you going?"

"Bathroom break," the chef de partie says casually, like they aren't in the middle of service and it's the most obvious thing in the world.

"Again? That's the fifth time you've left your station."

"Didn't realize I had to ask your permission to piss," Hector snaps, walking away.

"Listen here, you mouthy motherfu—"

Alexander cuts himself off and takes a deep breath in through the nose. He wants to lose it. He wants to erupt. Explode. Eviscerate everything standing in his way.

But then he catches a glimpse of Eden out of the corner of his eye, working twice as hard than usual to help her colleagues. Her sleeves are rolled up to just below her elbow. Her hair's pulled back into a bun, the sweat from hard work and concentration making the strands framing her face stick to her skin. If he loses control now, she'll have to work that much harder to make up for the outburst.

*People respond well to positive reinforcement, you know.*

Eden's words echo around in his skull. He mentally cringes as he prepares himself for what he's about to do.

"Nguyen," he says.

Rina looks up from her station, wide-eyed and probably expecting to be reamed out. "Y- yes, chef?"

Alexander pinches the bridge of his nose and sighs. "Good... Good job on that last order," he says, the compliment heavy and unnatural on his tongue. He cringes internally. *Ugh.* "Ease up on the strawberry topping a little, okay?"

Rina's face turns bright red, mouth dropping open. "Oh, um... Th-thank you so much, chef."

"Drenton, nice work on those steaks. The table gave their compliments. Focus on the orders for tables seventeen and twenty-one next. Er, please."

"Sure thing, chef," Peter replies, just as dumbfounded as Rina.

"Thatch, good pace. A little lighter on the dressing."

"Yes, chef."

"Lawrence, the arrangement on the last one was beautiful. Keep that up."

"Thank you, chef," Freddie says.

"Monroe?"

"Yes, chef?"

She's there at his side in an instant. Alexander can tell she's as tired as he is, but he can sense the determined fire within her.

"Can you take over for a few minutes?" he asks, dipping in to speak softer. There's less than a foot of space between them. "I'm going to talk to Hector in private. Might be a few. Don't freak out if there's yelling."

"Not a problem," she says, smiling. She's pretty when she smiles, but he can see how tight it is. There's still so much left unsaid between them, but this isn't the time and place to dwell on their near-kiss experience.

*It was a mistake. A moment of weakness.*

*It can't happen again.*

Eden wastes no time taking up the reins, calling out the next order that prints out. It's a seamless transition, almost like they've practiced a thousand times.

He finds Hector in the staff room, sitting at the small break table on his phone.

Alexander's blood boils.

"What are you doing?" he growls. "We need you out there. Why are you fucking off?"

"Would you relax? I'm just taking a break."

"People are working their asses off to make up for your incompetence. Get off your damn phone, or I'll—"

"Or you'll what?" Hector hisses, standing up. "What will you do, hm? Pass me over for yet another promotion?"

"You're a piece of shit, you know that? This is exactly why you didn't get the job."

"You sure about that?"

Alexander scoffs. "The fuck is that supposed to mean?"

"Sebastian personally tapped me for the position."

"And it was ultimately my decision to follow through or not."

"It makes me wonder why you'd choose that nobody over me."

"What?"

"You heard me. You were supposed to hire from within, Chen. That's what Sebastian said. Instead, you hired the first damn person to bat their pretty eyelashes at you."

"Be careful with what you say next."

Hector takes a step forward, deliberately getting up in Alexander's space. He's unafraid. Mostly just stupid, though.

"What did she do, hm?" Hector asks, voice dripping with venom. "It's pretty obvious she's your favorite. What did she do to earn that honor, I wonder?"

Alexander clenches his jaws so hard, he can hear his molars squeak against each other. The thinly-veiled implication leaves a bitter taste on his tongue. "Go home."

"What?"

Alexander stands straight, squaring his shoulders. Hector is quite tall, but he doesn't carry intimidation the same way. The redhead shrinks back, still wearing an expression of indignation.

"Go home," Alexander repeats in a low voice. "Before you say something you'll regret. One step out of line, Hector. One more step out of line and I'll fire you on the spot. I'll have you blacklisted from every restaurant from here to the other coast. I'll make sure you're stuck working at a Denny's for the rest of your miserable little life."

"You can't—"

"Yes, I can. Don't forget who I am. Sebastian might have taken you under his wing. He might own this restaurant. But the kitchen is *mine*, and you're at my mercy. I'm being very generous right now, so I suggest you go home for the night. When you come back tomorrow, I expect you to be on your best behavior. If not, I'll take you out with the trash myself. Do I make myself clear?"

The vein in Hector's temple twitches. "Crystal," he grumbles.

"Get the fuck out of here."

Hector stomps over to his locker to snatch up his things. He slams the door hard enough that it just bounces open again, exposing an old, tattered knife roll at the very bottom.

Eden's missing knife set.

Alexander doesn't have time to confront Hector about it. The redhead shoves his shoulder against Alexander's—it looks like it hurts him more than the latter—and pisses off for the night.

Alexander bends down to pick up the knife roll. He's enraged on Eden's behalf. He knows he should fire Hector immediately. Theft isn't something Alexander takes lightly. But it's been a long night, Hector is finally gone, and Eden has a fresh set of knives. A part of him is a little grateful that Hector had enough nerve to steal it. Eden truly deserves the new ones Alexander bought for her.

He'll make good on his promise. He's nothing if not a man of his word. One more screw up, and he'll make sure Hector is gone in the blink of an eye.

They get through service no thanks to Hector. Things cleared up really quickly the second he left. Food started moving again, and the work started to flow. Hector leaving was like taking a thorn out of everyone's side.

Easier to breathe, easier to function.

Nevertheless, Alexander needs a smoke.

While the rest of the staff finish off their cleaning duties,

Alexander takes a long, much needed drag on his cigarette out back. He knows he should quit. He's been trying to quit for a very long time, in fact. It's just that he hasn't been able to find the motivation to do it. He hasn't had the motivation to do much in general.

It's cold tonight. The evening air is still. The stars are out, bright and twinkling, the never-ending quiet of the universe weighing down on him. It's calming, he thinks, all that emptiness. It stands in complete contrast to the tumultuous state of his mind.

There's a lot going on in his head. Sometimes it's so loud, he can't distinguish thought from thought.

*Stupid new menu, I don't even want to make it. I have to figure out everyone's shifts for next week first. Shit, wait. I need to handle the food shipment by Monday or we'll be understocked. Is the cheese in the fridge about to go bad? Speaking of cheese: Roquefort. I don't like Roquefort, but Eden says to try it. Maybe I'll make a mille-feuille for her tomorrow.*

*Tomorrow. Hector will be back. Hector is a dick. Fucking asshole.*

"Chef?"

He looks up with a start. "Christ!"

Eden laughs, her smile apologetic. "Sorry. Didn't mean to surprise you."

"We need to put a damn bell on you."

"With a cute little collar and everything? I didn't take you for the kinky sort."

He glowers. "Shut up."

Eden laughs softly. "I'm *teasing*." And then, after a moment, "Are you okay?"

"Why wouldn't I be?"

"I was calling your name for, like, five minutes."

"Oh. Just spacing out. Don't worry."

Eden steps out to join him. She taps the tip of her shoe

against the pavement, picking at beneath her nails. "We're about finished inside. Just need you to close up."

"Sure, I'll be right there," he says, taking another deep drag of his cigarette.

"So, I was thinking..." She speaks gently, an adorable shyness about her.

For a moment, Alexander worries that she's going to try and bring up what happened in the office. He isn't sure if he's ready for that conversation. He doesn't have an explanation for his actions, only that he couldn't help himself. Something about Eden draws him in like a magnet. The more he tries to stay away, the more some invisible force drags him right back.

"We're going to trivia night tomorrow. I was wondering if you'd like to come."

This is officially the second time he's been invited to a non-work related event, but it's still as shocking as the first time.

"Who's *we*?" he asks, exhaling.

Eden stifles a cough, clears her throat. "Freddie, Peter, Rina, and me. It'll be fun."

"Thanks, but no."

Eden clears her throat again. She's doing her best to be subtle, hiding her mouth behind her hand. This time, Alexander clocks it.

*Ah, the smoke.*

He puts out his cigarette without a second thought. He's been meaning to quit, anyways. It's terrible for his palate. At least, that's the reason he gives himself.

"Why not?" Eden asks.

"I'm their boss. I doubt they'd want to see me during their off hours."

"So? You're my boss, and I'd like to see you in my off hours."

"Why?"

Eden smiles. "Well, we're friends, aren't we? That's what friends do. Hang out and stuff."

Warmth blooms in his chest. This is... new. He feels stupidly childish in his excitement, but manages to press it down.

"Careful," he says. "I'm starting to get the feeling that you like me."

She laughs, sheepishly glancing down at her shoes. "Shut up. Can you please come to trivia with me?"

Alexander chuckles.

*Oh, she's cute.*

"Well, I guess I could—"

"Trivia?" comes a voice from behind them. It's an old, cold voice that freezes Alexander all the way down to the marrow. "That sounds like quite the lovely distraction, my boy."

Alexander turns to see Sebastian standing there, one hand balanced on his polished redwood cane. The man is in his late seventies, but stands upright with incredible strength. His face is withered with time, wrinkles everywhere, with old, sage-like eyes. He's dressed in a bespoke suit worth thousands, accented with diamond cufflinks.

Sebastian gives Eden a friendly smile, but Alexander knows the truth.

There's nothing friendly about this man.

"Let's head inside out of this cold, shall we?" Sebastian continues, words sickly sweet.

Alexander knows it's not actually an ask.

# CHAPTER
## Eleven

Eden notices two things.

First, Sebastian looks like a snake who gave up halfway through the shedding process. No amount of fancy clothes and bejeweled accessories can make up for that.

Second, Alexander is uncharacteristically quiet. There's an edge to him, a tension he carries throughout his body that threatens to snap him at the knees, the elbows, the neck—basically anywhere that could give.

It makes Eden's anxious.

Alexander's nerves are contagious.

It doesn't take her very long to figure out who Sebastian is. Judging by the way Freddie, Peter, and Rina all scurried away after seeing him, Eden assumes that this man has authority over them. More so than Alexander, even, which can only mean one thing: she is face-to-face with the owner of La Rouge.

Sebastian drags a finger over the surface of the nearest prep station, grimacing in dissatisfaction. "It seems you've let things go since I've been abroad, my boy."

Alexander says nothing, keeping his eyes glued to the floor.

"Your name's Eden, is that right, my dear?"

She stands a little straighter, unconsciously positioned about a foot behind Alexander. He was the one who placed himself there, a discreet shield. "Yes," she says softly. "That's me. It's very nice to meet you, sir."

Sebastian smiles. It sends a chill racing down Eden's spine. "Such a lovely name. It's a pleasure to finally make your acquaintance. I must admit that Alexander hasn't said much about you. Such a shame to keep a pretty creature like you to himself, hm?"

Eden shifts her weight from foot to foot. "Oh, that's... that's very nice of you to say, sir."

"It's been a long day," Alexander says to Sebastian. "And it's her day off tomorrow. I'm sure Eden would like to get going."

Sebastian raises his barely there brows and smirks. "If that's the case, I'm sure I'm not keeping her from anything particularly important. Is that right, dear?"

"Well—"

"I've just gotten off a long flight from Paris, and I'm rather famished. Would you mind making me a little something? It'd give me an opportunity to get to know Alexander's sous chef all the better."

Eden notices Alexander clench his fists, the muscles in his jaw tensing, but she nods anyway. She gets the feeling that this isn't so much a request as it is a thinly veiled demand.

"I'd be happy to," she says. "Do you have any requests?"

Sebastian licks his lips, pulling up a nearby stool to sit upon. "I would like a Marseille- style shrimp stew to start, your take on a coq au vin for my main meal, and mousse au chocolat for dessert."

Alexander frowns. "I'll help."

The wrinkly old man raises a stern hand. "That won't be necessary, my boy."

"But that's a lot of work for one—"

"I'm sure our Eden can handle it. I expect nothing less for a sous chef of her caliber." Sebastian turns and grins at Eden. "It's not too much for you to handle, is it?"

Eden's heart is in her throat. Her palms are clammy and her breathing's shallow. She doesn't know if this is normal or not. If she declines, how suspicious will that make her look? But if she agrees to cook for him, will a restaurateur like Sebastian be able to tell just how inexperienced she is? Eden knows she's been relying on her palate more than her technique. And it doesn't help that Sebastian is sitting right there, judging her every move. She can fool the layman, but him?

She has no choice.

"It's not too much to handle," she says calmly. "I'll get started right away."

She's cooked her whole life, mostly out of her love for food, but also partially out of necessity. Parsons wasn't exactly a talented chef. In fact, Eden was fairly certain he'd never stepped foot in a kitchen in his entire life. To him, *buy-one-get-one-free* pizza deals from the local pizzeria was fine dining. He'd sometimes throw in a two-liter bottle of Diet Pepsi when he was feeling particularly fancy.

Eden realizes pretty quickly that this isn't cooking.

It's a performance.

She prepares her mise, she gets the necessary pots and pans ready on the stove, she concentrates on the different cook times for all three separate dishes at once. It's intense, trying to remember each individual recipe while working on them at the exact same time. To make matters worse, Sebastian never looks away.

It's honestly terrifying.

"So, my dear," Sebastian says casually. "Where did you work before this fine establishment?"

"A little Italian restaurant called San Ramo," she answers, flipping the chicken in her skillet to ensure even cooking.

"San Ramo," he echoes, a hint of haughtiness in his tone. "Never heard of it."

Eden tries her best not to let this shake her. She really did work at a restaurant called San Ramo, but the place no longer exists thanks to poor reviews about service and a failing health safety grade. She might have over exaggerated her responsibilities there, too. She was no more than a fry cook there, not a sous chef like she had claimed on her resumé.

She gives the shrimp, which are now sizzling in their own delicious juices, a quick stir to keep from burning on the bottom of the pan.

"And what would you consider to be your favorite meal?" Sebastian asks.

Eden really can't tell if he's genuinely interested, or trying his best to distract her. Judging by how deathly still Alexander is beside him, it's likely the latter.

"I'm a sucker for anything sweet," she replies, checking on the chocolate she has melting over a double broiler. The rough square pieces she'd chopped up are slowly but surely transforming into a rich pool of dark chocolate.

"Knew it," she thinks she hears Alexander mumble under his breath. It's barely audible.

Sebastian pays him no mind.

Eden plates the shrimp stew and adds a bit of orange zest on top for a hit of refreshing citrus. The shrimp—now a beautiful bright red amidst roasted garlic and fennel—radiates steam. The soup itself is more of a sauce, hearty and thick and zesty.

Next is the coq au vin. She's prepared a smaller batch in light of the fast serving time. It's as traditional as they come, but Eden honestly can't think of any way to make it 'her rendition.' She's added a side of white rice and places a savory chicken thigh atop of the mound, broth soaking into each individual grain.

The mousse is a pain in the ass, but Eden doesn't give up. As much as she loves to eat desserts, she has a hell of a time preparing them. Eden just doesn't have the patience. Mousse itself takes forever to whip up to the right consistency, and considering the fact that she has a million other things to worry about, she can't get it quite the way she likes. She tops it off with a healthy dose of whipped cream, sprinkling bits of hard chocolate overtop to cover up the fact that it isn't the prettiest thing to look at.

Eden presents all three dishes to Sebastian and holds her breath, her guts tied up in impossible knots. Sebastian looks less than impressed as he picks up a fork.

"Where did you study, dear?" he asks, stabbing a shrimp with more ferocity than necessary.

"The Gagnon-Allard School of Culinary Arts, sir."

"Just like you, my boy." Sebastian pats Alexander on the arm. It's hard for Eden to ignore how Alexander flinches away. "Who was your instructor? Wallace? Hilroy?"

Eden knows none of those names. "Zhao," she says, pulling from what she knows. Charlie Zhao was one of the only memorable instructors she had during her brief stint there.

"Zhao?" Alexander echoes.

She nods. "Yes. He taught me everything I know. I graduated a few years ago."

Alexander turns pale. Paler than she's ever seen him. He just stares, wide-eyed and bewildered.

*What's with him? Did I say something wrong?*

Sebastian takes one bite out of every dish, making sure to savor. He doesn't give any words of encouragement, nor does he provide any critique. He simply wipes his mouth on the back of a handkerchief he's pulled out of his jacket pocket—talk about fancy—before standing.

"Thank you for the meal," he says to her with a wide smile.

"It looks like my boy here's stumbled upon quite the diamond in the rough."

*Damn. What a waste of food.*

"Thank you, sir."

Sebastian turns to Alexander. "Full of potential, this one. I hope training her doesn't keep you too occupied."

"It won't," Alexander answers flatly.

"I know my arrival must have been out of the blue to you. But I had to come and check on my favorite student. I suppose kids these days don't like to answer their phones, hm?"

"Sorry. Won't happen again."

Sebastian nods. "Good. I'll check in soon to see how your progress is going. I hope you come up with that new menu soon. You know how much I hate to wait." He turns back to Eden. "You have yourself a lovely evening, my dear. I hope to see you again."

Eden forces a stiff smile. "Have a good night."

Sebastian walks away and exits through the back doors, the click of his cane against the tile floor growing softer and softer as he retreats. It's only when he disappears entirely that Eden feels like she can breathe again.

"Do you think that went well?" she asks Alexander, voice light and teasing. "I think he likes me."

Alexander doesn't bite. He's very obviously in a sour mood. "Clean up," he orders. "I'll drive you home."

"You don't need to do that. I can just take the bus—"

"It's late. They aren't running anymore."

Eden glances up at the clock that's nailed to the wall above the walk-in. He's right. Sebastian kept them behind for almost an hour and a half. Eden supposes she could walk, but it's freezing out and Alexander *did* offer.

"Alright," she says. "Give me two seconds."

Alexander doesn't reply.

The ride home is... *awkward*.

Save for the occasional direction, Eden doesn't say anything, and neither does Alexander.

His grip on the steering wheel is so tight, his knuckles are white. Eden can also hear him grinding his teeth over the loud rumble of the car engine. She debates about whether she should make small talk or not. Thank him for the ride. Compliment his car. Ask him why he looks like he's two seconds away from giving himself a heart attack.

She's only mildly embarrassed when they pull up to her neighborhood. It's in rough shape, the kind of place where a car like this will undoubtedly be jacked if left unattended for too long. Her apartment building doesn't look too bad from the outside, though the graffiti on the walls is less than tasteful.

Alexander pulls the car up to the curb and kills the engine. They just sit there. Eden isn't sure what to do. She tugs at the sleeves of her winter coat, mentally bracing herself to step out into the cold.

"Thank you for driving me," she says gently. "I really appreciate—"

"Why did you lie?"

The question is a punch to the gut.

It leaves her winded, so stunned that she forgets where and when she is. Eden stares at him. Alexander stares back. There's no give.

"I... I have no idea what you're talking about," she mumbles, throat closing up in discomfort. Her fight or flight instincts are offline.

"Why did you lie?" he asks again, firmer this time.

"I don't—"

"Your math doesn't add up."

"What?"

"Zhao. He retired nine years ago."

"Y-you're wrong."

"I know for a fact I'm not."

Eden crosses her arms over her chest. "What makes you so sure?"

"Because Charlie Zhao is my uncle."

Nevermind.

*This* is a punch to the gut.

"I was one of the last—" Alexander cuts himself off before he starts yelling. "I was the last student he ever taught, and I don't remember you at all."

Her blood is on fire. The voice in her head tells her to run, but her body has no strength left to move.

"So who the hell are you?" he asks. "Tell me the truth."

Eden's mouth falls open.

She can't think. She can't speak.

So she scrambles out of the car and *runs*.

# CHAPTER
## Twelve

Alexander gets out of the vehicle and follows her, alarmed. It's raining hard, droplets coming down as one heavy sheet.

"Eden, wait!"

She doesn't listen. She races into her building and all the way to the end of the hall, locking herself inside her apartment. She damn near clips Alexander's face when she slams the door shut.

He bangs his fist against the frame, frantic. "Eden? Let me in. Talk to me."

He regrets calling her out the way he did, but Alexander doesn't know a better way to broach the subject. The second she mentioned studying with Charlie, he knew. There was no possible way she was telling the truth. He needs to know. He needs to know because maybe— just maybe—he can help her.

A million and one questions race through his mind.

*What is she hiding? Who is she really? What the fuck is going on?*

"Eden?" he calls again. "Eden, please talk to me. I just want to know what's going on. Are you—fuck, I don't know—are you in trouble or something? Is that why you lied?"

"Go away," she says, her voice muffled by the door. The quiver in her words makes his blood run cold.

"I'm not going anywhere until you talk to me."

"Please, just leave." She sounds exasperated. Fearful.

"No."

"Why do you even care? Just fire me and get it over with."

Alexander chews on the inside of his cheek, holding back his frustration. He needs answers. "It's like you said," he says gently, carefully. "We're... We're friends, aren't we?" The word is heavy on his tongue, new and untested. "I just... I just want to help. I'm sure you have your reasons, but you need to talk to me. Everything's going to be okay. Don't hide, Eden. Let me in." And then, so soft that it's barely a whisper, "Please?"

Eden doesn't say anything for a long time. A part of him is worried that she's gone, that this is the last he'll see of her.

He breathes a sigh of relief when he hears her undoing the locks, the door creaking open only an inch. The edges of her eyes are red with the threat of tears, her lips chapped from all her worrying. Eden looks up at him and—*shit*—she looks so small and vulnerable and afraid.

"Tell me the truth, Eden."

She bites her bottom lip, looking defeated and on the verge of breaking down. "It's a long story," she mumbles.

"I've got nothing but time."

Eden pauses, regarding with the utmost suspicion. Alexander makes no move, desperate for her trust. If she doesn't entirely believe what he's saying, then he needs to prove through body language alone that she's not in trouble. He's here to help, not to be a foreboding presence—as hard as that might be for a man his size.

She eventually sighs and steps to the side, opening the door for him. "It's easier if I just show you," she says.

Alexander has no idea what that's supposed to mean, but he's thankful to be making progress.

He stares at the money on her coffee table. She's laid everything out, wads upon wads of cash in front of them.

"Holy shit," he mutters.

"I know."

Alexander sits beside Eden on the couch. It's small, and he's —well—tall and big and takes up over half of the space. Eden has her fingers laced together, hands placed atop her lap like a student preparing for a scolding at the principal's office.

He looks at her, bewildered. "You're sure you're not in trouble?"

She shakes her head. "No. I'm not in trouble."

"You don't owe someone money? Are you involved in... Shit, I don't know. Drugs or something?"

"No."

"Sex work?" he asks in a small, tight voice. "Trafficking? Theft? Are you on the run from the law?"

"No. Nothing like that. I've just been... saving."

Alexander takes a deep breath. He counts, makes an estimate. There's almost fifteen thousand dollars here, more or less.

"This should be in a bank."

"I know. But I..."

"What is it?"

Eden swallows. Alexander's entranced by the way her throat rises and falls with the action. He dares to reach out. Just this once. He gingerly places his hand on her wrist, just to show her that he's there and it's okay and that he's listening.

"Eden."

She takes a deep breath, closes her eyes, and gathers the courage to speak.

"*How old are you, sweetie?*" *the police officer asks her. The woman's crouched down so that she can look Eden in the eye.*

*Eden's never seen a lady police officer before, but she thinks she's very pretty. Eden likes her shiny badge and the way her radio looks attached to her shoulder strap. Eden holds up her hand, stretching out five of her little fingers.*

*"You're five, huh? I have a nephew who's five. That's a really cool backpack. Do you like Blue's Clues?"*

*Eden clutches onto her backpack a little tighter. She doesn't like Blue's Clues despite the animated dog character splashed across the back. She doesn't watch a whole lot of TV. Mostly because Mom always forgets to pay the cable bill or Dad's hogging the remote control because he wants to watch football. The backpack itself came from the thrift store. It smells like sour milk.*

*"Did you have fun at school today?" the police officer asks sweetly. "Did you get to play on the playground during recess?"*

*Eden chews on her nails, staring down at her worn-out shoes. She can still taste the Cheetos on her fingers. It was the only thing she had for lunch because it was all her mother packed for her. "Daddy says not to talk to strangers."*

*The police officer laughs. "That's really good advice. You're not supposed to talk to strangers, but you can talk to me. I'm a cop, and I'm here to help you."*

*The little girl shakes her head. "Dad says not to talk to cops. They're all bad."*

*The pretty police officer's face falls. She looks up at Mrs. Spellman, Eden's kindergarten teacher. She rises to her feet, the adults speaking in hushed whispers above Eden's little head.*

"How long has she been waiting out here?" asks the officer.

"Almost five hours," the teacher explains. "I make a point of staying with the kids until their parents show up. It's getting terribly late. I'm really worried."

"And you tried calling them?"

"Yes, several times. It keeps telling me that the number isn't in service."

"Do you know if she has any extended family in the area?"

"Not that I know of, no."

"Are you able to tell me what her home life is like?"

Eden stops listening at this point. Adults talk too fast and use words that are too big to understand. She keeps her eyes out on the road, waiting for the familiar shape and color of her Mom's red Toyota. Maybe Mom will buy her an ice cream to make up for the fact that she's late. She does that sometimes —buy ice cream to make Eden feel better.

She's been eating a lot of ice cream lately, especially after Dad yells at Mom.

Her mind is elsewhere. She really wants to go home to show Dad the picture she drew for him. Rachel, one of her classmates, lent her some glitter crayons to draw with. Eden's never made anything this beautiful. She's proud of her work and wants Dad to put it up on the fridge. Maybe he won't be so mad today.

"Alright, kiddo," the police officer says. "Would you like to come with me?"

"But Mommy and Daddy are coming. They said to be good and wait here."

She smiles, but there's something sad about it. Eden decides she doesn't like it. "We're going to try and meet your mother and father at the police station. It's getting awfully cold, don't you think? I'll treat you to a cup of hot chocolate when we get there."

Eden's tummy grumbles again. Her mother didn't pack her a big *lunch today, and it's getting really close to dinner time. Hot chocolate sounds yummy. How can she possibly say no?*

Alexander clenches his jaw, doing his best to keep his rage in check. "Then what happened?"

"They conducted a search, but there wasn't any sign of my parents. I wound up as a ward of the state, placed into the foster system. I bounced around from home to home and eventually wound up in the care of a man named Richard Parsons."

Alexander's stomach flips. An inkling of dread fills his guts. He doesn't like where this is going. "Did he... Did he hurt you?" he asks cautiously.

Much to his relief, Eden shakes her head. "No, nothing like that. He never laid a hand on me."

"Good."

She reaches out and takes Alexander's hand, giving his palm a gentle squeeze. He lets her. Alexander adores the feel of her fingers, warm and soft.

"Parsons was... Well, for the most part, he was good to me. Bare minimum effort, parenting-wise, but I was old enough to take care of myself at that point." She leans back into the couch cushions behind her. "The only problem was that I wasn't of age to take over financially. All money had to go through him."

"And?"

"Parsons had a very bad gambling habit."

Alexander looks to the money. "So you do owe a debt."

"No. Well, sort of."

"That makes no sense."

"I wanted to attend Gagnon-Allard for as long as I could

remember. It was always my plan to pursue my love of cooking, even after my parents went missing. So I applied for a scholarship. I didn't think I'd get it, but I did. I was over the moon."

Alexander's heart sinks. "Don't tell me he..."

She nods slowly. Sadly. "The money was sent to Parsons's account for safe keeping since he was technically my guardian. I went off to Gagnon-Allard, fully expecting him to have used the money to take care of my tuition. I really did attend. That wasn't a lie. I really did study with Charlie Zhao. I made it two weeks before I was called into the registrar's office. They told me that the payments for my program hadn't been made.

"So, I called Parsons to see what the hell was going on. Turns out, he'd spent it all. Every penny. Lost it betting on the ponies or something, not that that's important. What was important was that the money that was reserved for me was gone and I couldn't stay. There was no way the money could be retrieved. There was no way for my scholarship to be re-issued. I was forced to drop out."

Eden wipes her eyes with the back of her hand. "And it sucked. It really sucked because I loved all of my classes and I was learning so much and..." She glances at him. "And I met some really nice people there. Specifically one boy named Shang."

Alexander's face drops. Suddenly, everything clicks into place. He can't believe it.

The familiarity. The flashbacks he'd been getting. Everything makes sense and yet —at the same time— it doesn't.

"You were the girl," he realizes.

"You didn't seem to remember me when I first got here, so I didn't say anything. It was a long time ago, so I didn't think it would do any good to bring it up."

He stares at her, taking her in. "I remember more now," he

says slowly, images flitting through his mind. "I've been getting flashes here and there. Little, random things. You had a spatula in the shape of a whale."

Eden lets out a huff of a laugh. "Oh, shit. I'd totally forgotten about Toby."

He snaps his fingers and laughs—oh so gently—with her. "Right. Toby. I remember picking on you about naming the damn thing."

"You thought it was stupid."

He smiles. "I did. But then you proceeded to name all of your utensils just to spite me."

The girl from his memories has been here all along. It's no wonder Eden felt so familiar to him. Now he remembers. He remembers her bright smile and eagerness to learn. He remembers her sitting beside him in class, answering questions left and right. She was brilliant. She was the best of the bunch. A little bit of a sassy know-it-all, but Alexander remembers liking that about her.

And now she's here, lying her way into La Rouge with piles of cash on hand.

"How does the money fit into all this?" he asks, curious.

Eden swallows. "Missing persons cases never close. They just go cold. But I think... I think my parents are still out there. Somewhere. I was swept into the foster care system really quickly. Maybe they've been looking for me this whole time. So..." She gestures to the money. "I want to hire a private investigator. When I was younger, I heard about this PI, Maxine Kendo. She's apparently really, really good. The best PI in the world. She's solved hundreds of cold cases."

Alexander blinks, incredulous. "And she's going to cost..." He gestures to the money, too. "What? Fifteen grand?"

"Well, a little more than that, actually."

"What the fuck? That's so much."

"She charges per hour, and her rates are obviously much higher than the average PI because... Well, she's the best. My parents' case is over a decade old, so I'm sure there's a lot of information she needs to sift through. I need to have as much saved up as possible so that I can be prepared for however long this drags out. Hopefully not too long, but still."

"Christ."

"That's why I really need this job," she says, painfully honest. "It pays so much better than every other job I've worked, and it'll help me get to my goal faster." Eden tenses, casting her eyes to the floor. "I didn't want to lie to you. I really didn't. It's just... It's a vicious cycle. Without the education I need, I can't get the work. Without the work, I can't earn the money. And without the money..."

"You can't find your parents," he finishes.

She nods, solemn. "Being a chef... It's all I've ever been good at. Sure, I could work at a Dairy Queen or something, but who knows how long that'll take me. I was just desperate. I saw in the classifieds that you were hiring, so I applied. I swear I didn't want to lie to you, but I really, *really* need this job."

Alexander's quiet for a long while, turning everything over in his head. Yes, lying on one's resume is a terminable offense. If Sebastian finds out, Alexander will be in deep shit for hiring someone so under qualified. The smart thing to do is let Eden go. Maybe he can offer her a severance deal so she at least has the funds to find her parents. He supposes he can do that much for her.

But then again, it's *Eden*. There's just something about her, something inexplicable. She's got pure, raw talent. Eden can go far, maybe even further than he can. If she'd been given the same chances as him, they likely would have grown to be fierce rivals. It wasn't her fault that her dreams were squashed before she'd ever gotten out of the gate. The fact that she's self-taught and capable of running a kitchen all by herself? Even Alexander knows how much of a gem she is. And...

And he likes her.

He likes her more than he cares to admit.

He hadn't realized until now, but seeing her every day at work is a breath of fresh air. She makes it easier on him. Makes him give a shit. Getting through a shift is less of a slog when he knows she'll be there. Alexander shudders at the thought of firing her only to replace her with Hector—because seriously, fuck that guy. He wants her there.

"I believe you," he says.

"You do?"

"Yes. But—"

"I understand," she says quietly. "If you have to fire me, I'll understand. But if you don't, I promise I'll work three times as hard. I'll do whatever I have to do to keep this job. I love working at La Rouge. I really don't want to go, but—"

"You can stay."

"What?"

"You can stay."

"Is this some kind of joke?"

"Do I look like I make jokes?"

"But I'm not formally trained."

"I've never given a shit about formal education on a resume," he says simply. "What matters the most to me is if you can handle the heat. It's clear that you've got tons of practical experience, and you're a natural in the kitchen. You can't teach that shit in schools. I've had countless assholes walk through my kitchen thinking they were hot shit because they studied with *who-the-fuck-ever*. But when it came down to the rush and orders were piling up and it was time to dig deep, they weren't worth their salt. But you?" He gives her hand a squeeze. "You're something special, Eden. My kitchen hasn't run this smoothly in years and... And I really think it's because of you."

"Wow, I... I don't know what to say. But what about what happened to Amanda? Isn't this... hypocritical?"

Alexander nods slowly. "I realize that... If given another opportunity, I'd let her stay on, but there's nothing we can do about it now. What matters is keeping Sebastian from finding out about you."

"Right," she mumbles. "Right, okay."

"I'll let you stay, but on three conditions."

"Okay. What are they?"

"I want you to continue helping me come up with the new menu."

"Done. And the second condition?"

"Don't tell anyone that you didn't finish culinary school. It's quite frankly not their business to ask, but I know a few chefs at La Rouge who will make a bigger deal out of it than it is."

"Hector?"

"Hector."

"Alright. I don't plan on telling anyone. What's the third condition?"

"Let me be your teacher," he states. "Come in two hours early to help me with the menu, and stay two hours after for formal training. I'll make a sous chef out of you yet."

Eden beams, her sadness melting to give way to hope. "Can I, um..."

"What is it?"

"Is it okay if I hug you?"

Alexander nods, and she throws her arms around him to pull him into a tight embrace. He instinctively hugs her back, wrapping her up in his big arms. It feels absurdly good to hold her.

She's warm. She smells like vanilla. He doesn't understand why she feels so right. "Thank you," she says against his shoulder. "Thank you, thank you, thank you so much. I promise not to let you down. I'll work so hard, I swear."

"I know."

Eden moves away, and Alexander hates it. He doesn't stop her, though. He finds satisfaction in how relieved she looks.

"God, I really thought I was going to be job hunting," she admits, laughing nervously.

Alexander shrugs. "I guess it's your lucky day."

"Must be." She clears her throat. "So... Why 'Alexander'? Kind of stuffy, isn't it?"

He shakes his head. "It's getting late. Story for another time."

"Promise?"

"Promise."

"Okay."

Alexander rises and Eden follows, sheepishly picking at beneath her nails. She sees him to the front door of the apartment. Before he goes, she asks, "You never answered my question."

"Which one?"

"About trivia night. Will you come?"

He rolls his eyes. "I don't really—"

"Pretty please?" She clasps her hands together. "Please, please, *please*? You don't even have to really play. Just come and hang out. You can spend the whole night drinking, if you really want to."

Alexander sighs. He can't bring himself to say no. He just wants to see her smile.

"Fine."

Eden cheers, and it's the most adorable thing he's ever seen. "Here. Give me your phone."

"Why?"

"So, I can give you my number, silly. I'll text you the address of the bar so we can all meet."

He relents, fishing his phone out of his back pocket. Eden navigates the screen expertly, adding herself to his contacts before texting her own phone so she has his number. She hands it back, smiling like an idiot.

A gorgeous, pretty idiot.

"I'll see you tomorrow," she says.

"See you tomorrow," he promises.

He waits until Eden shuts the door before turning to leave. The second he gets outside, he lets out a huge exhale. This night has been... Well, it's been a lot. At this point, he just wants to go home and crash. Alexander's about to get back into his car when his phone chimes.

> Bea: Feel like coming over?

He sends a quick text back before slipping into the driver's seat. Once he hits send, he drives off, a massive weight lifting off his shoulders.

> Alexander: Hey, Bea. Sorry, but I think it's time we end this. It's been fun.

> Bea: Hey, no need to be sorry. We're both adults. I guess I better dust off the old Tinder account.

> Bea: Did you meet a girl or something? Just curious.

Bea: That brunette from your work was hot.

Alexander smiles to himself, the ghost of Eden's touch and the smell of her hair lingering like a dream.

Alexander: I 100% agree with you there.

Bea: LOL Happy trails, tiger.

# CHAPTER
## Thirteen

E den wanted to kiss him. She settled for hugging him. Now she's kicking herself for chickening out.

*Could have kissed him, Eden. You could have kissed him, but did you?*

*NoOooOoo.*

It all happened so fast. One second, she thought for sure she was about to lose her job. The next, she's at trivia with her friends the next evening and everything's completely fine.

The more she thinks about it, revealing her secret was going to have to happen sooner or later. She just didn't think it was going to be Alexander who figured it all out first. She's glad to finally be able to at least tell someone the truth. Still, she'll have to be more careful from here on out. The last thing she needs is to complicate matters further by telling people who have no business knowing.

The pub in question looks to be a rather decent place. More of a sports bar, if anything, what with massive TV screens turned to various channels like ESPN, the NFL, and the NBA. There are two distinct sections to the pub, the bar on the higher tier near the back, and the main floor one step down where tables have all been re-arranged specifically for trivia night. She spots Freddie, Peter, and Rina at one of the tables, having arrived before her.

"You made it!" Rina cheers, scooching over to pat the free seat next to her. "We thought you weren't going to show."

"It would have been super awkward if you hadn't," Peter mumbles.

Eden arches a brow. "Why would it have been awkward?"

"Because the boss man is here," Freddie supplies.

Eden doesn't know how she missed him, but she did. Alexander is absurdly tall and broad, so now that she knows he's here, her eyes lock onto him immediately like some kind of homing beacon. Everyone else disappears, and he's all she can focus on. Her heart skips a beat.

Eden's always thought he looked dashing in his chef jacket. But outside of the kitchen, dressed in a pair of dark jeans and a dark gray Henley that has no business being as tight on him as it is, he's...

Well, he's sexy as hell.

Especially so when he holds an entire tray full of drinks in one hand like it's nothing. Eden briefly wonders what she wouldn't give to be that tray.

*Down, girl.*

Alexander smiles at her, and she almost loses grip on reality. It's a barely-there sort of smile, the corners of his lips tugging upwards ever so slightly. Regardless, it leaves her speechless.

"You're here," he says warmly.

"I am."

"I'm glad."

She laughs. "Why would I invite you only to not show up?"

"Cruel prank?"

"I would never."

He chuckles. "Good."

Peter clears his throat. "Like, no pressure or anything, but do you think we could get to drinking? Very parched over here. Um, chef boss man, sir."

Alexander sets everything down and takes a seat next to Eden. He's treated the guys to some pretty high-quality beer, and he's got a glass of rosé for Rina, along with a gin and tonic for himself. There's one last drink remaining, a tall and narrow glass full of bubbly golden liquid. There are sliced strawberries submerged beneath a topping of vanilla ice cream. Alexander hands it to her.

"What is it?" she asks.

"A strawberry prosecco float. Who says vanilla ice cream can't be fancy?"

Eden smiles, very aware of how warm her cheeks feel. She chooses not to drink only because she knows how expensive cocktails can be. Five bucks per beer? Hell no. But since Alexander's treated her...

She takes a sip. It's utterly divine.

"Do you like it?"

"Yes, very much."

"Thought you might."

Rina claps her hands. "Okay, team. Here's the plan." She rises from her seat, taking charge of the situation. "We were this close to winning last week, but then someone decided to be a showoff and start calling out answers before they had a chance to think about it."

Freddie raises his hands in mock surrender. "Look, booze makes me overconfident."

"Overconfident, or stupid?" Peter chides.

"Shut up."

"Today's theme is film and television," Rina continues. "So, we better ace it this week or so help me God, I'll nag your ear off about it at work. Got it, Freddie?"

"Yes, ma'am."

"What's the prize?" Eden asks.

"A whole pitcher of beer and a basket of hot wings."

"We could just buy it, you know," Alexander says, ever the logical stick in the mud.

Rina, already a little tipsy and that much braver as a result, points an accusatory finger at Alexander. "That's no fun. Besides, victory makes it taste that much better. Capisce?"

Alexander puts his hands up in mock surrender, too, unwilling to piss Rina off. He gives Eden a side-eye, as if to say *yeesh*.

It makes Eden laugh.

Liquor has a fantastic way of making everyone friends. It's after the third round of drinks—that Alexander so graciously purchases for the table—that her other friends begin to warm up to him. Eden's immensely grateful. They were all so tense at first. Now, they look like they've been drinking buddies for ages.

As it turns out, Alexander and Peter get ridiculously loud when they've thrown back a few. They team up to relentlessly yell at the trivia night's host when he dares to contest one of their answers.

"Are you fucking kidding me?" Peter roars.

"What he fucking said!" Alexander adds, booming so much louder than the rest of the pub.

The trivia host winces, clearly no match. "Would you two please calm down?"

"Give him the point," Alexander demands.

"I'm afraid he didn't get it quite right."

"Because he forgot to add a *the* before the answer?"

Alexander snorts, pounding his fist down on the table rhythmically. "Give him the point! Give him the point!"

It doesn't take very long before people nearby join in on the chanting. Eden wonders if Alexander did that on purpose. It's astounding how charismatic he can be when he's yelling for the right reasons.

They get the point.

Unfortunately, they lose to the next table over in the lightning round. Rina still gets a consolation prize: a small basket of lightly salted fries. She munches away grumpily. Eden thinks she looks like a pouting hamster.

"Any pets?" Freddie asks. It's getting late, but none of them are willing to call it a night yet.

Eden shrugs. "I'm afraid not. My apartment building doesn't allow them."

"But if it did?"

"I'd love a dog."

"Big or small?"

"The bigger the better," she says with a grin. "Something with fluffy black hair, I think. I want to spoil it and cuddle with it all the time."

Rina nudges Eden in the arm with her elbow. "Save the cuddling for your boyfriend."

Eden laughs softly. "I'll keep that in mind if I ever end up with one."

She pretends not to notice Alexander's ears perk up.

Rina guffaws. "How's a gorgeous thing like you single?"

"Beats me. What about you guys? Any pets?"

Peter immediately pulls out his phone to show off a bunch of pictures he has on his camera roll. The majority of them feature a bright orange and white tabby. "This is Bubbles," he announces with pride.

"Bubbles?" Alexander mutters.

"Well, he's just so bubbly, so I think it fits."

"And you?" Eden asks Alexander. "Any pets?"

"No. I'm not home enough. It wouldn't be fair to them."

"Maybe get a fish?" Freddie suggests. "Super low maintenance."

"I'll pass."

Rina finishes her basket of fries, clearly dissatisfied. "You ever going to tell us who that leather babe was?" she asks Alexander.

He crinkles his nose. "'*Leather babe*'?"

Rina crinkles her nose, too. "Yeah, sorry. I just heard it."

"Oh, yeah," Peter says, raising a finger. "After work that one night."

"Scared me, to be honest," Freddie mutters. "Thought she was some assassin on her way to kick our asses."

"Your girlfriend?" Rina asks with a suggestive pump of her thin eyebrows.

"No. No girlfriend. We saw each other for a little bit here and there."

Peter and Freddie, in their drunken state, let out an overly dramatic '*oooooh*.'

Alexander rolls his eyes. "But that's over now."

"Oh, I'm sorry to hear that," Eden replies. Is this a smile tugging at her lips? But why doesn't she feel bad about the news?

"Don't be. It was very amicable."

"Well, that's...good. Yeah, I'm... Good."

Alexander smirks. "Prosecco hitting you a little hard there, Monroe?"

"What? No, of course not."

"*Sure*," he says dryly.

"Like you're one to talk," she teases, poking his cheek. "Look how red your face is. You've had, what? Three beers? You look like a tomato."

"I'll have you know it's called Asian flush, and it's perfectly natural."

Eden, bubbly and just on the other side of tipsy, giggles. "A cute, cute tomato."

He chuckles. "Oh, stop," he says, but there isn't any heat behind it.

"I should take a picture for posterity. Or blackmail."

"Blackmail? What could you possibly want to blackmail me for?"

"More paid vacation days, for one," Eden says, teasing. "Maybe a raise?"

"You already have fourteen paid vacation days a year, and your salary is more than generous."

"Yeah, but like... *More* of all that stuff, please."

Alexander snorts. "It's going to take a lot more than an embarrassing picture of me to get me to cave."

Her camera clicks. She's managed to steal two pictures of him, one mid-sentence and mid-blink, while the other shows off a partial smile.

"There," she beams. "Let me just forward this to the wait-staff. I *know* they'll love to see these in the group chat."

"Don't you dare!" Alexander reaches out and grabs the phone from her, holding it up and away. He fends her off, one hand on her shoulder as she laughs.

"Give it here!"

"Absolutely not!"

She's practically crawled onto Alexander's lap by the time she manages to get her phone back, feeling proud and very, *very* aware of how solid his body feels beneath her. Their eyes lock for a moment, the air around them electric.

"Anybody up for more drinks?" Rina asks, much louder than necessary.

Eden retakes her seat, suppressing her smile while Alexander shifts in his chair.

Peter mumbles awkwardly, looking between Eden and Alexander, then back to Eden again. "I don't know. It's getting pretty late."

Freddie pats him on the shoulder. "Come on. One more round, hm? What do you say, boss?"

"I think I'll pass," Alexander says, voice a bit hoarse. "Someone needs to be sober enough to drive you all home."

"Who's going to grab our refills?"

"Dibs not it!" Rina shouts, much louder than necessary, before bringing the tip of her index to her nose.

Freddie, Peter, and Eden immediately mirror the gesture, leaving Alexander the odd one out. He sighs, reluctantly getting up from the table to head to the bar.

"I've never been good at that game," he mumbles as he goes.

The second Alexander is out of ear shot, the trio lean in and practically swallow Eden whole.

"Holy shit, Eden," Rina practically squeals.

"What?"

"Uh, are we not sitting at the same table?" Freddie asks. "You two have been giving each other googly eyes all night."

"'*Googly eyes*?' What, are we seven?"

"You know what I mean!"

Eden can't stop smiling. "We haven't."

Peter rolls his eyes. "If you two look any more like lovesick puppies, I'm going to have to adopt you both."

"You're over exaggerating," she insists. "There's nothing going on between us."

"Really? You were basically dry humping his thigh."

Eden gawks. "Was *not*!"

"Freddie, baby, can you book me an appointment to see the

optometrist because Eden apparently thinks that I need my eyes checked."

"Guys, we're *not* a thing," she insists.

Peter squints at her. "I don't believe you."

"It's the truth."

"You're not interested in him at *all*?" Rina asks. "Because from where I'm sitting, y'all seem pretty dang cozy."

Eden squirms a bit. She didn't realize how obvious she was being. She mentally blames the alcohol. "I'm not interested in him. We're just... friends."

Someone behind her taps her on the shoulder. Eden turns to find a pretty young woman with blonde hair sitting at the next table over. There's actually a whole group of them, dressed up for a girl's night out on the town.

The blonde smiles. "Sorry, couldn't help but overhear. I was actually hoping to give him my number."

Eden flushes bright red. "Wha—Oh. Um..."

The woman scribbles her number down on a nearby napkin and passes it to Eden. "Would you mind giving this to him? We were actually on our way out. I wasn't going to say anything before because I thought you two were together, but—"

"Sure, I guess," Eden says in a mousy voice.

"Thanks, doll."

Eden's smile is obscenely tight. "Yeah. No problem."

Except it's definitely a problem.

"So, like, where's he from?" she continues on, twirling a strand of her hair around her finger as she eyes Alexander at the bar like he's a piece of meat at the butcher's shop.

"New York, I think?" Peter's the one who answers.

"No, no. Like, where's he *really* from?"

Eden crumples the napkin in her fist, her skin prickling. "Excuse me?"

"Oh, you know what I mean. Is he Korean or Japanese?"

A flicker of annoyance makes Eden work her jaw. "What's it matter?"

"He just looks *so* much like that guy from that K-pop group." She snaps her fingers, straining her two brain cells for a name. "Taehung? Or Mingyu? I guess it would be alright if he's Chinese, too, but..."

"You need to piss off," Eden snaps, slowly rising from her seat. "Right now."

"What's your problem?"

"Look, I'm going to give you the benefit of a doubt here and say that you're clearly too sauced to be thinking straight, but what you're saying is... Yeah, just ew."

"I just want to know more about him."

"Then how about asking for his *name* first?"

"You're making this weird."

"You handled that all on your own when you asked where he was *really* from."

"*Preach!*" Rina hoots.

"Give it to her, Eden!" Peter shouts.

"Run along, dollface," Freddie adds, gesturing a hand in a '*shoo*' motion.

Blondie scoffs. "Whatever, bitch."

The table of women leave just as Alexander returns with another tray of refreshments. He sets everything down, eyeing Eden curiously. She's seated on the edge of her chair, lip curled up into a pout.

"What was that all about?" he asks.

Eden stuffs the napkin into her jacket pocket. "Oh, nothing. Just asking where she got her lipstick from. Thought it might look nice on me."

He tilts his head to the side, giving her lips a once over. "I think you'd look nice either way."

Freddie and Rina do their best to hide their laughter. Peter rests his chin on his hand and dares to make kissing faces. Alexander's smart enough to ignore them.

And if Eden sits a little closer to Alexander for the rest of the night to ward off the interest of nearby tables, he certainly doesn't seem to mind.

They drop Rina off first, and then Freddie and Peter at their shared apartment.

Alexander drives her home next. The ride is nowhere near as intense as it was yesterday.

"Did you have fun?" she asks, mildly buzzed. Most of the effects of her drinks have long since worn off, but a warm haze lingers to fill her mind. She feels good. That, and the scent of his cologne works like magic on her. Something about him reminds her of the ocean. A little cold and dark sometimes, but with moments of shining brilliance, hidden treasures and vibrant life hidden somewhere deep below.

She wants to dive straight in.

"Yeah, actually," he says while taking a left turn. "Pretty fun."

Eden smiles, triumphant. "Told ya."

"Trivia host was an idiot, though."

"I mean, technically—"

"No, not *technically*. It was a poorly worded question open to interpretation. That was his fault."

She laughs, throwing her head back. "Oh my God, let it *go*."

He laughs with her. The sound of his voice vibrates straight through her, low and mesmerizing. "Do you think I did alright?" he asks. "With the others, I mean."

"You were great. Peter even said to me that you weren't as

bad as he thought. Don't tell him I told you that, though. He swore me to secrecy."

He chuckles. "My lips are sealed."

When they finally arrive outside her apartment building, Eden suddenly doesn't want to go. She's about to ask Alexander if he'd like to walk her in, just so she can spend a few more minutes with him, but he's already getting out of the car and circling around front to open the passenger-side door for her. He offers her his hand. She doesn't think twice and takes it.

They walk together, taking their sweet time venturing down the hall. Her shoulder brushes up against his arm, but he doesn't move away. In fact, he leans into the touch. His fingers ghost past hers, too many times to be considered an accident.

Something inside her is excited and bright, and Eden knows for a fact that it isn't the last remnants of prosecco. She gets to the door of her apartment and opens it, turning to look up at Alexander. He's inches away. Eden wonders when he'd grown comfortable enough to be so close.

She's not complaining.

"Do you feel like coming in for a cup of coffee?" she asks, doing her best to keep calm and appropriate, but fuck it's hard to do when he's so damn close and smells so good.

In all fairness, Alexander really looks like he wants to kiss her. Lord knows Eden really wants to kiss *him*.

He doesn't, though, and Eden's never been more disappointed.

"I should... I should probably get going," he says slowly, low and restrained. "It's getting late. And I need you sharp tomorrow."

*Ah, damn it.*

"Right. Totally understandable."

"Goodnight, Eden."

"Goodnight."

She closes the door softly, exhaling as quietly as she can. Her heart's pounding loudly in her chest, pulse so powerful that she can feel it in the tips of her fingers and toes. She supposes it's just as well. Alexander's just being responsible, and she can hardly fault him for that.

Eden turns to hang up her jacket and purse, toeing off her shoes. She's just about ready to head to the bathroom to take a shower when...

There's a knock at the door.

She whips it open.

"By '*coffee*,' did you mean—"

Eden grabs him by the collar and drags him inside. Their lips come crashing together.

# CHAPTER
## Fourteen

G lorious. That's the only word he can come up with to describe kissing her.

Alexander picks her up like she weighs nothing and relishes the way Eden gasps in surprise. She instinctively wraps her legs around his hips, arms circling around his neck and shoulders for support. Their lips slot together, a perfect fit, breathing each other in like their lives depend on it.

It certainly *feels* like their lives depend on it.

He pins her back against the nearest wall, suddenly winded when she rolls her hips against him, grinding against his stiffening erection. The languid moan he draws from her lips is downright sinful. Just the sound of her voice is enough to make him hard, so much so that it actually hurts not to take her then and there in the hall.

Alexander's never felt this out of control before. He strains against the throbbing stiffness in his pants, desperately trying to hold back out of fear of hurting her. With Bea, he was used to fucking hard and fast. That's how she liked it, and how he preferred it. But with Eden?

God, he wants to be gentle.

He wants to be gentle and take his time and savor every inch of her. He wants to run his fingers through her hair and tease her to the point of unraveling and give her everything she could ever ask for because she deserves no less.

But he also wants to have her wet on his cock and screaming his name and whimpering nonsense as pleasure overwhelms her senses. He wants to drag his fingers over her skin and mark her with hard kisses and hold her down as orgasm shakes her body.

He doesn't know which he wants more. Alexander wants her so badly, it almost tears him apart. He settles for exploring Eden's mouth with the tip of his tongue, eager to memorize her taste and savor the softness of her lips.

Even though he stumbles through her tiny apartment, bumping clumsily into furniture while drinking her in, Alexander's hold on Eden never falters. By some miracle, they make it to her couch, tumbling down together onto the cushions in a tangle of arms and legs. She rolls her hips against him again, and it drives him crazy.

She's so small, it's alarming, like handling fine crystal beneath him. He's constantly worried about crushing her, but she doesn't seem to mind him on top. In fact, she pulls him that much closer, eager for more.

Eden sucks on his bottom lip, raking her fingers through his hair like she's searching for a lifeline out in the middle of murky waters. She rolls her hips against him again, unleashing lava through his veins. Her hands are just as greedy as his, dragging down the front of his chest, wandering further to the front of his pants. Eden palms at his erection through the stiff fabric of his jeans, and he just about loses it.

"Eden—"

There's something ravenous in her eyes. Something seductive and dangerous. It's pure, unadulterated hunger. They're both chefs. They should know.

They move with purpose. Eden undoes his belt, he slips his

hands beneath her shirt. She gropes the front of his boxer briefs, he lightly squeezes her small breasts. He mouths at the delicate skin of her throat, she parts her legs that much wider. They breathe as one, panting and groaning and drowning in the pursuit of pleasure.

They've been dancing around each other long enough, even though Alexander has no sweet clue when the dance even began.

Was it the first day she arrived at La Rouge? Maybe the first time he saw her truly smile.

Perhaps it was when she took charge of his kitchen and he recognized a fountain of untapped skill. He can't be too sure. Right now, he doesn't care. Eden may be hungry, but he's ready to devour her whole.

She hooks her fingers over the waistband of his boxer briefs, the contact of her bare skin against his hips sending a jolt straight through him.

He stops and pulls away. "Wait."

Eden braces herself up on her elbows, concern written all over her face. "Shit. Did I hurt you? I'm sorry, I—"

"No, no," he assures quickly. "I just... Fuck. I think we should talk."

She brings her hands up to cover her eyes, mortified. "Oh, I'm sorry. Did you not want to—Shit, I thought—"

Alexander chuckles and cups her face, peering deep into her lovely eyes. Her pupils are blown wide open, her desire undeniable. "I want to, Eden. But I think if we're going to do this, we should do it right."

"What do you mean?"

He takes a deep breath. "I mean I'd like to take you out."

"Like, kill me or..."

He snorts a laugh. "On a date, dummy. Would you like to go to dinner with me, maybe?"

Eden giggles nervously, visibly relaxing. "But we work in a restaurant all day. Won't that be a bit too close to home?"

"You might be right about that."

Alexander sits up and pulls Eden over so that she's straddling his lap. It takes some of the strain off his cock, but he knows it's going to take a hot minute before he'll be able to settle down. Eden circles his neck with her arms and remains close. He can't get over how wonderful she feels pressed up against him.

"We can think of something else," he says. "But I do want to take you out. And I think... I think we should set some ground rules. Especially since we work together."

"And you're my boss."

"Exactly. I don't want you to feel obligated into agreeing to go out with me just because—"

Eden presses her fingers to his lips to stop him. "I don't feel obligated in the slightest," she states. "I like you, too. And I'd love it if we could do something together. Away from work."

Alexander nods. "Do you have any suggestions?"

Eden presses her lips into a thin line and crinkles her nose, appearing deep in thought. Alexander thinks it's the most adorable thing he's ever seen.

"When's our next day off?" she asks. "Have you already worked out next week's shifts?"

"I have, but I can move things around."

"It probably wouldn't be a good idea to go out on a weekend. The kitchen's going to need us."

"How about Tuesday? Restaurant's usually very quiet. The others should be able to handle it if we're both away."

Eden smiles. "Tuesday works great. I think the aquarium offers discounts then, too."

Alexander arches a brow. "The aquarium?"

She shrugs, sweetly shy. "I've always wanted to go, but I hate going to places like that all by myself, so—"

"The aquarium it is," Alexander says without hesitation. "I've never been to one, either."

Her smile outshines a thousand suns. "Really? You really want to go?"

"I do if you do."

"I can't wait."

Alexander leans forward to kiss her, unable to help himself. It's ridiculous how lost they get in each other's taste. When they finally pull away, Alexander is blissed out of his mind.

"You, um..." she mumbles, struggling to recover from her giddy thoughts. "Something about ground rules?"

"Oh, yeah." He clears his throat. "I think we should keep this between us for now. Until we figure things out."

She nods. "Sure, I get that. But I'm pretty sure the others already know."

"Do they?"

"Mentioned something about how we looked like lovesick puppies."

Alexander smirks. "Were we that obvious?"

"Pretty sure they were drunk when they said that, so I'd take it with a grain of salt."

"Duly noted."

"But yeah, I agree. I think we should keep it on the down low, too."

"No PDA in the workplace," he says sternly. "Nothing personal, but that's not something I'm into. Like, ever."

"Ever?"

"Ever."

"May I ask why?"

Alexander shrugs. "Work is work."

"Gotcha. I can respect that."

"Thank you. Anything you want me to keep in mind?"

"Yeah, but it's not so much a rule as it is a question."

"Shoot."

The tips of her ears turn pink. "You said that you and Bea had a... thing."

"That's right. We had a casual arrangement."

"How recently did that end?"

"Two nights ago."

"Wow, that's really recent."

"Yeah, well, I realized that I wanted to..." He trails off, not quite sure where his mind is leading him.

"So... I suppose you haven't had the chance to, um..."

Alexander smirks. "There's no need to be shy, Eden. Just ask me."

Eden clears her throat and tries again. "I suppose you haven't had the chance to get tested, have you?"

"I haven't. We always used protection, but I'll schedule an appointment and take care of it. What about you?"

"I dated a guy a few years ago, but I haven't seen anyone since. Too busy with work. I'm probably overdue for another test, either way, so I'll get one just to be safe."

"Sounds good."

"And... And if this doesn't end up working out—"

"Eden—"

"If it doesn't end up working out, I really hope we can still... Well, be friends, I guess. Because I think you're pretty great."

Alexander smiles. "Yeah. Me, too."

"You think you're great, too?"

"What? No. I meant—"

Eden throws her head back and laughs. "I'm messing with you."

"Why are you such a menace?"

"Someone has to keep you on your toes."

"I see."

"Good."

"Excellent."

"Peachy keen."

"Was there anything else you can think of?"

"Not right now. I'll have to let you know."

"Please do."

"Can we go back to making out now?"

He laughs, feeling better and lighter than he has in ages. "Fuck, yes."

Alexander knows he's probably being overdramatic, but kissing Eden is the best damn thing in the world. It was never like this with him and Bea. Not even for a second. With Bea, it was clinical and formulaic and rigid. But with Eden, he's never been so gladly out of his element before.

Everything about her excites him to no end. He feels like a teenager because it's only been two seconds into kissing her and he's rock hard again. Eden seems to know this, deliberately rotating her hips against him to send pleasure flooding through his body.

He knows it's too soon to do anything with her. He really likes her, and he doesn't want to mess things up by moving too fast. But at the same time, Alexander desperately wants her out of her clothes, splayed out in front of him, ready for him to have like a starving man at an open buffet.

The anticipation is torture. It may very well be enough to kill him.

He can't stop thinking about what she must look like underneath it all. Are her cute freckles exclusive to her cheeks, or are they hidden away like naughty little secrets, spread out across her skin like stars against the night sky? Where exactly will she allow him to leave love bites? Is that something she might be into? He pictures her covered in dull red marks on her breasts, the side of her neck, on each of her inner thighs.

He can't wait to have her. But for now, he needs to be patient. For now, he needs to savor what he already has.

He has the gentle curve of the small of her back. He has the smell of her vanilla shampoo fully memorized. He has her lips on his, tender and sweet. He has her pulse racing and breathing uneven, her excitement electric enough that he can feel it in the air.

He wants this to last forever.

He should know he's never that lucky.

Alexander's phone goes off four times in quick succession, a series of incoming text alerts startling them both.

"Ignore it?" Eden mumbles against his lips, practically pleading.

"Can't," he replies, wholly apologetic as he checks his phone with a squint.

"Who is it?"

"Sebastian."

The name is more effective than a sudden plunge into cold water. The mood is dead, kind of like the soulless creature living in Sebastian's husk of a body.

"I have to get going," he tells her softly.

"Are you sure you can't stay a while longer?"

Alexander thinks she's so sweet, she's going to give his heart cavities.

"Unfortunately. He's tightening his leash. If I don't answer, I'll be in deep shit."

Eden nods slowly, wearing a gentle and understanding smile. "Okay."

They readjust their clothes before Eden leads Alexander to the apartment door. They linger, giggling and smiling like children who've gotten away with something.

"Still helping me with the menu tomorrow?" he asks.

"Of course. I'll see you then, chef."

Alexander dips in one last time to kiss her chastely and—*ah, crap*—he can't remember the last time he felt this happy to be anywhere and this sad to be leaving.

# CHAPTER
## Fifteen

There's something lovely about walking into the kitchen to find Alexander busy at work, diligently turning something over on the stove in front of him.

It's his hands, she thinks. His big, strong hands and sturdy fingers that know exactly where to go and what to do. They're mesmerizing. What she wouldn't do to have his hands all over her—

*We're at work, Eden.*

It's truly a privilege to watch him cook. He's facing away, but this gives Eden ample time to admire the expanse of his broad back. The back that she was pretty much clawing at last night.

*Self control, woman. Ever heard of it?*

"Hey, you," she greets gently, not wanting to startle him.

Alexander turns to look at her over his shoulder. His smile is wide and warm, the corners of his eyes crinkling as he does. "Hey," he replies softly. "Have you eaten yet?"

Eden shakes her head sheepishly. "No, sorry."

"Figured." Alexander plates what he's been working on and sets the food down on the nearest prep table. "Pull up a stool."

Something blooms within Eden's chest as she sits down, eyeing the meal Alexander's prepared for her. Just a whiff of it is enough to have her stomach grumbling.

He's made her a chicken Florentine crepe. The crepe itself is thin and crisp, a beautiful golden-brown blanket around its savory filling. The rotisserie chicken is mixed in with bits of juicy mushrooms, chopped up spinach, and a very healthy helping of Italian blend cheese. Eden can smell the roasted garlic and the hint of nutmeg he threw in.

The first bite is like taking a bite out of heaven. She almost inhales the whole damn thing.

It's rich, it's buttery, it's perfect.

"Ah, wow," she mumbles, mouth full. "This is so good."

"You really think so?"

"Mm-hmm. You should be a chef."

"Hilarious," he says dryly. His smile betrays him.

*God, it should be illegal to look that handsome.*

She waits until she's devoured about half her meal before swallowing to ask, "What did Sebastian want last night?"

Alexander rolls his eyes. "Same thing he always does. Updates on the new menu. I BS'd my way through some suggestions. He's out of town right now checking on one of his other restaurants. He said he'd be in by the end of the month for a taste test. "

"But you don't have anything yet."

"Exactly."

"That's a dangerous game."

He shrugs. If Eden didn't know any better, she'd argue he looks defeated. Resigned.

It's sad, really. Eden can see the struggle in his eyes, the disinterest. She knows Alexander is talented, one of the best chefs of their generation. There have been countless news and magazine articles, as well as hundreds of reviews from some of the most esteemed food critics raving about his dishes.

So this apparent disconnect is confusing to witness. Something's holding him back.

She knows it, he knows it.

And if Sebastian knows it, Alexander's in trouble.

"What were some of the things you suggested?" she asks him.

"Mostly seafood dishes. Lots of lobster. Asshole food snobs love lobster. They think it's the fanciest fucking shit out there."

"Didn't they used to feed lobster to prisoners because it was so cheap?"

Alexander nods. "Back when they used to overfish and had an overabundance. Now, it's a delicacy."

Eden smiles. "I'm getting the sense you don't actually like lobster."

"I hate it. Takes too long to cook, hard to prep, pain in the ass to plate. I swear to God, if I hear one more complaint about portion sizes being a rip-off, I'll jump into the pot of boiling water myself."

This makes Eden laugh. "Never took you for a drama queen."

"Sorry. I don't mean to bitch so much. You're easy to talk to."

She suddenly feels drunk, even though it's a little before noon and she's never been more sober. There's just something about him—those hints of quiet sincerity and honesty—that makes her feel lighter than air.

Eden finishes off her lunch and pushes the plate to the side. "What was something you used to love to eat as a kid?" she asks.

"What?"

"I've never had to create original recipes before, but if I had to, I think it'd be fun to try and recreate dishes from my child-hood. Stuff that I haven't eaten in ages. My mother used to make this really weird hotdog and mac and cheese combination—she always drowned it in cheese—but it was the most delicious thing in the world. I've tried making it myself, but it's never quite the same. I think she had a secret ingredient in there somewhere. It's sort of fun to try and figure out what it is, like a nostalgia kick. Maybe that could work for you? At the very least, it'll help you get started."

Alexander leans against the counter, dipping in to regard Eden curiously. She can practically see the gears turning in his head. While he mulls it over, Eden stares at his lips. The lips that she was so hungrily kissing just last night.

*No, not at work.*

*Damn, this is hard.*

But it's too late. Now she can't stop thinking about how he picked her up. Dear *God*, she'd never been more turned on in her life. She was putty in his hands. A part of her wonders what it would be like to have him kiss her right here and now, pinning her against the nearest workstation so that she can reach down and—

"That's not a bad idea," he mumbles.

Eden inhales sharply, snapping back to reality. "Anything come to mind?"

He thinks. Really thinks. Eden can't help but notice how he sort of just... disappears. It gives her the chance to truly study his face. The hard edge of his jaw line, the way his lips wear a permanent pout, the way his inky black hair always seems frustratingly and impossibly soft. She wants to reach out to tuck a strand of his hair away.

She doesn't. She knows the rules.

So she sits there, fingers itching to touch.

Something sparks in Alexander's mind. At least she thinks so because he immediately moves to the walk-in to grab something. Eden thinks it's amusing how single-minded he can be sometimes. He'll stop everything at the drop of a hat to focus on whatever he needs to get done. His focus is admirable.

He returns with only five ingredients, not including the salt and pepper they have readily available at each cooking station.

Alexander's selected the best potatoes they have in storage, a medium-sized white onion, a hearty block of Reblochon-style cheese, a slab of fatty bacon, and has even retrieved a dry white wine from the downstairs pantry.

Eden's mind races. The ingredients are simple, but there are hundreds of different possible outcomes. She can't even begin to fathom what Alexander has in store for her.

He handles his knives beautifully. His grip is strong, but just light enough to offer the most flexibility. It isn't very long before he slices up generous bits of bacon and has it sizzling in a hot pan, fat melting away and frying all around the meat to leave it nice and crisp. In goes finely minced onion, and then a good cup or so of white wine to deglaze the bottom of the pan. Then it's the potatoes, which he's skinned and sliced with mind-bending accuracy.

Alexander pops everything into an oven-proof dish before covering the top with a hefty layer of cheese. He places it in the oven, but doesn't bother setting a timer. He's a skilled enough chef to know when it's done.

"Are you going to tell me what this mystery dish is?" Eden asks.

Alexander smiles. "It's a tartiflette," he explains. "My father used to make it all the time. Comfort food, for when I wasn't feeling well. It was one of the only things he didn't burn when cooking."

Eden sits up a little straighter. "Your father? Is he a chef, too?"

"No," he replies, suddenly stiff and rigid. "He was a mechanic."

"Was?"

"Can you check that the inventory was stocked?" he asks abruptly. "Before everyone arrives and it gets too busy."

Eden frowns. "Um, sure?"

"Thanks."

She gets up from her stool and slowly makes her way over to the walk-in. There's a detailed shipping chart attached to a clipboard hanging just to the right of the big metal door. It's a simple enough task to do, taking her all of thirty seconds to verify, so Eden can't help but feel confused. She still doesn't know what happened to him all those years ago. Eden wants to ask, but she's worried about sticking her nose where it doesn't belong.

*He'll open up eventually. Just give him time.*

When she gets back from her singular task, things are suddenly very awkward. She has no idea how she's supposed to move forward from here. Alexander, to be fair, looks no better off. She's half-tempted to break his PDA rule and make out with him in the walk-in to pass the time.

Unfortunately, Hector walks in, and it's suddenly so much worse. The redhead glares at the two of them, grumbling something under his breath that Eden's sure isn't anywhere close to a '*hello.*'

Freddie and Peter are the next two to show up. They're chatting about some kind of vet appointment for their cat. Rina arrives not long after, and then the rest of the kitchen staff arrive, immediately putting away their coats so they can get to their opening duties.

Alexander takes the food out from the oven and sets it down on the counter, scooping a small portion of the now creamy, cheesy, bacon-sprinkled potatoes into a smaller bowl for Eden. She doesn't waste time and takes a bite. It's piping hot against her tongue, but the slight burn is totally worth it.

"What do you think?" Alexander asks, looking very much like a child seeking approval.

"This is *amazing*," she says, already moving in for a second bite. It's honestly so good that she's speechless. She just wants to eat and eat and eat because it's just that heavenly.

He has an undeniable gift. Maybe they both do.

He tilts his head to the side. "How would you improve it?"

Eden smiles. "If you hit it with a bit of thyme and garlic, I think this could be a hit. I think you should add it to your new menu."

His smile is shyer, almost discreet. Eden wonders if it's because everybody's here now and he's not used to being anything but a hard-ass head chef around them. She thinks it's sweet, like his smiles are a private little secret just between them.

When Freddie, Peter, and Rina come over, he simply nods at them in greeting and walks away, getting ready to man the front of the line before service starts.

Freddie rubs his hands together. "What do we have here?"

"Can we try?" Rina asks.

Peter doesn't even ask. He's already stuffing his mouth full. "*Yum*. Did the boss man make this for you?"

The only reason she doesn't respond 'yes' with the utmost pride is because Eden's too busy trying to get a few more bites in. Some of the other chefs show up, curious and eager to give the dish a try.

The whole thing is devoured within a minute, not a scrap left over.

*A definite hit.*

# CHAPTER
## Sixteen

S omething's different.

Alexander isn't quite sure when it happened, but he realizes now that he'd been working beneath the heavy weight of a thick fog for years. It left his body languid and his mind cloudy. Unable to taste, unable to see, unable to care. But now?

Now he's excited, and he's starting to suspect his sous chef has something to do with it.

He almost breaks his own rule on numerous occasions throughout tonight's service. Eden's impossible to ignore. She's honestly the best kind of distraction, orbiting around him like his own personal comet. He finds surprising comfort in her proximity, assured by her constant presence like the rise and set of the sun.

Alexander doesn't think it's a problem until he realizes he's accidentally called out desserts before appetizers for table seven —a seriously amateur mistake in terms of timing—because being around Eden makes his whole body feel dopey. Maybe if she'd stop grazing up against him while he worked, he'd be able to focus.

On the other hand, he doesn't actually want her to stop.

As a matter of fact, what he really wants is to take Eden into the walk-in and kiss the ever- loving daylights out of her. What he really wants is to take her to the kitchen office, shut the door, and bend her over his work desk. What he really wants is to strip her down and see her in nothing but her chef jacket—

"Chef?" Peter asks.

"Huh?"

"We're closing up. You coming?"

Alexander blinks twice, suddenly realizing that the kitchen is quiet and the last few chefs are headed out the door. He can't remember the last time he got through a shift this easily.

Everything went smoothly, minor issues popping up here and there, but nothing he and Eden couldn't handle in an instant.

*We make a pretty good team.*

"Boss?" Peter waves a hand in front of Alexander's face. "Oh, shit. Hey, Rina? What are the signs of a stroke again?"

Alexander swats Peter's hand away. "I'm not having a stroke. Just thinking."

"Good, because my CPR's rusty."

"I'd rather you let me die than perform CPR on me."

Peter chuckles. "I'll keep that in mind."

"You guys go on ahead. I've got to talk to Eden."

"Is she in trouble or something? If it's about the broken pilot light—"

"Broken pilot light?"

"Yeah. I told you about it three times already. It's the reason my steaks haven't been cooking properly. I've been working on a half-broken element."

Alexander, for the life of him, doesn't remember any of these conversations. He folds his arms over his chest. A broken pilot light isn't the end of the world, but it's certainly an inconvenience. He's going to have to call the repairman to have the appropriate parts replaced, but there's no telling if they'll get here in time for the weekend rush.

The heavy clatter of a toolbox on a nearby counter catches him by surprise. He turns to find Eden by the stove in question, searching for the necessary tools she needs to fix it.

"What do you think you're doing?" he asks her.

"Building a spaceship," she answers sarcastically. Eden smiles at Peter. "Don't worry. I'll take care of it. You guys have a good night."

Peter nods. "See you tomorrow. You two be good."

Alexander frowns. "What's that supposed to mean—"

"Goodnight!" Eden says cheerfully, moving to close the door on everyone. She turns and leans against the locked doors, holding back a laugh. "Are you feeling alright? I've never seen you so spacey before."

He shrugs, unable to stop himself from smiling. "What can I say? It was a good day."

"I'm glad." Eden moves to the stove and starts taking the element off, along with the silver metal drip pan beneath it.

"You should really leave it for the repairman," Alexander starts.

"Relax. I used to fix these all the time."

"You did?"

She nods, tongue sticking out from the corner of her mouth in concentration. "The equipment we had at the place I worked before was at least thirty years out of date. I can fix this one up no prob—Ah, see? The pilot adjustment screw's just a bit loose. Can you hand me a slot screwdriver?"

Alexander shifts through the toolbox —it's a dusty old thing, hidden away somewhere in the darkest corner of the pantry down-stairs— but eventually finds what he's looking for. At least, he thinks so. Judging by the dissatisfied expression Eden wears, probably not.

"No, I said a slot screwdriver."

"What the fuck is that?"

"It's the flat one. Kind of looks like a spatula."

"You should have just said that in the first place. That's language I understand."

Eden giggles. "Of course, how silly of me."

Alexander holds up another tool. "This one?"

"No. That one's too thick. I need the three-sixteenth inch."

He holds up another, and then another, but to no avail. "You have to be fucking with me, right?"

"Unfortunately not," Eden teases. "Good thing you're cute."

She sidles up next to him, her arm brushing up against his. It's ridiculous how much Alexander likes her hands. They're small and cute, fingers slender and elegant. When she leans over to adjust the pilot screw, Alexander catches a glimpse at the bare skin of the nape of her neck. He has to fight the urge not to reach out and brush her hair to the side.

It's just that being near her does something to him, something he can't even begin to comprehend. Any sense of self-control goes straight out the window whenever Eden is near. It's an overwhelming feeling that he constantly has to keep in check because there's nothing he wants more than to have her lips on his.

He finds himself just behind her, one hand on either side of her on the stove edge. Eden works in the space between his arms, either unaware or perfectly content with his proximity.

When she's finished, she replaces the parts and turns the stove on to test. A low, gentle flame ignites, the issue officially rectified. Eden shuts it off just as quickly, satisfied with her job well done.

"There, as good as—"

She turns, her sentence fading into nothing. She licks her

lips, watching Alexander with an intense intrigue. They've drawn together like magnets.

He really wants her. She really wants him.

Alexander just might break his own rules. Just for her.

She whispers, "We should really..."

"What?" he whispers, just as soft.

"What, um..." Eden swallows, breathless.

Alexander takes a deep breath, soaking in the warmth of her body. His blood is on fire, and his heart is about to leap out of his chest. He adores how her cheeks have turned a light shade of pink, or the way her plump lips part in anticipation, or how her pupils are blown wide.

She drives him fucking wild.

"What were you going to teach me today?" she asks, finally mustering up enough courage to find her voice.

*Ah, right. Back to business.*

Alexander straightens his back and steps away. "Knife skills," he says, very much hating how gravelly his voice sounds. "Let's put your new set to work."

"I know my way around a knife."

"You do. But today, we're going to practice precision. Tell me, what's the difference between fine brunoise cut and a batonnet?"

Eden blanks. "I'm pretty sure those are just words you've made up."

"How exactly did you learn to cook?"

"By watching, mostly. TV shows and stuff. I know, it's kind of lame."

"No, it's actually quite impressive."

"It is?"

"You've picked up a lot of the beginner and intermediate techniques. It also helps that you have an amazing palate. Now it's time to get specific." Alexander tilts his head toward the walk-in. "There's a bin of vegetables that I set aside for you. They were about to expire, anyways, so you might as well use them to practice. Go grab them and come back."

Eden nods, her knowing grin sending sparks shooting up his spine. When she returns with the bin, she opens up her knife rolls. Alexander brings out his knives, too, preparing to demonstrate. A good teacher should be hands on, after all. Eden picks up her santoku, while Alexander opts for his chef's knife.

"I've been meaning to introduce you to Springsteen," she says, brimming with pride.

"You named it?"

"I named it," Eden confirms.

*God, her smile can light up a room.*

"Don't tell me you named—"

"Every single one. Yep! Would you like me to introduce you?"

Alexander laughs and shakes his head. "I have a feeling you're going to anyway."

"This is Clyde, Toby the Second, Henry, Daniel, Jack, and Zimmerman," she says, pointing to each one of her knives.

"And the bread knife?"

"Charlie. Rather fitting, right?"

He rolls his eyes. "God, it's a good thing you're cute."

Eden gently bumps him in the hip with her own. "Show me what the hell a fine bruno-thingy is."

Alexander demonstrates with a large potato, slicing with deathly precision and accuracy. "A batonnet is a rectangular prism that measures a quarter inch wide, quarter inch tall, and two to two and a half inches long. If you're making French fries, it has to measure a quarter inch wide, quarter inch tall, and three inches long."

"Does it have to?"

"That's how they test you in school. To make sure you're following instructions. You have to learn to measure by eye."

"Please don't tell me you're going to test me—"

"I'm definitely going to test you."

"What if I fail?"

"You won't."

"Your faith in me is flattering."

"Less talk, more learning."

"Yes, chef."

Alexander moves on to demonstrate a fine brunoise. He slices the vegetable into even smaller portions, edges sharp and straight, turning the batonnet into a small pile of perfect cubes. "A fine brunoise measures one-sixteenth, by one-sixteenth, by one-sixteenth."

"There's no way you can do that without messing up. That's puny."

He nods. "At Gagnon-Allard, your teacher brings around a little ruler to double check."

"People who are eating it won't care, though."

"True. But that's haute cuisine. It's still an art form. As pompous and ridiculous as it sounds, there are rules and expectations. It's what differentiates us cooking here and some soccer mom cooking in her kitchen."

"I guess."

Alexander gives Eden an encouraging pat on the back. "Give it a try. Let me go find my ruler."

She laughs. "Don't say that. You'll make me nervous."

"Don't be. You've got this."

She gets to work, practicing over and over again. Alexander knows she isn't half bad to begin with. Eden just needs some fine-tuning, a little nudge in the right direction. She's a natural, picking up on things much faster than he anticipated. He shows her how to properly do a paysanne fermière and a rondelle on a bias, and shows her the difference between a fine julienne and a regular julienne. Eden soaks up information like a sponge, her willingness to learn and improve evident in the way she handles her knives.

When she's all finished, she looks up at Alexander with wide eyes. "Well? How'd I do?"

He enjoys the long curl of her lashes, counts the faint freckles across her cheeks, admires the way her hair falls delicately before her brow. He doesn't understand how someone can be so beautiful, so sweet, so—

"Perfect," he answers.

Eden stretches her arms above her head and yawns, content. "Thanks. You're a pretty good teacher."

"And you're a pretty good student."

"Any other pieces of wisdom you want to impart tonight?"

"No, that's enough for tonight. Grab your coat and I'll drive you home."

He doesn't tell her that he lives almost an hour's drive in the opposite direction because he doesn't like the thought of Eden riding the bus so late. He's sure she's perfectly safe and smart enough to know how to defend herself if ever the need arose, but Alexander finds comfort in escorting her home. In fact, he looks forward to it. The ride may be silent, but it's comfortable.

When he's with her, he's at peace.

Alexander pulls up to the curb outside of Eden's apartment building and does a quick scan out the window. He doesn't like that she lives in a particularly unsavory part of town. There doesn't appear to be anybody around, though, so he doesn't have to worry about Eden running into any trouble.

"Hey," she says gently, sheepishly picking at her coat sleeves.

"Hm?"

"Thank you for today. I learned a lot."

"You're welcome."

"I have a question."

"Shoot."

"Now that we're not at work, can I please—"

Alexander reaches across the center console to take Eden's chin between his thumb and forefinger. He kisses her without hesitation, relieved to find her hungry lips on his.

Eden hastily unfastens her seat belt so that she can lean in further, clutching at his shirt like the ground beneath them is about to crumble from under her feet. The kiss deepens, devolving into something desperate and needy. Alexander circles her waist and pulls her over, allowing her to climb onto his lap, straddling him between her thighs. There's just enough room for her to fit between his chest and the steering wheel, but it's not like they want much space from each other to begin with.

Their tongues clash in a dizzying give and take. Her fingers wind up combing through his hair while he locks his hands together behind her back. When Eden grinds her hips against him, he knows for a fact that it's deliberate. She grins when she realizes just how hard he is.

"You're a tease," he grumbles, though there isn't any heat behind his statement.

"Sorry?"

"Don't be."

"Do you... Do you want to come inside for a bit?" she asks.

"I want to, but..."

"It's okay. I understand."

"I just want to do this right. I don't want to rush."

Eden smiles. "Tuesday can't get here fast enough."

He chuckles, brushing a strand of her hair behind her ear. "My thoughts exactly."

Eden kisses him one last time. "I'll see you tomorrow?"

"See you tomorrow, sweetheart."

She slips off his lap and exits through the passenger-side door, waving goodbye to him when she gets to the front door of the apartment complex. Alexander sits there until he's sure she's safely inside. That, and he needs to calm down a bit because driving with a hard-on is as uncomfortable as it gets.

# CHAPTER
## Seventeen

I ntuition. Clairvoyance. Sixth sense.

Eden can call it whatever she damn well likes, but the result is still the same.

Even before she walks into work, she can tell something is wrong. She feels tension deep within her core, the kind that makes her want to throw up whilst gasping for a full breath of air. At first, she worries she's coming down with something — maybe one of those 24-hour bugs that seems to be going around — but then she steps into La Rouge, spots Alexander, and suddenly understands.

She's never seen him quite this stressed before. He isn't angry or on the brink of erupting.

It's far worse than that. It's a quiet panic, one that has his face alarmingly pale, his nostrils flared, his dark eyes staring off into space.

Some of the other chefs are already here, looking to Eden in concern. "What's going on?" she asks Freddie, stepping forward.

"Palton's coming," he explains gravely. "Sebastian invited him, can you believe that bastard?"

Eden frowns. "Who?"

"You seriously don't know who he is?" Rina asks, a little

incredulous. "Simon Palton is one of the bitchiest, nastiest, most *up-his-own-ass* food critics out there."

Peter shakes his head in dismay. "He never gives a good review. The last restaurant he visited tanked shortly after he published his piece on them. The executive chef there had no choice but to retire because nobody else was willing to hire him afterwards."

"But it's only one review," Eden mumbles. "Surely it can't be that bad."

"Oh, it is. Palton's got a stupid amount of pull in the culinary industry. I'm talking connections to food producers, every kind of news outlet... He's been around for a millennium, so he's got his hand in fucking everything. He'll sink your career if he so much as believes you looked at him the wrong way."

Eden scoffs. "That's ridiculous."

She looks to Alexander, who's been silent this whole time. She can tell he's formulating a plan. He's calculating, considering his options. Even she knows there's no way out of this now. It's not like they can turn the food critic away—because that'd be a one-way ticket to guaranteed closure, especially considering that it was Sebastian who invited him—but Alexander doesn't look quite ready to split his focus between running his kitchen and making sure Palton has everything he needs.

This is a test.

"Alexander?" Eden says softly. "Tell us what you need."

He chews on the inside of his cheek, deep in concentration. "I need..."

"Anything," Peter adds encouragingly. "Just let us know."

"Yeah," Rina says with a nod. "I'm sure we can figure something out."

"We've got your back," Freddie assures. "Just give us the order."

Alexander takes a deep breath, wearing a genuinely appreciative smile. "Eden?"

"Yes, chef?"

"You'll run the line tonight. I'll be here in case anything goes wrong, but I'll be catering to Palton personally. The rest of you, business as usual. Give Eden your undivided attention. We clear?"

A chorus of, "Yes, chef!" echoes throughout the kitchen.

"Good. Now, get to work."

Everybody else scurries off, chatting amongst themselves as they prepare for tonight's service. It's going to be a busy one. There are three separate reservations of at least twenty people per party. It's also a Saturday evening, which means La Rouge will be packed full of weekend-goers looking for a reprieve from their regular nine-to-fives. If Sebastian really did invite Palton, then he chose the absolute worst time to do it.

Eden places a hand on Alexander's shoulder. "You've got this," she tells him.

He smiles. *Really* smiles. "Thank you, Eden."

Eden's run a kitchen before, just never on this scale and for so long. She's popped in here and there, taking charge whenever necessary, but she's used to Alexander coming back at some point to take back the reins. Those were little sprints, perfectly manageable in short bursts.

This is a marathon.

Her mind swirls with different table numbers, cook times, special orders that require different ingredients because apparently all of table six suffers from a gluten allergy—what are the odds? But she digs deep and keeps the kitchen running. It's not as smooth and meticulous as Alexander normally does it, but she's holding her own and that's really all that matters.

She's proud of herself, and rightly so. She's come a long way from her toy kitchen where she used to serve her father invisible food. Now she's running one of the toughest, most prestigious kitchens in the world.

*Mom and Dad would be proud.*

It's hard for Eden to resist checking in with Alexander as he personally prepares food for Palton. She hasn't had the misfortune of meeting the man, but she can tell just by looking at his order that he's a special kind of asshole. He's pretty much ordered every single dish off the menu, demanding all manner of substitutions and additions to each meal. If she didn't know any better, she'd swear Palton was making things overly complicated for the sole purpose of messing Alexander up.

He doesn't, though, because he's a genius. Alexander sends plate after gorgeous plate out to be served, piping hot and delicious.

From where she is at the front of the line, Eden can just barely see through the circular window of the kitchen doors leading out into the dining room. The back section is mostly empty—at Palton's request—so it's easy for her to spot the food critic in question.

The man looks, as impossible as it may seem, even scarier than Sebastian. One quick glance at the man is enough to send a chill down Eden's spine. He certainly appears the part of a food critic, dressed to the nines and sporting a cravat of all things. Eden wonders if she'll turn to stone if she accidentally makes direct eye contact with the man. She doesn't have too much time to worry about it, though, because another chit prints, and she has to return her focus to more important matters.

*Alexander's counting on me.*

"Can someone grab me the extra cilantro from the walk-in?"

he calls out, too focused on his salad arrangement to do it himself.

"I'll get it," Hector calls back.

Eden frowns.

She wouldn't bat an eye if any of the other chefs volunteered, but Hector? She's not naïve enough to believe he's doing it because he's a good sport.

Something's up.

"Hey, Peter?" she calls.

"What's up, chef?"

"Can you man the line for two seconds? I need to check on something."

"Sure thing."

Eden stalks to the walk-in and shuts the door behind her, effectively trapping Hector inside. She's caught him standing in between two of the produce shelves, one hand holding onto the cilantro in question, while the other is about to dump an entire handful of salt on top of the garnish.

It's an act of sabotage.

"What do you think you're doing?" she hisses. "The hell is the matter with you?"

"Get the fuck out of here," he snipes.

"You're not getting away with this."

Hector takes a step forward. He's not that much bigger than Eden, but having someone suddenly in your face is still very alarming. Hector looks vitriolic, the vein at his temple pulsing with rage.

"What the fuck are you going to do about it, hm?" he growls. "You going to report me?"

"As a matter of fact, I will."

Hector scoffs. "Figures you'd go running to him. There's nothing Chen wouldn't do for his little whore."

Before she even has the chance to process what's been said,

her hand shoots up. A gut reaction. She swings, dead set on slapping Hector from here to the other coast. He snatches her wrist and digs his nails into her skin, not hard enough to break but certainly hard enough to bruise. He clicks his tongue and shakes his head.

"What? Did you just try to hit me? That's assault, Eden. I could report you to Sebastian and have you fired."

"Wha—"

"Or maybe I'll tell him that you're a filthy fucking liar."

Eden freezes. "What are you talking about?"

"Did you seriously think I wouldn't figure it out? I've been doing some digging around. Nobody seems to know who you are. I waited for years for the chance to work at La Rouge. I studied under countless chefs to earn my place here. But you? Who have you trained with, hm?"

"I, uh—"

"Nobody, that's who. Because you're an untrained fucking *fry cook* who scammed her way into *my* job. You're an imposter who doesn't deserve to be here."

"Let go of me. Let go of me right now!"

Hector's grip tightens that much more. Eden tries to jerk away, but his hold is absolute. "The fancy job, the new knives, the private rides home... You've got Chen wrapped around your pretty little finger, don't you? Let's be honest. The only reason you're the sous chef is because you let him do whatever he wants to you."

"I don't—"

"Does he take you back to his place after work? Do you get on all fours and spread your legs for him like the slut you are?"

"Take that back."

"Or what? Say one goddamn thing and I'll expose you to Sebastian. And then not even Chen can do anything to protect his favorite little plaything."

Eden can't breathe. All she wants to do is strike Hector across the face. She wants to knee him in the groin, and hard.

But she can't. Violence, as much as she wants to claw Hector's eyes out, isn't the answer.

In fact, it could make things so much worse. Not just for her, but for Alexander. The last thing she wants is to cause more trouble for him. He's already dealing with so much. She can't afford to lose her temper and become a burden to him.

She takes a deep breath and stares Hector straight in the eye. This simply won't stand.

"You are a sad, pathetic little man," she says, the epitome of calm. "You can say whatever you want about me, but none of it's true. You just can't stand the fact that your career is stagnant and you don't have enough talent to climb your way up on your own. If calling me names and threatening me makes you feel like more of a man, fine. Knock yourself out."

Eden yanks her hand away and jabs her forefinger against his chest hard enough that it makes him wince. "You have a problem with me? You tell me. I'll cook circles around you, you snake. You think you can get away with it because I look like an easy target? I've got news for you, asshole, I've got a lot more fight in me than you think. But don't for a second think you can get away with dragging Alexander's name through the mud. He's twice the man you will ever hope to be. You're nothing but a little boy throwing a tantrum. So go ahead, do your fucking worst. Just don't be surprised when karma comes around to bite you in the ass."

"You little bi—"

The door to the walk-in swings open rapidly, sucking out all of the cool fridge air in one gust.

"Hector," Alexander barks, irritated. "Where is the— Monroe? What's going on here?"

Eden swallows, willing her racing heart to calm down. "Nothing."

Alexander doesn't believe it for a second. "Eden."

"Don't use the cilantro," she warns him before walking past him.

She's a damn fine chef and she knows it, fancy culinary school or no. When they get through service without a hitch, Eden knows it's because she's just that good.

# CHAPTER
## Eighteen

If Eden's distressed, she does a very good job of putting on a brave face.

Alexander isn't sure what happened, but he is sure that he wants to beat Hector's sniveling face into a pulp for whatever he did to her.

Unfortunately, he doesn't get the chance because the redhead storms out of the kitchen before Alexander can figure out what's going on. To make matters that much more complicated, he still has Palton to attend to. He can't afford to let Hector split his focus, no matter how much he's worried about Eden.

Alexander plates dessert, the final dish of the evening. He honestly can't remember the last time he's worked with this level of sweat-inducing attention to detail. He prepares the floating island, freshly whipped meringue floating in a crème anglaise topped with a dome casing of caramel he made from scratch. It might seem like a simple dish, but any number of things can go wrong.

If you don't whip the egg whites enough, they won't peak. If you add too much sugar, the whole thing becomes unbearably sweet. Producing the caramel is—in Alexander's opinion—a test of his patience because you need to get the temperature just right, add the right amount of butter, and kill the heat before you've got a burnt mess on your hands and ruin a perfectly good pot.

He wipes the sweat from his brow before picking the plate up. It's a good idea for the head chef to meet with a critic face-to-face, at least once, as a show of hospitality. Alexander hates this sort of thing, but what else can he do?

He picks up his plate and starts toward the kitchen doors, but Peter stops him before he manages two steps.

"Whoa, whoa, whoa, chef. Hold up a minute."

"What?"

Peter unties Alexander's dirty apron and replaces it with a fresh one. "Don't want him to think you're a slob, do we?"

Rina pops over with a mildly damp cloth and wipes at a small patch of his chef jacket where there's a bit of sugar powder. "Can't give Palton any more ammunition than he needs, right?"

Freddie comes up from behind and massages Alexander's shoulders. "You've got this, mate. Totally, totally got this."

A few weeks ago, Alexander would have told them all to piss right the hell off. He hates it when people are up in his personal space. It's uncomfortable and awkward and he feels like he can't breathe when crowded. And the fact that they're touching him so casually? Fuck no.

Definite no. Alexander hates being touched.

But he isn't as angry as he thought he'd be. Much to his surprise, he actually finds a small sense of comfort. Because these people are his... friends.

Yes, his friends.

They're not Sebastian.

They don't want anything from him. They just want to help. And Eden?

She's the cherry on top.

Eden approaches and very casually brushes her fingers through his hair to flatten it out a bit.

Everyone else is so preoccupied with primping him that they don't notice. It's almost intimate, her fingers gingerly grazing past his temple. Only he knows how her fingers feel scraping across his scalp. Only he knows what the look in her eye means. Eden doesn't even have to speak. He can tell what she's thinking off her smile alone.

*Make us proud, chef.*

He nods once, a silent conversation passing between them.

*I won't let you down.*

Alexander takes one more deep breath before stepping through the kitchen doors, dessert in hand.

Palton looks perfectly harmless at a distance. In passing, Alexander could easily mistake him with any number of generic-looking old men. His hair is white, his brow crinkled, and his fashion sense appears to have frozen in the '20's.

The 1920's, that is.

*Who the fuck wears a cravat in this day and age?*

Up close, though, it's a different story. Alexander thinks the AC in the back section of the restaurant must be busted or something because he swears the air drops several degrees the closer he gets to the table. Palton quickly goes from a harmless old geezer eating alone to something far more sinister. In reality, he's every chef's nightmare.

A food critic.

A *pompous* food critic.

*Ugh, the worst.*

Palton looks up and smiles. It's not a friendly smile. If anything, it's predatory—intended to lull his prey in until it's too little, too late.

"Ah, you must be Sebastian's boy," Palton says. The scratchy quality of his voice makes Alexander's skin crawl. "I've heard so much about you. And from my fellow colleagues, of course. There's not a critic out there with a complaint about your food."

"Thank y—"

"I, however, hold myself in much higher regard."

"What—"

"The fois gras was too salty," he says, launching straight into it. "The wine your waiter suggested was abysmal. A red wine with fish? I recommend your waitstaff undergo sommelier training."

Alexander simply nods, because what else is he supposed to do? He doesn't understand why Palton's just now bringing up these issues. Alexander could have had everything remedied at the drop of the hat.

No, he knows why Palton's doing this. The dickhead is trying to throw him off, rile him up. It's a power trip that Palton very clearly enjoys. It makes Alexander wonder what kind of sad, miserable life the man leads behind closed doors. If terrifying chefs is the only way he can get his rocks off, the poor bastard must be a pitiful thing.

Palton continues his little spiel. "Your escargot was much too oily. Your lobster was under-seasoned. Will dessert be just as disappointing, I wonder?"

Alexander places the plate down on the table. He's tempted to throw it right at the old man's face, but that's a one-way ticket to a ruinous review. He knows Eden and the others are only a few feet away, waiting with bated breath. He can't possibly let his temper get to him now.

That doesn't stop him from imagining it, though.

Palton picks up a clean spoon and makes a show of polishing it with his cloth napkin. Alexander knows for a fact that the silverware is spotless, polished twice specifically for the critic's arrival. Everything this man is doing is bullshit. Everything he's said is bullshit. There is nothing wrong with the food. They're works of art. Alexander wouldn't have sent them out otherwise.

Palton finally takes a bite of dessert. There's no considerable reaction. No twitch of the brow or purse of the lips. If Alexander thought Sebastian was hard to read, Palton is twice as hard to discern—plus three times as much of a douchebag.

"How is it?" Alexander asks.

"Passable."

Fuck it. At this point, Alexander's willing to take whatever barely-there-compliment he can get, just so the man will finally shut up and get the hell out of his restaurant.

Palton finishes off dessert—which Alexander takes as a good sign—before dabbing his lips delicately with the corner of his napkin. He extends a hand, gesturing to the seat opposite him. "Please."

"I'd rather stand. But thank you."

Palton gives Alexander a once over and smirks. "Sebastian was right about you."

"Right about what?"

He rises, adjusting his cravat. "That you're losing your touch. Maybe you should stick to cooking your *own* people's food."

Alexander clenches his fists, fighting the urge to implode. If sending Palton here was some kind of ploy by Sebastian to send him into a tailspin, it's on the verge of working. Sebastian didn't have to send a food critic to tell him his performance as of late was less than impressive. Alexander's reflective enough to recognize his own dissatisfaction. No, this is just Sebastian's way of adding salt to an already festering wound—one that Alexander's been trying to ignore for ages.

He doesn't love food anymore.

His passion is gone.

All of the pomp and circumstance, the hoity-toity clientele, the high expectations, the boss constantly breathing down his neck, the predictability of it all, the boring day in and day out, the constant complaints and need to micromanage and dealing with shitty employees and not getting enough sleep and—

He wants to quit.

But if he does, what else is he supposed to do? He's lost if he's not cooking. Food has been such an integral part of his life that giving it up would leave him lost.

Palton nods respectfully. "You have yourself a good evening, chef. I hope you look forward to my review."

He leaves without another word, abandoning Alexander to stew in his own silence. He wanders back to the kitchen in a trance-like state, on autopilot.

"How did it go?" Eden asks when he finally pushes through the double doors.

His chest constricts, the trapped air in his throat burning a hole through him. Everyone's staring at him, expectant. His shoulders are heavy and his head aches. Worst of all, Eden looks so damn hopeful that he can't bear to tell her the truth.

He just can't.

*She needs this job. She needs the money so she can find her parents. Go on. Tell her you fucked up and Palton's out for blood.*

"It was great," he lies between gritted teeth.

Eden makes a face. "What did he say?"

"Don't worry about it."

"Alexander." His name rolls off her tongue as a whisper. "Please?"

Alexander sighs. "He said... He said I should stick to cooking my own people's food."

"He fucking *WHAT*?" She rolls up her jacket sleeves, fists balling up tight. There's murder in her eyes. "I'll kill him. I'm going to kill him!"

"What's going on?" Rina asks from her station.

"That asshole said—"

"Nothing!" Alexander interrupts, hurriedly dragging Eden towards the kitchen office. He nearly has to pick her up and throw her over his shoulder to keep Eden from wreaking havoc. He slams the door shut before she can scream bloody murder.

"I need you to calm down."

"Calm down?" she exclaims, incredulous. "I'm not going to calm down. That asshole said—"

"I know what he said."

"I'm going to shove a whole chicken down his gullet!"

Alexander wraps his arms around her and pulls her into an embrace. He isn't sure if it's because it's the only thing he can think to do to restrain her or if it's because he's in need of comfort. Maybe it's a little of column A, a little of column B. Regardless, he feels her melt into his hold, her arms circling around his waist to hug him back.

"It's been a long day," he murmurs, soothed by her proximity. "Can we just drop it and go home?"

Eden's quiet for a long time, but her hug doesn't loosen. She has her cheek pressed to his chest, her eyes closed. She eventually takes a deep breath and sighs. "Is that what you want?"

He nods. "Please?"

"Okay," she says softly. "I'll save my chicken-cramming for another day."

This earns her a light chuckle. "Thank you. And thank you for taking care of the kitchen. It would have been impossible without your help."

"Of course," Eden replies. "We're a team, aren't we?"

His smile is tight, the weight of his guilt churning in his stomach. "Yeah."

Alexander sinks into the driver's seat, suddenly realizing how bone-tired he is. His feet hurt from standing all day. The skin between his fingers is itchy and dry from constant washing. His head feels so heavy, he's worried his neck is about to snap. All he wants now is to go home and curl up in bed.

And maybe have Eden curl up with him.

He relaxes almost immediately when Eden slides into the passenger seat. She hasn't even slipped on her seatbelt before he's cupped her face and moves in for a bruising kiss. He finds solace in the way she groans against him. He discovers heaven in the way she kisses him back, just as passionately.

Eden giggles when she finally pulls away. She brushes some of his hair out of his eyes and asks, "Ready to go?"

"Fuck, yes."

She snorts. "Seconded."

"Thank you again for your hard work. You're incredible."

"Can you say that again? I want to get a recording."

"Yet another piece of evidence for your blackmail pile?"

"You know it."

"You still have those stupid pictures of me. I've given you more than enough ammunition."

"Fine, I'll just have to secretly record you the next time you're doling out compliments."

Alexander rolls his eyes. "Let's get you home."

He already has the drive back to her place memorized. The traffic is nice and light, nothing but the golden glow of street lamps and the rush of wind over the hood of the car to keep them company. He's comfortable, he realizes, just being this close to her. It surprises him how simple it all is, being with Eden. Alexander could drive for hours and be perfectly content so long as he can turn to find her there.

"So," he says slowly, sorting through the tumultuous thoughts clogging his brain.

"So," she echoes.

"What happened? With Hector."

She shakes her head, not in the mood to speak.

"Eden. Don't think I've forgotten."

There's a long, heavy pause between them. She picks at her fingernails, gathering up the courage to speak.

"Promise me you won't do anything stupid," Eden replies quietly.

"Eden—"

"Promise me."

"Fine. I promise not to do anything stupid. Now tell me what Hector did to you."

"He called me a whore."

Alexander slams on the brakes, tires screeching to a halt. "He fucking *what*?"

The car behind them in traffic has to swerve to avoid crashing. The driver lays on the horn and flips Alexander off as he makes a hasty lane change to avoid collision.

"I took care of it," she insists hastily.

"You should have told me immediately."

"You had more important things to worry about."

"What's more important than y—" He cuts himself off. "I'm going to kill him. I'm going to break his face in and then I'm going to kill him."

She places her hand on his arm. "Don't."

"He can't talk to you like that. It's insubordination. It's sexist. It's—"

Another car passes them in a hurry, honking wildly.

"I know."

"What exactly did he say to you?"

Eden casts her eyes down to the car floor. "I don't remember.

Can we please just— Can we just go, please? We're going to get in trouble if we just sit in the lane like this."

"What. Did. He. Say?"

She swallows. "He... He said that I have you wrapped around my finger. That I'm your sous chef because..."

"What?" And then, so much softer, "What, Eden?"

"Because I'm your favorite plaything. That I spread my legs for you like a slut."

Something inside him snaps. Alexander's been holding back his rage for so long that he'd started to go numb. His heart is pounding a mile a minute. This is officially too much for him to handle. Between Sebastian and then Palton and now Hector... He's sure he might die at an early age due to stress.

The corners of Eden's eyes turn red with the threat of tears. "But it's not true. I worked... I worked really hard to get here. To *be* here."

"I know, I know."

Another car whizzes by, this time the driver rolling down the window to scream profanities at their stalled car. Alexander knows they have to move. This isn't safe.

It's also not safe to drive when he's on the brink of a mental breakdown because how dare Hector treat Eden that way?

His mind's already made up.

Hector has to go.

Alexander finds the strength, and—by some miracle—the control he needs to get Eden the rest of the way home without accidentally running any lights because all he sees is red. He parks by the curb, as always, and kisses Eden tenderly before she gets out. She gets out of the car and dips down, looking him in the eye.

"Don't do anything dumb," she reminds. "If I can't kill Palton, then you can't kill Hector."

"Who's going to stop me?"

"We can deal with it tomorrow."

"*I'll* deal with it tomorrow. You have Sunday and Monday off, remember?"

"Still, I—"

"I promise, Eden. Don't worry. I'll take care of it."

"But—"

"You just go home. You relax. You forget everything he said because none of it's true, you hear me?"

She nods slowly. "Okay."

"You're the most talented chef I know, so Hector's opinion means jack shit."

"Okay."

"Feel free to call or text me if you need anything, alright? Anything at all. I promise I'll answer."

"Alright." She manages a small smile. "Goodnight."

"Goodnight, sweetheart."

Alexander doesn't drive away until after Eden's safely inside. He sits there for a minute, maybe two, collecting himself.

He's never felt like this before. Insulted. Furious. Blood-thirsty.

What he wants is to drive over to Hector's place and give him a piece of his mind. No. That's still not enough. Alexander wants to tear him apart and then have Hector groveling for forgiveness at Eden's feet. Nobody gets away with treating his girl like—

His girl.

Eden.

Alexander lets out a shaky breath.

She's right. Violence isn't the answer. It isn't good enough. What he's planning is far, far worse.

Alexander pulls out his phone and makes several calls.

# CHAPTER
## Nineteen

S he gets the text just before noon on Sunday.

Alexander: Thinking of you.

Eden rolls over in bed and smiles at her phone, reading his words over and over and over again with the giddiness of a schoolgirl. Her thumbs fly over the screen, drafting up a response.

Eden: New phone, who dis?

Not two seconds later:

Alexander: It's me. Alexander?

She laughs aloud.

Eden: I'm just teasing you, dummy.

Alexander: You really know how to give a man a heart attack, huh? Thought I sent that to Sebastian or something.

Eden: lol nooooo don't die

Alexander: Too late.

Eden: I'll send help!

He sends a gif of a black lab puppy falling off a couch in a dramatic fashion, *#dead* flashing in bright white font at the base of the image.

Eden smiles so hard, her cheeks hurt. She can't even say that she minds.

Eden: So cute!

Alexander: Me, or the dog?

Eden: You know the answer.

Alexander: It's the dog. Don't worry, I won't take it personally.

She finally sits up in bed, nibbling at her bottom lip. She can't believe how much she actually misses him. It's been less than twelve hours since they parted ways, but deep down, she yearns to see him again. Like it's been weeks or years instead of half a day.

Eden smiles to herself.

Alexander: Have to go. Service soon.

She doesn't want their conversation to end, but she understands, nonetheless.

Eden: Have a good shift!

He sends another gif, this time of a little pug who's somehow got his bottom half stuck in a toilet bowl. Eden doesn't necessarily understand the message he's trying to convey, but it doesn't matter. It makes her feel all warm and fuzzy inside.

She eventually finds the strength to pull herself out of bed. She really does have to start her day. She may or may not spend the whole time thinking about a certain someone with inky black hair.

Eden visits the clinic on Monday. She's never particularly liked visiting the doctors—what with her fear of needles and whatnot—but Doctor Amy Henski is the epitome of caring. Eden's always thought the woman was pretty cool. She's got fun aunt vibes, the type that'll help you sneak out after curfew or let you sneak in a couple sips of her wine.

"There," Henski says. "You're all set. I should have the results to you by this evening."

"So soon?"

"I run the lab work downstairs, so we don't have to worry about long queues." Henski tosses Eden a cheeky wink. "Besides, I get the feeling you might want to know sooner rather than later?"

Eden's suddenly aware of how warm her face is. "I, uh... Well, yeah. Thanks."

Henski chuckles. "Who's the lucky someone?"

"Just a guy," Eden answers, unable to stop herself from smiling because Alexander isn't just a guy to her. "I work with him."

"Are things pretty serious?"

"Getting there, I think. I mean, I really hope so."

Henski smiles warmly. "Well, even if your results do come back negative, I would still like to encourage you to be safe. Have you thought much about contraceptives?"

"I used to be on birth control, but that was a few years ago. I'd been seeing this other guy, but I stopped once we broke up."

"Are you interested in going on the pill again?"

"Maybe. The stuff I was on made me feel awful. I'm a bit wary."

"Perfectly understandable. The pill isn't exactly one size fits all." Henski quickly walks over to her desk and opens up a drawer, plucking an informational pamphlet from within. She hands it to Eden. "Look this over and let me know if anything interests you. Condoms are the most convenient and inexpensive option, but they aren't guaranteed to work one hundred percent of the time. None of them are, really, but it should suffice for now."

Eden smiles. "Thanks, doc."

"I'll give you a call later when the results are in."

With that, Eden hops off the exam table and leaves.

She walks home, taking the opportunity to soak up some sunshine. It's a gorgeous day out, and tomorrow's forecast is promising to be even more beautiful. She passes by several small boutiques, paying the majority of them no mind. Eden's never been the kind of person to mindlessly window shop. She has much more important things to deal with than staring longingly at things she won't allow herself to afford.

That is, until she spots a dress in the window of a clothing store.

It's pretty. Prettier than anything Eden owns, at least. That really isn't saying much because her closet is abysmal to begin with, hardly anything worth gushing over. She's never been a clothes type of girl. The nicest thing she owns is her black chef jacket, and that had been a very generous 'business expense.'

She continues to stare, the delicate lace bodice flowing into the rest of the sundress. The capped sleeves would look cute on her. She could throw on the jean jacket she's stuffed somewhere at the back of her closet and pair it with some sensible flats. She wonders what Alexander would think if she showed up for their date in this little number.

*It'd make him wild.*

But then she looks a bit closer at the price tag pinned to the side and deflates. "A hundred-sixty bucks?" she mumbles to herself, incredulous. "What the hell is it made of?"

It's a lot for one article of clothing, and Eden simply can't justify the purchase. If she comes at it with a cost-per-use mentality, it's just not worth it. Sure, payday was Friday and she has more than enough in her account, but those hundred sixty dollars should really be going towards hiring Maxine Kendo. She's sure Alexander won't care in the slightest what she chooses to wear.

Except, *she* cares.

Eden wants to look good. Not just for him, but for herself. She wants to dress up and treat herself and feel confident. She wants to feel like a million bucks tomorrow.

But the pang of guilt in her chest keeps her from stepping inside the store. She needs this money. For her parents. She's so close to her goal that she can taste it. If she starts spending money on frivolous things, it'll feel like she's cheating. Like she's deciding that her parents aren't as important. That her own fleeting desires take precedence over finding her family.

How is she supposed to enjoy something that will only serve as a bitter reminder?

She could be a hundred sixty dollars closer to hiring a PI. Or she can buy a pretty dress for the sake of one day, one momentary lapse in resolve.

She eventually finds the strength to walk away.

*Maybe next time.*

When Eden gets home, her phone rings. It's the number from Doctor Henski's office.

"Hello?"

"Hey, Eden," the doctor greets. "Is this a good time?"

"Of course."

"Good. I just wanted to give you a call and let you know I got your test results back."

"Wow, that really was fast."

"I know, right? I get the feeling that the technicians at the lab like me."

"How does everything look?"

"All results came back negative," the doctor informs. "You're good to go."

Eden breathes a sigh of relief. She sort of knew she would be, but the confirmation is an extra weight off her shoulders. "Thanks, doc."

"Have yourself a good day."

"Yeah, you too."

When Eden hangs up, she feels instantly lighter.

S he wakes up the next morning practically buzzing with excitement.

*It's Tuesday!*

Eden can't remember the last time she was this excited to go out on a date. An *official* date. Inviting Alexander to trivia night didn't count because the rest of the gang was there, their trip to the knife shop was out of necessity, and she wasn't entirely sure how to categorize all the times Alexander has literally cooked her lunch before work. Surely he'd done that out of a professional concern.

So, yes. In her books, today is an official date, and she can hardly wait to get started.

She has to keep herself from skipping on her way out the building. It becomes a next to impossible task when she sees Alexander's car already pulled up to the curb, the man patiently leaning against the side of his vehicle.

He looks delicious. Alexander's clothes are darkly colored from his jeans to the conforming sweater he has on. There's an ease to him, one that she rarely gets to see when they're both in the kitchen. He breaks out into a charming, slightly crooked smile the second he lays eyes on her.

It makes her melt a little.

"Hey," she greets, for some reason feeling a million times shyer. She chalks it up to nerves.

"Hey yourself," he replies, dipping down to kiss her. He says it so sweet that Eden can't help but blush. "You look beautiful."

Eden catches a glimpse of herself in the passenger-side window. She would have looked utterly darling in the dress she saw the other day, but settled for a pair of comfortable white skinny jeans, her favorite white blouse with the frilliest of hems, and her cleanest pair of Nike sneakers.

She's comfortable. She feels *good*. In the end, she supposes that's all that really matters.

And if Alexander thinks she's beautiful, that just makes everything so much better.

She places her hands on his jacket and tugs at the fabric lightly. "Grey, huh? Truly a daring step into the world of fashion. Someone better call Anna Wintour."

"I have no idea who that is."

"Anna Wintour?" she repeats. "The editor-in-chief of Vogue?

The lady who everyone's pretty sure is the inspiration for Miranda Priestly in *The Devil Wears Prada*?"

"Oh, the Meryl Streep movie?"

"You know Meryl Streep, but you don't know Anna Wintour?"

He shrugs, nonchalant. "Meryl Streep is a great actress. I liked her in *Julie & Julia*."

Eden rolls her eyes. "Of course you'd watch a movie about cooking. Let me guess, you're a fan of *Ratatouille*?"

"You mean the health violation movie? I might be impartial to it."

Eden giggles. "You excited for today?"

"To stare at sushi? Of course."

She rolls her eyes, but has a hard time keeping a straight face. "Don't be such a party pooper. Come on. It's going to be so much fun!"

He chuckles, already reaching to pull open the passenger-side door. "Alright, alright. Hop on in."

The aquarium is as busy as one would expect for a Tuesday, which is not at all. Eden doesn't mind, though. This means there are no lines or busy crowds to worry about.

And when she reaches over to take Alexander's hand, he isn't as inclined to shy away. He holds onto her firmly, almost proudly, willingly allowing himself to be dragged from display to display by his girl.

She can't remember the last time she felt this carefree. This light and easy. And being with him... Being with him leaves her absurdly warm and fuzzy all over.

They visit the jellyfish, the dolphins, the little tide pool area where kids can gently pet things like starfish and minnows. It's at the otter exhibit that Eden takes pause.

The habitat is lush with plants and crystal-clear water. At the center, floating about peacefully on its back, is a singular otter with light brown fur. Its paws and tail are tucked in upon its fluffy stomach.

"This is Kiera," one of the nearby caretakers introduces.

"She's adorable," Eden replies.

"Where are the others?" Alexander asks.

The caretaker smiles sadly. "We normally have five other otters in here with her. Her partner used to be here, but he unfortunately passed a few months ago. She's become quite aggressive toward the other otters, so we've had to keep them separate for a while."

Eden frowns, watching the animal pitifully. The pang of something uncomfortable stings her chest. Kiera looks so lonely.

She, too, knows what it feels like to be alone. She knows what it's like to wait. For years and years and years. Never knowing, but always hoping. Maybe if she's good, maybe if she's patient, she'll finally find the answers she's been looking for. But perhaps the truth scares her, too. Just a little. It's only natural that the doubts would creep in.

What if her parents left her behind? What if they're dead? What if—

Alexander gives her fingers a quick squeeze. "You daydreaming?" he teases.

She smiles up at him, squeezing his fingers back. "Just thinking about lunch. Hungry?"

He nods, once again allowing Eden to drag him off toward the sea-themed food court area located near the front of the aquarium. It's nothing fancy. There's a burger joint, a pizza stall, even a small Panda Express.

"A bastardization of my people's food, but whatever," Alexander grumbles under his breath.

They find a seat at an empty table a few feet away from a massive fish tank. "Can't believe you got a fish burger," Eden says with a chuckle.

Alexander shrugs. "It was the only thing that looked remotely appetizing."

She rolls her eyes. "You and your high standards."

"Nothing wrong with having high standards, sweetheart."

"But what about the fish?"

"What *about* the fish?"

Eden gestures toward the tank. "Eating that in front of them? That's morbid."

He takes a deliberately large bite. With a full mouth, he mumbles, "Oops."

The smallest bit of mayo catches on the corner of his lip. Eden, suddenly emboldened, leans forward to kiss it away. She holds his gaze, relishing the deep, dark burn she sees in him. Eden licks her lips, more than happy to tease.

"Behave," he warns, voice suddenly dropping an octave into a delectable grumble. "You're going to get us kicked out."

Eden smirks and kisses him again, lightly sucking on his bottom lip. "Oops."

"Be good."

"I'm an angel. What could you possibly mean?" Eden leans forward, placing a hand on his knee. Her fingers itch to explore, but settle for grazing up the top of his thigh and stopping just shy of his front.

"You're playing a very dangerous game right now."

"Dangerous? How so?"

He places his food down and leans forward, too, his lips brushing past her ear to whisper, "Does teasing me in public like this turn you on?" His breath is warm against her cheek. It sends a shiver down her spine and fills her chest with a courage she's never experienced before.

"What if it does?" she asks, a challenge.

"Never took you for someone so naughty."

"Looks can be deceiving."

"Ah, such a fucking smart mouth."

"Face it, you love my smart mouth."

"Hmm..."

"What?"

"Just thinking about all the things I want to *do* to that smart mouth."

Her breath hitches in her throat. "You—"

"Tell me what I'm thinking right now. If you guess right, maybe we'll make it happen."

Eden's face fills with heat, her heart pounding in her chest. Her brain is about to melt. There are so many possibilities, so many scenarios. But one look from him, and she's a goner. Her tongue is a twisted knot. The fire pooling in the pit of her stomach has her unraveling at the seams. Alexander might have just broken her.

Alexander can sense her struggle and chuckles, tenderly kissing her cheek. "What are you being so shy for? You started it, sweetheart. Come on, venture a guess."

"What if I guess wrong?"

"I doubt you will." He presses his forehead to hers, the tips of their noses bumping up against one another. "Say it," he whispers against her lips. "Say it."

"I think..." Eden takes a deep but shaky breath. "I think you want to fuck me."

"Among other things."

She looks deep into his eyes and reads him like a book. "I think you want to fuck me hard. And then soft. All night, and then all morning. On my back. On my knees. You want to taste me. You want me to taste you."

"I think you want me to make you beg," he says, still soft and only loud enough for her alone to hear. "You want to be taken against a wall. In my bed. On the fucking floor. You want me to make you tremble. You want to be fucked so good, your voice gives out. You want to feel sore in the morning. Isn't that right, Eden?"

"Yes," she gasps, the word bubbling past her lips without a second thought.

Alexander kisses her once, like a promise. "I've grown tired of staring at fish."

"Me, too."

"Then let's get the fuck out of here."

Eden has never agreed to anything faster in her entire life.

There's simultaneously too much time and not enough of it. The drive back to his place is obscenely long. The need to have his lips on hers is ever-present, an addiction she can't shake.

They're in a rush, but they're also in the mood to slow down and savor. It leaves Eden in a delirious state of mind, wanting too much and getting too little.

He all but carries her up to his apartment after he parks the Audi in the building's basement garage. Eden wants to comment that this place is super fancy. Security gate, a doorman, and even assigned parking stalls? To her, that's peak luxury. She doesn't get much of a chance to speak, however, because the second he has his arms wrapped around her, their mouths are too preoccupied to get a syllable out.

Eden all but whines when Alexander has to set her down to fish his keys out of his pocket to unlock the front door. The second they're through—

It's a beautiful kind of chaos.

He pins her easily against the back of the door, mouthing hungrily at her neck. He sucks hard enough to leave marks. Eden doesn't care. In fact, she wants more. She wants proof against her skin, badges of honor to wear and show off to the world. She clings to him, tugs at his hair, wraps her legs around his hips as he easily supports both of their weight. Her skin is on fire, but she wants to feel so much warmer.

Alexander carries her over to the kitchen, setting her down on the kitchen island's marble surface. It's cold, but she's too enthralled in the task of lifting off his sweater to notice. The offending garment is tossed to the floor, forgotten.

He's a wall. Hard, solid, sturdy. Eden drags her fingers down his toned chest and defined abs, licking her lips as she eyes the large bulge in the front of his jeans.

"You have a very lovely home," she says, voice dripping with desperation.

"Care for a tour?" he asks, though it's very clear his interests lie elsewhere.

Eden shakes her head, panting. "Later?"

"Later," he agrees, moving in to devour her mouth once more.

There's nothing quite like his hands. Eden realizes just how much she adores them when his fingers slip beneath her shirt and he holds her firmly at the waist. It's almost a relief when he finally takes her shirt off, exposing the white lace bralette she has on underneath.

"Fuck," he hisses against her dainty collarbone, moving down to nip at her breasts over the delicate fabric. "Look at you. Did you put this on just for me?"

"Do you think it's pretty?" she asks, unsure why she's suddenly so self-conscious.

He smiles up at her, the corners of his eyes crinkling as he does. It makes her heart explode. "Gorgeous," he confirms. "You're gorgeous, Eden. Do your panties match, too?"

She nods, bashful. "They do."

He huffs, a sort of half-laugh that Eden can't quite decipher. "What?" she asks.

He rises, presses a kiss to her ear lobe. He murmurs, low and hungry, "I really want to ruin you."

Eden bites her lip. She can barely breathe as she rasps, "Then what are you waiting for?"

He hums, content, as he reaches behind her to help lift her bralette up and over her head. Alexander grabs at her small breasts, easily covering her with his massive hands. She shivers, both amused and aroused at how small and protected he makes her feel.

He leaves a line of kisses from her breasts down her stomach, marking her as he works his way down to her jeans. It's a wonder to watch his skilled fingers undo the front of her pants before tugging them off with great haste. All that remains is her matching white lace thong, one that leaves little to the imagination.

Alexander growls. "You're really going to kill me, you know that?"

"Sorry," she replies, breathless.

"Don't be," he mumbles, moving in to lick at her mound through the fabric.

Pleasure spears through her in a massive shock wave, the warmth of his tongue seeping through the lace. The throbbing wetness between her legs grows more and more unbearable with every second. But Alexander takes his time, mouthing at her through her thong with slow and controlled determination.

It's torturous.

It's heaven.

"Take it off," she commands, barely recognizing the sound of her own voice. "Take it—"

"Be patient."

Eden whines. "But I want—"

"I know."

"Please—"

"I told you. I want to ruin you."

Eden moans, lightheaded and babbling nonsense. It's enough to make her toes curl. She's sure she sounds pathetic, panting and mewling like she's in heat. She doesn't care. Neither does he. In fact, it's very obvious how much he's enjoying all this. He brings a hand up to graze his fingers up her inner thigh, slowly creeping toward her welcoming entrance.

"I want to see you on my fingers," he says. "Is that alright with you?"

"Fuck yes. Please hurry, I need—"

"What do you need, sweetheart?"

"You. Inside me."

He finally —*finally*— pulls her panties off, tossing them over his shoulder to be abandoned on the floor somewhere. Alexander sucks in a sharp breath, admiring Eden in full. He doesn't waste time with compliments. They've both waited long enough.

He presses a finger against her wet entrance, dipping down to tease her clit with a quick swipe of his tongue. A sharp gasp escapes her throat as electricity jolts through her, the heat in her stomach growing more and more intense. He draws tight circles with the tip of his tongue as he presses a single finger into her.

Eden moans at the stretch. It's nothing she can't handle, and her slick desire makes it easy to adjust. He inserts a second, this time curling his fingers to sweep over her sweet spot. Eden's hips buck involuntarily, desperation mounting.

"Oh, God," she pants, reaching down between her legs to comb her fingers through his hair. "Right there—*Fuck*."

It's almost too much. She's dizzy, overwhelmed by his touch and his tongue. He seems to know exactly what she needs and how she likes it, impossibly accurate and relentless in pursuit of her release. The hot coil within her grows tighter and tighter, threatening to explode.

And then it does, a bright wave of pleasure sweeping over her. She drowns in it, moaning languidly as she closes her eyes and enjoys the high. Her chest heaves, rapid breaths matching the rhythm of her heart. A sudden, satisfying exhaustion hits her soon after. Every inch of her body is alight with soft fire, satiation evident in the way she strokes his hair.

Alexander licks his lips, looking understandably smug. "I'm not done with you yet," he says firmly, lifting her with ease. Eden instinctively wraps her arms and legs around him, kissing him slowly as he takes them both down a long hall.

His bedroom is cooler than the rest of the apartment. Eden uses it as an excuse to cling to him for warmth. Their lips find each other like magnets, only ever parting when they're both in need of air. She stands at the edge of the bed, reaching down to palm at Alexander's hard cock.

"Your turn," she says, dropping to her knees.

"Eden—"

"I've been thinking about this all day," she mumbles, slowly undoing his belt and dragging down the zipper. She hooks her fingers over the waistband of his jeans and boxers, pulling his clothes free.

Her eyes widen as his cock springs forth. Nothing could have prepared her for the sheer size of it. It's big, just like the rest of him, but it's still a surprise. The tip is an angry red and leaking with want, the shaft thick and dauntingly long.

"Fuck, you're massive," she mutters to herself.

Alexander chuckles, carding his fingers through her hair. "You're just pocket-sized."

"May I?"

"Anything you want."

Eden starts with a lick across the head of his cock, testing the waters. He tastes a bit salty, but she doesn't mind in the slightest. After a while, she gets used to the taste. It's just so... *him*. She wraps her lips around the head of his cock and swirls her tongue around, delighting in the chesty groan she earns from above.

His grip on her hair tightens. Not enough to hurt, but certainly enough to keep control.

"Your fucking *mouth*," he mutters. "Fuck, Eden. Show me what you can do."

She complies, hollowing her cheeks to suck him down inch by careful inch. He's too big to take all the way, but she does her best. What she can't take into her mouth, she uses her fingers to wrap around her shaft. She pumps him slowly, working in tandem with her mouth to push him closer and closer to the edge.

"You feel amazing, Eden. So pretty with my cock in your mouth. Love how you—*ngh*—look on your knees."

Eden closes her eyes and enjoys herself, bobbing her head back and forth and sucking in earnest, listening to the litany of filth spilling from his mouth.

"Eden, I—" Alexander hisses. "Get up."

She releases him with a wet pop. "But I'm not done playing with you yet."

"We've got all night, sweetheart, but I want you. *Now*."

When he offers her his hand, she takes it, rising up from off the floor. He guides her to the bed and has her lie down, the cool sheets a welcome sensation against her sensitive skin. Eden lies on her back, head upon a soft pillow—his pillow that smells completely of him—watching with bated breath as he pulls a condom from the bedside drawer. Once he's rolled it on, he easily finds his way to her, lying on top between her open legs.

The furious rush they were in before has dissipated, making way for something sweet and slow. When they kiss again, it's tender and careful. The look in his eyes makes her heart flutter. He looks at her like she's precious, special, something to keep safe forever. She sweeps her fingers past his cheek, plays with his hair, smiles into the kisses she gives him.

"You still okay with this?" he asks gently. "Is this what you want?"

Eden nods and smiles, wrapping her arms around his neck. "Yes. Absolutely."

He lines himself up with her entrance and pushes forward slowly. The stretch is significant compared to his fingers, filling her so full, it actually makes her wince. He stops immediately, pressing an apologetic kiss to her cheek.

"Should I stop?" he asks, concerned.

"No, just—You're really big. I just need a second."

He nods, carefully cradling her body close. The golden glow of the setting sun through the bedroom windows paints his skin, allowing Eden to admire all of the hidden marks on his body. She notices a scar across the front of his right shoulder, leading up across his collar bone. It's faint, incredibly old, almost healed over. It's in this golden sun that Eden can count the freckles on his face. She's never paid attention to them before, not really. They're perfect imperfections, unique to him and him alone.

Eden shifts and settles beneath Alexander's weight, finally adjusting. She nods, smiling shyly. "I think I'm ready now."

"You sure?"

"Mm-hmm."

"Okay."

He starts slowly at first, pushing all the way in. Eden trembles beneath him, the air squeezing out of her lungs as he plunges deeper and deeper. She feels so impossibly full, she thinks she might break. But she doesn't. Something tells her Alexander would never allow that to happen. He throbs inside of her, but he's clearly holding back for her sake. When the head of his cock sweeps past her sweet spot yet again, something explosive erupts out of nowhere.

"Oh, *fuuuuck*," she whimpers. Her walls flutter around him as her whole body ignites into flames. The pleasure is all-consuming, knocking her thoughts from her mind.

Alexander huffs, stunned. "Did you—Just from me—"

Eden covers her face with her hands, embarrassed. "I'm sorry. You just feel so good, I—"

He chuckles, pushing her hands aside to pepper her face with kisses. "Don't be sorry, it's alright. Can I keep going?"

"Yes. Yes, please. I want to make you come. Give it to me rough."

"If you want it rough, you'd better hold on to me, sweetheart."

She does so, circling his neck with her arms. He rolls his hips against her, pace picking up in rhythm. The slap of their skin combined with the sound of their filthy groans is music to her ears. He snaps his hips into her relentlessly, searching for more of that sweet friction. The bed creaks in protest beneath them, but they show no signs of slowing down.

"Fucking God, your pussy feels so good."

"Fuck, I— Right there, oh God right *there*."

"So nice and tight for me. Spread your legs wider—that's it."

Eden can feel herself growing tighter, hotter, brighter. She can hardly breathe, and her heart is racing a mile a minute. "I think—Fuck, I think I'm going to come again. I'm gonna—"

Alexander claims her mouth, tongue sweeping over hers as he pins both her wrists above her head against the pillow. He fucks her harder, claiming her, pushing her closer and closer toward climax. When it happens, she moans into his mouth, quaking beneath his weight. He finds release, too, his muscles tensing as he spills over.

They lie there together for a while, nothing but the sound of their combined panting to fill the silence.

Eden's blissed out of her mind. "Wow," she whispers.

"Good?"

She laughs softly. "Amazing," she corrects.

"Come here," he orders, scooping her up in his arms.

They kiss for a few minutes, or maybe it's a few hours. Eden supposes it doesn't much matter.

She can't remember the last time she felt this complete.

# CHAPTER
## Twenty

"A little birdie told me they spotted you arriving to work in the Chef's car today," Rina teases, bumping her hip against Eden's as they work together to prepare her mise. "What's that about, hm?"

Eden shrugs, but it's very difficult to keep a straight face. "We're carpooling. Nothing wrong with carpooling, right?"

Rina sniffs the air. "And you both just so happen to use the same scented body wash now?"

"What are you, a bloodhound?"

"You're not exactly denying it."

"Less talk, more whipped cream."

Rina giggles. "Oh, God. You're even starting to *sound* like him."

"What's going on?" Freddie asks, sidling up beside them at the dessert station with a bin full of fresh strawberries.

"Eden and Alexander are *carpooling*," Rina explains with a suggestive pump of the eyebrows.

Freddie grins like the cat who got the cream. "*Ooh*, is that so?"

"You guys are being silly. Nothing's going on."

"Mm-hmm," Rina says, though it's very obvious that she doesn't believe Eden in the slightest. "Can we expect little baby chefs running around any time soon? We can dress them up in cute little aprons and hats!"

Eden rolls her eyes. "Do you hear that? I think someone's calling for me."

Freddie frowns. "I didn't hear anyth—"

"Bye!" she chirps over her shoulder, making a hasty exit towards the front of the line.

She goes about the rest of her opening duties, ensuring that everything is in its place and that the waitstaff know what substitutions are available in case guests aren't interested in the house special.

She's more than a little aware of Alexander's presence the entire time. It's like she has some invisible homing beacon on him. He's always at the edge of her periphery, demonstrating to the saucier how he wants tonight's gravy done or confirming the reservation of twenty with the maître-d'.

When his eyes glance up from his task, they lock onto hers in a heartbeat.

Eden glances away, grinning sheepishly to herself. She manages to bite back a giggle, the bubbliness rising in her chest reminding her of champagne.

Alexander eventually joins Eden up at the front line. She's chopping onions, her fingers curled expertly around the white vegetable to avoid any knicks. She keeps her eyes down on the chopping board, but she's a bit distracted by his warmth now that he's here. There's a gravity to him, one that she finds herself pulled towards.

"Did you have a good day off, chef?" he asks evenly.

She nibbles on her bottom lip. "It was alright."

"Only alright?"

Eden shrugs a shoulder, continuing to dice. "Not that it's any of your business, Chef, but I had a date."

"Was he a gentleman?"

"Kind of a jerk, actually."

Beside her, Alexander bristles. "Wha—"

"I saw the cutest stuffed whale in the gift-shop," she continues dramatically. "I had my heart set on it, but you know what happened? We blew right past the shop and went straight back to his place."

Alexander snorts. "I'm sure he feels bad. Probably just got distracted by something important. Maybe he'll go back and buy it for you as a present for your second date."

Eden arches a brow, grinning. "You think he'll want a second date?"

He doesn't answer, but Eden doesn't miss the way he smiles to himself. She holds back her laugh.

She's just about finished cutting up the onions when she feels the tension in her hair suddenly loosen, a soft snapping sound reaching her ear. Her elastic gives out, her locks falling over her eyes. "Ah, shit," she grumbles to herself. "Cheap dollar store crap."

Before she can set her knife down, Alexander is behind her, quickly combing back her strands with his fingers and putting it up again with a rubber elastic he must have been carrying around in his apron's pocket.

"Don't get onion juice near your eyes," he warns.

The brush of his fingertips against the nape of her neck sends a delightful shiver running up and down her spine. Her cheeks warm, the tips of her ears redden.

"Thank you," she whispers.

Peter, who'd just returned to his station with a metal bowl full of spices, clutches an imaginary string of pearls. "The fuck did I just witness?"

"Drenton." Alexander steps away, clearing his throat. "You're finally here. I need a word in my office."

"Am I in trouble, or..."

"I'm not asking again."

"Pray for me," Peter whispers to Eden as he walks past, following Alexander dutifully.

Eden's curious. As much as she wants to ask what's going on, she still has duties to fulfill. She diligently spends the next ten minutes preparing for their shift. They're just about ready to open the doors to La Rouge, the first few customers already waiting in an orderly queue just outside.

When Peter exits the office, he's practically buzzing with excitement. He rushes over to Rina and Freddie, speaking so quickly that Eden doesn't quite catch what they're saying.

"What's going on?" Eden asks them.

"You are looking at the freshly promoted chef de partie," Freddie announces, patting Peter on the shoulder.

She blinks, amazed. "Wait, what? What happened to—"

"Hector?" Peter laughs joyously. "Fired. Can you believe it?"

"Fucking finally, if you ask me," says Rina.

Eden frowns. "Fired? You mean—"

"We're going out for drinks tonight to celebrate," Freddie says. "Want to come? It's his treat."

Peter puts his hands up in protest. "Whoa, what? I didn't agree to that?"

"You're the one getting a pay bump, man. Treat us a little."

She spots Alexander exiting the kitchen office. He looks... Well, normal. Ready to get back to work.

"Congrats," she mumbles before brushing past her friends. "Please excuse me for a sec." Eden rushes over to the head chef, frowning.

"Yes?" Alexander asks casually. Too casually.

"What the hell happened?"

"What are you talking about?"

Eden grits her teeth. "Seriously? Now's not the time to be coy. You fired Hector? I told you not to do anything stupid," she hisses. "Why did you do it? And why is this the first I'm hearing about it? Aren't you supposed to run things like this by me first? As your sous chef, I'm—"

Alexander sighs, lowering his voice so that it's soft and impossibly gentle. "I had a number of legitimate reasons to terminate him. He said inappropriate things to you, his work performance was lacking, and..." He reaches behind him and retrieves her old knife roll, the one that had suddenly gone missing from her staff locker.

Eden frowns, taking the item from him. "He took it? Why didn't you tell me?"

"Consider the situation handled," Alexander says firmly. "Hector will never work in this industry again."

"What do you mean?"

"I have a number of contacts. Food critics, other chefs, restaurant owners... I called everyone I could think of to warn them that Hector might try to find a job with them. Let's just say he did not earn himself a stellar work reference."

Eden swallows, a bit shaky. "So you just destroyed his career? Just like that?"

"Hector was an asshole. He was given fair warning time and time again. He pissed off the wrong people, so this is what he gets."

An odd feeling brews in the pit of her stomach. A part of her is relieved. Yes, Hector was an asshole. He made her life miserable at work and said some truly awful things. She knows she shouldn't feel guilty, and yet... To have his whole career ruined just like that? Just because Alexander said so?

*Why do I have a feeling this is going to bite us in the ass?*

As if reading her mind, Alexander says, "He can't do anything to you anymore, Eden. As long as I'm here, you'll have nothing to worry about."

She nods slowly, only because she doesn't know what else to

do. What's done is done, and it's not like she particularly wants Hector to have his job back. Not after everything he's put her through. When the first chit prints on the line, she decides to let it go.

They have work to do.

It's smooth sailing tonight. Without Hector trying to sabotage them around every corner, things flow with ease and precision. Orders go out hot and ready, their chefs are able to keep their stations clean and clear, and the entire kitchen works as a well-oiled machine.

She leaves the line momentarily to head to the walk-in in search of more ingredients. It's a moment of reprieve in the small, cool space away from all the hood fans and the flaming gas stove tops. She locates what she needs and grabs a bushel of carrots by their greens when she hears the door open.

It's Alexander.

"Chef? Did you need some—"

Before she can finish her sentence, Alexander swoops in. He circles her waist with one big arm and dips her back, claiming her lips with a heated ferocity that makes her melt like butter over a high flame. Her skin burns against the cool air of the walk-in, pressure mounting between her legs. Her lips come away swollen and tender, her heart beating rapidly with a newfound craving.

"What happened to your *no-PDA-in-the-workplace* rule?" she teases, breathless.

He pauses, hovering barely an inch away, waiting on bated breath.

"Fuck it," he rasps before diving in for another heated kiss.

She giggles into their second kiss, clinging to the front of his chef jacket with one hand while continuing to hold onto her bunch of carrots in the other. He's got a strong, supportive hand on her back, steadfast and sure.

She melts into his touch, hooking a leg over his hip with a soft moan. Alexander's got her pinned against the nearest shelf. The frigid metal bites into her skin, but she's so consumed by his daring display, it's an afterthought. Eden rolls her hips against him, teasing his lips apart with the tip of her tongue.

"Making out in the walk-in, Chef?" she teases. "This has gotta be a health violation."

"Probably. Do you want me to stop?"

Eden grasps his collar. "Fuck no."

Before they can get back to it, Freddie's muffled voice cuts through their stolen moment of privacy from the other side of the thick fridge door.

"Has anyone seen Chef? Or Eden? Table nineteen just sent their dish back complaining that it doesn't taste right."

Alexander sighs. "Will the madness ever stop?"

Eden rolls her eyes. "Drama queen. We only have an hour left until close, just hang in there."

He presses a quick kiss to her forehead, mumbling something unintelligible as he leans his weight against her. Eden thinks he's cute when he pouts, like an oversized puppy that doesn't realize he's too big for her lap.

"Tell you what," she says gently, bumping the tip of her nose against his. "We're both off tomorrow, right? Why don't you come over and I'll make you dinner?"

This earns her a beautiful smile. Alexander is truly breathtaking when he deigns to try anything other than his permanent scowl.

"Really?"

"Oh, yeah. You can pick me up early and we'll go shopping for fresh ingredients."

"So you want me to join you while you buy groceries? Should we stop by the laundromat while we're at it? That way we can get a head start on your chore list."

Eden giggles. "Do you wanna spend the day racing shopping carts up and down the spice aisle with me or not?"

Alexander chuckles, the corners of his eyes crinkling as he grins. "I'm a grown-ass man, sweetheart. Fuck yeah, I wanna race shopping carts up and down the spice aisle."

# CHAPTER
## Twenty-One

He feels strangely giddy. Dare he say it, like a damn school girl.

Alexander can't say he minds.

There's something wonderful about being with Eden on their day off. It's just grocery shopping, but Alexander appreciates the normality of it. The simplicity. He doesn't have to be *on*, just present. There are no orders to give, no customers to deal with, no cooking times to worry about. All he really cares about as he pushes their metal shopping cart is watching Eden as she explores the rows upon rows of shelves for the ingredients they need for dinner.

It's easy being around her. Relaxing.

Eden rips into a bag of sour cream and onion chips, which she promptly sets down in the section of the cart meant for little kids to sit in.

"Oh my God," Alexander groans. "You're one of *those* weirdos."

She looks up at him, puzzled. "What?"

"You snack while you shop."

"So? It's not like there are rules against shopping while snacking."

"Don't you think it's distracting?"

"For who? Me or you?" Eden flicks her ponytail over her shoulder and hooks her arm around Alexander's, pushing forward down the chip and pop aisle. "Studies have shown that it's best to go grocery shopping on a full stomach," she continues matter-of-factly.

"Is that so?"

"Mm-hmm. That way, you don't buy unnecessary things just because you're hungry."

Alexander pauses while she skips on ahead, munching away as she browses the shelves. She only stops to consider the items marked for sale and never anything at full price.

Something protective stirs in his chest.

Her new chef jacket. The knife set. Her secret coffee tin that only he knows about.

One way or another, it always comes down to money with Eden, and that makes him a little sad. It's true that his parents taught him frugality, but this is on a whole other level. It seeps into everything she does, every decision she makes. A tiny voice in the back of his head—one that grows increasingly louder with every passing day—wants to change all that. He wants to *help*.

He just doesn't know how.

As they stroll down the aisle together, his mind works over-time. Alexander knows he could easily pay for that private detective—Michelle something? Maxine?—but he knows Eden too well. She'll protest wholeheartedly the same way she did when he bought her new knife set. A lump lodges in his throat at the memory of her tearing up, so overwhelmed she could barely speak.

*People don't do stuff like this for me. Ever.*

He wants to change that, but only if she'll let him. It probably won't go over very well if he comes barreling in flashing his cash like some asshole with a hero complex. Knowing Eden, she might be insulted by the presumptuous nature of it. Grand gestures... That's not what she needs or wants. It's not his style, either.

So he starts small.

Eden puts a box of premium pasta back on the shelf and moves on. Alexander picks it right back up and tosses it into the cart.

"What are you doing?" she asks, amused.

"Nothing. What else is on the list?"

Eden squints at him, the corner of her lips curling up into a grin. "Marshmallows."

"Pasta and marshmallows? The fuck are you trying to make?"

She giggles. "They're for two separate recipes, dummy."

"You're the dummy."

Before she has the chance to protest, he wraps his arms around her, kisses her firmly on the lips, and then lifts her up and sets her down in the cart.

Eden bursts into a fit of laughter. "Oh my God, what are you doing?"

Alexander pushes the cart forward. "What else do you need for dinner, chef?"

They continue going up and down the food aisles, collecting a wide variety of different ingredients. Alexander thinks of it as a puzzle. He sees the pieces that Eden's picking up, but for the life of him, he can't see the overall picture.

Gochujang, Japanese chili miso, chocolate chips, ketchup, garlic powder, graham crackers, sesame seed oil, and fresh shrimp straight from the tank. Every single time Eden tries to go for a cheaper version to save a couple of cents, Alexander immediately puts it back and replaces the item with something of higher quality.

Eden puts her hands on her hips. "Stop that."

"I don't know what you're talking about."

"Alexander—"

"Is there anything else you need?"

"Well, no, but—"

"Then we're off to the checkout!"

She throws her head back and giggles wildly as they race down the aisle. Neither of them care about the pointed looks they earn from startled shoppers nearby.

Even when she's pouting, Alexander thinks Eden's the cutest thing he's ever laid eyes upon. They're seated at her kitchen table, which is just barely big enough for two. Her dish —spicy miso grilled shrimp over rice—was delectable; equal parts savory, spicy, and filling. Now they're waiting for dessert, a rendition of campfire s'mores in a deep pie plate, which is baking slowly in the oven.

Alexander pokes her cheek. "Still mad at me?"

"No," she says, clipped.

"I don't believe you."

"I should have known you were going to try and pay for the whole damn thing."

Alexander rubs his neck, tilting his head from side to side to stretch his sore muscles. "I didn't think you'd wrestle me in front of the cashier. You should consider becoming a professional MMA fighter if this whole chef thing doesn't work out for you."

This earns him a sheepish smile, but he knows he can do better.

"C'mon, Eden. Don't be like that. I'm allowed to do nice stuff for my girlf—"

He stops himself before the word slips out, but Eden's already smiling brighter than the sun. "For your *what*?"

"Nothing."

"You were going to say girlfriend, weren't you?"

"N-no?"

"Holy shit, are you blushing?"

He clears his throat. "Absolutely not."

Eden practically throws herself out of her chair and hops onto Alexander's lap, straddling him between her thighs as she wraps her arms around his neck. She giggles, clearly pleased as punch. "You wanted to call me your *girlfriend*," she says happily in a sing-song tone.

He gently grasps her chin in his hand, tilting upwards to better stare at her lips. "Say it again," he orders, his voice a low grumble.

"Girl. Friend."

"You don't think it's too soon?"

She shakes her head. "I mean, you've fed me a gazillion times by now. I'm pretty sure in some cultures that means we're married."

Alexander knows she's trying to joke around, get a reaction out of him. Instead, he chuckles. "Hm…"

"What?"

He grins when she does. "I have a question for you."

"What is it?" she asks.

"If you're my girlfriend, wouldn't you agree that I'm allowed to treat you to things?"

Eden presses her lips into a thin line. "Maybe. Sometimes."

"*All* the time," he corrects.

"Why?"

Alexander pauses for a moment, thinking it over with great care. "There is literally no one else on Earth that I'd rather spoil. You're the only one I can think of who deserves nothing less."

She pauses, looking deeply into his eyes. Alexander can't tell what she's thinking. Is she about to argue? About to cry?

*God forbid it.*

Instead, she leans forward and kisses him tenderly, so soft and sweet that Alexander wonders how he got so damn lucky. She's the one who deepens the kiss, combing her fingers through his hair as she rocks her hips against his stiffening erection. Eden carefully pulls his shirt up and over his head, tossing the offending fabric away so that she can paw at his wide chest. His hands slide down to cup her ass, giving *just* the right amount of squeeze to make her moan.

"We only have five minutes before dessert's ready," she protests.

"I can do a lot to you in five minutes, sweetheart."

"Then what are you waiting for, *boyfriend*?"

He moves with purpose, hooking his hands around her thighs so that he can lift her up and lay her down on the kitchen table. The dishes have already been cleared, save for a pair of forks that clink together with the sudden movement. His skillful hands make quick work of the front of her jeans, tugging them off hurriedly before kneeling on the kitchen tile between her thighs.

They've already eaten dinner, but he's ravenous. With the time now sitting at four minutes and thirty seconds, he wastes no more time and dips down to enjoy his meal.

The *sounds* she makes. Alexander's so hard, it's almost painful.

He teases her with his tongue, his fingers; makes his business her pleasure. Eden reaches her peak just as the timer on the oven beeps. Alexander can't help but smirk at himself. He always knew he worked well under pressure.

"Mmph, thank you for that," Eden mumbles. "Sit tight. I'll go get dessert."

"I've already *had* dessert."

She rolls her eyes. "Cheesy."

Alexander reclaims his seat just as Eden returns with a piping hot baking dish. It's a layer of molten chocolate topped with a gooey marshmallow layer and a buttery graham cracker crust. She also retrieves a tub of vanilla bean ice cream from the fridge and a can of whipped cream...

Which she immediately sprays all over his chest. He's momentarily shocked by the cold, but then Eden gets on her knees with that mischievous glint in her eye that he adores so much.

"Food needs to cool," she reasons. "We've got time to kill."

"What a waste," he pretends to complain. "Hand me a napkin?"

Eden shakes her head. "I've got a better idea."

She advances, her hands resting gently on Alexander's knees as she leans forward to lick up the mess she's made. A delightful shiver runs up and down his back. It's safe to say he's thoroughly enjoying the view. Eden continues to lap up the whipped cream, working her way all the way down until she's face to face with his belt buckle. Nimble fingers pull him free of his pants. Before he knows it, she's taken him into her mouth with a content hum.

He lets his head tilt back with a relieved sigh. Is this what Heaven feels like?

No, not heaven.

Just Eden.

He curls his fingers into her hair and watches her work, her eyes closed in concentration as she hollows her cheeks and sucks in earnest. The warmth of her mouth surrounding him feels too good to be real, the tight coil deep within his core growing hotter and brighter with every pass of her exploratory tongue.

"That's it, sweetheart. Just like that. So fucking pretty with my cock in your mouth. You're gonna make me—"

Stars fly across his vision. His mind whites. A wonderful wave of euphoric exhaustion seeps into his muscles, his bones, his very marrow. Alexander watches with a grin as Eden rises, licking her lips.

"I think dessert's cool enough now."

He chuckles. "Goody."

His phone goes off. It's Sebastian asking for updates on the menu, the restaurant.

Alexander leaves his messages on read before putting the device on silent. Eden's the only one who deserves his attention right now.

# CHAPTER
## Twenty-Two

"Fuuuuuuck," she groans into her pillow.

It's Monday morning a few weeks later, and she has to work a shift tonight, but *holy cannoli cheese on a cracker* does she feel like Death incarnate. Eden's in so much pain, she can't tell if she's hungry, needs to vomit, use the toilet, or if it's just her cramps trying to knock her down several pegs.

In summary: not a pretty picture.

She rolls over in bed, clutching her stomach. Eden knows she's been blessed with relatively light periods. It normally only lasts three or four days, but the first day is always the worst. It's almost as if her body made a trade-off with some unnamed fertility goddess. In exchange for a short cycle, all of her monthly side effects are crammed together into one day.

Eden can normally get by on an ibuprofen or two, often with the assistance of a microwaveable heat pack. She's used to brute forcing her way through the day, as most women around the world are wont to do. She's got shit to get done, a kitchen to run.

What a shame her uterus is trying to *kill* her.

She never takes time off from work, never calls in sick—even though it's probably a health violation not to do so—but Eden isn't sure if she can make it through her shift like this. The pain's too great, and she's worried that she'll only get in everybody's way if she goes to work like this. So, after about five minutes of mental back and forth, Eden reaches for her phone on the bedside table.

> Eden: I don't think I can come in to work today.

It surprises her how quickly Alexander responds back.

> Alexander: What's wrong?

> Eden: Feeling sick.

Her phone starts to buzz. Alexander is *calling* her.

"Do you think it's the flu?" he asks the second she picks up. "Freddie called out sick, too. Stomach bug or something. I'm worried something's going around."

"This is definitely not a stomach bug," she croaks. "If you really need me to come in, I can—"

"No, no. It's fine. Tonight's going to be quiet, so it's nothing I can't handle."

"Okay, I'm sorry."

"Don't apologize. It'll be a good learning opportunity for Drenton. Get some rest."

"Thanks, Chef."

"Don't mention it."

The rest of the day is torture. She's hungry, she's angry— the textbook definition of hangry. Eden tries taking a hot bath, eating chocolate, doing some light stretches, but all in vain. She's just going to have to suck it up and nap it off like she does every month. She's curled up under several layers of her fluffiest blankets on the couch with the TV switched on to Jeopardy. The moment she's found a partially comfortable position to lie in...

There's a knock at the door.

"Good grief," Eden mumbles, dragging herself up with a groan. "The volume isn't even up all the way, Mrs. Jefferson!"

It's not Mrs. Jefferson.

"Do you not get along with your neighbors?" Alexander asks.

"She lives downstairs," Eden explains. "She's always yelling about how my TV's too loud or that I'm stomping around."

"Do you want me to have a word with her?"

He sounds so serious about it that Eden can't help but laugh. "No, please don't. Pretty sure she'd eat you alive. I'd prefer you in one piece."

"Your concern is greatly appreciated."

"What are you doing here?" she asks softly. "Aren't you supposed to be at La Rouge for closing?"

"Drenton can take care of it. He's familiar enough with the procedure by now. Besides, I wanted to check on you. Are you feeling any better?"

Eden's face flushes with heat. "Look, this is really sweet of you, but I'm... I'm not *sick* sick."

Alexander's brow furrows ever so slightly. "I don't understand."

"It's not a big deal."

"Is it serious?"

"Um, not really?"

"Because if I can help in any way, all you have to do is let me know."

"I'm on my period!" she blurts out, her face uncomfortably hot.

His face blanks. "Oh."

"Was that too much information?"

"No, no. It was just, uh..." Alexander scratches behind his ear. "You know what? One sec." He turns on his heels and retreats down the hall in a flash.

All Eden can do is stare at the spot he was once standing, heart pounding in her ear as her brain shifts into overdrive. She worries that she weirded him out. Periods are perfectly natural, nothing to be freaked out by. Eden's equal parts disappointed and angry when she returns to her spot on the couch. Their relationship is still pretty new, but she thought maybe Alexander was more mature than this. She sits there, quietly fuming.

Once she's feeling like her old self again, she's going to give Alexander one hell of an earful.

He shows up roughly twenty minutes later, entering the apartment without so much as a knock. Eden startles, standing up in a hurry. She's ready to jump down his throat about how insensitive he's being, but then she notices the plastic bag in his hand. Alexander sets it down on the coffee table, shifting through the contents.

"Sorry that took me so long," he says quickly.

"Where'd you run off to?"

"There's a drugstore about three blocks from here. I had to ask the pharmacy assistant for help. I didn't know if you had a preference for tampons or pads, so I got a mix of both, but then she mentioned something about a Diva Cup, to which I responded, '*The fuck is a Diva Cup?*'"

He continues to unpack the bag, setting everything down neatly. "I've also got a couple of chocolate bars for you—the expensive kind, because that cheap sugary shit's only going to make you feel worse—some ginger tea, and some Midol just in case you didn't have any on hand. Oh, and I also got you..."

Alexander pulls out a tiny plush dog. Its fur is made of black velvet, its eyes are wide and cute, and it has the most adorable floppy ears. "To make up for that stuffed whale at the aquarium."

She wraps her arms around his neck and hugs him tight, pressing her face against the crook of his neck. Eden's heart has never felt more full.

"Thank you," she whispers. "You're so... *Argh*. I don't even have the words. Amazing. Awesome. The best."

"I'll never tire of hearing you sing my praises." He hugs her back, pressing a light kiss against the top of her head. "Have you had anything to eat today?"

"Not really. I've mostly been napping."

Alexander makes a '*hm*' sound in disapproval. "That won't do at all. Get comfy on the couch. I'll make you something."

"Boyfriend, delivery boy, and now my personal chef? Do you have any idea how sexy you are to me right now?"

Alexander smirks. "I do it for the annual boyfriend-delivery-boy-personal-chef award."

He wraps her up in a cocoon of blankets, stamping a kiss to the tip of her nose before making himself right at home in her kitchen. Eden marvels at how comfortable he looks here. He knows where the utensil drawer is, he knows where she keeps her pots and pans. Eden observes in quiet fascination as he pokes around in her cupboards in search of ingredients, slipping on her hot pink apron with the cute cartoon cat design on the front. He grimaces when he sneaks a peek inside her fridge.

"Your fridge makes me sad," he comments lightly.

"*You* make me sad," she replies, even though she knows she doesn't make any sense.

He chuckles. "Hang on, grumpy pants. I know exactly what I'm going to make you."

Alexander works diligently and with such care that her heart can't help but flutter. He preheats the oven, saws off four thick pieces of sourdough bread, spreads a generous layer of mayo instead of butter before searing to a perfect golden brown in a pan. Once browned, he uses a single clove of garlic and rubs it against the bread, giving an otherwise boring piece of toast that extra herbal kick.

He's generous with the layers of cheese he applies—in this case, sharp cheddar and mozzarella—before he lays everything together, lovingly wraps the food up in a sheet of parchment paper, and pops it in the oven to melt. Once he's satisfied, he pulls the sandwich out and drizzles the top with the lightest trace of honey; a playful balance of sweet and salty.

Alexander plates up without pomp or circumstance, returning to Eden with the fanciest grilled cheese she's ever eaten in her entire life. He sits beside her, one arm slung over the back of the couch so that she can lean in against him as she munches away.

Eden moans. "Holy shit."

"Is it that good?"

"Mphf, *fuck yeah.*"

He kisses her cheek as he turns up the volume on the TV. "Good."

She eats, thoroughly famished, as they watch an episode of Jeopardy together. Eden answers a couple of questions while Alexander makes a good effort. If they played for real, he'd be at least two thousand dollars in the hole.

"God, I suck at this," he grumbles when he gets yet another answer wrong. "I swear I'm smart."

Eden giggles quietly to herself, her eyelids drifting close. She finds him so soothing that she can barely stay awake. She likes the warmth of his skin, the smell of his shirt, the way he gently strokes her arm as she drifts off. For the first time in a very long time, she doesn't go to bed counting the money in her coffee tin. Right now, she isn't concerned about urgently saving for the future.

When she's with Alexander, she has time to slow down, to relax. She can let go of her worries, be present and in the moment. When she's with him, she feels safe and warm and so impossibly content that she can't even put it into words. She adores everything about this man. Hell, she might even—

"Love you," she mumbles as sleep drags her under.

# CHAPTER
## Twenty-Three

*L* *ove you.*

She said it casually, in passing—like it was the most obvious thing in the world. Two simple words spoken in a broken sentence, but it still leaves Alexander's head spinning.

On one hand, it makes him feel good. Excited. He really, *really* likes Eden. He's never felt this strongly about anyone before, never felt this protective and adoring.

But it doesn't stop the doubts from creeping in.

Are they moving too fast? Is she sure she wants *him*? Alexander knows he's not a catch. He's moody, famous for his temper. It's one of the many reasons why he's never had a long-term girlfriend before. They don't tend to stick around for very long once they realize what a handful he is. There's the added issue of his demanding job. He's married to his work. The restaurant is basically his second home.

Will Eden leave when she realizes her mistake? Sure, things are good right now, but will she think he's worth the hassle when he inevitably fucks this all up?

Alexander's never stayed over at a girl's place before. Even when he was still seeing Bea, their dalliances never evolved into sleepovers. It was his way of keeping things separate, clinical. No need to worry about the morning after and the tiptoeing around each other and the awkward *'see you later maybe'* conversations when he left as soon as the deed was done.

But when he rolls over first thing in the morning to find Eden there beside him, he's never felt more at peace. He carried her to bed and tucked her in some time around one in the morning. He fully intended on leaving, but Alexander doesn't have a key to her apartment and he didn't like the thought of leaving her alone with the door unlocked.

He had every intention of sleeping on the couch so she could have some space, but Eden literally wouldn't let go of his hand. Alexander had no choice but to curl up behind her, not that he had any complaints.

She's hogged all the blankets, curled up in her own little burrito of warmth. All he can see is the tip of her nose poking out from beneath, as well as a few strands of her hair. He smiles to himself. She really is the most adorable thing he's ever seen.

He slings an arm over her and holds her close. The clock on the nightstand reads 5:00 AM. There's still plenty of time to sleep.

The next time he stirs, it's to the smell of bacon, eggs, and pancakes.

He reaches to his side, groggy and mildly disoriented, but finds Eden's half of the bed vacant. He can hear her humming a soft tune elsewhere in the apartment, so he rubs the sleep from his eyes and shuffles out of the bedroom toward the kitchen.

Eden is a sight to behold.

She's put on his black sweater, the one he'd worn yesterday and taken off in great haste last night. Her hair is a tousled mess, somehow effortlessly ethereal as it catches the sunlight. It doesn't appear that she's wearing much else. Alexander, naturally, is overcome with the strong urge to check.

While Eden flips a pancake, he slides up behind her and slips an arm around her waist. He brushes her hair to the side so he can kiss the part of her neck he just bared. Eden giggles, suggestively grinding her ass up against him.

"This looks delicious," he murmurs against her skin. "Feeling better?"

"Yes, a lot better. I wasn't sure what you wanted, so I made a bit of everything."

"I wasn't talking about the food."

She throws her head back and laughs. "Oh, wow. Can you be any cheesier?"

He chuckles. "Yes. I bought an entire book of awful pick-up lines to test out on you."

Eden snorts. "Why?"

"To make you laugh, of course."

If Eden keeps smiling like this, her cheeks are going to start to ache. "How do you like your eggs?" she asks.

"However you like them."

"I don't like eggs."

"Oof," he mumbles, pulling away. "That might be a deal breaker for me."

Eden rolls her eyes, but there isn't any heat behind it. "Oh, fuck off."

"How can you not like eggs?"

"I don't *not* like eggs. They're just not my favorite. I'd prefer not to eat them by themselves. Too eggy."

He crinkles his nose. "How would you describe this dish, chef? Oh, '*too eggy.*'"

Eden kills the heat on the stove and turns, playfully swatting at his chest. "This is bullying at the workplace," she teases, smiling wide.

"We're not at the workplace."

"So it's just bullying, then?"

"Face it, sweetheart. You like it when I'm a little mean."

"Maybe."

He places a hand on either side of her hips and presses her up against the edge of the kitchen counter. "Maybe?"

"I like it when you're in control," she clarifies. "Not when you're mean, per se. Though those two things tend to go hand in hand with you."

"You like it when I'm in control, huh?"

Eden nods, nibbling her bottom lip. "It's sexy. I love how you look at the front of the line, running your kitchen. It's distracting, really. It's a miracle I can get any work done."

"That so?"

"It's your hands that do me in, though."

"These hands?" he asks, slipping his palms beneath her sweater—*his* sweater. He pulls up at the fabric and realizes something. "Are you—"

"Not wearing a bra? Yeah."

He finally kisses her, grumbling, "You're a fucking wet dream."

"You're welcome."

Alexander lifts Eden onto the kitchen counter and moves in to claim her mouth, kissing and licking and breathing her in. He ignores his throbbing cock to instead focus on her. Her moans are like a siren's song, hypnotizing and intoxicating. She grips his hair at the roots and holds him where she wants him. He adores the way her body feels pressed against his.

If he died this instant, he'd die a happy man.

"Mm, Shang—"

He freezes.

It feels like he's taken a punch to the gut.

"Don't call me that," he says with way more force than he intends.

Eden stiffens, startled. "Oh, I just thought—"

He shakes his head. "Sorry. I just... Please don't use that name."

She frowns, understandably confused. "Why?"

"I don't want to talk about it."

"You said that last time, too. You said you'd tell me when you're ready."

"Well, I'm still not ready."

"But Shang, I—"

"Stop it." He pulls away with a huff.

The mood's ruined.

Eden bites her bottom lip, a flicker of annoyance ghosting past her hazel eyes. She closes her legs, suddenly bashful. "Do you not trust me or something?"

"It's not that."

"Then what?"

"That name. Everything it represents. It's not something I want to deal with. Ever."

"Everything it represents? I don't understand."

"You don't have to."

She gawks at him. "What the hell happened to you? What made you—" she gestures at him, "like this? Are we really going to have a fight over a name?"

"Leave it alone, Eden. It doesn't concern you."

Her jaw tightens. "What even is this?"

"What?"

"Us." The word lingers in the air, heavy and pointed.

"Eden—"

"If this is... I'm your *girlfriend*. You said you wanted to do this right. I assumed you meant..." Eden huffs, growing more and more agitated. She hops off the edge of the kitchen counter and stares up at him. "I assumed you meant trying to be together for real."

"That's what I meant, yes."

"Well, then I hate to break it to you, but that means talking to me. About everything. But if you don't trust me enough, then—"

"What are you saying?"

Eden gets up and pulls her hair up into a messy ponytail. "Shit," she hisses. "Shit. Maybe this was a mistake."

"It's not a big deal."

"Not a big deal?" she snaps. "You have two fucking names, and you won't tell me why. If Alexander were your middle name, I'd get it, but it's not. It's a *stage* name. Why are you hiding who you really are? I don't... I don't know you."

"Don't say that."

"But it's true!" She shifts her weight from foot to foot. If Alexander didn't know any better, he'd assume she's seconds away from making a run for it. "The boy I knew in culinary school was sweet and gentle and loved to crack jokes. But you..." She licks her lips, struggling to find the right words. "You're intimidating as fuck. You turned into someone that everyone's afraid of pissing off. That doesn't just happen."

He clenches his fists tight, remaining perfectly still. "Are you afraid of me, Eden?"

She chews on the inside of her cheek. "I'm afraid that you won't be honest with me when it counts. I don't ask for a lot, but I need honesty. Parsons lied to me about spending my scholarship money. My parents lied to me about coming to pick me up. I don't think I can handle you lying to me about who you are." Eden approaches cautiously, daring to reach out to press a hand to his chest. "You can trust me," she whispers. "I'm literally trusting you with my job, to keep my secret. Why can't you trust me, too?"

"It's not about trust. I can't talk about it."

"Why not? I don't want to be with someone that doesn't—"

"I said I can't! Just fucking leave me alone!"

Eden winces, and he hates himself that much more for it.

He knew he was going to screw up, he just didn't think this soon.

"Jesus."

"I'm sorry. I didn't mean—"

She casts her eyes to the floor. "I think you should get going."

"Eden. Fuck, Eden, no. I'm—"

"I'll see you at work."

"Eden, wait—"

"When you feel like talking to me, let me know. If not, don't worry about it. We'll just pretend that..." She doesn't finish her sentence. "Please. Just go. We need space or whatever, before we say something we both might regret."

Not knowing what else to do, Alexander grabs his jacket and leaves.

He drives home in silence. The first thing he does is trudge over to the nearest stash of cigarette cartons he has hidden behind one of the fake plants on his shelf, whipping a cigarette and light out in a flash.

He takes a long drag and welcomes to burn in his lung. He'd been trying so hard to quit.

Fuck, fuck, *fuck*.

He knows he could tell her. He could reveal the truth. He doubts that Eden will judge him because—bless her soul—she's an angel and she'd never do such a thing. But it's not that simple. It's not that easy because the past, his past... It hurts to even think about it. He's spent a decade learning to swallow the guilt, to ignore it until it's a dull sensation in the pit of his stomach. Talking about it, revisiting those old memories...

Paris. His parents. Sebastian. The rain. The last time he saw his father. He just wants to be rid of the pain. Sharing that part of his life with Eden... He's not willing to do it. He doesn't want her to see him for what he is.

A little boy too afraid to return home.

A coward.

A fuck up.

# CHAPTER
## Twenty-Four

Eden wants to kick herself until her shins are purple with bruises. She's thought about it long and hard since leaving this morning.

She shouldn't have pushed. She realizes she overstepped, that she shouldn't have tried to make Alexander talk about his past if he wasn't ready. What happened to him—whatever it was —must have been traumatic. She was wrong to demand the truth from him, wrong to make him so uncomfortable.

She simply thought that—maybe—they were close enough now. They'd been together for a couple of weeks. How was she supposed to know when it was a good enough time to ask him for the truth?

She talks herself into circles. On one hand, she doesn't want to stress him out. But doesn't he care enough to at least try to talk to her? She shouldn't feel this guilty for wanting to get to know him, to understand him.

Eden decides she'll apologize to him when she sees him at work. Mainly because she feels bad about leaving things the way she did. Maybe they'll be able to salvage—whatever it is that they are.

But if not? If not, she'll have to deal with the mess she's made. She doesn't want to imagine how fucking awkward it's going to be now, how awful and strained and downright embarrassing. What if he hates her now? What if he wants nothing to do with her? Alexander could fire her on the spot, if he wants. But will he?

God. She wants to be anywhere else in the world but here. But if she suddenly calls in sick again, she knows Alexander will see right through her ruse. That'll only make it more unbearable to show up to work.

A fine mess, indeed.

"Fuck me," she grumbles to herself as she steps through the back doors of La Rouge.

The first person to greet her—thankfully—is Peter.

"Heads up," he warns. "Chef's in a *really* bad mood."

Eden chews on the inside of her cheek. "Do you know why?"

Her chef de partie shrugs. "The man's a mystery. I was hoping you were the one with answers. He hasn't even told us what the night's specials are, but he's so grumpy that I'm too afraid to ask."

"I'll talk to him," she offers.

Peter pats her on the shoulders. "Thanks for taking the bullet. I'll get a head start on funeral arrangements."

Eden rolls her eyes. "Drama queen."

She finds him in the kitchen's corner office, Alexander's massive frame haunched over the cramped desk in front of the restaurant's work laptop. They use it to submit produce orders, send off payroll, organize the month's shifts, deal with customer reviews, and—in this particular instance—reply to a particularly angry email from one Hector Trisko. Eden's only able to catch a glimpse of the first few lines over Alexander's shoulder, but it's more than enough.

*I'm going to make sure you pay for what you did. Did you really have to destroy my career? Nobody's willing to take me after the lies you've spread. I hope you rot in hell you chi—*

"How long are you going to stand there?" Alexander asks, not looking away from the screen. His tone is flat, tinged with bitterness.

"What is that?" she asks.

"Hector's threatening to sue me for defamation."

"Seriously?"

"Do I look like I'm joking?"

Eden puts her hands on her hips. "He can't sue you for giving a poor reference. It's not your fault he's a shit employee."

"I'll deal with it, Monroe. It's none of your concern."

She bristles. "The hell is your problem?"

"I don't appreciate you riding my ass!"

"And I don't appreciate you pushing me away!"

"Would you give it a break already? Everyone's pissing me off, and I've got too much shit to deal with today."

"And what about me?"

"What?"

"If I piss you off, will you do the same to me what you did to Hector?"

Alexander balks. He looks like he's been stabbed. "Do you really think so little of me?" He sounds impossibly small. "If this is about this morning…"

"Of course this is about this morning."

"Eden, look—"

A knock at the door interrupts them both. It swings open, revealing Sebastian on the other side.

"Ah, there you two are," he says, sickly sweet. "In the middle of a meeting, I see. I hope I'm not interrupting."

Alexander stiffens. "Actually, I need to speak with her alo—"

217

"You're not interrupting," Eden says quickly.

Sebastian smiles. "Might I have a word?"

"Sure. I'll give you two some privacy."

"No, dear. I mean I wish to speak to you."

Eden holds her breath. "Oh, um..." She glances at Alexander, who appears just as concerned as she feels. What the hell does this wrinkly old sea cucumber want with her, of all people? "Of course, sir," she says slowly.

"Come. We can use one of the tables in the dining room." Sebastian turns to leave, expecting Eden to follow on his heel.

She takes a single step forward before Alexander catches her hand, frantic. "Eden, wait."

She slips out of his grasp. "Not now."

"Eden, just—"

She shuts the door as she walks out. End of conversation. She can't handle this right now.

Sebastian has chosen a small table in the back corner of La Rouge, one with a frosted glass partition beside them to block them from view of the kitchen. Eden wonders if it's deliberate. It probably is. The table is meant for two, so it feels strangely intimate to be sitting across from him. Again, probably a deliberate move on his part. Like he knows how to get under her skin, purposefully placing himself within her personal bubble. He can feign innocence, of course.

After all, this is just a little chat they're having. Perfectly pleasant and friendly. But Eden knows better. Her gut tells her that things aren't as they seem.

"How are you enjoying your time here?" Sebastian asks, voice velvety smooth.

"It's been fantastic," she answers.

*For the most part. It'd be better if my boss wasn't such a dickhead. A handsome, sexy dickhead.*

*God, I hate him.*

*No, I don't.*

"I've been very impressed with you, Eden," Sebastian continues. "I'm curious, what are your plans for the future?"

"My future?"

He checks under his fingernails for non-existent dirt. "I'm sure you're aware of all the accolades Alexander has earned over the years. Several Michelin stars. I'm sure you're aware that it's like winning an Oscar for people like us."

Eden nods, admittedly impressed. "Yes. He's... quite amazing." Deep down, she knows she means it.

"Olivier, Pock... They were all, at some point, protégés of mine. They all owe their success to me."

"Is that so?" she asks. She isn't interested in the slightest.

"Have you ever thought about running your own kitchen, my dear?"

"Sometimes. Maybe one day in the future. It's always been a pipedream for me."

"What if I told you it didn't have to be a dream for much longer?"

Her stomach flips. "I beg your pardon?"

"You have a great deal of potential. I would love the opportunity to truly help you shine." Sebastian pulls out a slim white envelope from the inside pocket of his jacket and slides it across the table. "I'm sure you're aware that La Rouge isn't the only establishment I own. I have a number of restaurants scattered throughout the world, several of which I think you'd be a perfect fit for. All you would have to do is pick."

Eden opens the envelope and finds a single check inside. She's never seen so many zeros in front of the decimal place before. "What is this?"

"Your signing bonus," he explains simply, like it's a stupid question.

"This is... incredibly generous of you, sir."

It really, truly is. The check could pay for a PI like Maxine Kendo two, maybe even three times over. Eden could finally afford a nice apartment, all the delicious food she wants to eat, all of the pretty dresses her heart could ever desire.

Sebastian smiles. "Think of it as an investment. And that's also on top of your yearly salary, which I assure you is quite competitive. You'll make the same amount that Alexander earns in no time at all."

Her hands can't stop shaking. She wants to pinch herself to make sure this is real. "I don't know what to say," she admits.

"You don't have to accept the offer right away. Please think on it, though I personally wouldn't take too long. Things tend to move fast in my line of work."

"Who will be Alexander's sous chef? If I accept, I mean."

"There's no need to concern yourself with finding a replacement. With the way things are going, I doubt there will be any need to..." Sebastian trails off, laughing gently. "Don't mind me. Just the ramblings of an old man. Please let me know your answer as soon as possible. Hold onto the check. To serve as inspiration."

Eden slips the check back into the envelope and then stuffs the envelope into the pocket of her apron. "Thank you, sir. I'll definitely mull it over."

"That's my girl. Thank you for your time, dear."

"You as well."

"Best get back to the grind, then. I think service has started."

"Um, right. Thanks."

She gets up and walks back to the kitchen, so frazzled that she doesn't notice Alexander standing anxiously on the other side at first, clearly waiting for her.

"What did he want?" he asks, voice raspy. His brow is twisted with worry, and his cheeks are a little flushed. He looms near her, like he wants to reach out, but forces himself not to.

Eden takes a deep breath. She doesn't know how to begin. Even though it's a flimsy piece of paper, the check in her pocket weighs a million tons. If she accepts Sebastian's offer, she'll finally have the money she needs to find her parents. She'll have everything she could ever need.

But doubt creeps in and infests her mind. What if she can't do it? Alexander makes running a kitchen look easy. What if she can't pull it off, Sebastian realizes she's full of shit, and he fires her due to incompetence? She'll end up right back at square one. She'll have left her friends behind.

She'll have left *him* behind.

What will this mean for them if she accepts? If she doesn't? Eden's too overwhelmed to deal with any of this right now.

He tries again, so soft and sweet and genuinely worried that Eden wants to cry. "Are you okay? Did he say something to you?"

"I'm fine." She takes another deep breath. "What are the specials tonight?"

Alexander shifts in his spot. "Eden."

"The specials. What are they?"

"The salmon filet," he says slowly. "And the fois gras."

She brushes right past him. "Okay. Let's get to work."

She pretends not to notice the way he opens his mouth to speak, just to think against it and close up again.

# CHAPTER
## Twenty-Five

This is the worst shift he's had in weeks.

The restaurant is slammed. Peter is understandably adjusting to the responsibilities of his new role, so things aren't running as smoothly as they could be. And worst of all?

Eden won't look at him.

Not once.

The orders won't stop coming in, his cooks are swamped, and this god-awful pain in his chest every time Eden ignores him just won't go away.

He knows he needs to apologize. He *wants* to apologize. For his behavior, for being standoffish, for being an irredeemable asshole. He knows he shouldn't have yelled at her, made her feel like she wasn't worth letting in. It's just that he can't find the time to pull her aside and explain himself.

And then there's Sebastian. His unannounced appearance has thrown Alexander through a loop. He desperately wants to ask Eden what they talked about, what was said. She appeared quite shaken when she returned from her one-on-one with the restaurateur. All he wants to know is if she's okay, if she needs him for—anything, really.

He only gets more and more frustrated as the night goes on. He can't help it. Nothing's going right. Dishes are sent back, customers are dissatisfied with wait times, and the dishwashing machine in the pit keeps getting clogged up with all manner of food scraps and bent straws.

Things with Eden are off-kilter, too. He can feel it. They're working on the same sinking ship, trying to bail it out, but they're not working together. He talks over her, she talks over him, sometimes giving conflicting information to the other cooks. She sends out food before Alexander's ready, he holds back when she needs to clear chits. He can't count the number of times they've almost had run-ins with one another, literally stepping on each other's toes.

They need to be better than this. Should be better than this. What's supposed to be an organized dance is now a free for all.

His eruption is inevitable. A long time in the making. All the signs are there: the piercing headache behind his eyes, the tension in his shoulders, the rage boiling in his stomach. Part of him—the weaker, pathetic part deep down—wants to curl up into a ball and sleep it all away.

The other part of him knows that it's easier just to explode.

It just so happens that Rina is the unfortunate soul caught in his line of fire when he finally does.

"What are you doing?" he hisses at the top of his lungs. "I can't serve this when it looks like pig slop."

Rina tenses, very much a deer caught in the headlights. "But I've been making the sundaes this way all evening."

"You're drowning the damn thing in caramel sauce. Who the fuck approved that?"

"I did," Eden hisses.

"It needs to be consistent," he snaps back. "We can't have people come in one week expecting a goddamn caramel river, and the next week only receive a drizzle. That shit is what makes people think we're skimping on ingredients."

"It's not that big of a deal. We need more caramel to balance the sweetness."

"That's not for you to decide. We're going off the goddamn recipe *I* wrote."

"Maybe your recipe needs to be revisited because the way *you* make it tastes like ass."

"The fuck did you just say to me?"

"You heard me. It. Tastes. Like. Ass."

"Take that back."

She crosses her arms. "No."

Peter tries to step in between them, trying to ease some of the tension. "Mom, Dad. Let's not fight, okay?"

"Shut the fuck up, Drenton!" Alexander and Eden both shout at the exact same time.

Eden rolls her eyes with a huff, turning on her heel to stomp off to the walk-in. Alexander follows without hesitation, unwilling to let this go. The door closes shut on them, trapping them in the small confines of the refrigerator.

"Go away."

"What the hell is your problem?"

She whips around with alarming speed, forcing his back against the frigid door. "You. You are my problem."

"Jesus, you're impossible."

"*I'm* impossible? You can't make it two minutes without berating your employees."

"I wouldn't have to berate them if they'd just do their fucking jobs."

"Mistakes happen. They happen all the time. Tearing a person down isn't going to help in the slightest. Rina looked like she was two seconds away from crying!"

"Then maybe she's not tough enough to be in my kitchen."

"Why does anybody have to be tough? I didn't realize that

being tough was a requirement to work in a fucking kitchen. But I guess that's what the mighty Alexander Chen needs to feel like a man, or whatever the fuck grumpy asshole persona you decide to use when you wake up in the morning."

"Don't fucking go there, Eden."

"No, I'd better not. Lord knows it won't do me a bit of good."

"I told you already. I'm not fucking ready to talk about it!"

"Yes, you've made that perfectly clear!"

"What the fuck are we even fighting about?"

"I don't fucking know—"

He cuts her off with a bruising kiss, pressing her up against the nearest storage shelves. Her hands fly up to his chest, clinging to his jacket as a gasp bubbles past her lips. He isn't sure what compels him to do it. Alexander hates seeing her upset; would do just about anything to make her feel okay. Eden sounds like she's going to cry, and it breaks his heart in two. She's like this because of him. God, he couldn't possibly hate himself more.

She shoves him away, their lips ripping apart.

It's more painful than a slap.

There's a ringing in his ears, but it's almost inaudible over the hard rush of blood pumping through his skull. The lights of the kitchen are too fucking bright. His skin is feverish and sore. He has never experienced exhaustion quite like this before. He feels like he's witnessing everything happen from two inches left of his actual body. No matter what he does, he can't get a grip.

It's too loud and it's too quiet. His body feels too heavy, but he also feels untethered and about to float away.

He wants to scream. He wants to cry. He wants to put his fucking head through the dishwasher.

Then something occurs to him. It's a sudden moment of clarity.

Staring down at Eden, he wonders how the fuck he got here. He thought she was the last person in the world he'd ever raise his voice to. He hates it. He doesn't mean to, nor does he want to continue. And yet here they are, at each other's throats, screaming like there's no tomorrow.

And for what?

He can't remember when being angry became his default setting. He can't remember how La Rouge became more important to him than the people in his life. He can't remember where Shang stopped and Alexander began. This job, this place, has chipped away at him for years. The constant grind, the never-ending orders, the relentless scrutiny of his every move.

He's alive, but he's dead. Hollow on the inside with nothing left to give. The demands of the job have drained him of all he has. He's in so much pain and under so much stress that he can't remember what life was like before Sebastian dug his claws into him.

He can't do this anymore. He won't.

Especially not if it means going up against Eden.

For once in his life, he's found something too important to him to let La Rouge and Sebastian destroy.

He might have done that all by himself. Something inside of him finally breaks.

"I'm done."

Eden blinks. "W-what? What do you mean?"

He doesn't mean to shut down, but he does. It's like his brain has ceased all functions for the sake of self-preservation. He processes nothing, the next few minutes a blur. He doesn't register sound or time or movement. All he knows is that he can't stay a moment longer.

He doesn't remember getting in his car.

He doesn't remember Eden calling after him.

He doesn't remember driving home.

He doesn't remember pulling out his phone and dialing a number he hasn't called in over a decade.

The phone rings five times before a woman answers. "Hello?"

Alexander clears his throat. "A-Ma? I... I need help."

# CHAPTER
## Twenty-Six

A lexander doesn't show up for work the next day. Or the day after that.

Or even the day after that.

The sinking feeling in Eden's chest won't go away. It's so intense that she isn't sure if she needs to vomit, cry, or scream. Maybe some kind of combination of all three, though she can't be quite sure.

It's hard for her not to worry. He up and left in the middle of service and hasn't been back since. She sent him a couple of texts asking after him, but they've all gone unanswered.

She wants to throw up because this feeling is all too familiar.

Waiting for her parents. Wondering when they were coming home. Sitting alone as the sun set with a ton of unanswered questions. Feeling anxious. Wanting to cry, but trying so desperately to be brave. Something's probably keeping them. She just has to be a good girl and wait.

She's angry, too. Not at him, but herself.

Now that she's had some time, she has nothing but ample opportunity to reflect on how wrong she was. How selfish, how childish, how cruel and unthinking.

She pushed him too hard. She kept poking and prodding under the excuse of wanting to get closer when she should have recognized his boundaries and respected them. Just because she's shared her secrets doesn't mean she has a right to his.

It's just that she's scared of not knowing. Not knowing means she feels out of control.

She's spent half her life not knowing about her parents, and it's instilled this deep, ugly, twisted insecurity within her very marrow. It's an insecurity that she wasn't fully aware of until now, and she feels that much more of a fool because of it.

Eden knows it's a poor excuse, but she can't rationalize it any other way.

She comes to work on the fourth day and finds that he still isn't there. She enters the kitchen office, but there isn't any sign of him. It's at this point that she really starts to panic. Alexander wasn't in a good state of mind when he left, and he sped away too quickly for Eden to get through to him.

She sits down in his office chair and sighs, resting her elbows on the desk before her. No one ever chooses to stay. No one ever chooses her.

Is it because she's broken? Is it because she's not good enough? Why else would people just throw her away?

There's a soft knock at the door. Eden nearly jumps out of her seat. "Alexander—"

Freddie pokes his head into the office, offering an apologetic smile. "Nope, sorry. Just me."

Eden slumps in her seat. "Oh."

"How're you doing?" he asks, moving to lean against the edge of the desk. Freddie folds his arms across his chest and observes her, calm and patient.

"I'm fine."

"Why don't I believe you?"

Eden shakes her head, too drained to keep up her brave face. "I made a mistake."

"With Chef?"

"I said some things that I shouldn't have."

"That can happen sometimes."

"No, I knew better. But that didn't stop me from pushing."

"Must have been pretty serious for him to dip on us like this."

Guilt twists in her stomach like a knife. "Yeah," she mumbles.

"Have you tried reaching out to him?"

"Several texts, but I haven't heard anything back. I'm afraid that if I try again, I'll be overstepping. More than I already have."

"I've seen the guy blow up before, but never quite like that. Do you think he might..."

"What?"

"Try something stupid."

Eden swallows. Now she really does want to puke. "Like hurt himself?"

"I don't know. Maybe. Himself, or someone else."

"God, I don't know." She starts to shake. "All he said was, '*I'm done.*' I have no idea what he meant by that. Does he mean he quits? Does he mean he's done with me? I just..."

"Hey, hey," Freddie coos, rubbing her gently on the back. "It's okay. Everything's going to be fine."

"What if it isn't? What if I've ruined everything before they've even begun?"

"Eden, deep breaths, hey? Deep breaths."

She follows his lead, inhaling through her nose and exhaling through her mouth. She feels fucking pathetic. She wishes she could take everything back.

"Look," Freddie says gently. "I don't know what's going on between the two of you or what's happened, but I can tell how much you care about each other. Sometimes we say and do things that can hurt those closest to us."

"But I should know better."

"Yes. But you're not perfect, Eden. Nobody is. Sometimes our emotions get the better of us. Sometimes we have lapses in judgment. It happens. Everyone makes mistakes. But what do we do after?"

Eden's jaw tenses. "We learn. And apologize."

Freddie nods. "Give the man a bit of space. You both need to cool off. Once you're both ready, then you can move forward."

"Thank you. I really needed to hear that."

"No problem, love."

"When did you get so smart?"

"I've always been smart. I know I may come across as the comedic relief of our little group, but I can promise you that I have a lot of wisdom to offer."

"Clearly."

"I was in the Army, you know. I've known my fair share of Alexander-types."

Eden sits up a bit straighter, intrigued. "You were in the Army?"

"Yeah. Enlisted out of high school. Not out of a sense of patriotism or anything, but because I wasn't ready for a life without structure and order. Found myself amongst a lot of like-minded individuals, a lot of whom had tempers like our favorite head chef here. Some of them were... deeply troubled, I guess you could say."

"How did you... I don't know. Bond with them, I guess? I'm sure it was imperative in that line of work."

Freddie shrugs. "By being patient. Everyone's got a backstory. Everyone has scars they need to heal. It's just that, for some, those scars can't be found on the skin. Some people never opened up to me, and that's okay. We could function together, work together, get the job done. Some of them did, and that was great, too. It definitely made the job easier, having that kind of rapport. But at the end of the day, nobody owed me any explanations. And it quite frankly wasn't my place to play detective and demand answers. Relationships have to be organic, not forced. Otherwise they don't last."

Eden nods, Freddie's words striking a chord with her. "I see that now."

He pats her on the shoulder. "He'll come around. You'll see. Just give him time."

"Yeah. I'm going to do that."

"Service is going to start soon. You feel like kicking tonight's ass?"

People come and people go. At the end of the day, she only has herself. She feels too much, loves too hard. Maybe that's why people leave her. Maybe she's too clingy. She demands too much. That's probably what makes it hard to be around her.

But if she puts on a smile and keeps marching forward, it'll leave no time to dwell on the past.

"Absolutely," she answers quietly.

She gets through service even though it's the weirdest feeling in the world not to be working by his side.

His absence is jarring, like she's missing a part of herself. She just doesn't feel right.

Closing routines have become second nature to Eden. She double checks that everything's been cleaned within an inch of its life—just in case the health inspector decides to make an impromptu visit—and then she makes note of all the ingredients they're running low on.

Alexander is usually the one who approves inventory orders, but she has to do it herself since there's no telling when he'll come back to work.

*If* he comes back to work.

Her mind is a haze. The last couple of days have been rough. Unable to sleep, haunted by the harshness of her own words.

Haunted by the look in Alexander's eyes as he left, empty and cold and lost. Haunted by Sebastian's offer, using every second since to doubt if she's even worth such generosity.

Eden wants to talk to someone about it, to make sense of it all, to find her place and her footing. Part of her wants to take the deal. Part of her wants to run as far away in the opposite direction as she can. She doesn't know what she wants anymore. A lot has changed recently, too much and too quickly. This sudden shift in the winds has her directionless, frantically staring down a storm she can see approaching.

The only person she wants to talk to about the offer won't return her texts. The only person she wants to talk to at all, she needlessly hurt.

*God, I hope he's okay.*

"Eden," Rina calls from the doors. "We're headed out. Need a ride?"

"No, thank you. I've got a bit of work to finish here. I'll see you all tomorrow."

"Don't work yourself too hard," Peter says with a light laugh.

"See you tomorrow," adds Freddie as the trio walk out the door.

And then it's just her, in the middle of the quiet kitchen without a clue as to what to do next. She pulls out her phone to see if she's missed any messages, but there are no new notifications waiting for her. With a heavy sigh, she types up one last message. One that's sincere, one that's understanding.

> Eden: I'm sorry. I know you probably don't want to talk to me, but can you at least let me know if you're safe? I promise not to bother you anymore, if that's what you want.

She sends it off without a second thought and stuffs her phone in her pocket before grabbing her coat and locking up.

The bus ride home is a miserable one. Long, draining, and the seats smell a bit musty. It's a relief when she arrives at her stop, located just a few blocks from her actual apartment building. She walks the rest of the way, pulling her thin jacket closed over her chest against the cold night. She's brisk in her journey home, shivering the whole way.

It's when she sees an Audi parked out front that she takes pause, her heart suddenly in her throat.

Alexander sits on the curb side, long legs extending out before him. He doesn't look angry. He doesn't look sad. It's like the fire within him has been snuffed out.

He just looks numb.

*I'm done.*

Eden holds her breath and cautiously takes a seat next to him, the cold of the pavement seeping through her work pants and biting at her skin. She doesn't say anything. Neither does he. Eden contemplates asking how he's been, but one look and it's fairly obvious.

Alexander's in rough shape. Not as bad as she expected, but his weariness is almost palpable.

There are dark circles beneath his eyes. His normally luscious black locks are knotted and a little greasy. He smells like an ashtray.

Eden's the first to give in and speak.

"I'm sorry," she whispers. "I'm so sorry. I overstepped and I didn't respect your boundaries and I promise never to do that again. But I'd also understand if you... If you don't want to keep seeing me. I said things I shouldn't have and... Fuck. I was a lot more eloquent in my texts." She laughs bitterly.

"You sent texts?"

She glances at him. "Yes? A good dozen. I was trying to check up on you, but you never answered."

"Broke my phone," he replies curtly.

"You what?"

"My phone. Broke it." He runs a hand through his hair. "I was... angry. I called my mother and she... She has that effect on me. So I broke my phone."

Eden swallows, incredulous. "Your mother? What—" She stops herself. It's none of her business. If he feels like sharing, great. Until then, she's learned her lesson about prying. "I was really worried about you," she says instead. She chews on the inside of her cheek to keep from crying. It doesn't help. Her eyes feel hot with the threat of tears, the mounting pressure inside her skull too strong to fight against any longer.

"You said you were done. Did you mean with me?"

Alexander shakes his head, frustrated. "No, I—Ah, shit. I'm sorry. I know how bad that sounds. Please don't cry, Eden, I—"

It's too late.

It hits her like a runaway train.

Frustration, followed by a quick and heavy dose of alleviation.

She sobs into her hands. "Do you have any idea how scared I was? You left. You just *left.* You said you were done and you drove off and didn't answer my calls and I thought—" Her voice is shaky. It's squeaky and pathetic and cracking all over the place. "I was so worried. What if you got in an accident or something? What if you were hurt? Dead in a ditch somewhere? There would have been no way for me to know if you were okay or not and I—"

It suddenly occurs to her that a runaway train isn't a good enough analogy. This hits much harder. Deeper.

Darker.

"I don't want to have to look for you, too!"

The silence that follows is brutal.

"Shit," Alexander mutters to himself. "Fuck, Eden. I forgot all about—"

She shakes her head, trying to shake herself free of the thoughts. "No, no. It's fine."

"It's not fine."

"I don't want to make this about me. I'm just glad that you're alright."

"Eden?"

"What?"

"Can I hug you?"

She nods quickly, eagerly. No sooner is she wrapped up in his arms.

Every ounce of stress she has bottled up in her body evaporates. She feels safe. She feels good.

She feels like she's home.

"I'm sorry," he murmurs into her hair. "I wasn't thinking. I shouldn't have left the way I did—"

"Don't apologize. You have nothing to apologize for."

"Yes. Yes, I do. You're important to me, Eden. I shouldn't have shut you out."

"You only did that because I carried on the way I did. I shouldn't have pushed you."

"That's no excuse to stonewall you. It's just... My brain shut off. I wasn't thinking because I couldn't."

"You don't have to explain yourself to me. Not unless you want to. I'm just so glad you're safe."

"This was just a stupid fight."

"Yeah. Really stupid."

He breathes her in. Eden melts into his touch.

"Jesus," he grumbles. "You're freezing. Do you want to go inside?"

"Yes, please," she mutters through chattering teeth.

They end up on her couch. He sits forward while she straddles his lap, chest to chest, arms draped over his shoulders as they continue to embrace.

They're like this for a long while, holding each other. Recharging. They say nothing. Neither of them has the energy to start. Eden knows they have a lot to talk about still, but for now, this is fine.

He rubs his palms up and down the curve of her back. She closes her eyes and rests her face in the crook of his neck.

"I should have said that I quit," he says softly. "Not that I'm done. That was a poor choice of words."

"You quit?"

"That place... I think being at La Rouge makes me crazy."

"You're not crazy."

"It makes me *feel* crazy. I feel like..." He tilts his head back and rests it against the back of the couch. "I feel like I was always going to explode. It was just a matter of time. I'm just sorry that you had to see it. I'm sorry that I didn't reach out sooner. It wasn't my intention to frighten you."

All Eden can do is nod. She doesn't mind. Sure, in the moment, it had been frightening to see him leave. But Alexander's here now, and that's what matters most to her.

"Are you really alright with that?" she asks softly. "I'm not questioning your choice. I just want to know if you've thought this through."

"I haven't. That's why I needed some time away. To think. I thought working on a new menu would help inspire me. Turns out, it's even more of a drag. Honest to God, the only time I felt even remotely okay was when I was cooking with you."

Eden smiles gently. "Do you mean that you're done with La Rouge, or cooking in general?"

"I don't know. Maybe both. It's kind of terrifying." He sighs. "It's *really* terrifying. This is all I've ever known. Food is my passion. *Was* my passion. I can't imagine doing anything else with my life, but I also know that I can't keep doing things like this. I'm... I'm tired. I'm exhausted. I need a break. From all of it."

She sits back and takes in his face. She believes him, can see the fatigue in the lines of his face. She's personally experienced burnout once or twice, but what Alexander's going through...

This is on a whole other level. A devastating one.

"Whatever you need," she tells him, cupping his cheeks in her hands. "I promise I'll be here. Not pushing. Just... here."

"Thank you, Eden. I needed to hear that."

"What now?"

"I'm going to visit my mother," he says. "She lives upstate. That's why I called her."

Eden blinks. "Oh. I thought you said—"

"That I broke my phone after? Yeah, uh... I was just in a bad headspace."

"H-how long will you be gone?"

"I'm not sure yet."

Her stomach flips. "So you *are* leaving."

Alexander holds her a bit tighter. "No, sweetheart. I'll be back before you know it."

She sets her jaw. She's heard this particular song before. But she swallows her fear and forces herself to nod. She can't be selfish. Not right now. It's so obvious that he needs this, this time and distance to heal and recuperate. She can't make this about herself.

"I understand," she mumbles. "Just promise to get a new phone so we can keep in touch?"

"I'm buying a new one first thing in the morning."

"When do you leave?"

"Tomorrow. Right after I hand in my formal resignation to Sebastian."

She sucks in a sharp breath through clenched teeth. "Oh."

"What is it?"

"Nothing."

"Eden."

"Let's focus on you, yeah?"

"Your needs aren't second to mine, sweetheart. We're both going through some shit. Does this have to do with your meeting with him?"

She nods, hesitant.

Alexander sits up a little straighter. "What did he do? Did he say something to you?"

"He offered me a job," she recounts quietly. "Gave me this massive check saying it would be my signing bonus. He wants me to be a head chef at one of his other restaurants."

He stiffens, hard as a rock beneath her. The dark edge of a quiet fury tenses his muscles, a flicker of something hateful flashing across his eyes.

Not at her, of course. Never at her. It's an anger for her. "What did you say?" he asks, voice low and strained.

"That I'd think about it. But..."

"But?"

"It doesn't feel right. Working for him." Eden picks at beneath her nails, unable to concentrate otherwise. "He's always rubbed me the wrong way. The way he talks and says nice things, but it always seems pointed and condescending. Or the look in his eyes. He creeps me out, and as much as I want to run a restaurant one day, I definitely don't want to be under his thumb. And I've... I've seen how he stresses you out. How he treats you. I would never willingly work for a man like that."

"You're not just saying this because it's what I want to hear, is it?"

"No, of course not. I genuinely feel this way. I think I'm... Yeah. I'm going to decline. I would have done it sooner, but I wanted to talk to someone about it first. And you were really the only person I wanted to talk to. But now I'm worried he'll be bitter about it. Like he'll make my life at La Rouge a living hell if I stay."

"If he does, I'll make him regret it."

"Alexander—"

"I'm serious, Eden."

"I'm sure he won't," she says, more to herself than to him. "It'll be fine. I'll word it super politely or something."

He's clearly dissatisfied with the answer, but has no response. He settles for kissing the tip of her nose.

"Will you promise to text me when you get there?" she asks after a while.

"I promise."

She holds onto him for a little while longer, relieved to find the weight bearing down on her chest has subsided. Eden doesn't want him to go, but she also understands that this is what he needs.

The only thing she wants is what's best for him.

Even if that means they have to be apart. Even for just a little while.

# CHAPTER
## Twenty-Seven

Pulling into the driveway of his childhood home is surreal. Everything in Bellingham, Washington is the same, but it also isn't.

The porch swing is still there, but its white paint job has been chipped away from years of exposure to wind and rain. His mother's rose garden, the one tucked directly in front of the porch, is still here, too. But it isn't as grand or as vibrant as it used to be. It's entirely likely that Chen Xu Hong simply doesn't have time to tend to the garden anymore. Especially since looking after her husband has become a full-time occupation.

*No thanks to me.*

The neighborhood is nice and quiet. They live in a polite little cul-de-sac deep in the suburbs of Chicago, so the roaring sounds of the city that Alexander is used to is effectively non-existent. It's a nice change of pace. Peaceful, calm. But as he approaches the front door of the house, he knows his momentary respite won't last for long.

He rings the doorbell, listens to it chime inside. A part of him panics. He still has time to turn around and drive back to the city if he wants to. He definitely wants to.

The door opens.

It's too late to retreat now.

He has to dip his head down to look Xu Hong in the eye. It's startling how different she looks. Older, wiser. Tired. The rich black hair he remembers her having is now peppered with white and silver, especially at the temples. Her face has aged elegantly, fine lines and wrinkles at the corners of her eyes and brow. Her lips have thinned out, but they still wear the same gentle smile.

She reaches out to hug him, patting him comfortingly on the back. "Welcome home," she whispers.

Alexander hugs her back. Holding his mother feels like a foreign experience, but is somehow familiar all the same. He doesn't know what to say. He's not even sure if there's anything to say. So he settles for hugging Xu Hong and tries not to think about how alarmingly small and frail she's become.

"How was the drive?" she asks, hooking her arm around his to guide him inside.

"Not bad. Nice and light."

"Good. That's good. I heard there might have been delays on the I-43 due to construction."

"Must have missed rush hour."

"I see."

Alexander feels... weird. It's evident that neither of them particularly gives a damn about the traffic. They're talking about nothing.

But at least they're talking. Thirty seconds in and nobody's screaming, so Alexander's going to count that as a win and roll with it. It's a new world record for them. His phone call the other day lasted only fifteen seconds before Xu Hong demanded to know why the hell a stranger was calling her so late claiming to be her son.

*Aiyah, this is one of those scams, isn't it? You're not going to trick me out of my social security number!*

Her initial inability to recognize his voice had hurt him, but he understood all the same.

He had barely recognized her voice, too.

Time tends to do that to a person's memories.

And the distance he chose will forever be his burden to bear. The guilt has been eating away at him for years, but he's here now. He's here now and in some small way, he's proud of himself for that.

"I'm glad that you're here," Xu Hong tells him as they enter the living room. It's a rustic space, decorated like they live out on a ranch somewhere in the midwest. Alexander knows that his mother was originally born and raised in South Carolina in a rich farming community that boasted fields of gold wheat and corn. Maybe decorating the house this way makes her feel more comfortable, more at home.

"I'm sorry to be an inconvenience," he says, muttering under his breath. He doesn't know why he feels the need to tip-toe around the subject. He called his mother, practically hyperventilating not even twelve hours before.

"I'll show you to your room."

"I know where my room is, A-Ma."

"We turned it into an office space after you..."

He clears his throat. "Right."

Looks like they're going to tip-toe around things, after all.

"All of your stuff is still there," she assures. "We just had to turn my old office space into a room for your father since he can't use the stairs."

He takes a deep breath. "How is he?"

"A royal pain in my ass."

"Unsurprising."

Xu Hong chuckles. "He's good. He was actually very happy to hear that you were coming to visit." And then, much softer, "He's missed you a lot. We all have."

Something sharp stabs him in the chest, his fight or flight instincts finally kicking into high gear. He thought he was ready for this. He thought he was finally strong enough to come home and face his biggest fears, face the family he'd left behind. But now all he wants is to make a break for the door.

He could do it, too. It'd take four or five long strides and he'd be back outside in a jiffy.

It's not like Xu Hong is in any condition to chase after him anymore.

That thought makes him sadder still. Xu Hong used to chase him up and down these very halls when he was a boy, always able to catch him and drag him off to take his bath. Now Alexander's biggest worry is that if he does bolt and Xu Hong runs after, she might slip on the hallway rug and tumble and hurt herself. He honestly isn't sure when she became so fragile to him.

All parents do, he supposes, at some point or another.

"Let's put your things down," she suggests gently. "Then we'll go and see him, hm?"

Alexander nods, throat impossibly dry.

He's shown to his room. It used to be the guest room/storage room when he was a boy. Now it's full of his things, all neatly preserved. Almost like he never left.

His posters are still here, hanging on the walls. Alexander wonders if Xu Hong put them up all by herself, or if she had Uncle Charlie help her get to those particularly high places. There's a shelf full of his old trophies, too, all covered in a thin layer of dust.

There's one from the time his school's soccer team won first place at state. There's one from the time he earned the top academic award in the eighth grade. There's also a plaque from the local Chicago chili cook off that he won with Uncle Charlie when he was only thirteen years old.

He smiles at his things, thinking back with a warmth he

hasn't felt in ages. It's odd how much of a guest he feels like in his own home. He was a part of its history, but now he feels too far removed.

Alexander sets his bag down—it's got a few shirts, clean pants, and notably nothing to do with cooking—at the foot of the bed.

He steels himself for what's about to happen next.

It's long overdue. He can't keep running from his past forever.

Xu Hong takes him back downstairs and guides him toward what has now transformed into Li's room. It's understandable that he'd be relocated to the first floor where it's easier to get him in and out. Alexander distinctly remembers sending a healthy check to install an elevator, but Xu Hong had declined citing the lack of enough support beams throughout the house.

He sends money often, knowing full well that Li was the main income owner of the household. It was true that Xu Hong had a nice pension plan in place from her brief time as the local mayor, but with all the medical bills and household upkeep... Sending them a part of his salary every month is his way of helping out, even if it's distant and impersonal.

Li lies in the center of a custom-ordered bed, one designed with an adjustable bed frame so that he can choose to sit upright or lay flat with the touch of a button. The room is very much like the living room, full of color and woodwork for a nice cohesive, welcoming feel. In the opposite corner is an electric wheelchair, tucked away to recharge. It's an older model, not too flashy and without all the bells and whistles.

"The prodigal son returns," Li says with a good-natured chuckle. The term stings, but Alexander knows he deserves it.

"A-Ba."

"Come here. Let me look at my boy."

Alexander approaches slowly, like he's afraid. Deep down, he *is* afraid.

Xu Hong aged with grace. Li, on the other hand, looks like an entirely different person.

Alexander remembers a man who towered over everyone in the room. Someone with a big, commanding voice who was able to charm everyone he came across. Alexander remembers a father with snark and sass. A man who knew what he wanted and lived by no one else's rules. He remembers a man who ran his mechanic shop with an iron fist, taking no prisoners when it came to half-assed jobs.

That sounds awfully familiar. Alexander figures he must get that part of himself from Li. Who knew he had so much of his father's heart in him?

The man before Alexander looks nothing like the man he once knew. Li is a lot smaller, skinnier due to loss of muscle. His hair is almost completely gray, and his face sags in several places. His eyes are the same, though. Full of kindness, full of mischief. When Li smiles at him, there isn't a hint of sadness or disappointment or anger like Alexander thought would come to pass.

There's nothing but forgiveness.

Alexander sits down on a vacant chair next to Li's bed, Xu Hong sitting directly next to him in another. He leans forward, allowing his father to reach up and brush his fingers up against the faded scar on his cheek.

"This healed nicely," Li says fondly. "That's too bad. I hear chicks dig scars."

Alexander wants to laugh. He wants to cry. He settles for a wistful smile. "My girl seems to like me just fine."

Li gasps. "You have a girl?"

"Is that so hard to believe?"

"Is this like the time you said you had a girlfriend in middle school, but she turned out to be imaginary?"

"You're never going to let that one go, huh?"

"You just didn't want me to chaperone you to the school dance."

"Because you were going to get all dressed up in that ugly velvet suit of yours and insist on taking pictures."

"It's a rite of passage, son."

"I don't believe you for a second."

"What's her name, then? If you haven't made her up."

Alexander smiles. "Her name's Eden. She's my sous chef."

Xu Hong chuckles. "Oh my. A workplace romance? What's she like?"

"Feisty," he replies, easily imagining the fire behind her beautiful eyes. "Tough. But sweet, too. She can cook circles around me."

"I like her already. We'd love to meet her one day."

"Yeah. I want you to meet her, too."

A heavy pause falls over them. Alexander isn't sure what to say or do. He doesn't know how to begin. What is he supposed to say after a decade away without so much as a phone call? He'd left in such a hurry after the accident, blinded by his shame and guilt and anger. But he's older now. Wiser. A whole lot less brash and impulsive, as hard as that may be to believe.

This is a Band-Aid that he needs to rip off.

"I'm sorry," he blurts out, unable to meet his father's gaze. "I'm so sorry. For everything. I should have listened to you guys. I should have listened to Uncle Charlie. Sebastian was a mistake and you told me as much, but I wouldn't listen." His face warms with remorse, vision blurring with tears he has no control over. He's a little boy again, no longer a man. "I shouldn't have gone to Paris. I shouldn't have—"

Xu Hong hushes him, gingerly rubbing his shoulders while

Li places a hand on his son's lowered head.

"Stop it, son," Li says firmly. "What's done is done. There's no point beating yourself up about the past."

"But you're like this because of me."

"No. I'm like this because that asshole got drunk behind the wheel and swerved into our lane."

"You wouldn't have been out on the road if I hadn't asked you to pick me up."

"Shang."

Alexander cringes. It all comes rushing back to him.

The flight from Paris to New York is roughly eight hours and twenty minutes non-stop. Shang's butt is sore from sitting so long. He's grumpy, too, because he's running on less than an hour of sleep. Who's idea was it to allow crying babies onto planes again?

Li meets him at international arrivals just like he said he would.

His mother is noticeably absent.

"Is Mom still—"

"Pissed? Yeah."

Even though Shang expected as much, his chest still stings. He hasn't spoken to Xu Hong in over a year and a half. The phone works both ways, of course, but it's pretty obvious that he inherited his mother's stubbornness.

It's another twenty minutes of awkward standing around while they wait for his suitcase at baggage claim. Shang doesn't know what to say. Neither does Li. Small talk feels like a waste of energy. Besides, there are people around. The one consistent thing in Shang's life growing up was the fact that his family never aired their dirty laundry in public. Arguments were reserved for behind closed doors, never out in the open.

*This is why when they finally hop into Li's old clunker of a Ford truck and the doors close, Shang isn't at all surprised when his father blurts out, "You need to apologize to your mother."*

*He sighs. "Here we go."*

*"Don't give me attitude, son," Li snaps in Cantonese. He merges onto the highway. It's raining so hard that the wiper blades can't keep up. "This isn't up for debate."*

*"I don't understand why you can't be more supportive!" Shang snaps right back. "Sebastian's already made me chef de partie. He's promised to make me a sous chef in less than a year."*

*"That man is bad news."*

*"He isn't. He's done more for me in six months than Uncle has my whole life!"*

*"Sebastian is using you! Why can't you see that?" Li reaches into the door-side pocket and pulls out a page ripped out from a magazine. "What's this, ha?"*

*The page lands on Shang's lap. It's a picture of him, posing behind a carefully set prep table with knives and assorted spices and prepared plates of food. Just below the image is a caption that reads:* 'Chef Alexander Chen, the next great prodigy?'

*"What's wrong with your real name?" his father demands. "It's a good name. A strong name!"*

*"Sebastian doesn't think that it's marketable."*

*"Marketable? What's that supposed to mean?"*

*"You wouldn't understand."*

*"Then explain it to me!"*

*"I'm already enough of an outsider. Do you really think someone who looks like me has a chance of being taken seriously doing what I do?"*

*"Don't change for them! You are more than enough!"*

*"Do you have any idea how many times they told me to go back to China? Or to stop fooling around and go back to making dumplings? I've never even been to China!"*

"Don't listen to them!" his father snaps.

"Or what about all the times when they start making references to that dumb Disney movie? I'm so fucking sick of people telling me to 'be a man.'"

"They're in the wrong. Not you!"

Shang groans. "Would you just—"

It happens all at once.

The flash of oncoming lights. The screech of tires. Shattered glass, warped metal. The impact is so powerful, it forces their truck to roll, landing top-side-down in the ditch. He hits his head so hard, he blacks out.

When he opens his eyes again, he wakes up in the hospital. He's never experienced pain like this before. An open gash across his cheek. Both his arms, broken. Ribs, cracked. He doesn't understand how he's alive.

His mother's soft sobs bring him back to reality. She's at his bedside, weeping into her palms. If she's here, then where's—

"Dad?" he rasps, panic rising in his chest. "Where's Dad?"

Xu Hong shakes her head, body trembling too hard to even speak. Shang fears the worst, but the truth is so much crueler. There aren't enough words to describe his guilt and shame.

"I'm sorry I didn't come home sooner," Alexander mutters pathetically. "I know you're mad at me."

Xu Hong shakes her head. "We were never mad at you," she whispers.

"Disappointed, then."

"Never," Li says. "We just didn't want to see you throw your life away."

"We've always wanted you here," Xu Hong adds. "But we

knew you had to choose to come back. Nobody could force you."

"I regret taking as long as I did."

"Let the past stay in the past," Xu Hong coos, brushing some of Alexander's hair out of his eyes. "All that matters now is that you're here."

"Still. I'm so sorry."

"There's nothing to apologize for."

"It was an accident," Li reminds. "It wasn't your fault."

He smiles weakly, understandably drained. "I love you both."

"We know," Li says with a smirk.

Xu Hong curls into him and hugs him tight while Li squeezes his hand. Alexander's still shaky, but he feels a million tons lighter. Bubbly, even. Like all of his troubles are starting to evaporate and rise into nothingness. He didn't know how much he needed his family until this moment. It's startling how much Sebastian has managed to rip away from him.

But not anymore.

"How about you wash up?" asks Xu Hong. "I'm steaming a marinated crab as we speak. We can have dinner and you can tell us all about your job."

He grimaces. "Or lack thereof. We, uh... We have a lot to catch up on."

"Forget the job," Li mutters. "I want to hear more about this imaginary girlfriend of yours."

"She's not imaginary."

"Uh-huh."

"She's real, Dad."

"Sure, sure."

"I'm serious."

"I'll believe you when I see her."

His mother smiles, kissing him on the temple. He closes his eyes and relaxes. He's safe.

He's home.

# CHAPTER
## Twenty-Eight

Alexander: I'm here. I miss you.

Eden reads his text over and over again until the words are seared into the back of her eyes. She misses him, too. A lot. Eden can feel it in her bones, in the way she constantly looks to her left expecting him to be there. She's sure she'll have the kitchen running smoothly, but there's no denying how different it will feel being at the front of the line all alone.

Except she's not alone. Not really.

Sebastian pulls her into the kitchen office as soon as she arrives at La Rouge, seething. His eyes are bloodshot with controlled rage, the vein at his temple pulsing.

"What's the meaning of this?" he asks, holding up what she assumes is Alexander's resignation letter. "Did he say anything to you? Where is he?"

"It's as much of a surprise to you as it is to me," she says in as even a tone as she can muster.

"That ungrateful little..." Sebastian grumbles something under his breath. What it is, Eden can't be sure, though she knows it's likely nothing flattering. "No matter. I was going to get rid of him sooner or later."

"W-what?"

"Don't worry about it, my dear. It's just business."

Eden's stomach flips. She doesn't believe Sebastian for a second. She gets the sense that this is a lot more personal than he's letting on.

"Have you thought much more about my offer?" he asks, shredding Alexander's letter into tiny pieces before carelessly tossing it in the nearby garbage bin.

She steels herself, standing that much straighter and holding her head high. "I have."

"Excellent. Which restaurant would you like to run? Obviously La Rouge is now available to—"

"Actually," she says quickly, "I've decided to decline."

Sebastian freezes. Insulted. In disbelief. He looks like he's been slapped clean across the face. Eden wonders, ever so briefly, if she should.

"You *decline*?" he echoes, words dripping with something cold and cruel.

"Your offer was most gracious," Eden replies politely. "But I believe such an opportunity should go to someone much more deserving. I still have a lot to learn in my role as sous chef, and I cannot confidently say that I will be able to lead an entire restaurant at my current skill level."

She's stiff in her delivery, but only because she's rehearsed her little spiel in the mirror too many times to count. A deliberately crafted speech designed to be polite, but direct. Sebastian has one of two options: accept, or lose his shit. Eden sincerely doubts he's willing to come out as the true snake in human flesh that he is, so it comes as no surprise when Sebastian relaxes into a smile.

A venomous smile, but it's better than the alternative.

"I hope you understand how rare my offer is," he says slowly. "I could turn you into a star, my dear. Even greater than Alexander ever was. Under my tutelage, there isn't anywhere in the world you can't go without someone knowing your name. Think about it a little harder, Eden. Fame, fortune, your own restaurant, even your own cooking show. Alexander never liked the spotlight. But you? You could shine, my dear. Brighter than anyone else. I could give you everything."

Eden bites down on her tongue. There are only two things she really wants: to find her parents, and to be with Alexander.

And she isn't willing to sacrifice herself to Sebastian to achieve either of those goals.

Faking her way into the sous chef position at La Rouge had been a means to an end. Signing on with Sebastian permanently had never been in her original game plan.

She forces a smile. "Like I said, sir. I'm afraid I will have to decline. But thank you."

Sebastian's expression darkens. "I will not ask again, Eden."

"And I won't answer again."

"Then you leave me no choice."

"Pardon?"

He turns toward the office door. "Hector, my boy. Come on in, please."

Her stomach lurches as she spots a familiar tuft of red hair and a smarmy grin walking into the small space. There's triumph in Hector's eyes. Eden has never wanted to punch someone more.

"What's going on?" she demands, unable to shake the uneasiness in her tone. She's outnumbered now, and Hector has made no secret of his distaste for her.

"I was curious to learn about Hector's termination," Sebastian says simply. "Alexander normally informs me of such things. I reached out to learn the full story."

"There was always something about you that bothered me," Hector sneers. "Nobody seemed to notice, but I did. I did some digging, asked around. Alexander isn't the only one with connections. I called a few schools, but nobody knows who you are." He folds his arms across his chest, puffing it out like he's won. "You never went to culinary school, Eden. You lied. And now Alexander isn't here to protect you anymore."

Sebastian shakes his head. "I was willing to overlook this when I first found out. You clearly have talent, and I'm all for defending my head chefs for the sake of my restaurant's reputations. But now that you've declined..."

Eden blanches. No words come to mind. Her guts are in a knot and her stomach is seconds away from throwing up her breakfast.

She could beg. Beg to keep her job, beg Sebastian to overlook her lack of formal education, beg them not to tell anybody.

But she knows better. She's too smart and too proud and too strong to let people like Sebastian and Hector walk all over her. It's all business to them. Soulless and calculated and all for the sake of climbing to the top to rake in the cash. And even while having a steady paycheck with a healthy excess to save away to help find her parents, Eden has never seen food the way they do.

Food is beautiful. It brings people together, feeds both the stomach and the soul. Her happiest—and admittedly few— memories are of her and her parents at the dinner table, feasting on the simplest of meals while enjoying each other's company. Her happiest memories are of her and Alexander in the kitchen together, learning from each other, feeding each other. Working for Sebastian will only taint what food and cooking means to her.

"What do you have to say for yourself?" Hector asks, so clearly pleased with himself, it's almost painfully infuriating.

"Thank you."

"What?"

"Thank you. For helping me realize what a garbage place this is." Eden takes off her apron and tosses it at Hector. He doesn't catch it in time, so it hits him square in the face. "I quit," she announces proudly before turning to leave.

"Well, looks like the head chef position's all yours," Sebastian says.

"I can't wait to get started," Hector replies.

Eden doesn't bother sticking around to listen to the rest of their conversation. She follows in Alexander's footsteps and walks straight out the door.

She's free.

The gravity of the situation doesn't really hit her until she returns home and proceeds to count her tin of hidden cash. She does this every day, at least once—sometimes more than that when she's particularly anxious—as a sort of soothing ritual. Eden counts and counts and then she counts again, the sinking feeling in her chest spreading to her core.

She's two grand short. Just two thousand dollars away from what she needs to hire Maxine Kendo. A measly two thousand away from finding her parents.

Tears sting her eyes as a pressure builds inside her skull. She was so close.

Eden sits on the edge of her bed, exhausted and a little shaky, convincing herself that there's nothing she could do. She doesn't know what this will mean for her future. Knowing Sebastian's slimy nature and Hector's vindictive streak, they may very well drag her name through the dirt and blacklist her all over town.

Even still, leaving was the only option, especially now that the jig is up. Especially now that Hector is back. Especially now that Alexander isn't there. She can always find another job. She's scrappy that way. But still, the pang of knowing how close she came seeps into her marrow and leaves her bitter inside.

"Stupid Sebastian," she grumbles to herself as she lays her head down on the pillow. "Stupid Hector."

Eden isn't entirely sure when sleep takes hold of her, but the next thing she knows, her phone's blowing up with all sorts of messages.

> Rina: Saw you storm out… Where are you? Are you okay?

> Freddie: Hey, love! Just checking up on you. Text me back soon!

> Peter: WHY THE FUCK IS THE GINGER BACK I CAN'T—

> Peter: EDEN PLEASE TELL ME YOU'RE COMING BACK!

> Peter: OH GOD HE'S IN CHARGE!?

> Peter: I WISH FOR A SWIFT AND PAINLESS DEATH I—

She doesn't have the strength to text them back just yet. She knows she needs to tell her friends the truth sooner rather than later. Lord knows Hector will have no problem spewing all sorts of hate. A part of her is worried that her friends will come to resent her just as Hector had—though he was always a spiteful little bitch—but still.

What if Rina, Freddie, and Peter think she's full of it? What if they can't bring themselves to forgive her? She needs to reach out and be honest with them.

But not now. Not when she's tired and adrift and unsure what to do next.

She sends them each a quick message to say she's fine and that she'll explain things later.

Eden rolls over in bed, partly sleepy, partly grumpy. She should have known Hector would be back to stir the pot. Rats always find a way to survive, after all.

There's really only one person she wants to talk to right now, but she isn't sure if Alexander is busy or not. She sends a quick text to double check.

> Eden: Hey, can I call you?

> Eden: If not, it's not a big dea

She doesn't even finish typing up her sentence. Her phone starts to ring, a familiar name popping up on her screen.

He's FaceTiming her.

She quickly runs her fingers through her hair to brush it out and wipes the weariness from her eyes before answering.

"You don't have to ask for permission to call me, sweetheart," he says the second she picks up.

*God.*

It never ceases to amaze her how handsome he is. Alexander actually seems refreshed for a change, like he's managed a decent night's sleep. His hair is pulled into a half-up, half-down situation, giving Eden ample time to take in the hard line of his jaw and the thickness of his neck. It's then, and only then, that she realizes he's shirtless.

Shirtless and sweaty.

*Yum.*

"I didn't want to disturb you," she says with a light giggle, snuggling into her pillow. "I know how much you hate texting."

"My thumbs are too big."

"What are you doing right now?"

"I was just out for a run."

"Didn't take you for much of a jogger."

"I don't like to run in the city. Too much going on. Streets are quiet here, though, but I'm really out of shape."

"You? Out of shape? Have you passed a mirror lately?"

"You flatter me."

"Where are you now?"

"Just got back to my parents' house. I'm on the porch." He moves the phone in a way to show off his surroundings. There are manicured lawns and expensive SUVs in most driveways and houses lined up in neat little rows. The sun looks to be setting where he is, painting the sky a soft pink and orange. The house in question looks lovely, the epitome of suburban life.

Eden laughs. "I believe you. How are things? With your parents, I mean."

"Good, actually. Better than I thought. Wait. What time is it? Aren't you supposed to be at the restaurant right now?"

"It's a long story."

"I've got time."

"You should go home before you catch a chill. I don't want you to get sick."

"Aww, you worried about me?"

"Always."

"What happened, Eden?"

"I don't want to stress you out."

"You *do* understand that not telling me stresses me out more, right?"

Eden takes a deep breath. "I told Sebastian I wasn't going to take his offer. He wasn't very happy about it."

"And then what happened?"

"Well, then he brought Hector in and—"

"Hector?"

259

"Yeah."

"What the fuck?"

"I'm..." Eden shakes her head. "Hector found out. That I didn't go to culinary school. I don't know if he had any hard proof, but I was so stunned that I didn't deny it. I just kind of left after that."

"Oh, Eden, are you okay?"

"Yeah, as weird as that might sound. I'm just tired."

"I'm sorry, sweetheart. I know how important that job was to you."

"Don't be sorry. I'm sure I'll land on my feet."

"I should be there with you."

"No. I don't want you to worry about me."

"I always worry about you."

Behind him, Eden can see the front door to the house swing open, a flood of golden light pouring out onto the porch. She can just make out the silhouette of an older woman.

"I thought I heard you out here," the woman says. "Who are you talking to?"

"Eden," Alexander answers.

"Oh, I want to meet her. Let me see!"

"No need to grab, A-Ma!"

There's a bit of a shuffle, but the phone's camera eventually falls on her face. Eden sits up in bed, smiling in the hopes of making a good first impression.

"Hello, ma'am," Eden greets. "It's very nice to meet you."

"Oh, you weren't lying when you said she's gorgeous. Hi, dear. Please, just call me Xu Hong."

"What's happening?" comes yet another voice, this time from a gruff sounding man.

"Li, look! *Hěn piàoliang-ah!*"

The next person Eden sees is an older gentleman with silver hair and bushy eyebrows.

She's inside their home, she realizes, catching a glimpse of Alexander's childhood surroundings. The man—Li—smiles. He sits rather stiffly in a high-back leather armchair.

"She *is* very pretty! Looks like you're not an imaginary girlfriend, after all."

"Jesus Christ," Alexander grumbles somewhere in the background. "Can I please have my phone back?"

"Yes, but only if you put on a shirt," Xu Hong replies. "You're going to catch a chill."

"That's what I said," Eden notes with a light laugh.

"Go on. Upstairs with you." Xu Hong turns to face the screen. "Sorry about him. He's always been such a stubborn boy."

"That's alright. I can handle it."

"Shang tells me you're a sous chef."

*Shang.* Eden's smile tightens ever so slightly. She promises herself she won't push, not again, even despite her confusion and burning curiosity.

"Um, yeah," she says quietly. "I mean, I *was* a sous chef. I actually quit earlier today."

"Oh, I'm sorry to hear that."

"Don't be. La Rouge just wasn't a good fit for me, that's all."

"Such is the way of life, isn't it?" Li says with a chuckle. "There's no need to worry, though. When one door closes, another one opens. That's what I always say."

"I suppose this means you have a lot of free time on your hands now, eh?" Xu Hong asks.

"I guess so."

Li and Xu Hong exchange a look, grinning to one another.

"If that's the case," Xu Hong starts, "you're more than welcome to come stay with us for a little while. I'm sure Shang would love your company. Lord knows we'd love to get to know you better."

Eden blinks, flushing in surprise. "That's really generous of you, but I wouldn't want to impose."

"Nonsense, dear, we'd love to have you." Xu Hong turns to shout over her shoulder. "Isn't that right, Shang?"

Alexander's returned, dressed in a tight light grey shirt that shows off the width of his chest and his ridiculously strong arms. Eden thinks it's a significant improvement over the rest of his black wardrobe.

"A little privacy, please?" he says curtly, taking his phone back from his mother. His parents laugh as he moves down what looks to be a long hall, leaving to be in a separate room. "I'm sorry about them. They're as chaotic as I remember them being."

"I don't mind. They seem really sweet."

"You're more than welcome to, by the way. To visit. Stay. Meet the parents in person. If you want."

Something giddy bubbles within her chest. "I'd love to, but that's a pretty big step. Are we ready for something like that?"

"We will be. When I tell you everything."

"Alexander, if you're not ready—"

"I want to. I can tell you in person when I pick you up?"

Eden smiles wide, breathing suddenly that much easier. "Yeah," she whispers. "You know what? Yeah. Come pick me up. A little time away from the city might be good for me, too. I'll pack a bag."

"Awesome. I can't wait to see you."

"Me, too."

They pause, both smiling like idiots.

"Hang up, dummy," she says, holding back a laugh.

"No, you hang up."

"Oh my God, we're not doing this."

"Then hang up first."

"Maybe I will."

"Do it," he dares.

She can't bring herself to. "No, you."

"Oh my God," Li sighs dramatically somewhere in the background. "I will pick myself up out of this chair and hang up for you."

Alexander chuckles. "I'll see you soon, sweetheart."

"Alright, alright. I'll see you soon."

She ends up hanging up first, but it's no matter. She rolls over onto her back and beams at the ceiling. Today might have started rough, but the promise of seeing Alexander soon makes it a million times better.

# CHAPTER
## Twenty-Nine

He knocks on her door, smiling wide when she comes to answer. She throws her arms around him in an instant, pressing her face into the crook of his neck.

"You're here early," she mutters against his skin.

He breathes her in. "I might have floored it so I could see you."

"You shouldn't speed."

"Sorry."

Eden giggles. "No, you're not."

He laughs with her. "No, I'm not." He plants a chaste kiss on her forehead. It's a bit ticklish because his stubble is coming in, but Eden can't say that she minds. "Can we talk inside?" he asks.

"I'd rather do this on the doorstep."

"Oh, uh... Okay?"

"I'm kidding, dummy," she says with a light giggle. It's a nervous little sound. "Come on in."

Eden guides him over to the couch, sitting down directly next to him so that she can play with his hair. It's an exchange of sweet touches, gentle caresses. He has a hand on her knee while she brushes the hair at the nape of his neck.

All is calm, all is right. He closes his eyes and collects his thoughts. He had the whole drive back to the city to think about it, but now that he's here, he doesn't know what to say.

She gives him all the time he needs.

And bless him, he *tries*.

His mouth opens just to close again. His brain is running Windows XP and he desperately needs his thoughts to load, but no words come to mind. There's just so much to go over, he doesn't know where to start.

"Let's try an easy question first," she offers.

"Yeah, okay. I think I can do that."

"How was the drive?"

He makes a sound, a half-sigh, half-laugh. "It was fine. Good. Traffic was nice and light."

"And how are your parents?"

"They're well. My mother's very excited to meet you."

Eden smiles. "I'm excited to meet her, too." And then, very softly, "Why don't you use your real name?"

He chews on the inside of his cheek. It's time to rip off the Band Aid. "It was Sebastian's idea," he starts off slowly. "To make me more... palatable."

"Palatable?" Her expression draws tight. "I'm not going to like where this is going, am I." It's a statement, not a question.

"Look, I don't think I can get through this while sugar-coating things."

"I don't expect you to." Eden takes his hand, gives his fingers a squeeze. "I'm listening. I'm here."

"I'm used to people taking one look at me and already having made assumptions. Sometimes they're good, and some are... not so great. There's no way to escape it. They see me at surface level first, and everything else comes second. They see my name on a resumé, in an article... and it's more of the same."

"That's not fair," she grumbles.

"Believe me, I know. But that's how the world works."

"So Sebastian made you change your name to fit in?"

"In a way, yes. '*It's easier to pronounce*,' he said, or some other bullshit line."

"It's literally one syllable versus four," she says with a scoff. "That's so fucking dumb."

He shrugs a shoulder, weariness clear in his eyes. "Yeah, well... I was impressionable back then. All I wanted was to fit in, to belong. You have to understand, Eden, I wanted to be a chef so badly. It's all I've ever wanted to do. Food, cooking... It brought me so much... *joy*."

Eden gives his fingers an encouraging squeeze. She knows all too well.

"I was willing to do anything if it meant I could stay in Paris. Cook and train at one of Sebastian's restaurants. Not everyone in the haute cuisine scene is closed-minded, but there are a handful of very loud and influential individuals who'd prefer a certain level of... purity."

Eden glowers. "You mean..."

"Yeah. It's as bad as it sounds."

"Well, I say they can shove it up their racist assholes."

"I agree with you there." His face grows sullen. "I felt like Sebastian was giving me a fresh start. It gave me the opportunity to reinvent myself. The chance to be good enough, to be *more*."

"But you *are* good enough," Eden insists.

"I can see that now, but at the time, I didn't believe it. I was young and eager to impress. I wanted to prove to the world that everything they could do, I could do better. There was no shortage of nasty comments, but I did it, Eden. I came out on top and showed them all wrong."

She offers him a small, sympathetic smile. "You said... you said you didn't like everything the name represents. What did you mean by that?"

"The other day at La Rouge... You were right. Alexander is a persona. One that I've hidden behind for ages. Nobody knows about the massive wedge it forced between me and my family, how it drove us apart. I chose Sebastian over my family, only for him to strip away everything that made me *me*."

He swallows hard, his chest unbearably tight. "The guilt I feel... I can't escape it. I've felt obligated to Sebastian for so long, but at the same time, I regret leaving my family behind. I don't know how to be myself when I'm at work, but I don't know how to exist as Alexander anywhere else."

"That sounds exhausting," Eden says softly.

"It really fucking is." He chuckles bitterly. "I don't know who I am if I'm not cooking, Eden, but I don't know if I can go back to that place. I'm lost and confused and..."

"What is it?" she whispers.

"The only time I feel even remotely okay is when I'm with you."

Eden grasps at the collar of his shirt and pulls him in for a kiss. He leans into her, realizing just how much he's missed the taste of her tongue and the softness of her lips.

"Thank you for telling me," she mumbles, her forehead pressed to his. "I know that couldn't have been easy."

"I *do* trust you, Eden. I do. Please never doubt that. I'm just... not really good at the whole *heart-on-my-sleeve* thing."

She smiles gently. "If my opinion counts for anything, I think you did very well."

"You mean I get full marks?"

"Oh, definitely. A solid ten out of ten for communication."

"I'm sorry I pushed you away."

"And I'm sorry I pushed you into pushing me away."

"I'll do better going forward. I promise."

"Me too."

"Does this mean you forgive me?"

Eden nods. "I forgave you ten minutes ago."

He chuckles softly. "Hey, can you do me a favor?"

"Anything."

"Will you... Will you call me by my name?"

She beams, her face brighter than the sun. He realizes just how fitting her name is. She's his ray of sunshine, his garden of Eden. She's a breath of fresh mountain air. She's the warmth of a calm fire in the middle of a dark winter evening. She's absolutely everything to him, so when she opens her mouth to say his name, the world suddenly clicks into place and makes sense.

"Shang," she whispers, so soft, so sweet.

Eden kisses the tip of his nose again.

She kisses the corner of his mouth.

She kisses him fervently on the lips.

He kisses her back, lightheaded and alleviated and so damn overjoyed. He wraps his arms around her waist and pulls her onto his lap so he's straddled between her thighs, mouthing hungrily at her lips, down her jawline, the front of her throat. He sucks hard, leaving marks on her skin as a reminder to himself that she's here. She's really here and she's his and he's never been happier.

It doesn't take long before a tight heat begins to grow deep within his core, his cock throbbing with desire. Eden grinds her hips against him, sending pleasure shooting through his system. He'd be perfectly happy to keep kissing her, but he needs more. He craves more. Judging by the way Eden clings to him, fingers carding through his hair as she groans and rotates her hips, she needs him just as much.

"Can I take you to the bedroom?" he asks, gruff and barely in control.

"Yes," she blurts out with a gasp. "Yes, please."

He lifts her up and carries her down the hall, mouth never once leaving her. He doesn't have time to take in her bedroom, choosing instead to zone in on the bed tucked into its corner.

He sets her down gingerly on her back, eagerly pulling off her clothes. He kisses every inch of her bare skin that he can get his lips on, only taking pause once she's fully naked beneath him.

"You're fucking gorgeous," he murmurs, committing her form to memory. There's something ethereal about the way the moonlight paints her curves.

He tosses off his own shirt, cool air hitting his overheated skin. He shimmies out of his jeans and boxer briefs, too, practically aching to be in her arms again. When he returns, he settles near the foot of the bed so that he can rest between her legs, kissing the insides of her thighs.

Eden lets her head fall back against her pillow as he moves in to tease her entrance with the tip of his tongue. She tastes a bit salty, but not in a bad way. He drinks her in, eager for more, flicking his tongue over her clit in a way that makes her toes curl and her back arch.

"Shang!"

He doesn't recoil when he hears his name this time. It's still weird to him, but he knows he'll get used to it. Especially if it's her calling his name.

"I'm right here, sweetheart."

"I need—"

"Tell me."

"Your fingers. Please, I want—"

"Don't worry, I've got you."

Eden's nice and slick, so he's able to slide two of his thick fingers inside with ease. He curls them, working her sweet spot while his tongue drives her wild. The sound of her wanton moans has him impossibly hard, but he's perfectly happy to stay where he is. Eden's a sight to behold, an honest to goodness work of art. He regrets not getting to do this sooner, but he understands how invaluable the short time away has been. He sees everything clearer now.

He meant what he said. He wants to be better. For both of them.

Eden whines his name, her walls tightening around his fingers. "Shang."

"Come, sweetheart. I want to feel you come. Come on, Eden."

A string of curses falls from her lips as trembles wrack her body, pleasure leaving patches of her skin flushed with arousal. He removes his fingers and licks at her quivering entrance, savoring her juices.

"Good girl," he hums, getting up onto his knees. "Condom?"

"Bedside drawer," she says between pants. "Check the expiry date, though."

He retrieves the item in question and verifies. "They're still good. Been a while since you had to use these, I take it?"

Eden chuckles, bringing a hand up to hide her face. "Hush. I've been busy at work. My old boss used to keep me at all hours. Didn't leave much time for a social life."

He slips the condom on, returning to his place between Eden's soft thighs. "Your old boss sounds like an ass."

"He is, but it's a good thing I like him anyway."

"I'm going to put it in now. Is that alright?"

Eden circles his neck with her arms and pulls him down for a quick kiss. "Yes. Yes, please."

He moves slowly, mostly for his sake because Eden feels so fucking good, he might come then and there. The head of his cock is particularly sensitive, pleasure sparking from nerves to nerve. It's almost enough to leave him winded and seeing spots, but he holds off.

He wants to show her just how much she means to him.

His pace is slow, the drag of his cock against the ribbed walls of her pussy excruciatingly delightful. He continues to mark her delicate skin, works up a sweat to see her so completely undone. Open-mouthed kisses mix the sounds of their languid groans, their animalistic grunts, their passionate pleas for *more please fuck more.*

Suddenly emboldened, Eden hooks a leg over his hip and uses the momentum to roll them over. She looks like a fucking goddess riding him, hair a beautiful mess as her perfect tits bounce with her movements. She rolls her hips, coming down on his shaft in a way that nearly leaves him blind with ecstasy.

"You're so fucking beautiful, Eden."

"God, you feel so good."

"You like fucking yourself on my cock?"

"Yes, Shang. You make me so—*ngh*—fucking wet."

"I'm going to make you scream my name. Let's see if we can piss off the neighbors, hm?"

Eden leans forward, the new angle nearly sending him straight over the edge. She presses her forehead to his, their hot breaths ricocheting off each other's cheeks.

"Eden—"

"I want you to come," she mewls. "I want you to come. I want to make you feel good."

"I'm really close."

"Me, too. Oh, God, I'm—"

He grabs her by the waist and rapidly fucks up into her, snapping his hips and burying himself deep inside. The delicious friction sends them both hurtling, the tight coil in the pit of his stomach exploding like a million fireworks all at once. It's the sound she makes that he truly delights in, a half-sob, half-gasp as her climax rushes through her.

They ride the high together, eventually falling limp in each other's arms. Time passes them by as they kiss lazily, contently.

"Do you have any concealer?" he asks after a while.

"Uh, yeah. Why?"

"You might want to cover those up," he teases, tapping one of the many hickeys he left on Eden's neck. "You know. Before you meet my parents."

Eden blushes and laughs. He laughs with her. Never at her.

Shang has never felt so wondrously complete before.

# CHAPTER
## Thirty

Eden makes it up the first two steps of the porch before Shang takes her hand and gives her fingers a gentle squeeze.

"Are you sure about this?" he asks.

"Yes."

"Are you really, really sure?"

"Yes? You're kind of freaking me out, to be honest."

"Sorry, it's just... My parents are really, um..."

"Use your words, honey."

"They can be a lot. Like, *a lot*. I'd be doing you a disservice by not warning you beforehand."

Eden giggles. "I'm sure I can handle—"

The front door to the house swings wide open, a stout older woman bursting forth like someone's lit a fire under her ass.

"*SHE'S HERE!*" Xu Hong screams, loud enough that Eden actually flinches. Eden quickly finds herself swallowed up in the woman's embrace, her face pressed to Xu Hong's bosom. She smells of gingerbread cookies and peppermint. For a second, Eden thinks she's hugging the embodiment of the Christmas season itself.

Even though it's the middle of March.

"Let me get a good look at you," Xu Hong says, grasping

273

Eden by the shoulders. Eden's never really enjoyed the spotlight, and this sudden rush of attention has her cheeks and the tips of her ears burning red. "Shang was right. An absolute beauty."

Eden grins, shooting him a sideways glance. "He said that?"

"He's been talking non-stop about you."

"*Mom.*"

"Come on in, darlings. Let's get you settled. I'll introduce you to Li later. He's down for a nap right now. His meds make him sleepy, unfortunately."

The first thing that Eden notices is the smell of something delectably aromatic wafting from the open-concept kitchen. It's a mix of rich herbs that Eden can't even begin to name.

"It smells wonderful in here," Eden comments aloud.

"I'm making us pork soup dumplings for lunch," Xu Hong explains. "An old family recipe, passed down to me by my grand-mother, and passed down to her by her grandmother. Hopefully I'll be able to pass it down to you one day, hm?"

The comment is friendly enough, but full of suggestions that Eden isn't entirely prepared to deal with. A part of her really wants a future with Shang, but things are still very new. Eden knows it's just a recipe, but it's the implication of it that has a warmth blooming in her chest. It would mean that she's one of them. And the only way she can officially be one of them is if Shang pops the question and only if Eden accepts.

But surely they're a ways off from that, right? It's much too early to be entertaining thoughts like that.

What they have is really new, a little fragile, a baby bird just learning to spread its wings.

No need to go swan diving off the deep end quite yet. They agreed to go slow. And despite that, this all seems so fast.

No. There's no need to rush at all.

Sensing her discomfort, Shang clears his throat and gently

places his hand on the small of her back. "Come on, sweetheart. I'll show you upstairs. And Mom?"

"Hm?"

"I think your pot is boiling over."

Xu Hong mutters a soft '*aiyah*' before scurrying off to the kitchen.

Eden follows Shang up the stairs and down the hall, entering the bedroom with a sense of wonder. As far as childhood bedrooms go, this one doesn't exactly scream out of the ordinary. There are band posters and family photos and little knick-knacks scattered about. A typical teenage boy's room, one frozen in time. It's a little cramped, but that's only because Shang has long since outgrown the space. Eden wonders how on earth a man of his size is able to fit in the double tucked into the corner of the room.

The singular double bed.

"I'll sleep on the couch," Shang says.

"Don't be silly. We can share."

"Are you sure? I want you to be comfortable while you're here."

"I'll be comfortable as long as I'm with you."

Shang gives her the smallest of smiles. It's sweet, almost shy. Eden's suddenly overcome with the urge to pick him up and hide him away in her pocket, as impossible as that may be. She moseys on over so she can circle his waist with her arms, holding him tight.

"I've been told I snore," he protests with a chuckle.

"And I've been told that I could sleep through a hurricane."

"I'm a blanket hog."

"That's fine. I sleep better when it's cool."

"I also talk in my sleep, too."

Eden laughs. "Do you *want* to sleep on the couch? It sounds an awful lot like you're trying to convince me not to share a bed with you."

"No, never. Believe me. I just want to warn you that this is what you're signing up for." He gestures to himself. "A snoring, blanket hogging, sleep talking mess."

She tilts her chin up and glances at his lips. "I'm all in."

Shang dips down to kiss her chastely, and Eden can't help but notice how different he is the farther from La Rouge he gets. It's a subtle change, but one she latches on to. He's always been leagues gentler with her compared to everyone else, but especially so now. Tender, adoring. He's still strong and solid, but he's uniquely soft around her. Only for her.

Eden really loves it.

As Shang leans away, Eden gives chase, unwilling to let go of his lips. Her attempt is cut short, however, when Xu Hong calls from the kitchen.

"Shang! Can you do me a favor?"

He sighs. "What is it?"

"Can you run to the farmer's market for me? I forgot that I put in a fresh order for scallops. I need it for dinner tonight."

Eden stands up on her toes, suddenly excited. "You guys have a farmer's market around here?"

Shang smirks. "Uh, yeah?"

"Can I come? I've always wanted to check one out."

"You've never been to a farmer's market? Seriously?"

"Never had the time." And then, much quieter, "Or the money."

A flash of sad understanding sweeps past Shang's dark eyes. He nods once before taking her hands, giving her fingers a gentle squeeze. "Then what are we waiting for?"

It's flipping *cold* this mid-March day, but Eden uses this as an excuse to hold Shang's hand nice and tight.

He, in turn, stuffs both their hands in the pocket of his jacket.

She retaliates by bumping up against him as they walk, arm sealed to arm.

As it turns out, this offers him the perfect angle to press kisses into the top of her hair.

The indoor farmer's market isn't that busy—it's almost noon and a Thursday, so really what was she expecting?—but there's still plenty to capture her attention. There are two sections, an outdoor area where vendors' booths are lined up beneath white tents to shield from the cold, as well as an indoor area occupying what looks to be a decommissioned ice rink. There are even more booths there, circling around the perimeter with items on display.

It's overwhelming at first. Eden wants nothing more than to run from stall to stall, checking out all the different goods people have to offer. But she also wants to keep holding onto Shang's hand. She's a child in a candy shop, and he's her anchor.

There's all manner of things here. Stalls full of homemade fudge piled high behind glass. Hand-painted art pieces on carved wood. Fresh fruits and vegetables lovingly grown by local farmers. There's an artisan who's crafted an entire display of cheese, the packaging stamped with the business' adorable little logo of a cow jumping over the moon.

Shang zeroes in on a wheel of parmesan. He asks if he can purchase a smaller wedge, to which the vendor says he can.

Eden, meanwhile, is suddenly distracted by the glint of

something shiny in the stall not three feet away. There's a printed banner draping over the front of the booth, the business' name on full display: Jane & Cass Jewelers. Every inch of surface space is covered in all sorts of rings, bracelets, earrings, necklaces, and hair pins. There's one bracelet in particular that catches her eye, an intricate piece of silver and gold intertwining one another.

"That's a couple's bracelet," the woman standing behind the counter explains. She has a name tag pinned to the front of her shirt: Jane. There's a man beside her, too, and Eden assumes that he must be Cass.

"Crafted it myself," he states with pride. "The pieces come apart, so you can keep one band and give the other to your partner."

"It's lovely," Eden replies and means it. It really is a gorgeous peace. Simple, elegant. She can easily imagine the silver portion of the bracelet around Shang's wrist, gold one on hers.

"You seem like a sweet girl," Jane says. "Tell you what, I'll give it to you for half off. Call it eighty bucks?"

Eden's smile is stiff. She appreciates the offer, but money's always been a terrible pinch point for her. A mental block. An impossible mental barrier that she can't figure out how to climb over. She's spent so long collecting every penny, hoarding every dollar, that it just doesn't feel right to spend it on something so frivolous. She's always been this way. With food. With that dress she saw in the window. Small, trivial things in the long run. Especially compared to her overall goal.

But this time is different. Because this time, it wouldn't be just for her.

Eden glances over her shoulder and notices Shang wrapping up business with a different vendor. A warmth blooms in her chest as she watches him interact with the little old man behind the counter. There's an ease to Shang that wasn't there before. A kindness in the way he smiles and indulges in a bit of small talk.

She wants to get him something. As a way of saying thank you. For giving her a chance at La Rouge, for her new knife set, for being a shoulder to cry on. As a way of showing how much she appreciates him. For his strength, for his ambition, for his patience and tenderness.

Eden puts her hand in her pocket and feels the outer edge of her wallet beneath her finger. She has a decision to make.

They get back to the house in time to see Xu Hong making a fresh pot of chrysanthemum tea. Li is seated in his electric wheelchair at the table. He smiles wide when he lays eyes upon Eden.

"Caught yourself a lovely one, son," he says fondly. "It's so wonderful to meet you, Eden."

"It's nice to meet you, too."

He raises his eyebrows, noting her light accent. "A Texan gal? Whereabouts did you grow up?"

"Houston for a little while, and then Austin until I was eighteen."

"I remember Austin very well. Used to travel there all the time."

"You did?" she asks as she takes a seat next to Li at the table. Shang pulls out her chair for her—like an absolute gentleman —before joining Xu Hong in the kitchen to deliver the final ingredient needed for lunch.

Li nods, and Eden can recognize Shang in the corners of his eyes and the shape of his nose. It occurs to Eden that Shang looks a great deal like his father. They have the same dark eyes and straight nose.

"I actually met my wife in Austin," Li says. "I was visiting an old friend. Almost missed the bus, so I was running like a mad man to catch it. Guess who I ran straight into?"

Eden laughs, looking over to Xu Hong. The woman has her hands on her hips, shaking her head in dismay.

"Cussed him up and down for it," Xu Hong says sternly.

"And I fell in love in an instant," Li adds. "I was only in town for a week, so I did everything under the sun to convince her to give me her number."

Xu Hong rolls her eyes as she expertly picks up a soup dumpling and deposits it into Eden's bowl. "This guy just wouldn't take the hint."

"I'm guessing he wore you down eventually," Eden says thoughtfully.

"Boy, did he ever. There's just something about that Chen family charm."

Eden gives Shang a sheepish smile as he sets down a plate of food in front of her before taking his place in the chair to her left. She knows all too well what Xu Hong's talking about. It's not hard to notice that Shang doesn't say a whole lot, but he doesn't appear to be displeased. Eden wonders if he's just busy taking it all in, treading lightly.

They dig in.

Eden can't remember the last time she had soup dumplings this flavorful. It takes much too long to prepare the meal from scratch, so whenever she has a craving for it, she buys the frozen kind from the local grocery store. But it always comes out a bit soggy and flavorless. This, on the other hand, is an explosion of ginger and green onion and salty soy sauce with Chinese vinegar. Nothing really beats home cooking.

"How is it?" Xu Hong asks. "Do you maybe want a fork?"

"Oh, no. I'm all good, thank you."

"It's a little nerve-wracking having professional chefs at my table."

Eden laughs softly. "This is excellent. Really, really good."

Shang nods in agreement, quietly muttering, "Just like I remember it."

They eat in silence for a bit, but it isn't uncomfortable. Eden actually likes it. She can't remember the last time she sat down for a family meal. There's more than just soup dumplings to enjoy: an entire collection of garlic-fried broccolini, fluffy jasmine rice, and a big plate of shrimp chow mein to help themselves to. She enjoys the simplicity of the moment, likes how Xu Hong patiently feeds her husband extra pieces of pork while Shang loads Eden's bowl up with extra veggies.

"What were you doing in Austin?" Eden asks Xu Hong curiously.

"I was studying at the University of Texas at the time."

"What was your major?"

"Political science."

"That's amazing," Eden says and very much means it.

"I thought it would help me get a law degree. Honestly, I thought I was going to be a lawyer after I graduated from Yale, but I decided to give the political track a go. I served as a mayor for several years."

"I had no idea. That's actually really cool."

"More like time-consuming," Xu Hong says, a hint of something sad ghosting across her eyes.

Eden notices how Shang shifts in his chair, eyes glued to his plate. It appears she's unknowingly touched a nerve.

"Pass the bok choy," he says gruffly.

"What about your parents?" Li asks. "They live in Austin? Or are they nearby."

She freezes. Eden knows he means nothing by it. There's no

way he'd know the truth unless Shang told him already, but Eden doubts Shang would even bring up the issue out of respect.

"I'm not sure, actually. I haven't seen them in a very long time."

The back of her neck suddenly feels very warm, not because she's flushing with embarrassment, but because Shang has placed a tender hand there. She leans into his touch out of pure instinct, drawn to him and the quiet comfort he offers.

"Embarrassing stories!" Li declares, words slicing through the awkward tension like a knife. "I demand embarrassing stories about my son."

Eden breaks into a grin. "Only if I get to hear embarrassing stories about his childhood in return."

"You drive a hard bargain, little lady. Consider it done."

"Oh, let me go get the photo album!" Xu Hong says with a gasp, jumping straight out of her chair. "He was the cutest baby. Had the biggest ears *ever!*"

Shang pinches the bridge of his nose. "Someone please kill me," he grumbles, but there isn't any heat behind it.

Eden, for one, has never been more delighted.

Her stomach hurts from laughing. It's genuinely painful. She's curled up in a tight little ball, holding back fits of laughter. It's much too late to make so much noise, but her newfound wealth of information about Shang's unfortunate emo phase is still fresh on her mind.

"You're a little gremlin," he says affectionately as he climbs into bed. "I should have destroyed these pictures when I had a chance." He slides up next to her, and Eden wonders how in the world she feels so safe in his arms.

Eden rolls over and buries her face against his chest. "You're sure you're comfortable? I can sleep on the floor if—"

"Out of the question. Fourteen-year-old me would be freaking the fuck out right now if he knew he was going to have a girl in his room."

"Ah, I guess we owe it to fourteen-year-old you, then."

Shang kisses her forehead. They're really starting to become Eden's favorite kind of kisses. Especially when he curls his fingers against the nape of her neck, playing with her hair there.

"Your mom was right, by the way."

"Hm?"

"You really were the cutest."

"Yeah, but then puberty hit me, and I was a gangly freak through all of middle school and high school."

"You weren't that gangly."

"I'm pretty sure I was lopsided until I was sixteen. My arms were two different lengths."

"Do you think we would have been friends if we went to the same school together?"

"Maybe? I was kind of a quiet kid. Couldn't talk to a girl to save a life."

Eden laughs, snuggling in closer. "I think we would have been friends. The kind with secret handshakes and friendship bracelets."

Shang hums. "That sounds nice."

She sits up and smiles. "I actually have something for you."

He props himself up on an elbow. "Oh?"

"Yeah, hold on." Eden climbs over him like a damn tree, fishing through her pockets. "Will you close your eyes? And hold your hand out."

"Why?"

"Because it's a surprise."

Shang smirks, doing exactly as instructed. "Why are you so adorable?"

"Genetics," she offers up as a reply.

"Can I open them yet?"

"No."

"Now?"

"You're impossible. Yes, now."

He does, eyes immediately falling to the silver twist of metal now on his left wrist. Eden holds up her own to show off the other half, a bashful smile on her lips. She thinks it suits him. Silver is cool and hard and poised like he is, like the reflection of a full moon glowing off the surface of a lake. Gold is warm and bright and soft like she is, like the sun shining over endless fields with the promise of summer.

"Do you like it?" she asks softly.

"Was this what you were doing at the farmer's market?"

Eden nods. "I saw it and... I don't know."

Shang takes her hand and pulls her onto his lap, kissing her cheeks, the corners of her lips, a line down her jaw. "I love it, Eden. Thank you."

He wraps her up in a tight hug. Eden circles his neck with her arms and squeezes him back, kissing the crook of his neck.

She can't even begin to describe how happy she is.

# CHAPTER
## Thirty-One

W hen Shang wakes up the next morning, he discovers
that he hasn't hogged the blankets. He's hogged *her*.
He's got his arms slung around Eden's torso, his long legs
tangled in her slender ones. She fits up against him like a dream,
her ass tucked perfectly up against his front. He's so unbeliev-
ably comfortable, he'd personally prefer to close his eyes and
drift off for a few more minutes, happily drowning in the scent
of Eden's hair.

Unfortunately, his dick doesn't get the memo.

Shang thinks he can will it away, but then Eden shifts her
position slightly, grinding up against his throbbing length. Eden
stirs, humming a sigh.

"Good morning to you, too," she says, teasing.

He kisses the back of her head. "Go back to sleep."

She doesn't, though. Instead, she deliberately backs her ass
into him and moans, snaking a hand back to caress his cheek.
"Come on, honey. Let me help you."

Within an instant, Shang's senses are on high alert. Little
sirens inside his head go off. He can't deny his aching cock any
longer, but knows that they're in a less than ideal location. He
knows just how loud Eden can get. He actually prefers it. But

with his parents' home, Shang can't pull out his usual stops to make Eden scream his name.

"We're going to have to be quiet," he whispers, reaching around to slide a hand down the front of Eden's cotton panties. Eden muffles a groan as Shang parts her folds with his fingers. "Fuck, you're already so wet for me."

"Shang—"

"I've got you, sweetheart."

He does little more than brush his fingers up against her clit, but it's enough to make her body tremble beneath him. He draws slow circles against her, amused by how she's struggling to keep her volume under control. The knowledge that he's able to reduce her to a babbling mess with just his finger makes him painfully hard. He grinds his cock against her ass, the friction he finds almost maddening. It's close, but never enough. Eden writhes and whimpers and it's enough to make him go insane.

"Beautiful," he murmurs into her ear. "Love how you move against me."

A moan rips from her throat as climax hits her, wave after wave of pleasure causing her muscles to spasm. Shang has to place a gentle hand over her mouth to stifle the sound. It's for him and him alone. His teasing hand comes away wet with her arousal. He's never been quite so proud to see such a mess.

"Your turn," she mutters, turning over. Shang, for one, doesn't complain in the slightest when she pulls the band of his underwear down to let his cock spring free.

Eden kisses him lazily as she wraps her fingers around his shaft, stroking at an easy firmness. Shang doesn't mind the mild coldness of her hands or the hint of morning breath or the fact that they're definitely making too much noise.

He's in heaven. He supposes he'll always be, so long as he's with her.

Shang lets her take control, setting the pace. It's maddening just how close he gets only for Eden to ease up at the last second. It's wonderfully cruel. It leaves him wanting more, just within reach. She's prolonging this, he realizes. The glint in her eye tells him that she's having more than a little fun.

"Eden," he rasps. His voice sounds foreign to his own ears. He sounds desperate.

"Relax," she coos. "Relax, honey. I'll help you."

He gasps against her lips as she continues her loving strokes, the tension in the pit of his stomach growing tighter and tighter with every pass. "Fuck, I'm going to—"

"Come on. That's it."

Shang reaches down to come in his own hand, drunkenly kissing Eden like she's ambrosia.

He'd gladly starve if it meant he could drink the taste of her lips forever.

He eventually slips out of bed, pulling on his shorts, to tiptoe down the hall to the bathroom to wash up. When he comes back, Eden's curled up in bed—his bed—looking like something out of a dream. Shang crawls back under the covers, pulling her close.

If his heart was any happier, it'd burst.

"Someone's in a good mood," Xu Hong comments as she traipses into the kitchen.

Shang flips the bacon he's working on, gesturing to the full French press on the kitchen island. "Help yourself. I can't remember how you take your coffee."

"Black is fine, thank you."

"How do you want your eggs?"

His father chuckles as he wheels into the room. "Anything other than scrambled would be great," he says. "Your mother can't poach an egg to save a life."

This earns a light slap across the back of his head, though Xu Hong's fingers barely connect. "Hush."

"Is Eden still asleep?"

Shang nods, moving over to pay attention to the Hollandaise—he's made it from scratch, of course—warming over a double broiler. "She's used to night shifts. I can go get her."

"No, no," Xu Hong says with a quick wave of her hand. "Let her sleep. We wanted the chance to talk to you, anyways."

Shang grimaces. "About?"

"Nothing serious, don't worry."

He moves about the space, re-familiarizing himself with his childhood home. He spent countless hours here as a boy, learning to bake, learning to cook, watching with wide-eyed fascination whenever Uncle Charlie came over to whip up some new creation. This is the exact stove Shang caused his very first grease fire—it was promptly smothered out—at the tender age of eleven. This was where Shang would agonize over every ounce of flour, every tiny gram of salt needed for seasoning. He doesn't remember when he got to the point where he could measure by eye and sound and taste. It just came to him, somewhere along the line, a skill picked up after hours upon hours of practice.

He places two dishes down, one in front of each of his parents. Breakfast today consists of eggs benedict over a fried piece of ham on a toasted English muffin, drizzled over with buttery Hollandaise sauce and a side of bacon, grated hash browns, and a pitcher of orange juice to wash it all down.

Shang doesn't say it, but it warms his heart to see his parents dig in, the looks of delight on their faces sparking something within him he long thought dead.

"What did you want to talk about?" he asks.

Xu Hong glances over at Li before grinning. "Well, as you're probably unaware, it's going to be our fortieth wedding anniversary."

"Today?"

His mother nods. "Today."

"Congrats," he says, doing his best not to be stiff and awkward. He's been away for so long, he'd forgotten entirely.

"We were going to tell you a little earlier," Li starts, "but we got a little distracted playing catch up."

"Tell me what?"

"We're hosting a little party," Xu Hong explains. "A small get-together. Tonight. Here."

Shang shifts. "Do you need me out of the way or—"

"No, no. We very much want you here."

He sighs. "Oh, alright. Good. Thank you. Who's, uh... Who all is coming?"

"Oh, just the boys," Li says fondly. "Bobby, Edwin. A few of your mother's old colleagues."

Shang swallows. "Uncle Charlie?"

Xu Hong's smile is tight but sympathetic. "He said he'd be making an appearance, yes."

He sets his jaw. "I see."

"I think it'll be good for the two of you. To see each other."

Shang doesn't say anything. Everything that's happened... It's a lot. He supposes it's a lot like ripping off another bandage. If he could face his parents, surely he can face the mentor he'd let down.

"There's another reason why I bring it up," Xu Hong continues. "I just got off the phone with the caterer I hired for the party."

"Oh?"

"It appears there was some last-minute scheduling issues. They've given me back my deposit back, but I'm without anyone to—"

"I can help," Shang offers without hesitation.

"Are you sure?"

"It's no trouble."

Xu Hong smiles and pats Shang on the arm. "Thank you so much, dear. I know I'm asking for a lot on such short notice, but..."

"What's short notice?" comes a sleepy voice.

Shang looks up and immediately smiles when he sees Eden shuffle in. Her hair's an adorable mess, and he wouldn't have it any other way. He pours her a fresh mug of coffee, instinctively moving in to kiss her temple while wrapping an arm around her waist.

"They're having a party tonight to celebrate their anniversary," he explains.

Eden's eyes widen. "Oh, congratulations, you two!"

"They were just asking me if I'd be willing to cater."

Eden peers up at him, half-surprised. "Of course you'll help."

"I already said—"

"And I'll help out, too!"

Li chuckles. "That's alright, kid. We can't ask a guest to work."

"But it's okay to ask *me*?" Shang chides.

"You don't count."

Eden looks at Xu Hong and Li. "I really wouldn't mind. I love working with him. And it'd go much smoother if he had a helping pair of hands. *Someone* has to keep an eye on him."

"If you're sure," Xu Hong says. "Well, I guess we'll look forward to it."

It feels good to be in command of a kitchen again, even if it's a small one and it's only the two of them. It doesn't get his blood pumping quite the same way. There's an undeniable thrill that comes when orders arrive non-stop. There's something magical about working in a full-scale kitchen, surrounded by noise and smell and bright industrial lights overhead.

But this is still nice. Better than nice, actually. It's comfortable and calm and... *fun.*

Getting to unabashedly flirt with his sous chef is definitely a bonus, too.

This is a dance he's done a hundred thousand times. Except this time, the rhythm's different. There's no need for pomp and circumstance, no need for excessive flair or stress or the pressure to perform. This is a dance he enjoys. Shang and Eden waltz around one another, just as they've done before, but with an ease and an acceptance that this is more than enough. There's beauty in the process.

As they put the cannoli in the oven—everything lovingly made by hand—he realizes that he starts to feel it again. This pull to something lighter, something inexplicable. Working for Sebastian had snuffed his passion out, leaving him in the dark for the longest time. Shang doesn't understand how he didn't see it sooner. Sebastian was *this* close to sucking him dry, a hollow shell of himself. He'd been drifting down a dark path for so long, it was a wonder that he didn't crash and burn sooner.

He doesn't really know where this new path is leading him. It's scary, really, not knowing what the future holds in store.

"Behind," Eden announces as she moves the tray of stuffed mushrooms directly behind him.

Shang watches her work. She's always had a hypnotizing effect on him, though he's only just realized to what extent. Eden works with a smile, totally in her element. Shang thinks she belongs in the best kitchens out there, to own her own restaurant one day. He isn't just being biased, either. She's really just that good.

The path forward may be scary, but as long as he's with her, there's no doubt in his mind that it's the right one.

The party's in full swing by eight. It's not a huge crowd, but it's still large enough to leave his stomach unsettled. He's not... good with people. Employees, fine. He can order them around all day long and not have to worry about them the second they punch out. But these are some of his parents' oldest friends. Most of them knew Li before he was in the chair. Shang isn't sure if he can handle being out there, knowing full well that everyone else knows who he is and what happened.

"I'll go bring the crab tartar out," Eden offers. "Are you sure you want to stay here?"

Shang nods, and that's all Eden really needs. She understands perfectly, bless her soul.

Shang misses her the second she disappears out to the dining room.

He mills about, cleaning as he goes. He's always been very methodical like that. A clean workspace is a safe workspace, after all.

"Shot up like a bamboo shoot, eh?" comes a gruff man's voice from behind.

Shang freezes for a second, gathering his wits before turning to face Charlie. He's aged. A lot. Shang has no idea why it surprises him so much. Charlie's hair has turned gray, and his beard to match. His eyes sag with wrinkles and unspoken burden. His uncle has his hands stuffed in his pockets, appearing just as uncomfortable as Shang feels.

"I've always been this tall," Shang says lamely.

"I'll have to take your word for it." Charlie clears his throat before jerking his thumb over his shoulder. "That's your girl?"

"Yeah. Eden."

"She looks familiar."

"She was a student of yours for a little while."

"Ah. Can't say I remember her."

"It was a long time ago."

"Yeah. A long time ago."

As far as awkward conversations go, this one takes the cake. Even the one with his parents hadn't been so bad. At least he had his guilt to do all the talking—not to say that he doesn't feel guilty about the way he left things with his uncle, but it isn't quite the same.

Shang hurt Charlie in a different way, one that hit his pride.

"I'm sorry," Shang says, giving it a try anyways. "I should have listened to you."

Charlie shakes his head. "I don't really want to talk about it."

Shang frowns. "O—kay?"

"When Xu Hong told me you were going to be here, I spent the whole night trying to figure out what I was going to say to you." Charlie sighs. "I know it's foolish, but I'm still very upset, Shang."

"I understand. I am, too. At myself."

"Do you remember what you said to me before you ran off to Paris?"

Shang shakes his head. "I don't remember. I was... angry."

"You said I *was a worthless teacher of no value.*' You said '*I was just an old man clinging to my father's glory.*' I think you said my food tasted like ass, too. Just in a more colorful way."

Shang winces. It's coming back to him now. The things he said in anger were a blur to him. He doesn't remember anything other than seeing red, of feeling so upset and frustrated and furious that he couldn't breathe. He may not recall what was said, but Charlie does. Those words hurt his uncle far more than Shang had ever realized.

"I'm sorry."

"I quit afterwards, you know. After you left."

"I heard."

"I didn't realize that I'd failed you until it was too late."

"It wasn't your fault. I was a dumb kid."

"Regardless, it was a really bad time for me. For all of us, after you... My best student and nephew wanted nothing to do with me. My best friend was paralyzed. I had to watch as my sister tried to pick up the broken pieces." Something in Charlie shifts from sadness to quiet rage. "You have no idea how many nights your mother cried on my shoulder, kid. Do you have any idea how hard it was to watch her struggle to keep it together? All she wanted was a phone call and you couldn't be fucked."

Shang's throat squeezes tight as a stinging pressure builds behind his eyes. "I know," he chokes. "I know I fucked up. I'm... I'm trying to make it better."

"Your parents may have forgiven you. That's what parents do. But I'm still fucking pissed, Shang. It's... Shit. I need more time. What you did..." Charlie rubs a hand over his weary face. "I'm sorry. I know this probably isn't your idea of a great family reunion, huh?"

Shang swallows to keep himself from crying. None of this is fair. Sebastian took so much from him, and Shang still has to suffer the consequences. A part of him wants to be defensive, to use Sebastian as an excuse. But the other part of him knows he needs to own up to it, that some of his decisions were entirely his own. Shang hurt his loved ones, intentionally or not, and he can't expect everyone to forgive and forget no matter how much he wants it.

"I understand," Shang says quietly. "All I can do is say I'm sorry and try to be better."

Charlie nods solemnly. "I'll get there. I just need time."

"I'm sorry for the things I said. I don't think your food tastes like ass."

"Thanks, kid." Charlie clears his throat and straightens his back. "I'm, uh... I'm going to get back to the party. See you out there?"

"Yeah, uh... maybe."

Charlie disappears, and Shang's never been more thankful for the quiet that follows.

It takes him a few deep breaths before he stops shaking. Things with Charlie aren't ideal, but perhaps with time, it'll get better. Shang's making an effort, and right now, he tells himself that's enough.

"Shang?"

He turns when he hears the sound of Eden's voice. It's warbled, like she's nervous or afraid. Concern shoots straight through him when he notices her brows pulled together in worry. He rushes over, the instinctive need to protect overcoming his senses.

"What happened, sweetheart?"

Eden looks down at the envelope in her hands. Shang hadn't noticed it before. "Your mother, she..."

"What's going on?"

"I said I didn't want to be compensated. I was more than happy to help with the catering, but she insisted."

"She paid you?"

Eden nods, sniffling. "Mm-hmm."

Shang's nothing but confused. "And that's... bad?"

"No. It's a really good thing. She says she has an envelope for you, too."

"Okay, then why do you look like you're about to cry?"

"Because..." Eden sucks in a shaky breath through clenched teeth. "She gave me two grand, Shang. I finally have enough to hire Maxine Kendo."

# CHAPTER
## Thirty-Two

E den stands by the car, Li seated directly beside her on the driveway. They watch the back and forth in silent amusement.

Shang pushes the envelope back toward his mother. "I told you, I don't need you to pay me."

Xu Hong pushes the envelope right back. "I'll hear none of it. I'm paying you for services rendered."

"This is too much."

"Nonsense. This is what I would have paid the caterer had he shown up."

"The bastard was over-charging you, then."

"Would you just take it?"

"Absolutely not."

"Take it!"

"No. I'm not exactly hurting for cash, A-Ma."

"Well, then think of it as making up for all the red envelopes you've missed."

"Aren't I too old to still be getting red envelopes?"

"You're always going to be my baby."

"*Mom.*"

"*Son.* You're not supposed to refuse a gift. I thought I raised you better."

"Oh dear God, why are you like this?"

"I will stuff this down your pants, mark my words!"

"Why do you have to make everything sound so threatening?"

Eden leans over to whisper in Li's ear, continuing to watch the exchange unfold. "Are they always like this?"

Li rolls his eyes and chuckles. "You have no idea, kiddo. You have no idea." While Shang attempts to keep his mother at arm's length, literally sticking his arm out like in those old black and white slapstick comedy movies, Li leans over to whisper to Eden. "Do me a favor?"

"Anything," she replies.

"Take care of him for me, okay?" Something sad but accepting flashes across the man's eyes. "I don't know how many more years I've got left in me."

Eden shifts, uncomfortable. "Don't talk like that, Li."

"Just hear me out. It's something we all have to deal with, eventually. I'm not saying it's going to happen right this second, but one day, I'm not going to be here, and I need to know that my boy's in good hands." Li smiles gently. "He's got a short temper, as I'm sure you know. It takes a lot to coax him into talking about his feelings. But the way he looks at you... That's how I know you'll be the one who can do it. So take care of him, yeah?"

She nods, both warmed and resigned by Li's words. "I was planning on it," she admits.

"Thank you, kid."

Shang approaches the car with a sigh, the envelope stuffed into the back pocket of his jeans. Xu Hong is right behind him, looking downright triumphant. Eden stifles her laugh.

"You guys should pop into the city soon," Shang suggests. "Just be sure to call first."

Xu Hong nods. "That sounds wonderful. Maybe I can finally convince your father to go shopping for a new chair."

Li huffs, affectionately patting the worn-down material of his armrest. "What's wrong with Ol' Sparky?"

"I think the fact that you have to call it *Ol' Sparky* is enough of an answer."

"I don't have to call it Ol' Sparky. I just think it's a cute name."

"Mm-hmm. Yes, dear."

"Don't '*yes dear*' me."

"Okay, dear."

There are hugs all around before Eden and Shang get into the car. They wave through the windows at Xu Hong and Li, who remain in the driveway until the car is well and truly out of sight.

Shang threads his fingers between hers and brings her hand up to his lips, kissing her knuckles. "Are you ready?"

She nods slowly. It hasn't quite hit her, what she's about to do. She's been waiting to take this next step for literal years, and now that she finally is, a part of her worries that it's too good to be true.

"As I'll ever be," she mumbles.

E den's never seen the inside of a private investigator's office. All she has to go off of are those old-timey black and white movies she's seen. Parsons usually hogged the television, but on the rare nights he worked late and she was alone, Eden liked to help herself to his DVD collection. She always had a soft spot for detective mysteries, especially the ones with happy endings.

Maxine Kendo's office is spacious and bright, a far cry from the things Eden's seen in movies. She and Shang occupy the guest chairs in front of a large mahogany desk. On the other side: Maxine Kendo.

She's a small woman. A *really* small woman. Maxine barely comes up to Eden's chest. She has a lovely dark complexion and wise eyes. The glasses she sports makes them look massive. There's a stillness to her, one acquired through many years of practice and observation. Eden is both calmed and unsettled by the woman's presence, eager for her help, but mildly unappreciative of the way the PI seems to be making a study of her and Shang.

Maxine shuffles a few documents around on her desk. "I believe I have your story straight now. Such a sad case. You're a resilient one, I can tell."

Eden swallows. "Thank you."

"And you're sure you have no living relatives left?"

"No. It's just me."

Maxine hums, stroking her chin. "And everything about your parents' disappearance is in the files you provided?"

"Um, yes. That's everything I've got."

The woman nods. "Very well. Now, I may be good at what I do, but a missing person's case that's this old... Well, let's just say I don't want you to get your hopes up."

Eden's breath catches in her throat. "But you'll take the case?"

"Yes, I shall."

"H-how long do you think it'll take?"

Maxine smacks her lips, tilts her head to the side. "You must have patience, dear girl. I'm an investigator, not a magician. I give you my word that I will dedicate my focus to finding your parents as quickly as possible."

Shang reaches over and places a hand on the back of her

neck. He doesn't say anything. The comforting warmth of his palm against her skin is more than enough.

"I will get in contact with a few of my sources," Maxine continues. "Multiple sets of fresh eyes may help a great deal."

Eden stands, so excited and anxious that she's two seconds away from vibrating straight out of her skin. "Thank you. Thank you very much."

When they get back outside, Eden realizes her legs are Jello and she can hardly stand. It was all over so fast, so quickly. Ten plus years of saving, of waiting—and now it's out of her hands. There's nothing left to do. It's up to Maxine to find her parents. Or not.

She'd rather not dwell on it.

Shang takes her hand and guides her back to his car. "Would you like to go back to your place, or mine?"

She squeezes his fingers. "What would you prefer?"

"I'd prefer wherever I can be with you."

Eden hums contently. "Yours, then. And then mine. And wherever else we find ourselves."

She closes her eyes and relishes the way he kisses her forehead. She likes how he takes care of her.

And take care of her he does.

They went straight to Maxine's office upon leaving his parents' place, so they haven't had a real chance to decompress. The first thing Shang does is take Eden to his bathroom, lifting her with ease and setting her down on the counter. He kisses her slowly, tenderly, all while slipping her out of her clothes while the shower heats up and the bathroom slowly builds up steam.

Her skin burns, but in a good way. She wants so much, hungry to feel his hands on her. Anywhere, everywhere. Shang seems more than willing to give, peppering kisses against her cheeks, the crook of her neck, down along her shoulders. She likes the gruffness of his hands, feels very much like a dish he's preparing. He handles her with the utmost care, stroking and kissing and massaging her arms and legs and breasts.

She's completely naked, exposed. She's never felt safer. The only reason she whines is because Shang's still fully clothed, and it's so terribly unfair. Shang chuckles. It's like he can read her mind. He parts for a second to give himself enough space to shuck his shirt off. Eden all but paws at him, her fingers tracing the hard lines of his chest and abs.

God, she could just sink her teeth into him.

"Prime Wagyu beef," she mumbles to herself.

"Did you just compare me to a cow?"

"Only the best kind, I promise."

Shang huffs a laugh. "Weirdo."

She palms at the obscene bulge in the front of his jeans. "Yeah, but you like it."

"I do," he says without hesitation. "Here, move over. I've got condoms in the medicine cabinet."

"Actually—" Eden places a hand on his chest. Licks her lips. "Do you think we could maybe try without?"

Shang smirks. "What? Really?"

"I've, uh... I've been taking birth control."

"Since when?"

"A little while," she admits, heat spreading across her cheeks. "After I went to see my doctor, we talked about, um... options. But if you don't want to—"

"I want to," he says quickly. "But only if you're sure you want me."

"I'm sure. Do you want me?"

"I'd want you in a million different lifetimes, Eden. Without question."

She leans in and captures his mouth, sucking languidly on his bottom lip.

His hands are careful but greedy, grasping at her like some kind of lifeline. Eden loses herself in his touch, in the strength of his arms and the way his moans vibrate straight through her and leave her breathless. She huffs a sigh of relief when he finally shimmies out of his pants, long, hard cock nudging her inner thighs. Her heart beats so hard, she can feel her pulse in the tips of her fingers and toes.

She wants this.

She wants him.

Now and forever.

Shang lifts her into the shower, presses her right up against the tile. The shower's been going long enough that it doesn't come as a cold shock. Eden hooks a leg over his hip, eager to feel him inside her. He looks so fucking handsome, hair wet and clinging to his face and neck. Eden used to laugh at books that described a person's skin as glistening, but not anymore. She gets it now.

She can't believe that he's all hers.

He kisses her, lips slotting into place. He sweeps his fingers over her folds, teasing her entrance.

"So nice and wet for me," he hums. "I'm going to make you feel so fucking good, sweetheart. Would you like that? Want me to fill you up?"

Eden shivers, electricity arcing from nerve to nerve. "Y-yes. Yes, Shang, I do."

He rubs the head of his cock against her clit, torturously teasing. "I don't know. What do good girls say if they want my cock?"

"Please," Eden almost shouts. "Please, I want—"

"Use your words. Come on, sweetheart. I know you can do it."

"I want your cock in me," she whines. "Fuck me like you own me—"

A loud moan rips itself from her throat as Shang presses into her. Splits her open.

Stretches her to the fullest.

It feels so good, it's almost blinding. All she can focus on is the way he thrusts in and out of her, makes her take his full length just to pull back and do it all over again. The sound of wet skin on skin drives her up the wall, but nothing makes her lose it quite like the way Shang grunts with each snap of his hips.

Feral. An animal. A man on a mission.

"'*Like you own me*,'" he growls. "You really know how to drive me fucking crazy, Eden."

"Shang—"

"What is it, sweetheart? Don't tell me I'm too much for you."

"No, never. I want—"

"What? You want what? You close already?"

Eden both loves and hates the pride in his voice. "Cocky bastard," she murmurs, too dizzy to see straight.

He grins. "Yep, that's me. This cocky bastard *owns* you and your tight little pussy. Look how well you take me, sweetheart. Like you were made for me."

"*Fuck*—" It's a whine. It's a whimper. It's desperate and choked off and needy.

He grips her waist and fucks her hard against the shower wall. "You sound so fucking hot, Eden. Come on. Take it. Fucking take it."

Her back arches as she climaxes, drags her nails across his back, waves of pleasure washing over her so hard and fast, she thinks she might collapse.

Shang doesn't let her, though. He holds her steady through her orgasm, still pumping his cock into her in pursuit of his own pleasure.

"Ah, fuck," he groans against her lips. "Jesus Christ, Eden, I think I lo—"

They come undone together, riding out the high while clinging together well after the water's gone cold. This probably wasn't the most efficient shower they've ever taken, but it certainly was the most fun.

"Did you..." Eden pants, licks her lips. "Were you going to say something?"

Her heart is pounding. Not just because of the mind-blowing shower sex, but because she's pretty sure Shang almost said that he... Maybe she's dreaming?

"Let's get out before we get all pruny," he says, kissing her cheek.

Eden doesn't press him. She supposes that he'll get there when he gets there. He's already made progress in leaps and bounds. If he needs time, she'll happily give it to him. Right now, she's exactly where she wants to be. They towel off and share the hair dryer, all the while stealing kisses wherever they can find them.

For two weeks, they're as happy as can be, falling into a new rhythm together.

And then Eden gets a call from one Maxine Kendo.

# CHAPTER
## Thirty-Three

They head out to Houston on the first available flight. Eden feels strange, gripping onto the piece of paper that she used to hastily scratch down the address Maxine managed to acquire. Eden's impressed with the woman's efficiency.

Eden doesn't recall her childhood home, but the area is familiar to her. And to think that all this time, her mother never truly left.

Shang parks the rental car next to the curb in front of a small, rundown bungalow. It's not exactly a rough neighborhood, just a poorer one. The front yard is small and narrow, tall grass and plentiful weeds growing wildly against the waist-high chain link fencing around the perimeter. The blinds are closed, moss covers the roof, and leaves collect in the gutters.

"Are you sure you don't want me to come with you?" he asks gently.

Eden swallows. Her heart's beating so fast, she can't distinguish the beats. Her palms are cold and clammy. In truth, she desperately wants Shang to come with her, but this is a conversation that she needs to do alone. She nods her head, gives his hand a squeeze, and musters up all the strength in her body to finally step out of the vehicle.

The climb up the front steps of the wrap-around porch that

may as well be Eden's Everest. Her hands tremble, her heart is in her throat, and the air feels too cold and too thin to take in a proper breath. She's spent almost two decades thinking about this moment, dreaming about the day she finally reunited with the family she lost. Now that the moment's upon her, Eden's not sure if she can go through with this.

She raises her hand to knock on the door and pauses to take a deep breath.

"Come on, you can do this," she mumbles under her breath.

Then she knocks.

One.

Two.

Three.

"What do you want?" a woman's voice snaps at her from the other side of the door.

"Ms. McAuley?" Eden says uneasily.

The door opens, but only an inch. A pair of old hazel eyes peeks out to greet her. "Who're you? If you're trying to sell me something, I'm not interested."

Eden presses her lips into a thin line. "Ms. McAuley, I'm Eden Monroe. I... I think I'm your daughter."

The woman doesn't react the way Eden expects her to when she delivers the news. In fact, she doesn't react *at all*. "What do you want? Money?"

Confusion swirls through her. "N-no, ma'am. I'm just here looking for answers." Eden's guts are tied up in impossible knots. This isn't how she imagined things would go. "I don't understand," she mumbles. "I was five when you forgot to pick me up from school. I've spent years searching for you."

Ms. McAuley's lip curls up into a sneer. She finally opens the door fully, offering Eden a good look at her hunched, willowy figure. She always imagined her mother as the embodiment of warmth and sunshine. This lady is anything but.

"You mean Johnny? That son of a bitch wasn't your father, he was just my boyfriend at the time."

Eden isn't sure if she wants to pass out or cry. She feels like she's five years old again, confused and scared and desperate for answers.

"Why didn't you pick me up?" she asks, her voice thin and on the verge of breaking. "I waited for you for hours."

There isn't a lick of sympathy in Ms. McAuley's face. Her features are hardened with indifference, wrinkled with her passive cruelty. "I had you when I was sixteen," she explains, emotionless. "Your real father—the rat bastard—said he'd take responsibility. That he'd be there for us. Filled my head with dreams of a happily ever after. But what does he do the second you were born? The fucker skips town."

Eden's chest is painfully tight. She's torn between feeling sympathetic and angry. "Then what happened?" she urges, dying for the truth no matter how much it's going to hurt.

"I met Johnny, the guy you thought was your father. I let myself think maybe this time would be different. He took care of us for the most part. He had a steady job, a good head on his shoulders, but that son of a bitch didn't stick around for very long, either. The day he broke up with me, I realized there was no way I was going to be able to take care of you. I dropped you off at school and..."

"You abandoned me," Eden realizes aloud. "You didn't forget about me. You *chose* to leave me."

Ms. McAuley shrugs. It's startling how cold and cruel she's capable of being. "I figured you'd be in better hands with the state than slumming it with me. I could barely take care of myself let alone a child. Besides, it looks like things worked out for you, didn't it?"

Eden takes a step back, shaking her head in disbelief. She can't believe all the sleepless nights she wasted wishing to find this woman. She can't detect a hint of remorse or even a sliver of regret.

They say that daughters are supposed to be reflections of their mothers, but she's glad that isn't true in her case. In spite of everything, Eden isn't cold and calloused. She's worked hard for everything she has. She's determined and hard working, she's kind and she's loyal. Her mother's right. Things did work out for Eden. All the hardships she's had to endure, all the endless waiting...

She came out the better person.

Eden stands there, silent for a long moment as she organizes her thoughts. This isn't how she wanted things to go, but maybe it's for the best. She doesn't see any point fighting for someone who clearly doesn't want her in the first place. There's no point choosing a family that left her to fend for herself when she can go back to the car and find comfort in the family she's found.

She stands a bit taller, holds her head up high. She still wants to cry. Not for herself, but her mother. It's such a shame the woman will never get to know her. Eden's fine with it. She has someone very special who will cherish her a million times over.

"Thank you for answering my questions," she says evenly.

"That's it? That's all you wanted?"

"Yes, thank you."

"Wait!" Ms. McAuley eyes the rental car parked by the curb. "Do you have twenty bucks to spare? Gas prices are through the damn roof."

Her audacity would turn a lot of people off, but Eden doesn't bristle. Eden pulls out her wallet and pulls out a couple of bills. She counts it out slowly. Instead of giving her twenty, she slips a hundred even into the woman's hand.

Eden smiles politely. "Consider this a parting gift," she says softly. "I hope you have a good rest of your life." She turns on her heels and leaves the way she came, sliding into the passenger seat in a hurry.

Shang watches his girlfriend expectantly. "How'd it go?"

She finally cracks. The flood gates open, and there's no holding back. Eden cries and cries and cries, a wash of emotions threatening to drown her.

Anger. Disappointment. Bitterness.

*Relief.*

The entire time Shang hugs her, kisses her, whispers sweet nothings to help her get through it. It takes her a good ten minutes of bawling her heart out before she manages to find some semblance of calm.

Because yes, this fucking sucks, but at least she has something she didn't have before.

Closure.

"Let's go home," Shang murmurs against her cheek.

Eden nods.

*Home.*

She likes the sound of that.

# CHAPTER
## Thirty-Four

E den has a hard time getting up the following week. And the week after that. The bed she shares with Shang is the only place she feels safe, second only to the secure hold of his arms around her.

She knows she should get up. Take a shower. Eat. But her mind is in a haze. It's clouded by a heavy fog that won't part.

She mentally scolds herself.

*Get over it.*

But she can't.

It's just that reality has finally snapped into place. No more questions about where her parents went, no more wondering about what happened. They *chose* to leave her. Nothing is going to change that, and all those years of wishful thinking were nothing but a waste.

*They didn't want you.*

Eden knows this probably isn't the best way to start off their relationship. She doesn't want Shang to see her like this. She's stronger than this. Tougher. Made of steel that learned to forge itself. Everything she has, she worked for. With the exception of Shang, she's never accepted gifts from anyone. She frowned upon free handouts. She wasn't someone to be pitied, to be coddled.

So why can't she find the strength to move? To eat? To do anything other than breathe and exist?

Deep down, she's scared. Scared that Shang will leave her if she stays like this too long. What if he decides she isn't worth the trouble? What if he thinks her wallowing is too much? It'd be so easy for him to call things off. What if he decides she's too much of a burden just like her parents did? It'd be easy for him to walk out the door and never come back. Eden knows she's a mess. A mess that just isn't worth it.

*Get up. Please get up.*

It's an insidious thing, this voice in the back of her head. It's loud, borderline deafening. Inescapable. It compounds every doubt she's ever had, every single one of her insecurities—keeps her trapped in a clusterfuck of noise that only she can hear.

*He's going to leave me.*

*Just like my parents did.*

*Because at the end of the day, I'm nothing.*

She didn't expect to be set off this hard. In all honesty, she felt perfectly fine on the flight home. Normal, even, right up until cold reality hit her like a runaway semi. Now she can barely roll over in bed because what does it matter? What does *any* of it matter? Nobody wants her, so she may as well lie here and keep from bothering anyone. If she stays quiet, if she doesn't move a muscle, she doubts that anyone will even notice she's gone. Her parents certainly didn't give a shit enough to care, so why waste her breath?

There's a soft knock on the bedroom door.

"Sweetheart?"

Shame rips through her chest, shearing her lungs and shredding at her heart. Eden's been camped out at Shang's apartment for weeks now, and she feels God-awful about it.

*You're such a fucking burden, Eden.*

*Why does he bother putting up with you?*

The bed dips beneath her, then comes the gentle weight of his hand on her shoulder.

"Do you feel like going for a walk with me today? It's a nice day to visit the park."

He speaks so tenderly, it almost makes Eden cry. Hell, she *does* cry. She doesn't have the energy to sob, so it's up to gravity to make her burning tears fall and soak into his pillow. She wants to respond, but she's too trapped in her own mind to form sentences. Her body and mind are bogged down, numb to everything around her. She feels suspended in time and space, drowning in place while treading water with *just* enough effort to take another breath.

When she doesn't answer, he tries again. "Rina called. She, Freddie, and Peter wanted to know how you're doing. They invited us to trivia night at the bar again if you're feeling up to it."

"You can go," she mumbles, barely audible past her cocoon of thick blankets.

There's a long pause. She's faced away, so she has no idea what expression he's wearing.

*He's probably annoyed with me.*

*I bet he regrets being with me.*

When his weight leaves the bed and the sound of his footsteps retreat out into the hall, Eden isn't surprised. It hurts like hell because—yeah—she saw this coming, but she can't blame him, either. She's just as frustrated with herself if not more. Shang is used to the bright, bubbly version of her. This isn't what he signed up for. He deserves a girlfriend that he doesn't have to baby or constantly check up on.

*See? He's leaving, just like I knew he would.*

His voice reaches her ears, but his words are muffled by the distance he's put between them. It sounds like he's on the phone with someone, but Eden can't be sure.

"Hey, Rina... No, I'm afraid not. What? Tell Drenton to stop screaming in the background, I can't hear you... Next time, alright? Yeah, you too."

Much to Eden's confusion and dismay, Shang returns to bed. He climbs under her protective mountain of covers and holds her close, her back pressed flat against his chest as he presses kisses to her hair.

"Stop," she pleads, her voice thin and weak. "I haven't showered."

"I don't care."

She squirms, tries and fails to push him off. Her skin is uncomfortably tight. "Leave me alone."

"No."

"Go away, Shang!"

"Is that really what you want?"

Eden whimpers. "*Yes.*" She's lying, of course, but Eden can't help but wonder if it'd be easier if he gave up. She doesn't know if or when her slump's ever going to end. Right now, it feels eternal.

Despite this, he holds her even tighter. "I'm not going anywhere, sweetheart."

"But *why*?"

"Because."

Frustration bubbles to the surface, nothing but anger filling her chest. "That's not a fucking answer!"

"Eden—"

"Just leave. I'm not worth it, alright?"

"Don't say that. You *are* worth it."

"No, I'm not."

"Yes, you are."

"You're being really fucking annoying, Shang."

"You'll have to forgive me, sunshine."

Eden yells into her palms. "Just *go* already."

"No."

"Why not?"

"Because I love you."

His confession knocks the air out of her lungs. Her head spins, the rest of the world dropping out from beneath her. Were it not for the safety of Shang's strong arms, Eden wouldn't be able to tell up from down.

"You... You what?"

"I love you, Eden," he whispers, pressing a tender kiss to the nape of her neck. "Just because things are hard right now, that doesn't mean I'm going to give up on you. Love doesn't pick and choose. You were there for me, and now I'm going to be here for you."

She *bawls*. There's no controlling it, no point in trying to keep it inside. She's sad and lonely and grieving, but she's also relieved and overjoyed and so damn in love. It's an overwhelming concoction of emotions that she wades through all at the same time.

"I know you're hurting, sweetheart. If I could take your pain away in a heartbeat, I would. You're just going to have to deal with me being annoying."

Eden manages to roll over to face him, her lip trembling. "I didn't mean it," she mumbles. "I'm sorry, I didn't mean it."

"It's okay."

"It's not. I'm so pathetic right now."

"You're not pathetic. Trust me, I've been there. I've said my fair share of mean things when I was at my lowest. But you're more than welcome to yell at me if it'll make you feel better."

She shakes her head, wipes her teary eyes with her hands. "No. No, you don't deserve that."

"You're my whole world, Eden. Never forget it."

"O-okay..."

"There's something I want you to do for me."

"What is it?"

"I want you to take all the time you need. I'm not going anywhere."

Eden can't believe how lucky she is. He's so strong. So resilient.

It takes a bit more convincing, but Shang eventually helps her into the shower, washes her hair, dries her off with the fluffiest of his towels. He carries her back to bed, allowing her to curl up close as he places his laptop between them and puts on a movie. *Ratatouille*—because of course. Eden's only half watching, but the adorable animations and the sound of the characters voices bring her comfort. What she enjoys the most are Shang's occasional comments.

"So unrealistic," he mumbles. "Real ratatouille takes three hours to make. Ego would have been waiting forever."

Eden's heart feels a little bit lighter. She's far from making a full recovery, but she *is* getting better. She manages a half-laugh as she presses her face against his chest, soothed by his presence. When she's with him, she knows she's never truly alone.

# CHAPTER
## Thirty-Five

I t takes her another week. She feels guilty, taking so much time, but it's not like depression has a start and end date. There's no timer counting down, no set time period that draws a hard line between her lows and highs. She wakes up that morning expecting to have yet another repeat of the day before. Maybe she'll manage a walk around the house. Maybe a nap or four.

But she feels better today. Lighter. The clouds are parting. She's going to be okay. And if not, she knows she always has him to lean on if she needs to.

"There's my sunshine," Shang greets her with a genuine smile when she finally manages to shuffle into the kitchen. He rises from his seat at the table, abandoning the paperwork he has spread out over the surface. Shang wraps his arms around her and presses a flurry of light kisses to her cheeks, her forehead, the tip of her nose. "How are you feeling?"

"Better," she mumbles against his shirt. "Much better."

"I'm glad to hear it. Take a seat, I'll make you breakfast."

"I'm not that hungry." He looks her dead in the eye and holds her gaze until she finally relents. "Alright, fine. Maybe I'm a *little* hungry."

Shang perks right back up. "I'll make your favorite."

"Belgian waffles with strawberry compôte?"

"No, a single hard-boiled egg. Of course Belgian waffles with strawberry compôte."

"You really know how to spoil me."

"An honor and a privilege, I assure you."

Eden gives his butt a light pinch before takes a seat at the kitchen table and watches Shang shuffle around his kitchen. Wonder of wonders, he's *humming* as he cooks. Eden isn't sure what the tune is, but it makes her all warm and bubbly inside to see him so at ease.

She takes the opportunity to plug in her phone. The last time she bothered checking it was just before visiting Xu Hong and Li's upstate. It takes a few minutes, but once it has enough juice, her phone turns on.

A sudden bombardment of notification sounds erupts not long after.

"Holy crap," she breathes, frowning at her screen.

"What is it?" Shang asks, though he doesn't sound entirely interested.

There must be a hundred different texts waiting for her, spread out over the time she went away, all increasing in frequency and alarm. They're mostly from Peter, though there are a handful from Rina and Freddie, too.

Peter: SOS

Peter: HECTOR IS RUINING EVERYTHING PLEASE CALL ME

Peter: I SWEAR TO GOD HE'S WORSE THAN ALEXANDER

Petor: EDEN!? EDEEEEENNNNNNN!!!!

Peter: I'M GOING TO QUIT. I'M GOING TO QUIT I CAN'T STAND THIS ASSHOLE.

Peter: OH MY FUCKING GOD PLEASE EDEN SAVE US WHY DID YOU LEEAAAAAAAVEEEEE

Peter: HAVE YOU BEEN KIDNAPPED OR SOMETHING? DO I HAVE TO CALL 911?!

Freddie: Hey, love! Can you please give us a call or a text or something so we know that you're alright?

Rina: Yeah, the whole kitchen staff is pretty much ready to leave en masse. Can you give us a call? We're worried about you. I tried calling Alexander. He says you're not feeling well?

Peter: It has come to my attention that writing in all caps is considered yelling. I wasn't aware of this.

Peter: BUT NOW THAT I AM, KNOW THAT I AM DESPERATELY YELLING FOR YOUR HELP PLEASE AND THANK YOU

Eden turns to Shang. "I think something's going down at La Rouge."

He shrugs. "Not my problem anymore."

"The restaurant might not be, but don't you care about our friends?"

Shang turns, chewing on the inside of his cheek. "Yes. But I don't know what we'd be able to do for them."

"Maybe we should meet up with them. They seem kind of worried. It'd be nice to see them, don't you think?"

He nods slowly. "Yeah. It would."

"Great. I'll give them a call."

P eter flings himself across the sticky bar table and sobs.
"Hector is a demon. I swear to God he was born in the fiery pits of hell and clawed his way up to the mortal realm to wreak havoc upon us. That's why his hair is red, you know. It's imbued with the flames of the underworld and full of tortured souls!"

Shang pats Peter on the shoulder twice; straight faced, though Eden can tell the gesture is full of genuine sympathy. "That's rough, buddy."

They're back at their usual bar, at their usual spot. Trivia night was postponed because the host came down with an unfortunate case of the stomach bug. Eden doesn't mind, though. She knows her friends really need this opportunity to catch up and vent.

Eden stares in a mixture of admiration and horror as Rina downs her pint of beer in five large gulps. Eden figures her friend must have been an absolute delight at college parties.

"He actually yells at the customers," Rina says with a grimace. "*Yells.* Even you didn't do that. He got right up in one of the guest's faces and screamed bloody murder. *'You're an imbecile'* this and *'You wouldn't know good food if you shat it out on a plate'* that. It was a nightmare to watch."

Shang shrugs. "I made sure never to send out dishes I thought were unsatisfactory. Never got a complaint that I know of. From the guest's side, at least."

Freddie scoffs, tossing back his fourth shot of tequila. "And that's just how he treats our patrons. He's an absolute monster to all of us. I don't think Kay's gone home once after a shift without crying. Laurie told me she's got her two-weeks' notice written up and ready to print. She's just waiting to hear back from another restaurant so that she isn't without a job."

Peter sits up straight, suddenly very serious. "We have to murder him."

Eden chuckles. "Funny."

"No," Freddie says, "he's right. Hector needs to go."

Rina nods in agreement. "We can lure him behind the restaurant and stab him."

"But my knives are my babies," Peter says. "I say we knock him on the back of the head with a tenderizer, stuff his body into the corner of the walk-in freezer, and burn the whole damn restaurant to the ground."

"Christ," Eden says, looking between her friends. "You're all joking, right?"

"Yes," the three of them grumble bitterly.

Eden knows they're lying.

Shang leans back in his chair, casually draping an arm over Eden's shoulder. She likes how he twirls the ends of her hair around his finger absentmindedly.

"I'm sorry you guys are going through this," he says. "If you need a letter of recommendation or something, I'd be happy to write it for you. Although I'm not sure if my name holds much weight anymore. Sebastian's probably put my reputation through the meat grinder already.

Freddie grimaces. "Yeah, we heard. It's all the culinary magazines have been covering lately."

Peter pulls out his phone and opens up a browser tab. "This was on the front page of Gastronomica."

Eden takes the phone and reads aloud, "*The Rise and Fall of the Infamous Iron Chef, Alexander Chen. Once the poster boy for the culinary arts, Chen has plummeted from the upper echelons of fine dining after an explosive tirade and exit from his multi-award winning restaurant, La Rouge. Sources confirm that the Michelin Star chef has struggled for years with alcoholism, drug abuse, and violent outbursts due to unchecked anger issues—*" She shoves the phone back into Peter's hand. "What the fuck kind of bullshit is that?"

Shang places a gentle hand on the back of her neck. Eden's almost lulled into a state of calm by the warmth of his palm, but she's just too angry.

"Sources," she bites out. "What fucking sources?"

"I wouldn't be surprised if Sebastian paid someone off to talk to the reporter," Shang says simply.

"Why are you so calm about this? You should sue for libel."

He shakes his head. "I'm tired of fighting that man. I want nothing to do with Sebastian. It's a blessing in disguise. Now I don't have to go through the trouble of burning the bridge myself."

Rina shifts in her seat. "So that means there's no chance of you coming back to La Rouge?"

"No."

A silence befalls the table. Eden can't stand to see her friends so glum.

"There are plenty of other restaurants in the area," Shang says, trying his best to be helpful. "I'm sure you can find jobs elsewhere."

Freddie blinks. "You haven't heard?"

"What?"

"Sebastian's in the process of buying out the neighboring restaurants to cut down on the competition," Peter explains grimly.

Eden frowns. "How many?"

Rina swallows. "All of them."

Eden's heart leaps up into her throat and immediately plummets into the pit of her stomach. "How... How is that even possible? Is that even allowed?"

Shang clenches his jaw. "Sebastian's got the money and the

connections. That's how he came to own La Rouge. He bought the restaurant across the street, had the menu priced well below what the original owner could afford and then drove the man out of business. He had no choice but to sell. Then Sebastian bought him out and wound up with two restaurants on the same block. He does that everywhere, not just here. It's how he got his foothold in France and Spain."

Freddie crosses his arms over his chest. "You don't sound horribly upset."

"Sebastian handled the business side of things. I just wanted to cook. What he did to boost revenue was his business."

"Well, well," comes a sultry voice, "look at you admitting to having a cold, black heart."

Eden turns in her seat, peering up at a gorgeous woman with jet black hair and distinctively thick brows.

"Bea?" Shang asks, sounding very much startled. "What are you doing here?"

Eden tries to ignore the twist of jealousy that fills her chest when Bea casually pulls up a chair and sits next to Shang at the table. She doesn't know the woman well enough to make judgements, but this doesn't stop Eden from putting a hand on Shang's knee. Just in case.

"I was in the area and thought I'd pop in for a drink," Bea states simply. "Maybe seven. I think I deserve it, now that I'm being laid off at The Lunchbox."

Shang frowns. "You're being laid off? Oh, wait. Uh, everyone, this is Bea. Bea, this is Freddie, Peter, Rina, and Eden."

Bea smiles. "Lovely to meet you all."

Eden flushes, warmth spreading to her cheeks. She feels kind of bad. Bea doesn't seem all that terrible. Perhaps her jealousy is misplaced.

"You're being laid off?" Shang tries again.

"Yeah. It's nothing as nefarious as what you've been talking about, though."

"You were listening in?"

"Maybe a little." She takes a sip from the beer bottle in her hand. "No, the restaurant owner's retiring or something. Wants to spend more time with his family now that he's in his seventies."

"That sounds sweet," Rina comments.

"It is, but it means that he's selling off the restaurant, which means *I'm* out of a job. It's fine, though. Being a chef wasn't really my thing. I might take some time off to find some other passion." Bea takes another sip of her beer. "I doubt it's going to sell. The location's a real hole in the wall. Literally. A part of the building caved in in the 60's, and that's when they turned it into a bar. And it's the most decrepit part of town, too. I wouldn't be surprised if they decide to just demolish—"

Eden stops listening. Her mind is in overdrive. She has an idea.

Shang wants a fresh start. Her friends need new jobs. Eden wants to see everyone happy.

"We should buy it," she says, quiet at first, like she doesn't trust her voice to carry her message. She clears her throat and commands everyone's attention. "We should buy it and start a new restaurant."

Her suggestion is met with stunned silence.

"Are you serious?" Shang asks softly, like he isn't sure if he heard correctly.

"Why not? I know that I still want to be a chef. That's never going to change. But there's no way in hell I'm going to work for Sebastian ever again. If he's buying up restaurants left, right, and center, the chances of me finding another job outside of his influence will be next to impossible." Eden turns to her friends. "There might be an easier solution than murdering

Hector in his sleep. Why don't we just take matters into our own hands?"

Rina is the first to perk up. "That kind of sounds amazing."

"It's already set up as a restaurant, so we'd have all the necessary appliances to start us off," Eden continues. "Nothing a fresh coat of paint and some redecorating won't fix."

"What would we cook?" Freddie asks, a curious brow raised. "Hector has destroyed my love for French cuisine."

Peter nods. "And it's not like a pricey restaurant in the rough part of town exactly screams accessible, either."

Everyone looks to Shang, who's been quiet the entire time. His brows are knit together, and his lips are pressed into a thin line.

A small voice in the back of Eden's head tells her that this is the time to panic, that he isn't onboard with this idea at all.

"Comfort food," he mumbles.

Eden's eyes widen. "What?"

"We could... We could come up with a menu of our favorite comfort food." There's a spark behind his eyes, something alive and electric and hopeful. "Stuff we loved as kids. Cheap but hearty meals that everyone can enjoy. Something filling. Something that families from all walks of life can enjoy. Not just snobby food critics with stupidly small portions."

Peter shifts in his seat. "What about Sebastian?"

"Fuck him."

"But where are we going to get the money to buy the restaurant?" Freddie asks.

"I think you're forgetting that I'm *technically* a celebrity chef," Shang says, matter of fact. "I can shell out what we need to purchase the restaurant, pay for renovations and upgrade—"

"And hire staff?" Rina asks.

Shang nods. "Tell everyone who's still at La Rouge that they'll have a job with us if they want it."

A thrill shoots straight through Eden as she listens to Shang speak. He's the same, but not the same. There's something vibrant about him now, renewed and passionate.

"Are we really doing this?" she asks, beaming.

"I'm all in if you are," Freddie says.

"Me, too," Rina adds.

"Me, three!" Peter declares.

Eden takes a deep breath, willing herself to contain her excitement. "What are we going to call the place?"

"Just keep the name," Bea suggests. "Locals know it well enough, already. Might as well use its existing reputation to give yourselves a head start with its old customer base."

Shang holds up his drink. "To new beginnings."

Everyone else holds up their drink and cheers, "To new beginnings!"

# CHAPTER
## Thirty-Six

The Lunchbox needs more than a little elbow grease. Shang wouldn't be surprised in the slightest if Gordon Ramsay walked in to admonish its condition on a surprise episode of *Kitchen Nightmares*. The place is downright filthy when the owner hands over the keys, little thought or consideration offered after the signing of the papers. The guy looked done with the place, eager to clap his hands clean and head off to whatever adventures awaited him.

The Lunchbox was their problem now.

The wallpaper is faded and yellowing in places from years of sun exposure. The tile floors are somehow sticky and slippery at the exact same time. The tables and chairs in the restaurant front are so old, Shang's worried that the furniture might collapse if a customer puts their full weight on it. The carpet is equally precarious. He doesn't want to think about when it was last given a thorough wash. Probably never, but Shang wants to try and be positive about it.

On the first day, they get right to it. A complete overhaul.

Peter, Freddie, and Rina remove the furniture from the front of the restaurant, tossing everything into a waiting truck they've hired to drag everything to the dump. They'd donate it all, but there's honestly very little that can be spared. Once the area is clear, the plan is to rip up the carpets and wallpaper. They've left the front doors open, but the restaurant lights off. The whole place needs some fresh air.

Shang and Eden are in the kitchen out back, surveying their new domain. It's a lot smaller than La Rouge. But it's all theirs, a little kingdom of their own.

The majority of the appliances left over at The Lunchbox are in surprisingly good condition. Not as fancy or as big and impressive as what Shang's used to, but it's more than enough. They make sure to test everything—Shang doesn't want to run the risk of a grease fire—and come across a couple of snags. Minor issues. Easy to fix. Especially because his girl's got nimble fingers and an eye for these sorts of things. She isn't afraid to get her hands dirty. It's a good thing, given the ghastly mess of old food crumbs and oil behind the fryers.

He loves watching her work. The way she zones out and concentrates on the task at hand. Sometimes she hums a little tune, content in the simplicity of manual labor. Scrubbing, scraping, polishing. He doesn't understand how Eden can look so angelic on her knees, sleeves rolled up and covered in sweat. She glances up at him and smiles, the corners of her eyes crinkling.

Then it occurs to him just how in love he is. Shang's so in love, it hurts. He honestly can't remember the last time anyone made him feel his whole. It's a miracle he has her.

He never wants to let her go.

They each contribute at least one dish to their new menu. It's not an extensive list, just a handful of favorites that are not only delicious and filling, but affordable as well.

Peter makes the most mouthwatering *shucos* on heavenly soft long bread buns, buttered and toasted to perfection before being topped with halved hotdogs, guacamole, cabbage, mayonnaise, tomato sauce, chili sauce, and mustard. It's both crispy and soft at the same time, a perfect combination of textures in one's mouth. It's honestly the perfect dish for anyone looking for a quick but hearty meal for lunch.

Freddie brings fish and chips to the table. Simple, delectable, but hardly anything to scoff at. He makes sure to use a beer batter to bring out the subtle flavors of the fresh halibut he uses. It's then fried to golden perfection. The fries are lovingly cut and seasoned by hand, optional Cajun spice in a small serving bowl to the side. He never skimps on the portion sizes, either. The fish is massive, and he makes sure to pile fries so high, a few always fall off the expo line.

Rina contemplated making a classic pho from scratch, but eventually decided on her and her sister's personal favorite *gỏi cuốn*—savory braised pork, massive prawns, soft vermicelli, cucumbers, lettuce, and diced carrots all wrapped up in a pretty rice paper blanket. The way she plates everything makes the dish look like a masterpiece that's too good to eat. Most people do, however, eat it eventually, because it'd be a right shame to waste such an amazing meal.

Eden makes her mother's macaroni and cheese. The cheap, boxed shit from grocery stores doesn't even begin to compare. She comes in early to make the macaroni from scratch, rolling and kneading pasta dough with deft hands. The cheese sauce she uses is also made from scratch, generous helpings of butter and cream and sharp cheddar—a sprinkle of salt and pepper and oregano, too—melting into one cohesive concoction she then pours over her recently boiled pasta. She makes every bowl to order, placing everything in cute little ramekins they found on sale, popping it into the oven beneath the broiler so that the butter-coated bread crumb topping can turn a beautiful golden brown. With a bit of chopped bacon and fresh green onions sprinkled on top, it's arguably one of the most demanded dishes at The Lunchbox.

And then there's Shang. He doesn't struggle to come up with something to contribute.

Ever since leaving La Rouge, ever since being here—with the woman he's sure is the love of his life and all of his friends—his mind's been overflowing with ideas. Dishes from all around the world. Simple things. Complex things. There's a little bit of everything for everyone.

He cooks on a whim, spurred on by the oddest moments of inspiration. It's what makes The Lunchbox's specials menu so...

Well, special.

It's a strange feeling, but he's getting used to it. Feeling like he belongs. Sometimes it's overwhelming. Sometimes it's heartwarming. His kitchen has transformed from a place of cutthroat ambition to one of love and support and creativity.

Shang's never been happier.

With Eden at his side, he feels invincible.

H is parents come to visit, just as they promised. Shang and Eden take the night off so that the four of them can sit together at the back of The Lunchbox, enjoying their meal. It's been a while since they had a family dinner together.

Li enthusiastically shows off his new wheelchair.

"It even has a seat warmer!" he exclaims, showing Eden the button that adjusts the temperature settings. "I mean, I can't exactly feel it on my ass, but it's wonderful for my neck and shoulders. Oh, and look here." He presses another button. The wheelchair gives out a soft *beep beep*. "Now people will know to get the hell out of my way when I come barreling down the sidewalk."

"Yes," Xu Hong hums. "Barreling down the sidewalk at eight miles per hour."

"Careful the cops don't catch you," Shang chides. "I'm pretty sure that qualifies as drag racing."

Li puffs out his chest and grins. "Fuck the police. I'd like to see them try to catch me. Besides, Eden will back me up if it comes down to a fight."

Eden giggles. "You bet."

"Attagirl. We'll be unstoppable."

Shang rolls his eyes. "You're really not helping me set the mood, Dad."

She turns to him and arches an eyebrow. "Mood?"

"I've been trying to build to it all evening, but Dad won't stop talking about his fancy new toy."

Li snorted. "I'm sorry, okay? I'm just super excited."

Xu Hong huffs. "Oh my God, Li. We get it. Bells and whistles and all that. The anticipation's been killing me."

Eden frowns. "Shang, what's—"

When she turns to face him, she finds him down on one knee with a ring box in hand, opened to reveal the massive shimmering diamond inside. The centerpiece is surrounded by a circle of tiny sapphires, the band itself made of white gold.

Eden's mouth drops open.

Somewhere in the background, Shang swears he can hear Rina scream, "Holy fuck it's happening! Everyone shut the fuck up!"

"Shang," she breathes, initial shock melting away into the sweetest, most beautiful smile he's ever seen.

"You have made me happier than I've ever been in my entire life," he starts, voice unwavering. "You challenge me. You know when to push, you know when to hold back. You make me laugh like no one else. You make every day so much brighter. I didn't realize how lost I was before I met you. You helped me come back to my family. You helped me make friends. You helped me find my passion again. I love you so much, Eden. I want to spend every waking moment with you. So will you do me the honor of letting me be your husband?"

She whispers a teary-eyed, "Yes," before throwing herself at him, kissing him hard and happily in front of the entire restaurant. Shang's only vaguely aware of the loud applause that follows, too elated to notice much else other than Eden in his arms.

He slips the ring onto her finger and marvels at how she's his entire world.

"Drinks are on me!" Li declares, much to everyone's delight.

It's after-hours, and the restaurant sign says they're closed, but their colleagues and close friends all stay for the after party. Shang's buzzed. Not on alcohol—he hasn't taken a sip—just on life.

Fuck, he can't remember the last time he felt this good.

Laurie, Rina, Bea, Xu Hong, and Kay surround Eden, all eagerly catching a glimpse of her ring.

"It's massive!" Laurie gawks.

"It was my mother's," Xu Hong explains. "It's been in the family for generations."

"It's beautiful," Eden says, smiling.

Shang can't help but smile, too. His beautiful little fiancée. His little future wife. He'd buy her a million different rings if she wanted because that's what she deserves.

Freddie pats Shang on the shoulder. "Peter owes me a hundred bucks."

Shang huffs. "Were you betting that she wouldn't say yes?" he asks, mildly offended.

"No," Peter grumbles. "We had a bet whether or not you'd give a sappy speech."

"My speech wasn't sappy."

"It was a *little* sappy," Li notes.

Eden laughs and holds Shang close, wrapping her arms around his waist to press her cheek against his chest. "I thought it was perfect."

Shang presses a kiss to her hair. "Thank you, sweetheart."

Bea coos. "You two are so sweet. I think I might have cavities now."

"Where do you think you'll have the wedding?" Rina asks. "And when? And how?"

Peter nods. "It has to be on a beach. Super romantic and very popular these days."

Eden grins. "I'm sure we'll figure it out. We've got plenty of time."

Li beams with pride. "I'm proud of you, kid. She's a real catch."

"Thanks, Dad."

"So," Xu Hong says with a click of her tongue. "I hope you know I'm expecting a lot of grandchildren."

Shang feels his face flush with heat. "*Mom.*"

"At least two. Maybe three. I want to spoil them rotten."

"We're not even hitched yet. Can't we—"

"Hop to it!"

Shang chuckles, hiding his embarrassment. "Jesus, Mom. Would you relax?"

"If your first born's a boy," Peter states, "you'd better name him after me."

Freddie gawks. "Excuse me? You better name him after *me*. I'm clearly their favorite."

Rina raises her hand immediately. "I call dibs naming it after me if it's a girl!"

Shang's about to protest, but Eden pats him on the small of his back. "Just let them have this."

Despite his groan, he's the happiest he's ever been.

# CHAPTER
## Thirty-Seven

**One Year Later**

It's a sweltering morning in May. They have to be at the restaurant early to let the repairman in. They've been having issues with the restaurant's AC unit, and the last thing they want is to cook while they're cooking.

But first, coffee.

By the time Eden hops out of the shower and gets fully dressed, she finds Shang at the kitchen table. He's got his laptop open, papers strewn everywhere with a frown knitting his brow together.

She comes in from behind and wraps her arms around his broad shoulders, placing a kiss on his cheek. "Good morning, my love."

"Mmph," is the noise that comes out of his mouth. Eden's learned that her new husband isn't, in fact, a morning person. He merely likes to *pretend* he is.

"It's my turn to make breakfast," she says with a giggle. "Any requests? I've been craving Pad Thai tacos again."

"First thing in the morning?"

She shrugs. "What? Like there's a rule saying we can't?"

It's then that Eden glances at all the papers on the kitchen table. There are a couple of formal letters, some article clippings, printed screenshots of online slander. Upon further inspection, Eden realizes that Shang has been looking at poor reviews for The Lunchbox.

Not just one or two of them, either. *Lots* of them. Hundreds upon hundreds of one-star reviews on Yelp and Google complaining about anything and everything from food arriving at the table cold, ridiculously long wait times, general uncleanliness of the restaurant and bathrooms, crappy service, and so on. None of it makes any sense, of course, because they haven't even been open long enough to have earned this many complaints.

"What is this?" she asks him. She flips through a couple of the pages. Most of these reviews look fairly recent, posted within the span of a couple of hours last night while they slept. "Where'd these all come from?"

"I'm not sure, but it's nothing to worry about, sweetheart. I'll take care of it. I'm sure I can get them taken down."

"The Lunchbox is just as much my baby as it is yours. If someone's trying to drive our business under by posting a barrage of fake reviews..." Her thoughts suddenly click into place. She turns to face him and frowns. "Do you think it's Sebastian?"

Shang sighs, chugging his mug of black coffee. "I wouldn't put it past him."

"He's done something like this before, hasn't he? Driven other restaurants out of business."

"We don't have any proof that it's him."

"What if we could *get* proof?"

He arches a brow. "It sounds like my little wife has a plan."

"Hell yeah, I do. Where'd I put Maxine's number?"

He storms into La Rouge with a thick manila folder tucked beneath his arm.

It's empty in here. A ghost town when it should be the middle of dinner rush.

"So much for wanting to make a scene," Eden says, half-joking. "And here I thought we'd at least have a couple of witnesses."

"It's just as well," he replies. "We don't need witnesses to destroy them."

Eden nibbles her bottom lip. "Damn. I forgot how sexy you can be when you're a little mean."

He swallows his amusement. "Save it for later, sweetheart."

"The fuck do you think you're doing here?" Hector sneers, storming out of the double doors that lead into the dining section from the kitchen. "Get the hell out of my restaurant!"

Shang doesn't even flinch. He steps forward, standing at full height with his chest proud. "We're not here for you. Bring me Sebastian."

Hector's cheeks turn as red as his hair, a deep, furious crimson. "How dare you—"

Eden presses her hand to his face and pushes him aside. "Move along, bucko. We've got business to take care of."

Shang follows dutifully into battle, not even bothering to look Hector in the eye as he passes. Hector isn't worth a grain of salt, let alone his acknowledgement.

They find Sebastian squirreled away in the kitchen office, hunched over the little desk inside. There are maybe four or five other chefs at work, milling about with nothing to do. One glance at the kitchen is all it takes for Shang to know La Rouge is severely understaffed.

"What are you doing here?" Sebastian snarls.

"We're here for an apology," Shang replies evenly.

His former employer scoffs. "You've both come back to grovel, have you? I'd never take either of you back in a million years."

"No," Eden corrects, crossing her arms. "We're here for an apology from *you*."

"From me? For what?"

"For trying to sabotage our new restaurant with fake reviews," Shang says, holding up a finger as he counts off Sebastian's offenses. "For releasing false and defamatory information about me to be published in Gastronomica, and for forcing us to deal with the shriveled up asshole that you are."

Sebastian stands, but he's the furthest thing from intimidating. Shang and Eden have him boxed in with nowhere to go.

"I don't know what you're talking about," he seethes. "And even if I did, I'd never apologize to the likes of you."

Eden tilts her head to the side, nonchalant. "We're giving you one opportunity, Sebastian. Shang's letting you off the hook easy. All he wants is an apology for the years of mistreatment you subjected him to. I personally wanted to lock you in the walk-in until you were a popsicle, but he made me see reason."

The vein at Sebastian's temple throbs, threatening to burst. "I will never apologize to hacks like you. You're both a disgrace to the culinary world!"

Shang sighs, glancing over at Eden with a shrug. "Go ahead, sweetheart."

She grins. "With pleasure." Eden quickly reaches into her pocket for her phone and sends off a quick text.

"What are you doing?" Sebastian demands. "You're both

wasting my time. Leave the premises at once, or I'll have the police escort you—"

Shang slaps down the manila folder he's been carrying onto the desk. It flips open, hundreds of documents spilling out from inside.

Sebastian's eyes are bloodshot, his nostrils flared. "What is the meaning of this?"

"*This*," Shang begins, "is courtesy of a friend of ours. A private investigator, as a matter of fact. She's managed to trace every single one of those fake reviews back to you. She's also unearthed a handful of connections that you have in the industry—food critics, reporters, other restaurateurs, ex-employees—who are willing to testify about all of your shady dealings."

"Shady dealings?" Sebastian snaps. "I won't stand for this slander!"

"You can deny it all you want," Eden says, "but we've got all the evidence we need to prove that you've been underpaying staff, sabotaging competition, and even paying reviewers to give your restaurants a boost in ratings to justify price hikes in your menus." She holds her phone up. "I just sent a message to our PI to release everything to the press. Had you apologized like we asked..."

Shang smiles. "Thank you, Sebastian. I'll admit that I'm grateful for the help and mentoring that you provided me earlier in my career. I wouldn't be the chef I am today without you. But everything after that... After you stripped me of my name, drove a wedge between me and my family, almost ruined my passion for food, telling me everyday that I'd be nothing without you... I realize now that it was all bullshit. Everything that I am—that's all me, my friends, and my loved ones." He slips a hand around Eden's waist. "I hope you have a nice life."

Eden peers up at him with a grin. "Ready to go?"

"After you, sweetheart."

Sebastian's too stunned to speak. To argue. Hell, to even *breathe*.

Shang and Eden leave without another word, their fingers laced tightly together.

# CHAPTER
## Thirty-Eight

"You have to sharpen your knives before service every single time," he instructs. "It's dangerous to work with a dull blade. Can you tell me why?"

Amanda looks up from the notes she's been writing. "Because dull knives encourage you to apply too much pressure. If you slip, you could seriously end up cutting yourself."

Shang nods. "Good. Very good. I'm impressed with your progress this past week."

"Thanks, Chef," she says. "I'm really glad you're giving me the chance to learn. I was honestly surprised when you called me up the other day."

He scratches behind his ear. "Yeah, well... We're not at La Rouge anymore. I don't give a shit if you're formally trained so long as you follow instructions and pull your weight."

Amanda beams. "I won't let you down, Chef."

"Good. Then that concludes your last training shift. Be here bright and early tomorrow for service."

"Yes, Chef."

"Yo, Shang?" Peter calls from the line. They're starting prep even though they won't be open for another hour.

"Yeah?"

"Some dude's out front asking for you. Says he's your uncle?"

"Charlie's here?"

Shang wipes his hands on his apron and slips through the double doors from the kitchen to the dining area. He's gotten used to the cramped space. They can only hold a fourth of the tables that La Rouge can, but he doesn't mind. Less tables means less orders to drown in during rush. Less orders means he can take his time perfecting every dish before he sends them out. It's a nice change of pace.

A man stands by one of the front tables, admiring the décor. The walls are a charming mustard yellow, numerous picture frames hanging from the walls. Every one of his kitchen staff chipped in, bringing in pictures of them when they were still in culinary school. The man seems particularly fond of one. He's in it, along with his dark-haired nephew standing just in front of him.

"I remember that day," Uncle Charlie says. "You spent hours on your hair."

Shang rolls his eyes, but there isn't any heat behind it. "We both know I got my father's ears. Have to hide it somehow."

Uncle Charlie chuckles. "Very true."

"What are you doing here?" Shang asks softly.

"Wanted to check on you. Word around town is that this is the place to be."

Shang smiles, pride filling his chest. "I guess we're doing alright."

"Humility? Surprising, coming from you."

He shrugs, shoving his hands into his pockets. "I think Eden brings it out in me."

"That must be it."

A pause falls over both of them. It isn't uncomfortable, per se, just a little heavy. "I wanted to apologize," Uncle Charlie says finally. "For how I spoke to you at your parents' party. I realized I was being a hypocrite."

Shang shakes his head. "Don't worry about it. It's in the past. Let's just move forward."

"My, how you've grown. You're certainly a bigger man than I."

Shang takes a few steps forward and claps his uncle on the shoulder. "Hungry?"

"Famished."

"I'll whip something up for you before we open."

"Are you sure it's not too much trouble?"

"It's no trouble at all."

It's a few days before Christmas, but the restaurant's been closed all week. Eden knows that it's one of the busiest times of the year for restaurant workers, but it never sat right with her, having them work with the holidays right around the bend. Since they're business owners now, they're more than capable of giving their employees some paid time off. That way, everyone can spend time with their loved ones without having to worry about making hourly.

Eden's gone all out on the decorations this year. Massive pine tree in the corner, decked out with all sorts of ornaments and tinsel and lights and candy canes. Naturally, they bake up a storm together, so the whole damn building smells of cinnamon and nutmeg and spearmint. They're going to be spending Christmas Day with Li, Xu Hong, and Uncle Charlie upstate, but the days leading up are just for them.

She's seated on the couch in front of the TV, watching *Elf*—a classic to end all classics. Eden spins her wedding ring around her finger, again and again and again. She adores the weight of it, the shine, the brilliance. Most importantly, she adores the man who gave it to her.

*I hope he gets back soon.*

The apartment door swings open. Shang walks in, wrapped up so tight in his scarf and oversized winter coat that Eden can't help but laugh. There's snow in his hair, covering his shoulders. His cheeks and nose—the only parts of his face poking out from under his scarf—are red from the cold. He sets down two bags of food on the kitchen island as he toes off his slush-covered boots.

"Well, that was a fucking nightmare," he says.

Eden hops up from her spot on the couch and makes her way over. She can feel the frigid air from outside wafting off of him. She squeals when Shang leans down to kiss her, his frigid lips against hers.

"Give me your warmth," he murmurs, nuzzling in.

She shivers, playfully trying to shove him off. "Your hands are freezing!"

"Come on, sweetheart. Lay a little sugar on me. I braved the outside world so you could have a stocked fridge."

Eden snorts. "Oh, *thank you*. I'm sure you won't benefit from having food at all. Totally for my benefit." She kisses him anyway, delighting in the way his chuckle rumbles through her.

Shang shrugs off his coat and scarf, tossing everything over the back of the kitchen island stool. It doesn't take him very long before he's wrapped his arms around her again, pulling her close. Eden presses her face against his chest and kisses just over his heart.

"What do you want for dinner?"

"I don't know. What do *you* want for dinner?"

"Are we going to do this every single day?"

"There are so many options. How am I supposed to choose?"

"I will literally cook anything for you."

"And I'll literally cook anything for you."

"I picked yesterday, so now it's your turn."

"Oh my God," Eden says with a giggle. "Ugh, fine. Can we please have katsu pork curry over rice with a side of sweet corn?"

"Anything for you, chef," he says with a grin, making his way over to the kitchen.

He stops short when comes to the dinner table, spotting a little rectangular box with a white bow made of soft ribbon placed neatly atop. There's a tag attached to it, too. It has his name on it. "Sweetheart, what's this?" he asks over his shoulder.

Eden holds her breath, barely able to contain her excitement. "An early Christmas present. You should open it."

Shang arches an eyebrow, squinting at her suspiciously as he undoes the ribbon. "What are you scheming?"

"Who says I'm scheming?"

"I can smell it."

"Oh, *really*?" Eden asks with a laugh. "Quit being a dummy and open it already."

"Fine, fine. But if this is some kind of prank—" He looks inside the box and stops mid-sentence. Shang glances back up, his eyes wide. "*Is* this a prank?" he asks softly, a whisper.

Eden shakes her head, smiling wide. "Not a prank. I wouldn't joke about this."

He picks the slender object out of the box, marveling at it. His eyes water, his expression caught between awe and confusion. "A pregnancy test?" he rasps. "Wait, are you…"

She stands up from the couch and makes her way over, blushing. "Yeah, I am." Eden swallows. "I know we've only talked about it in passing, but—"

"I'm going to be a father? I'm going to be a…" Shang beams, a soft laugh bubbling out of him. "I'm going to be a *dad*?"

Eden giggles, elated beyond words. "You're going to be a dad."

He wraps her up in his arms, holding on like she's the most precious thing in the world. She *is* the most precious thing in the world.

"I love you," he whispers in her ear. "I love you so much."

She cups his face in her hands and kisses him tenderly. "I love you so much, too."

### Epilogue

**Five Years Later**

"Careful, careful," Eden says to the little black-haired boy climbing the stairs in front of her. He's determined to carry the tray all by himself, though Eden makes a point of carrying the glass of freshly squeezed orange juice to keep it from spilling.

"I'll be careful, Mama. Don't worry."

They make it all the way down the hall to the master bedroom. It's early. Far too early for breakfast, technically, but Liam's eager to surprise his father on Father's Day with a meal he prepared all by himself.

Well, mostly.

His clumsy little hands couldn't quite flip the pancakes just right, so most of them were broken lumps of unevenly cooked batter. The sunny side-up eggs frantically turned into scrambled eggs. It was a quick save. Totally on purpose, he'd argued. The toast was burnt around the edges and somehow perfectly soft in the middle.

Eden isn't sure how her son managed that last one.

Her husband is wide awake, though he hid his face beneath one of the many pillows they had to give their son the impression that he was still sleeping. It was kind of hard to sleep through all the banging of pots and pans downstairs in the kitchen, despite Liam's best efforts to cook as quietly as possible to keep things a surprise.

"Happy Father's Day, A-Ba!"

Shang makes a show of snorting awake. He stretches, yawning wide. He wears a goofy grin as he says, "Well, isn't this lovely? How did you know I wanted breakfast at five in the morning?"

Liam places the fold-out tray across his father's lap and climbs onto the bed, sitting comfortably next to Shang in the crook of his arm. "Do you like it?" Liam asks.

Shang takes a few bites and rubs his stomach. "Oh, wow. This is... delicious, sweet pea."

Liam beams. "Do you like what I did with the eggs?"

Eden actually has to turn away to keep from laughing. Shang's all smiles, but she knows the look in his eyes.

It's horror. Thinly veiled, at that.

"Is that... Did you add sardines?" he asks, keeping his tone as level as possible.

"Yep! You always say that the best dishes come with secret ingredients!"

"I did say that, didn't I?"

"Aren't you going to finish it?"

Shang's smile stiffens, but only slightly. "I will, don't worry."

"You better not leave a single crumb," Eden teases as she sits down on the other side of her husband.

Shang gives his wife the side-eye. Eden pretends not to know what it means.

"Need to pee," Liam says as he climbs off, heading toward the bathroom on the other side of the hall. "Can we call Grandpa and say Happy Father's Day when I'm back?"

Shang nods. "Sure thing, sweet pea."

Liam scampers off and Eden bursts into a fit of laughter, covering her mouth with her hand. "Oh, this is too precious."

"My poor palate," Shang mumbles. "You didn't give him a hand *at all*?"

Eden shakes her head. "Said he wanted to do it all by himself." She taps the edge of his plate. "Come on, honey. We don't want to disappoint him, do we?"

Shang leans over and kisses his wife on the lips. "Just you wait until Mother's Day."

"Why does that sound like a threat?"

He simply shrugs. Eden is only a little bit worried.

Shang forgoes the rest of his mushy pancakes and instead places his hand over Eden's stomach. Her belly is getting bigger by the day. She's about four months along and practically glowing.

"How's she treating you this morning, my little wife?"

"Not bad," Eden says fondly. "I think our little girl's giving me a break from all the morning sickness." Eden runs her fingers through Shang's hair. "Now, eat your breakfast. It's *bring-your-kid-to-work* day, and I, for one, am interested to see what havoc he'll wreak in our kitchen."

Shang lets out a soft groan, but there's no denying his smile.

C ontrol. That's what he likes the most about running his own kitchen.

Everything has its place. Everyone has their roles to fulfill. Everything is measured and timed and seasoned.

He likes his knives dangerously sharp—it's dangerous to work with a dull blade—and he likes his waiters to pick up orders the second the plates hit the line. He's never bothered with a chef's hat because they're quite frankly pompous as fuck and it's hot enough in here as it is. He keeps his apron clean and the sleeves of his white chef jacket rolled up to just below his elbows.

Trained at the prestigious Gagnon-Allard School of Culinary Arts. Four Michelin stars under his belt. He's the pristine image of the world—class chef everyone believes him to be. He used to be the great and mighty Head Chef of La Rouge, Alexander Chen.

Now everyone just calls him Shang, chef extraordinaire and one of the greatest culinary minds of his generation. He's not so scary. He's actually a pretty fun boss to work with. Way nicer than he used to be.

But right now?

Right now, he's too busy watching his son to pay attention to the chits printing out.

Thank God he has his lovely wife to man the line.

"I need the dishes for tables four and seventeen," Eden announces clearly over the roar of the hood fans and the sizzle of skillets over low flames.

"And I need dessert!" Liam declares, reaching up to the dessert station to help himself to a chocolate covered strawberry.

Shang swoops in and picks his son up. "Come on, sweet pea. Can't you see Auntie Rina is working?"

Rina giggles, placing another chocolate-covered fruit in the center of Liam's palm. "Oh, I don't mind."

"She doesn't mind," Liam confirms to his father.

Peter winks at Liam. "So, do you think you'll grow up to be a chef like us?"

"He's too young to be thinking about those sorts of things," Shang says firmly.

"I want to be a food critic," Liam announces, much to Peter's exaggerated dismay.

"You *what*? Oh, the horror."

Liam laughs—bright and beautiful—just like his mother. Shang's heart has never felt more full.

"Hey, did you see this?" Freddie asks, handing Shang his phone. It's open to a recent article from Gastronomica, the title bolded and centered.

## *MICHELIN STAR RESTAURANT* LA ROUGE *TO CLOSE: WHAT WENT WRONG?*

A few years ago, the news might have left Shang with a bitter sense of amusement. There's nothing wrong with indulging in some well-deserved schadenfreude. Knowing that Sebastian has finally come face-to-face with his comeuppance should leave Shang feeling relieved. He should feel anger for all the turmoil that man put him through, should feel regret for the way things unfolded.

Instead, he simply shrugs and hands the phone back. He's proud to say that he's moved on. All that matters is what lies ahead. The future holds untold possibilities. There's no sense in allowing the past to bog him down. He has his new restaurant, his friends, his darling family... La Rouge and Sebastian aren't even an afterthought now that he's *free*.

"Alright, little buddy," Shang says, blowing a raspberry against Liam's cheek. "Let's let everyone work and grab some ice cream, hm?"

Liam gasps, his face lighting up like the Fourth of July. "Yay!"

"Oh, chef?" Eden calls out to her husband.

"Yes, chef?"

"I'm going to need a kiss on the fly before you go."

He chuckles, indulging his sweetheart—because why ever

would he not? He dives in for a quick peck on the lips, the lunch rush be damned.

Freddie stares at them both, salad in hand. "I think I have cavities."

The happy couple only laughs.

Eden mans the line expertly, calling out orders as chits print off. The rush is starting to pick up, but his wife is a chef in her own right. She works with precision, and she never sacrifices her flare. Every meal she plates is a work of art; generously portioned and an explosion of flavor.

Every time he looks at her, he falls that much more in love.

If someone had told Shang he'd be happily married with a son he adored, another bun in the oven, a restaurant he could call his own, and a team he'd do anything for, he would have rolled his eyes. He thinks about all the different choices that brought him here, all the different steps he took like those of a complicated recipe. He's a different man than he was a few years ago, and he suspects it's all thanks to her.

In the end, it didn't matter how much he sharpened his knives or how well he seasoned his dishes. He realizes now that he was missing a secret ingredient all along: a little dash of love.

*THE END*

If you liked *Knives, Seasoning, and A Dash of Love*, please be sure to leave a review on Goodreads to support this indie author!

# ACKNOWLEDGMENTS

Look, Mom and Dad! I'm officially a published author—my name's on the cover and everything!

Shang and Eden's story is very dear to my heart, and I cannot believe that I finally get to share it with the world. There are so many people that I would like to thank, without whom I very likely would not have been able to see it through.

Brittany, thank you for taking a chance on me. Without you, my dreams would never have come true. All it takes is for the right person to say 'yes' and you are 100% that person. You are an absolute inspiration and I cannot thank you enough for your hard work and dedication to the literary field. Every story you help to publish makes the world a much better and brighter place.

I would like to thank Kirsten, Kira, Tristen, and Joy for being the most supportive beta readers anyone could ever ask for. I'm sorry for breathing down your necks while watching you leave comments in my manuscript like a madwoman; I was just too excited.

I would like to thank my husband for putting up with all my late-night imposter syndrome rants. You are my Fated One in this life and every one hereafter. Thank you for believing me during moments when I couldn't do it myself.

VIV! Thank you so, so, so, *so* much for the beautiful cover art. I'm so honored that you've helped me bring Eden and Alexander to life. It goes without saying that I think all of your work is amazing and I really hope we get to work together again in the future!

Lastly, I would like to thank one very specific lightsaber-wielding fandom. Without your encouragement, this book might have never seen the light of day. I have met and made many of my dearest friends through this community and I cannot thank you enough. You all taught me that I'm not alone, and I'm here to say neither are you.

After having spent the last five years as a ghostwriter, let me tell you it's an *amazing* feeling to finally be able to claim my own work. Hundreds of stories under my belt, but this is the first one I get to call mine. Excuse me while I go happy-cry in a corner.

Thank you all so much for reading!

# ABOUT THE AUTHOR

Katrina Kwan is a Vancouver-based author, actress, and ghostwriter. She graduated from Acadia University with a Bachelor of Arts in Political Science with Honors in 2017. When she's not busy writing, you can sometimes spot her in bit parts on TV!

Follow her on Twitter to stay up-to-date on all of her upcoming projects.
You can also subscribe to her newsletter here.